THE
UNDOING
OF
ARLO

KNOTT

By Heather Child

Everything About You
The Undoing of Arlo Knott

THE UNDOING OF ARLO KNOTT

HEATHER CHILD

orbit

www.orbitbooks.net

ORBIT

First published in Great Britain in 2019 by Orbit

1 3 5 7 9 10 8 6 4 2

A CIP catalogue record for this book is available from the British Library.

ISBN 978-0-356-51074-3

Typeset in Minion Pro by Palimpsest Book Production Limited,
Falkirk, Stirlingshire
Printed and bound in Great Britain by Clays Ltd, Elcograf S.p.A.

Papers used by Orbit are from well-managed forests and other responsible sources.

MIX
Paper from
responsible sources
FSC® C104740

Orbit
An imprint of
Little, Brown Book Group
Carmelite House
50 Victoria Embankment
London EC4Y 0DZ

An Hachette UK Company
www.hachette.co.uk

www.orbitbooks.net

She said: For God's sake, good knight, go your way, and abide not with me, for ye may not deliver me. Thus as they spake together the dragon appeared . . .

From *The Golden Legend or Lives of the Saints*,
compiled by Jacobus de Voragine,
Archbishop of Genoa, 1275

Part 6

SNAKE EYES

Thirteen (years old)

I picked up where Mum had left off, rasping out an abrasive rhythm with the sandpaper block as my arm glided back and forth. An aroma of wood began to creep out from beneath the paint dust and I stopped, letting the shower of particles drift earthwards. Flecks of white dotted my navy-blue sleeve, a whole nebula of them. Right here on my jumper, I'd collected a galaxy of stars too numerous to count. I took a deep breath and blew them all away.

At this height, the roof was so close you could pick the moss from between its tiles. Although I was going through the motions of sanding, it was really about getting caught when Mum re-emerged through the back door, the gratification of hearing her panicked cry:

'Arlo!'

'What?' I exclaimed, in feigned innocence.

Once I was on solid ground, her anger-fright softened. She assured me that I was more than capable of smoothing and painting the entire fascia by myself, but also very good at holding the ladder. Taking my head in both hands, Mum peered into my eyes, making me blink.

'I can't see anything,' she said, letting go, 'but don't try that again without goggles. Your eyes are important.'

Once she had ascertained that no paint was threatening my corneas, she planted me firmly on the patio and clambered back up the ladder herself. Since builders were so expensive, she had taught herself household maintenance using manuals found in charity shops, struggling to understand the diagrams but sticking at it. DIY was not my favourite activity, but it did come with the most treats: already we'd had a second breakfast of pain au chocolat, and there was a packet of Rolos with my name on it.

I gripped the smooth sides of the ladder and winced at the music. As we were proper builders, we had the radio on an eighties station at full blast, and Mum's breathy tones were just audible singing 'Lucky, lucky, lucky' in time to the rasp of the sandpaper. I hoped Rob was not in his garden thinking this was my music. He was a year older than me, and ever since he'd moved in I'd been determined to hang out with him. The previous day I'd been upstaged by his neighbour on the other side, a grungy, annoying boy called

Tristan, who had flaunted his new CD player, complete with Oasis album, and had shown off a bronze, speckled frog he'd caught in a bucket.

Who'd have thought someone as cool as Rob would care about a frog? But he was more into animals than I'd anticipated. Tristan reeled off a few facts about tadpoles, suddenly the expert, as the amphibian crouched wetly in my new neighbour's hand, and all I could do was slouch off home and kick at the hydrangeas, wondering if there was any novelty value in the fat, orange-edged slugs that patrolled our borders.

My eyes strayed again to the clustering blue flowers and the damp soil beneath. Holding a ladder, it occurred to me, is the most pointless task. The ladder isn't going anywhere. If anything, it was supporting me. I was leaning against it. Would the weight of a thirteen-year-old really make any difference?

'Are you there?' Mum called down.

'Yes.'

'You're a star.'

The words fell, warm and familiar, as from a hot tap. The sun came out, and I glowed with happiness. A whole summer ahead, and mostly without my sister Erin. Being a tremendous egghead, she was off on some gifted student programme, a precursor to her degree. I was officially man of the house.

The idea that I was also a bit of a mummy's boy is not one that would have occurred to me at the time, though I certainly knew how to gain her approval, how to use my winning smile to best advantage. As my dad would have said, had he seen us even once during those years, 'Never neglect your fans.'

I looked up towards Mum's paint-splattered jeans and the basket of sandpaper hooked over the ladder, but a cascade of dust made me return my gaze to the flower beds and the neighbour's wire partition, where neither side had replaced a missing fence. Although it was only August, plants were sprawling drunkenly under the weight of their own growth, going brown underneath. There was moisture in the air, muscular sunshine with the threat of rain. The Victoria plum buzzed with wasps, burdened with green-purple fruit. I saw something move amid the weeds, not the rustle of a bird but a purposeful glide. It took a minute to realise I was watching a coil ooze around a stem, tapering into a tail, its flesh black and glistening.

'Mum,' I yelled instinctively, 'there's a slow-worm!'

'What?'

'A slow-worm, in the garden.'

'Darling' – her tone was half-laughing, full of affectionate disbelief – 'are you sure? They're practically endangered.'

She turned back to the eaves.

'There's one here.' True to form, it was moving slowly, cutting a neat undulation through the violets, towards the gap in the fence. If I didn't act fast it would belong to the family next door. There was a big plaster tub discarded on the lawn. It would take only a second to trap it, and then I'd have my own slow-worm. Already I could see myself unveiling the bucket to show Rob, while Tristan looked on in mute defeat.

The wood grew hot under my hands. Mum was singing again, tapping the block as she reached for the next section, shaving off snowflakes which fell into my hair. I didn't dare take my eyes from the creature. I was willing it to stay put, ready to shout at Mum to come down. It remained shining like oil, giving me hope that it was basking in the sun and in no hurry. Then, the moment I blinked, it started to move. An agony swept through me, and I clutched the wood so hard my fingers hurt, some swirl of underthought gathering imperceptibly. Finally I yelled, 'Just one sec,' and dashed over to the bucket, slipping on wet grass, and dived into the border. While I was still airborne, the slow-worm shot away, so fast I couldn't quite believe it. My hands thrust down among the leaves, filling my fingernails with dirt. It had vanished.

'Are you there?'

'Yeah,' I called back on autopilot, hearing both Mum's words and mine as though there was a time delay. When I turned, she was reaching across to the right. The ladder went to the left. I saw one wooden foot leave the ground, as the imbalance went beyond the point of correction. It was like watching a film, something that couldn't be true.

There was bewilderment in my mum's cry, as she realised

she was going to fall. Her left hand scrabbled at the edge of the tiles, the other dropping the block and reaching for a piece of drainpipe – far too slowly, it seemed to me, as though it wasn't remotely urgent – plucking at the plastic before letting it slip through her fingers. She plummeted, still clutching one tile she'd pulled from the roof, like a dentist who'd extracted a brownish incisor. The tile shattered on the patio.

I was still holding the bucket, my insides solidified with horror. My mother groaned. I ran over. There was no blood. She looked more dazed than hurt; she was trying to roll over. 'Get an ambulance,' she said. I took more precious seconds to digest her words, and I think I even asked, 'Are you okay?'

No need to dwell on that scene longer than necessary. The ambulance was slow coming. At the hospital, I watched the nurse lift a chunky receiver to dial my nan, before repeating the process to call the switchboard at Erin's summer school. She gave up trying to get any coherent information from me on the whereabouts of my estranged father. It's all there in little crystallised sensations: greasy magazines in the waiting room, medical people coming in to ask me questions, and the brief mortification of trying to use the water cooler and yanking out the whole stack of cups. These memories can remain a snowstorm, a blizzard, like the white paint still caught in my hair. There is no need to examine every single flake.

My sister arrived, hours later, hardly believing she'd been

called home. She asked me what happened, even though I heard the nurse telling her. I stayed quiet, hoping the guilty heat was not reddening my cheeks. Erin soon started crying.

'Stupid Mum,' she said. I was angry at her for that, but didn't trust myself to speak. Instead I pretended to sip my cup of ice-cold water, and tried to stop hearing the sound of a tile smashing on concrete.

They let me see her, much later, lying in a bed that smelled of our drawer of plasters and bandages at home. It seemed like a trick, as though she was in fancy dress, or playing a role on stage, only there was no audience but me, and the other cast members were machines and bags of fluids. With great liberty, the nurses touched my shoulder whenever they spoke to me, while I sat in the chair and bit any parts of my thumbnail that had dared to grow beyond the quick. It didn't matter what their expressions said, or how quietly they murmured. I would stay with her until she was well enough to come home, and that was that.

Thirteen

In the end they gave me another chair so I could make a sort of bed. The nurses chided even as they took pity, telling me I wasn't helping anyone by hanging around, that I shouldn't really be there without an adult. The blanket was fibrous and smelled of chemicals, but I wrapped myself up and listened to the strange tings and coughs and nocturnal shufflings of the hospital.

The next day, Nan crouched in front of me, a barely perceptible groan escaping her lips. I could see her eyes were softened with crying, her features almost liquid with lack of sleep. She sought my hand and flattened it between her leathery palms, examining my chewed fingernails with their telltale traces of dirt. I withdrew, folding my arms, and she sighed.

'There's nothing heroic about gluing yourself to that chair. What would she say?' A nod towards the bed. 'She'd wonder why you weren't looking after Erin and me, wouldn't she?'

Mum's lips were slightly parted and the colour of slate. My nan was right. She seemed to sense the change of heart beneath my frown.

'I've packed some things from your house . . . we can stop at Asda and you can tell me what cereal you like.'

With great reluctance I found myself following her spongy sandals until the bleak corridors spat us out at an underground car park, where I climbed into the cream Mini she'd owned since before I was born. It was so rusty. I tried not to press down with my feet in case the floor fell out.

The next few days felt as flimsy as the paper plates Nan used for our meals – an impulse purchase at the supermarket along with my Frosties. Her house was in a satellite village a short drive from Croydon. From the garden you could hear birdsong rather than sirens, and milk was still delivered in glass bottles. The village centre was pretty and had a duck pond listed in the Domesday Book, but Nan lived in an estate of modern houses clad with ugly yellow stone and full of spindly furniture. It was for visiting only, not for living in. Every ornament was precarious, every bathroom bottle a mystery.

Whenever we returned from the hospital, Nan would be instantly at a loss, wondering how to entertain us. The evenings became segmented into parcels of time, of making and eating dinner, watching a television programme – often an agonising soap opera – and then the awkward no man's land before bed. All three of us were in a state of shock, and I felt oddly lethargic; my normal energy quashed, my appetite minimal.

One evening, in desperation, Nan went to the attic and found a board game. We didn't even play these at Christmas any more. The faded box challenged players to find their way through Goblin Wood; it must have predated any of the games I'd heard of. It had been years since I'd played anything except *Tetris* and *WWF Superstars* on my Game Boy. Once we'd found the dice, I miserably threw six after six while she declared, 'Look at you, on a winning streak.'

I was glad both to win and to get it over with, and so, by the look of it, was Erin. My sister went back to feigning interest in the instruction booklet for her chunky Nokia, a gift for university she'd hardly looked at until now.

The board games reminded us uncomfortably of Dad. Perhaps Nan had forgotten they were his thing. I remember the selection he amassed – which must have gone with him when he left – of every new game, with no torn or dog-eared boxes and no missing counters. They were pristine, every part lovingly curated. His favourites were those that managed to break out of two dimensions, such as Mousetrap and Hungry Hungry Hippos. Erin, being five years older, had done her time with the dice, so it was generally me and him, huddled around the dining room table whether it was rainy or sunny outside.

On one occasion the neighbour passed us an ancient game called Beat the Wyrm, in which knights had to quest their way towards a maiden while avoiding squares with dragons, but most of the pieces had been lost and there was only one knight remaining, a pewter Saint George with a red cross on his smock. I clutched it in my sweaty palm as Dad folded up the board in annoyance. 'You may as well keep it,' he said. 'That's one way to beat the wyrm: lose all the pieces.' Instead we pitted my knight against an array of characters from his brand-new DC Comics game, till he made Superman fly across to the finish line, much to my annoyance, and then told me I was a sore loser for disputing the shortcut.

His sense of fun, as well as his enthusiasm for big dreams, was what I liked best about him, though he lost points for hogging the spotlight, playing the fool in front of my friends or saying things for shock value. He once told my sister I was an accident, shrugging in a weren't-we-careless kind of way and then laughing uproariously. Erin didn't giggle, and for once I appreciated the way her pensive expression never varied. The statement lingered until Mum had a go at him, proving it was true.

I think it was my sister's mobile phone, rather than the board game, that gave Nan the idea to try and contact him. It required a special trip to our house to get one of his letters, as none of us had his number. When she rang, I hovered just

13

outside the lounge doorway, so I could see her pushing her finger into the tempting spirals of cord as she dialled. She sounded ridiculously surprised when someone answered.

'Oh hello,' she said. 'Is this Jeremy? Oh, I had this down as his . . . well, he's written "cell phone". His agent? I see. Can I speak to him please? I'm Louise's mum. Louise? His ex-wife? She's had an accident. I'm here with his children.' A long pause followed in which Nan occasionally drew a breath but was cut off before she could interject. 'Well, it was a fall. I'd rather talk to him if it's all the same. But surely . . . If you could give me their number . . . It's a what? Oh . . . well, if you could pass it on then. Yes. We'll do that. Thank you. You too.'

She told us later that he was ill. I could have questioned this, but somehow it figured – or rather, him not being able to show up figured. Five years of near-complete absence had slimmed down my mental picture of him into something half-formed, tiny enough to live in the curls of the signature that concluded his occasional letters.

Every day that passed felt less real, and the surgical scent of the hospital never left my clothes, though how it got into my pyjamas was a mystery. At Mum's bedside I stared at her face for so long that it stopped looking familiar, more like a mask that needed peeling away. It was discoloured and a little swollen, which didn't help. I was allowed to take her hand – sometimes encouraged to – and it felt strange, not cold but cooler than usual. She always had such warm hands. I didn't believe in the old adage of 'cold hands, warm heart'. Warm hands, heart and everything else.

Closing my eyes each night, the colours became brighter, more vital, but more terrifying. They were the green-blush bruise of plums, the cloudy white of a plaster tub against a night-black slow-worm, yellow grass and pink patio. The moment was magnetised, and every molecule of my being ached towards it, every second of the day. If only I hadn't moved. If only I'd kept my bulk against the ladder, stopping that first awful gap appearing beneath its right foot. I could have ignored the slow-worm and waited till Mum came down. The Rolos were still on top of the fridge as far as I knew, unless by then we'd had a break-in and they were sticking together the jaws of some burglar. The yearning to return to that scene was so powerful my body became riddled with aches. I would force myself out of bed each morning with the creakiness of an eighty-year-old and eat breakfast only to appease Nan, finishing bowls of Frosties that became soggier and more disgusting the longer I took to eat them.

If I could go back, my eyes would never leave the ladder. I'd sing along to Kylie and Madonna and Tiffany and hold on all day, all night if necessary. I'd only move when she climbed down, wiping sweat and sawdust from her forehead. By now, I was seeing rungs on trees and street lamps. The dreams began to pull me around, to stretch and warp me. I remember quite clearly the process of torturing myself, the way that sleep became a punishment. If Mum would only awaken, then I'd make it up to her.

Erin started driving the Mini to the hospital, having been put on the insurance at great expense. Increasingly Nan was staying at home, only joining us every other day at most. It was tiring her out, she said, and we later found she'd been battling her own long-held fear of hospitals, one I would grow to share.

You'd think my sister and I might have bonded during such a time, but she has always been bad at communication, and neither of us felt much like talking. Plus, I was scared. Ladder accidents were common, apparently, and no one questioned me about what happened. But my sister was annoyingly smart and more than capable of teasing out the truth, given half a chance.

On that particular day, one I would rather forget, I could tell something was different. Even the hospital had a sense of wrongness, a strange smell of ginger in the corridor and a child in tiger face paint lying on a stretcher, struggling to breathe. The heating was turned up too high, and Nan broke away for a lie-down in a waiting area, saying she felt dizzy. Sure enough, we were told that Mum had been moved to a private room, which had never happened before. I was reassured slightly by Erin not seeming to think anything amiss – she had undergone many more meetings with doctors, and was even now being beckoned away while I was allowed to make a beeline for Mum's bedside.

Seeing her in the mornings filled me with both sadness and solace. I totted up all the things she'd need to be told about when she recovered: the folding bed, the Frosties, the Mini and that no one had done any stationery shopping for the new school year. Erin came in and closed the door. She stood in silence for a while as the machine breathed in and out. I sat peacefully in the chair and was surprised at her stiff posture; she was poised, as though ready to run.

'What did they want?' I asked. The previous day an elderly doctor had spent at least twenty minutes telling us about Mum's condition – I learned the words 'traumatic subarachnoid hemorrhage' later on – and his notion that her brain was in bad shape. I sensed the others had heard it before, and I tried to be heartened by the effort he was making to explain it to me. When football players got over injuries they were out of action for ages, so I took the speech to mean her recovery would take a long time. I was prepared for that. 'It's why they call them *patients*,' a cheerful nurse had told two restless children the day before.

What I did not expect was Erin giving a dry sort of cough and telling me that she and Nan had completed the paperwork, and they were going to turn off the machines.

'It's what the doctors think we should do,' she went on, looking slightly puzzled at my lack of reaction. 'There's no point keeping her on life support for ever.' Of course not, I thought, just until she heals. 'They've been saying it for weeks,' she continued, her face growing blanker. 'We've been

17

putting it off. Especially Nan, as you'd expect. But it's . . . draining. She doesn't want Mum to suffer any longer. It's going to happen today, once the right people get here.' Her hand ground together the buttons of her shirt. 'Aren't you going to say anything?'

Why should I? It was ludicrous.

'Do you understand what will happen?'

With a cold thread of horror, I realised her eyes had fixed onto a little flick-switch – the kind of thing you might see in a pilot's cockpit – on the breathing machine by Mum's bed. Yesterday the doctor was pointing it out to her, though I didn't hear why. Now I understood. They were going to turn off everything that was keeping her alive. She would have no chance to heal. In short, they were going to kill her.

Now I look back, I realise my sister was partly to blame. Is that ungenerous? Her defining feature was maturity, every member of the family telling her she was a sensible, responsible girl since her early teens, yet she didn't play this scene in a very mature way. She should at least have encouraged me to say my goodbyes. Instead she seemed frustrated that I didn't understand.

'This is the main switch,' she said, gravitating closer.

Perhaps it is unfair of me to dwell on this, since inside Erin an emotional maelstrom must have been raging. I, of all people, understand the need to do difficult things quickly, to smash through the clinging embrace of your thoughts and take action.

Her eyes flitted to Mum's closed, waxwork face, then to me, full of that light I had come to recognise as her own personal satisfaction at being the adult – her confidence that she could handle anything, no matter how hard. 'Maybe we shouldn't draw it out.'

'No,' I said, and stood in her way.

'Don't you understand? We have to stop her suffering.' There was a rasp in her voice, tears gathering as she approached what she feared most, the moment she wanted behind her. A glance at the door, then she went for the switch. I slapped her hand away.

'Arlo, you're making it harder.'

'Leave her alone.' I was Mum's only protector.

When she tried again, fury coursed through my veins. This was life or death, happening so fast that all reason left me and I started seeing hostility on Erin's face, aimed at Mum. They'd never seen eye to eye and now she was showing her true feelings, her jealousy. I might have been a few inches shorter, but there were muscles in my arms, while hers were weedy. Her hand was stretching out, shirt sleeve falling back to show pale freckles. I fell over myself to get between her and the switch, then I grabbed her wrists and twisted her down, but she curled in on herself and escaped my grasp. She tried to get round me, using her height, and I planted my feet on the floor.

'Stop it, Arlo!'

She wouldn't quit. It was like we were children again, her

whole weight pushing into me, but she was surprisingly easy to manhandle, my anger growing alongside her determination. Those bony arms were easy to press and bruise, easy to grab and swing. I knocked her into the wall and somehow she wound up on the floor, eyelids fluttering. Seeing her dazed filled me with a combination of satisfaction and anxiety. I backed away, blinked and then suddenly she was up again. A cry of shock was wrung from my throat as she tried to get past me, but instead ran into my fist. It felt good to hit the firm flesh, so I did it again, jarring my hand. It was the first time I'd really noticed the bone structure of a face. I split her lip, hardly aware of my own strength. When I saw the blood, I was alarmed. I drew back.

'Sorry. I didn't mean to . . .' The feeling was so poisonous I wanted to scratch it away, knock myself out to stop it. My knuckles had made contact again and again. What was wrong with me?

Then I looked up. To my astonishment there was no blood. I was sure it had been there, that tinge of iron, but the smell was gone, her lip a hard, unbroken line. She was standing quite calm and cold, and I could see the blows hadn't been as hard as I'd thought. At least she'd give up, now she could see how things stood. Or would she? Her forward drift began with hesitancy, then became determined, and I saw her eyes fixed on the machine. Didn't she learn? It was as though nothing had happened. I had to get in the way again, and it wasn't pretty. I lost count of how many times my fists flailed, fingers seizing wrists, an elbow, the bed, the rubber point of my trainer making contact with something that felt like a deflated football. I thought I'd broken her bones, gone too far, but a second later she was back on her feet. Bloodless. The tears a trick.

That last time it happened, I just stared. The situation was so insane that if she'd knocked on her skull and said, 'Made of plastic, dickhead,' I'd almost have believed it. What could I do? I stared too long. She moved and her finger reached the switch. 'No!' I screamed, desperate to move but rendered immobile by what was happening, at her hand reaching other buttons, slapping at the monitor so it went black, the uncanny quiet settling over my mother where she lay. 'Turn it back,' I yelled, but she did not, and by then my first scream had drawn a nurse into the room.

'Oh,' she said, her voice filling with anxiety as she realised what Erin had done, 'you should have waited for the doctors.'

'We didn't need to.' She sounded whispery, defensive.

It was hard to tell which one of us the nurse was restraining, as my sister seemed to collapse against her while I struggled for a second longer towards the machines. Then, as though my skin had become a sieve, my energy flowed away. The nurse eased an unbloodied Erin into a chair, called the doctors, then turned to me. Unexpectedly she crouched, encircled me with a kindly arm and said, 'It's okay, it's probably best this way.' I wanted to fight her, make her swallow these words, but something about the curve of her shoulders and the scent of hot skin and perfume from within the nurse's uniform made me bury my head in the blue fabric and soak it with involuntary tears. Two consultants arrived and busied themselves removing tubes and pressing buttons while, curled into a ball, I listened to the sound of things shutting down.

Thirteen

The bus ride from school was forty minutes, sometimes an hour. Inevitably, my room became my cave, a safe place with a lockable door. The imaginary television set was on the wall about six inches above my desk.

These were the weeks of Unreal Events: my mother's funeral full of relatives asking, 'Does he speak?' and not realising that, if I didn't paper it over, my hideous, all-encompassing hatred of the world would squirm and coil and spit poison in their faces. Then there was the aftermath, the condolence cards finally thrown away, and Nan marshalling friends to help clear our old house, which would have to be sold to pay the mortgage. She filled her attic and garage with our stuff. Her downstairs study became my domain, and Erin was installed in the large, dusty-pink guestroom. I stayed out of everyone's way, coming home from school and closing my door, living, where possible, on snacks from the tuck shop.

It was only when I heard Nan on the phone to solicitors that I realised selling the house meant it would be gone for good. Foolishly I'd assumed we would return one day, and that it would always be possible to drop in and find things I had misplaced – old shoes or accessories for my Game Boy. I felt a slow-burn dizziness at being untethered from the home where I'd grown up, and it took until early November, when Erin was finally preparing to begin her undergraduate course – half a term late – for me to realise that this beige limbo was hardening into permanence.

I wandered from room to room when Nan was out, testing the house like a new item of clothing, struggling to get comfortable. There were scents I could not identify, areas I sensed were out of bounds. I didn't understand the purpose of the airing cupboard, or why Nan kept sheets and pillowcases there in dry suffocation. In the dining room, the key to a locked cabinet slouched in its ornate keyhole, ready to stand up and guard five small trophies for ballroom dancing. More than a year would pass before Nan resumed the activity that gave her so much pleasure, popping out to the club on Wednesday nights.

'Untimely' was the word she used to describe losing her only child; a mild, sing-song word that didn't do justice to the tragedy of parting with someone she'd put half her life into raising, someone younger and more vital than herself, and the crucial mid-link in our generational chain. If Erin and I had troubled ourselves to look, we'd have noticed the signs that Nan was not really coping: the napkins laid out for a meal that hadn't been cooked, toilet rolls in knitted covers beside a loo that had to be flushed with a bucket. Small mechanisms kept working, while bigger ones buckled.

It was only supposed to be a temporary solution. Nan tried repeatedly to contact my dad, fuming at the cost of calling the States, but he was in some sort of clinic, and she could only seem to leave messages. Bereavement, she felt, should drive even an estranged father back to his unfortunate progeny.

'He might want to have you over in America,' she said one evening, after another fruitless call. The idea was like a bad smell, and even brought a choking cough to my throat. I looked over to Erin for support, but her expression was neutral, thoughtful – probably contemplating whether she'd get to attend some fancy stateside university. I vowed silently that if they tried to make me go across the pond I'd run away, or at least make Dad's life hell until he sent me back.

Nan was unfailingly kind, and there was never any question of us being welcome in her house, yet we started to see the face that was left behind after those sporadic childhood visits. She slept badly, and I found a stockpile of valerian tablets under the sink. 'Named for me,' she joked, and it took me ages to work out this was because her name was not Nan but Valerie.

She would often get tired and, if a phone call made her lift her swollen legs from the footstool, there would be irritability in her tone. For some reason, Erin tended to bear the brunt of these mood swings. My sister would be curled up innocuously in an armchair, only to have her reading interrupted with barked questions, such as whether she knew how to hand-wash clothes in a bathtub, should there be no laundrette at university. Or, much to my delight, she might be told her hair was looking rather greasy.

While Erin was subjected to scrutiny, most of my misdemeanours went unnoticed. Yet I'd been so cherished by my mother that I still felt short-changed. Making my own lunch and clearing up the toast crumbs, for instance, would previously have warranted several words of praise, while Nan took it for granted that I could look after myself. Judging by the look of astonishment on her face, she also considered my request for a TV rather bold, though I would not have thought twice about asking Mum.

'You should be outside,' she said, 'not getting square eyes.' With a smile, the back door was held open until I went into the garden, instantly enveloped by the candy-like perfume of roses. I paced up and down on the grass, unsure what she expected me to do. Some minutes later there were raised voices, the door burst open and Erin almost fell out. I'd picked a bad day to ask about the TV. Nan was in a volatile state, no doubt worsened by the unfamiliar prospect of having to see a teenager off to university.

By this time Erin had a car – an old Polo bought for a few hundred pounds – and I was profoundly jealous. She had her freedom, so now as I watched her sink onto a stone bench I said, 'Go on, cry.'

Normally she was rather inscrutable and emotionless but, much to my horror, she now burst into tears. Erin was a quiet weeper, her face turning meaty and tilting away. A few irrepressible sobs and gasps for air were all that punctuated the flow. In what I felt was a great act of generosity, I went and stood beside her. Not sat, just stood. I thought back to the hospital room. She was even thinner and paler now, her hair in a tight ponytail and her body caved in as though protecting a soft animal hidden in her shirt. It was a tall order to leave home and find new friends only weeks after Mum's funeral.

'It's all right,' I said, sighing briskly with the effort. Birds twittered in the trees, and lorries rumbled by on the A-road. Erin stopped crying and just sat, perfectly still, hands folded, as though willing herself into another dimension.

Until that moment, I'd hated her, despised both her and Nan almost as much as I loathed the whole universe. But when I looked at her eyes, so dull, so uninterested in meeting mine, I found myself murmuring, 'I'm sorry, for what it's worth.' Who owed whom an apology? It did not seem to matter any more. Her head snapped round.

'For what?'

'For that day.'

She pulled the fabric tight over her chest, and I was afraid she'd announce that the kicking had cracked a rib. To my surprise it turned into a shrug.

'You did make a scene.'

This was not how I would describe it. For some time I'd tried to convince myself that the beatings had somehow happened inside my head, a side-effect of the stress. But the burn was still in my muscles, too real to be denied. It puzzled me that I'd been unable to inflict proper injuries on Erin. Perhaps grief and confusion had made me weak, so my blows fell like leaves, though they felt powerful enough at the time. Didn't I smell the blood on her lip? In quiet confusion, I'd picked a fight some weeks ago with boys from the rougher school who stood at the same bus stop, unbeknownst to my nan, just to prove I could land an effective punch. Much to my satisfaction, I came off the definitive winner, creating a pleasing ripple of respect among my classmates.

'Did I?'

'You yelled so much the nurse ran in,' she said distantly. Then a shudder ran through her body. 'I wish I'd held off and let them do it.'

She stood and walked straight into the house, not looking behind her. Some part of me had been gearing up for a more complete apology, an acknowledgement of the dark ugliness of it all, and a tentative plea to be forgiven. But the moment had passed, and I was left amid the irregular birdsong, the weary autumn insects.

Had I been less self-absorbed, I might have realised that my experience of Mum's death was only a sliver of what really happened. In the middle of that horrible decision-making process was Erin, trying desperately to live up to her responsible persona, using her voice of quiet calm and scientific detachment. Were they fool enough to believe it? Obviously they had been, or she would never have been dragged into the discussions, so when she was faced with the switch, the very switch, she could not bear to wait another second. It took me back to the memory of her lighting the candles on her own birthday cake, some time ago, when Mum was in bed with flu. The match sparked into a sulphurous whiff, and my sister muttered 'No excuses now,' before extinguishing her eighteen candles in one steady breath.

She went off to university the next day, cramming bags into the little Polo. As I waved her off, at Nan's insistence, I spotted a dead bee on the pavement, huge and fluffy. Instinctively I picked it up; but before I could show it off, a pain spread into the soft skin between my index and middle fingers. Can dead bees still sting? The agony was affirmative. I hurled the insect over the front garden and pressed my hand between my thighs.

Then the sting was gone. I looked down and what the hell did I see but a small black and gold lozenge of fur, temptingly curious on the tarmac, where it had been an instant ago. Erin's car drove out of sight, and Nan went inside. This time I knew there was no explanation for what I was seeing, unless it was that in this house, in crystallising limbo, I had gone insane.

Thirteen

What's done is done. One of many statements of resignation I heard fall from my nan's lips. For her, professional and wholehearted acceptance was a survival technique. But what was done was clearly not done. That bee had reappeared, and when I flexed my fist, tracing the line between my knuckles where the sting had spread out, it was also hard not to be reminded of the blows I'd landed on Erin at the hospital, that seemed to do no damage.

I started my tests with shortbread. A friend of Nan's had brought it back from Edinburgh in a jar decorated with thistles. Nan was rationing it out to me, one rectangle a day, already eyeing up its pretty container for her teabags. I put a piece on the saucer, licked the crumbs from my thumb, then picked it up and threw it across the kitchen. I turned my back, then spun round. The shortbread had not returned to the plate.

On my second attempt I made sure not to see where it landed, but again there was no reversal. It smelled buttery and delicious and, unable to wait any longer, I grabbed it from the cooker's hob where it had fallen and crammed the whole thing into my mouth. Maybe the trick only worked with dead bees.

In my distracted state I tried to put away the jar without getting a good grip. It hit the floor with a smash that echoed off the cupboard doors, scattering fragments all around. My groan of frustration soon followed. Nan would blow a fuse. What was the matter with me? Clumsy people were the worst. The last thing I wanted was to become one.

Then the miracle. I froze, not believing what I was seeing, afraid my slightest movement might tilt the universe a second time. The jar was back on the counter, perfectly intact.

For some moments I stood and stared insanity in the face, reaching out to touch its cool, bone-smooth surface, traced delicately with blue-green thistles. The crash had been loud, but five whole minutes passed without Nan coming downstairs to investigate. A conclusion loitered on the edge of my thinking, like someone too embarrassed to knock on the door. Was regret a muscle?

With some trepidation, I tipped the jar off the work surface once more, watched it shatter, then rued it for long enough to see it reappear. I could almost feel myself pulling the object, wishing it had not broken, and then I was back at the previous second, as though it had never happened. Like a sneeze, my eyes snapped shut involuntarily, a purely physiological reaction. There was no sense of rewinding or seeing the jar fly upwards like a small, ceramic spaceship. I let the container fall, then regretted it back to the work surface, again and again. I lived in that instant for who knows how long, until it seemed my eyes were two thistle-shot globes of white, smashing and re-forming with the jar.

I became so mesmerised that I made a mistake, ironically enough. Because my throat had gone dry so many times, I paused after one smash to get a glass of water. When I crossed the kitchen again, I found it impossible to make the shards come together. I squatted beside the breakage, screwed up my face and hissed, 'Come on, come on,' and nothing happened. I ended up sitting on the floor, picking at odd chunks of shortbread within the mess, and that's where Nan found me.

'Arlo?' She was aghast. 'What are you doing?' It must have looked as though I'd failed to get the lid off and had destroyed the jar to get at its contents. Her fury I could handle, but there was a crack in her voice, frailty and sadness breaking through. She had so few nice things. So little had cheered her since Mum's death, and she'd not found it easy looking after a child again, especially one who was making it so hard.

The muscle had failed. There was nothing I wanted more than to leap back and avoid this awful, heartfelt, verbal thrashing, but my mind was too muddled, and it seemed like Nan was just repeating herself, tears pricking her eyes anew. I ran off to my room, and things were cold between us for more than a week.

This new phenomenon felt like another component of loneliness slotting into place. I went to sleep with my usual sense of impending doom, expecting to see Mum's lilac lips, the drip-tube slithering in the corner of her hospital room, Erin carrying a ladder, the grass growing slippery and rotten beneath the linoleum and, since the funeral, the sneezes of the flu-addled vicar, black dresses, synthetic organ music and odours of wood and lilies. They were like chess pieces, and the only difference from one night to the next was the combination in which they would move. But that evening the board was deserted. I slept through a flatland of blissful nothing, as though I'd been cleared out and was ready to start again. For now, I could forget the slow-worm that was still out there somewhere, gliding through dark gardens.

As I washed my face the next morning, my skin felt clear, rubbery and young. For as long as I could remember, both parents had insisted that Erin and I could achieve anything we desired, as long as we wanted it enough. Dad believed this passionately, still having stars in his eyes, and my sister solemnly ploughed the advice into her academic life, reaping top grades as a result. Was this new talent, if that's what it was, born of the sheer power of wanting? Maybe other people could do it as well, if they were sufficiently tuned into the energies of the universe.

Every schoolbag is heavier than needed, containing textbooks hauled back and forth, too much stationery, cards to swap, gadgets and gizmos, enormous lunchboxes and weighty questions. I joined everyone who had, tucked somewhere in their bag, the issue of normality: what is it and, whatever it is, am I it? Unfortunately, my fight at the start of term had backfired and made people slightly wary of me. Plus, there was a rumour that one of the boys I'd battered had a brother in the sixth form who was going to make me pay.

Admiration had turned into suspicion, not helped by the fact that one or two loose-lipped teachers had been telling people my mother had died over the summer. People seemed to think it was a car crash, and I didn't correct them. Mates from previous years had grown distant now that I lived a long bus ride away. They hung out in groups and went quiet when I hustled my way in. Though I didn't see it at the time, I'd become the unwanted friend who would always be there, whether he was invited or not.

When I was around, everyone's freak-radar seemed to be on high alert. It was no time to be caught doing anything weird. I tested out my ability on small things. Listless in lessons, I pricked myself with a compass and watched the drop of blood appear and then vanish, muttered a swear word and then sucked it back in before the teacher's head could turn.

What was the point of it? I spent some time ticking off seconds in the back of my exercise book, entertaining myself by keeping time frozen at 14.09 on my digital watch. All I had to do was undo the last second I'd ticked off. Did this make me a time traveller? If so, it was a raw deal, being able to go back a whole second. No matter how hard I tried, I couldn't go back to 14.08. I couldn't remember how it felt to make earlier ticks, the exact pressure of the pen on my fingers, the movement of air round my face, and how many breaths I'd taken. Nice work, I told myself, after living in 14.09 for a while – you've made this long, boring class last even longer.

The lesson was information technology, taught by any teacher who had spare time. I spun around on my swivel chair, stumped by the last of the worksheet tasks. The room was full of carbon dioxide, hot breath emitted by the machines. I felt a sudden desperation, a sadness that I was damaged and no one could help me. It did not feel like madness; it was too mundane.

The teacher, a young woman called Miss Tepper, appeared at my shoulder.

'Ha, stuck on the bonus question? Don't worry, no one gets it.' Her fingers on my mouse were long and white, their nails shiny with clear varnish. They would be soft, a little moist. Something about the situation made me tremble, inconvenient things happening in my trousers. 'Have a little play with this . . .' She moved the mouse to the top left, so the name of a tool appeared. 'Do you see it now?'

I wound up my fists into spirals, Swiss rolls of meat under the table. With a gargantuan effort, I went back two sentences in time.

'The bonus question?' I cut in quickly, and went to *Edit*, finishing the task.

As they shot up, her eyebrows lifted my mood. In those hormone-fuelled days, misery and elation were two sides of an ever-flipping coin, but this was an unexpected high.

'Exactly. Well done.' A flash of Hollywood-perfect teeth. 'You should be very pleased with yourself, Arlo.'

I put my hand on hers, leaving it just long enough for me to savour the milk-fat texture of the skin, but reversing before her smile had time to disintegrate. It was so exciting, so wrong.

'I am.'

Fourteen

A teenage boy raised on the internet porn of later years might have done bad things with a gift like mine, but I was a good kid, if you dug deep enough, and my longings were really quite innocent. In any case, the retribution for any sin I could have committed was swift and excruciating, and went by the name of Glen.

He was the older brother I had been warned about, a mountainous boy who already had a part-time job at his dad's building company. I'd become adept at avoiding him, especially since the Victorian building in which we were educated had several entrances, still with 'Girls' and 'Boys' lovingly chiselled into the Portland stone. I would step down, spot those half-closed, murderous eyes, pull back and hotfoot it along the corridor, leaving by a different door, safe until the next time it happened.

At that age our egos were like sleeping lions – one poke and they would roar and rage out of control. In a fight I'd witnessed just a day or two before, the hapless initiator was left squealing 'I take it back, I take it back' as his face was ground into the bark of a tree. Luckily – and I'd never appreciated it so much – I *was* able to take it back, as long as the breath of it still lingered in my lungs, the pattern of movement in my muscles. I tried to sense which area of my brain was lighting up to make it happen, but it was too instinctive, and too quick; a sort of rocking sensation, like going backwards over a speed bump.

Regret still seemed to make it happen, especially when it was involuntary. Sometimes I'd trip or knock my knee and find I'd gone back a millisecond without noticing. But more often I was doing it deliberately, hardly needing to repent a kick of the football before it was back at my boot. It helped to be undertaking an action, no matter how small – even yawning was easier to undo than staring into space. I needed to be able to picture it in my mind, feel its memory in my body. The past was quicksand, and it was only possible to recover what rested for a split-second on its surface. I practised speaking aloud, keeping a phrase fresh and ready to dissolve, hearing it tickle in my ears. The trick was to pick the right moment to leap backwards, and not get too cocky.

Of course, in the first year after Mum's death, I failed in this entirely.

The day arrived when I could avoid Glen no longer. Staring into those acid-brimming eyes, I remembered that consequences did exist, that it was foolish to have imagined I could enter the lair of this monster day after day and not get caught. It happened on the school bus, which was a massive curveball since Glen normally got a lift. I'd gone upstairs and chosen a seat towards the back, failing to notice who was sitting behind me. Too late I realised that a couple of his mates had covered my exit. Once the passengers had thinned out, Glen stood up in the aisle, hardly swaying, and beckoned.

With all my might, I rifled through my mind, looking for those first steps onto the bus, but there were blurs, snatches of conversation, too much noise. Panic rose in my throat. You don't run away from these things, but I tried anyway, only to get a smelly jumper-arm in my face and nicotine-stained fingers grabbing my wrist, pushing me down. So then it started, my attempt to fight someone who could raise a breeze-block wall and was built like one himself. The first blow hit my cheekbone and dazed me so much I could hardly see; the others landed on my jaw, shoulder, solar plexus. Time is supposed to slow, in these instances, but it was over in a flash, and the long bit was sitting on the seat afterwards, licking blood from my front teeth and feeling something inside me die with every pitying but voyeuristic glance. Everyone else on the bus got off before me, Nan's village being the last stop.

By the time I was sliding a key into the front door, my face was resin-hard – damned if anyone would get a flicker of emotion out of me – but soon I was seeking Nan in the kitchen, disappointed to find her boiling the kettle and chatting to her dancing partner Brian. They burbled rather than talked, musing on the price of lime and soda and the benefits of a sprung floor. I abandoned all hope of getting her attention and slunk off to my bed, lying face down on the pillow, moving only when beaten by the need to breathe. Mum's cool hand should have been on my forehead, her arms wrapping me in an embrace I could sink into like a bath. My attention furled into a point, focused on those rippling black coils in the garden weeds.

Don't look. Undo. Hold the ladder.

I screwed up every cell in my body, till colours flashed and pains rippled through my head. What did a migraine feel like? The tension passed as I gave up, knowing it was fruitless. If waves of regret could have washed me so far backwards, they would have done so already.

Some gift. It was there to mock me, time throwing a few breadcrumbs into the lap of a starving man. My fists bunched up the sheets, tearing them from the mattress, and I lay with lights winking behind my eyes in a sort of waking dream, watching my mum's jewellery drawer open and inhaling perfume from the seventies as brown glass brooches regarded me with scratched facets. Where were they now?

For the next few days, I kept my head down and let my cuts heal. Then I sought Glen out at lunchtime as he was crossing the tarmac. My fear came in short, sharp, paralysing bursts, noted and ignored. As he paused to flick fag ash off his trousers and find a piece of gum, I planted my feet and said, 'Sorry.'

Brute satisfaction spread over his features. There was no reason I would go up to him and apologise, now it was all over, putting myself unnecessarily in harm's way. He translated it into the only realistic explanation his imagination would permit, that I'd been so cowed by his beating I wanted to genuflect even further. His lips would chew their way towards telling me to fuck off, and then . . .

What he did not realise was that, before I said sorry – and I repeated this process several times whenever the mood took me – I would ready myself, and from my cloud of meekness would emerge a kick to the crotch so vicious, and wracking his face into such a look of agony, that something must have ruptured. I dared not let it last more than a second before yanking myself back to the instant before the kick, when the muscles along my leg were just tensing and my weight beginning to shift. I'd see a shadow of confusion fall across his features as he tried to make sense of my smile – was I trying to make friends? – and we'd go through the usual process of him telling me to fuck off and continuing on his way, never knowing I'd just busted his balls.

It was vicious, petty and deeply unsporting, but so was Glen. I made sure he was alone when I wanted to kick him, so my own reputation would not be damaged by other kids hearing me seem to apologise. It may have swelled his bully's ego, but that was a small price to pay for the confidence it gave me in my abilities. When I was a small child and had the usual dreams of flying, I would scud along at bus-shelter height until I could be absolutely sure the power would not desert me halfway up an office block. But kicking Glen in the balls gave me mastery over gravity. No longer did I fear losing my gift at the most crucial time. It felt as physical and natural as snapping my fingers, only I clicked something inside my brain instead.

In the absence of friends, I played with the present moment, and school became less real by the day. Once my confidence had bedded in, I didn't hesitate to heckle the head if his assembly went on too long. 'Wrap it up, mate,' I'd groan. 'Why don't you and the litterbin just get a room?' The shock and ripening outrage afforded me a fleeting satisfaction, before I was forced to retract it. Another easy win was to sit in teachers' chairs and rifle through their desks, turning up fags and odd bits of alcohol and once a cola-flavoured condom, always able to dash to my seat just before they appeared. It was so wrong, yet such a delight to see Miss Tepper's beautiful jaw drop open when I asked her to confirm if I was experiencing a growth spurt . . . down there. She was far more interesting to me than the girls who giggled and shuffled in corridors, who folded together as tightly as those paper fortune tellers they were always making. Yet sometimes they would lift their arms to adjust ponytails and I'd get a whiff of some fruity shampoo, the exotic bounty of the Body Shop, and it was as if I could just reach over and tumble into whole new depths of wrongness. Thankfully, though, I never went that far, or no amount of undoing would have wiped their looks of horror from my memory. In any case, it was hard to feel lustful when I was busy testing the efficacy of different shoes – football boots wrung out an especially fine note of agony – on Glen.

This was the true purpose of my mental power, the ability to beat the crap out of life without ever being punished, to give me the wriggle room I needed for my roving, wrecking-ball rage. Even as my report cards filled with hostility, I knew I was wasting my potential. Erin may have been the gifted child, but I could still outpace most of my classmates without breaking a sweat. Teachers who'd known me in year seven lamented the waste of a formerly promising student. Mock GCSEs came and went – a mockery – and by year eleven I'd clocked up two suspensions and a place on some sort of red list for potential exclusion. If I made it to exams, I would fail spectacularly, though it would never be spectacular enough for my liking. Exams were small stones to throw in the face of fate. The world had swallowed up my mother, and it refused to do the same to me. I wanted to press buttons and see buildings disappear, to smash and burn and run, hurling everyone out of the way, leaving the village and all I knew behind.

It seems the powers that be are tickled by a force of pure destruction, knowing it will always obliterate the perpetrator in the end, because everything I wanted was delivered on a plate, the week before Christmas, when someone I'd hoped never to see again came to the door.

Fifteen

It was impossible to think about Dad at Christmas without finding myself aged seven again, the fir tree pricking my cheek as I crouched in the dark, startled by the sound of raspy breathing. I remember it perfectly: the lamp came on, and the figure in the armchair leaned forward in his limp Santa suit, cotton wool beard hanging down like a bib. The year before he'd been doing Pinter at Salisbury Playhouse, but now he was reduced to minimum wage at a department store, his lap filthy with floor grime from tiny trainers. Most disturbing was the way he looked at me, like someone too tired to care for a pet they had formerly loved. His voice was low and sonorous, burrowing into my head.

'Stare at the grotto for too long,' he intoned, replacing his glass on a sticky patch of sherry, 'and the letters of Santa rearrange themselves . . . into *Satan*. Bit of a coincidence, isn't it? Partial to a red suit, tempts parents to lie to their children . . .'

Imagine my little face falling. That's what Mum must have done from behind, where she'd come noiselessly down the stairs.

'Jeremy!'

He looked up.

She drew me away, sending me upstairs with a quick squeeze that promised more comfort to come. Since I'd always assumed that Santa was a game of dressing-up for adults, she needn't have worried. Mainly I was relieved that no one had asked what I was doing downstairs in the first place. I'd been halfway through getting away with one of the naughtiest and most scheming things I had ever attempted: peeling Erin's label from a gift – a bracelet, it turned out – and writing 'To Mum, From Arlo'.

Now, in my mother's eyes, I'd had a traumatic, coming-of-age disillusionment and was handling it with admirable stoicism. The next morning I soldiered on, even as she plied me with a large chocolate milkshake for breakfast, extra gifts and constant hugs. Some of the crackers wouldn't snap, but cause and effect pulled cleanly apart. Instead of punishment for messing with the gifts, I got the only thing I'd ever wanted on that festive day: to sit in an empty chair at the head of the table.

Dad's toxicity wasn't my fault. He'd fed the part of himself that craved applause until it became insatiable, something that ate into him in turn. As mince pies disappeared from the shops, Mum withdrew all her former indulgence of his bad behaviour, and he was soon living elsewhere, taking us out for weekend trips that we hated.

I was not sorry when he came to say he'd got a job in Los Angeles, a part in a new drama, playing the evil British guy. He loved that kind of role and was hoping it would lead to a movie career. I'd seen pictures of him as a young man at acting school, wearing a white T-shirt and braces, and sometimes a flat cap. He loved playing the classics: Strindberg, Chekhov and even Wilde, and despised Brecht. He'd never seemed interested in TV. Most of the actors he admired were stage players like himself, though he had a soft spot for Stephen Fry in *Jeeves and Wooster*. As we saw him off at the airport, he gave a little salute and said 'Cheerio,' already tuning up his arch-Britishness, turning away from us towards a more appreciative audience.

Nan must have been in the back garden, and it took me a while to respond to the pained raps of the antique knocker. I kept hold of my Game Boy as I went to the door, then nearly dropped it when I saw who was there. Dad was inching back from the mat, making a play of shyness. He was smaller than I remembered, his hair more salt than pepper, a scarf loosely encircling his neck above a double-breasted coat of faded aubergine. A small, tasteful suitcase on wheels was rocking by his feet, half-concealed behind his legs. It was as though a celebrity had turned up at the door, mock-humble but vigilant for signs of excitement, for acknowledgement that he was no ordinary guest. A smile dared to flicker.

'Hello, young fellow,' he said. A ridiculous way to greet your teenage son after so many years of absence. The strangest thing was the immediate familiarity of his voice, still stagey beneath the faint hoarseness of a winter cold. I said:

'Fuck the fuck off,' then reversed it.

Next, I swung a neat right hook. Pretty painful for me. Pulled it back.

Slammed the door in his face. This one I kept. Slightly sated, I opened the door again.

'Please,' he said, 'I only want a word.'

I could give him a word. But all this reaction was pure knee-jerk. My heart wasn't in it, numbed by the weirdness of the situation. So I let my father enter and seat himself in a high-backed chair where I could observe him silhouetted against the bay window. He took off his coat and, since no one had offered to take it, rolled it up and patted it down like a button-eyed puppy beside his feet.

'So you've been living here since . . .'

'Since.'

'Ah, yes. I was so sorry not to have been . . . to come to the funeral at least.'

'Why didn't you?'

49

A question that buckled him into a more tragic pose on the chair, knocking out a sigh.

'Those were dark times, dark times. All that hope and anticipation just crashed me. I was a train wreck, in the clinic six months, all kinds of needles and counselling, then I wasn't myself.' He scratched the side of his long nose. 'By the time I got my head above water it seemed rather too late. A shock, when I found out.'

To me, these words were rambling, cryptic, but Erin and I later discovered he'd had some sort of breakdown during his big break, the top billing that had finally come his way. He'd had to quit halfway through filming, and ended up in rehab. In the role of his life, his boots were hastily filled by another actor.

'So why are you here now?' I folded my arms.

'Okay,' he said. 'Okay, the letter from your school made it sound like you'd had a bit of trouble.' Our eyes met. So this was what had got his rehabilitated backside on a plane to England. Nan must have forwarded one of the missives from the headteacher, or maybe she sent the lot.

'So?'

He breathed out annoyance.

'So I'm trying to do the right thing, finally, if you could get it into your thick head . . .'

'You're here to make me study?'

He ignored this, instead pulling out a card wallet. Was he going to give me a handout?

'I was a mess, Arlo. I'm sorry. It was bad timing for you and Erin, but I'm okay now. I'm better than okay. I'm getting good money on the commercial circuit. Information films too. Have you heard of neuro-linguistic programming? What about Rutgers Applesauce? Well anyway, lots of promising stuff . . . and I've met an amazing lady.' The wallet flicked open to reveal one of those snapshots from a novelty photo booth, lovingly encircled in a gold heart, depicting a girl I would have happily pursued myself: ash-blonde and willowy, a healthy Californian blush on her cheeks. 'We've got a great condo, city views, south side. The schools are great there – I checked.'

With a jolt, I realised where this was going.

'The schools? You mean . . .'

He hesitated, obviously having planned a longer speech. 'Well, do you want to?'

Despite my scathing tone, the idea chimed interestingly. Los Angeles was big and sparkly, and it would be no bad thing to get away from Tupperware and spider plants and the odour of the fish fingers we'd had for tea. My life in LA played out like a movie at speed: Dad's immaculate chrome kitchen, the headache-bright orange juice that was not to be sipped from the carton, a bed with a new-smelling duvet in tasteful grey stripes. Brilliant sunshine and a tan like his, a million miles away from the pallid rectangles of the bay window, through which I could now see Nan dragging a black wheelie bin. It kept getting stuck on the uneven paving of the path, lid rattling as she struggled to dislodge it.

'What about Erin?'

He leaned in, elbows on knees, hands hanging loosely in the gap between. I noticed the large veins, the white edges of his nails.

'Erin too, once she's finished her finals. You can come after GCSEs so it's not too much of a disruption. Crysta goes to her parents in Vermont for the whole of July, anyway.'

'Crysta?'

The name made me recoil. Wake up and smell the mid-life crisis, Dad.

'Come on.' He sounded suddenly impatient. 'Don't keep me hanging.'

It had been two years and four months now since Mum died, and during that time he'd been acting and going to parties and fucking this Vermont girl and not getting on a plane or even calling, since he always said in his letters he wasn't a phone person. Eye contact, that's the key to communication. I made it now, willing him to see that my fifteen-year-old voice box could in no way articulate all the anger I felt towards him, for leaving in the first place and for coming back now, when his conscience had finally turned in its grave and told him to re-grasp the reins of parenthood.

Outside, Nan circumnavigated the gatepost at too acute an angle and the bin crashed over, spewing Asda bags and squashed-up boxes of cereal. It was too quiet to hear, but looking back I think there was a voice at the back of my head, nudging me to stand up at that point, ignoring Dad's cries of 'What? What are you doing now?' and making me stride out to get my hands filthy with rubbish juice.

He was Santa this Christmas, bringing me a tempting offer, but who would he be next year? Nothing had changed. He would always speed away towards his dreams, pushing everyone out of the way. Was that really who I wanted to be? The future had always looked so jagged and tangled, but in those brief minutes something seemed to settle. When I went back inside I'd find the right words to explain to him that someone here still needed me, and I'd only just realised how much that mattered.

As I took over from Nan, righting the wheelie bin while she tugged her cardigan closer and looked at me with wary surprise, I thought I heard it again: the whispering echo, so fragile, promising I'd get out of childhood in one piece, promising a new path.

Eighteen

Just beyond Winterbourne House, on the edge of campus, a track led through sparse woodland to an unexpected lake, its bulrushes like lollipops. Under clouds that had the soft glow of painted Renaissance skin, I gave my face to the mosquitoes, feeling the light touch as they landed and then took off once more, as though rejecting me.

When the day came for me to pack my boxes into Nan's old cream Mini and be driven to Birmingham, she could not hold back a few tears, even though we'd both been dreaming of this moment for ages. Things had been better between us since I'd stepped in, belatedly, to relieve some of the pressure of household tasks. Once or twice, much to my satisfaction, she'd even radiated that same gratefulness I'd become accustomed to enjoying from Mum. The respectable row of C grades I managed to pull out of the bag also went down well, and surprised me a little too. While outwardly I'd pretended not to care, that visit from Dad had changed my attitude entirely. From my messed-up, foggy brain, a plan of studying psychology condensed. What other subject would give me the insight I so desperately needed into the human brain? At A level I quietly applied myself to getting decent grades, beginning to understand why the French, geography, history, physics and other subjects of younger years had failed to interest me. What I'd really been learning was how to survive.

Now the autumn air was soft and still, and I could hear the lapping of the lake as I took a short cut towards university halls. It was sheer joy to have been thrown into a jumble-sale box of young people, cooking odours, too-loud music from tinny stereos and beer already building up in the two large fridges. After the isolation of the village, it was sensory overload. I smashed through the confines of my old self to become everyone's mate, the wiry, upbeat guy – a little too energetic, a bit rude – but laughing, always laughing. Mine were the Lambrini bottles lined up like skittles by the bin, and mine the lasagne that exploded all over the kitchen. I bought a black beanie, a little too small, and rammed it on top of my rebelliously long hair. Yes, I became that guy who wore a hat, never realising that girls would have to factor it very seriously into their calculations when deciding whether to sleep with me.

These days I was so keen to plunge forwards with life that

it was easy to forget my actions could be reversed. There may have been times it happened involuntarily: I'd be trying to cross a road and find my foot a few inches further back than I thought, just as a taxi skimmed too close to the kerb. Perhaps my gift was never meant to be anything more than a split-second flinch, operating at a subconscious level, and I'd been wrong to train or strain it into anything more. It straightened my path in life, though in dreams I ran rat-like through a labyrinth of possibilities.

'Arlo,' said the girl I'd had my eye on. 'Have I got that right? I'm Chloe, from Orkney. Chloe Glove.'

She was quite formal, neat in her tartan shirt, hair in a shiny black plait. We'd had one Introduction to Psychology seminar together, and were now recognising each other after a few drinks in someone's kitchen.

'I don't need your life story.'

Why did I say that? I was aiming for lightly facetious, but it came out harsh and I could see her face shutting down. The urge to leap back was too much.

'Chloe Glove.'

My best smile. 'A very fitting name.'

Amazingly, she'd not heard it before. Where had she been living? Well, up in Orkney, as I'd already been told. Later that night, snuggled in a dishevelled single duvet as she went to the sink, I thanked my lucky stars that I'd saved the banter and plucked our introduction from the brink of disaster.

It wasn't long before I had a box of tricks that made me quite successful on dates. For instance, it was quick and easy to identify a girl's favourite band, then click back a notch and say, 'Not a patch on Zeppelin, though.' Or I'd ask what she was thinking, repeat it back, and it worked like magic. In retrospect, this may have made me a weapons-grade arse, but at the time I saw it as harmlessly impersonating a mirror, attracting only those narcissists who really wanted to sleep with themselves.

Since I've never been a numbers person, and my loan seemed like boundless wealth, it came as a complete shock to find, midway through the second term, that I'd spent my entire balance and was plummeting into the red. University is the first time you properly spend your own money and, apparently, choosing beer over baked beans too often is not sustainable. I toyed with the idea of getting a job, and let a greasy burger bar application form sit on my desk for a week, but then someone bought a freezer pack of Mini Milks for the kitchen, and it gave me a better idea.

The splintery feel of the sticks inside the lollies took me back to the last time I'd made easy money, at a school fete with Nan. Between the usual offerings of tombola, guess-the-weight-of-the-teddy-bear, splat-the-rat and trace-the-metal-hoop-along-the-wire, there was an innocuous tray of sand studded with lolly sticks. Ten pence a go, find the red end, and win 50p. I didn't realise how easy it would be. Pick the wrong stick, undo that, and choose another until you hit the red one. Every 10p investment yielded a fivefold return. I managed several wins before the boy was irate enough to ban me.

Surely, thought my hungover student's brain, this principle could be scaled up to something like, say, the National Lottery. The promise of several million pounds was enough to bring me back to the idea of training. But was it even possible? My current record was only one minute and ten seconds, achievable if I did some simple, sensory action like tying shoelaces slowly, feeling the soft squash of fibres, the plastic ends digging into my fingertips. One minute, ten seconds. I watched the lottery draw on the cubic television in our kitchen, washing a mug with great care, feeling the warm water, scenting the lemon of the washing-up liquid. But even if I reversed, seeing the sludge on the mugs reappear, it was still only a minute or two before the draw began, and to get to the shop and get a ticket before sales closed would require an hour and a half, perhaps longer.

Something less ambitious was needed, and I'd already checked through the Yellow Pages for the address of the nearest casino, a short bus ride away. It was a bingo hall too, the smell of catalogue perfume and biscuits wafting through a window where someone warbled, 'Fifty-five, snakes alive . . .' My inexperience with such places must have shown on my face as I stepped onto the curly plastic mat, and the doorman chuckled at my hesitation.

'I dread to think where you keep your wallet,' he joked, gesturing to my skinny body. 'In you go.' He waved me through to a counter, where I was ID'd thoroughly and allowed to exchange a tenner for plastic counters, slid across the cash desk by a woman who looked curiously at my torn jeans, as though I was a kid who'd taken a wrong turn.

Pink rope lights led me into a hall with the atmosphere of a bowling alley or cinema complex, all fast food and industrial floor-polishers, though there was not a basket meal in sight, only waitresses in neat black trousers. I looked around the various islands, and dealers stared back with knowing, predatory eyes. My heart was beating so fast it made me jittery, but I was determined not to show it. I went to the roulette table, telling myself I was Bond, James Bond, and wondering whether to get a drink, as this was going to take some time.

A little ham-fisted, I placed half my chips – just in case – on number 18. The ball was tossed onto the wheel, which the croupier spun with a graceful, practised movement. No breathing until it ceased its rattle, coming to rest on a different number, and then I mentally yanked myself back so the chips were in my hand again. What number had it been? I couldn't quite . . . but it had definitely been red.

'All on red, sir? Stack 'em up!'

This time I got it. Fourteen, or was it forty-one? Forty-one! Relax. Do it again.

Delight from the croupier. 'Are you sure you haven't done

this before?' A wink at my beginner's luck. 'You're charmed. You're making your fortune, young man.'

Then, later: 'Oh, you really are charmed, aren't you? How exactly are you doing that?'

So long as I didn't sneeze, or do anything to affect the croupier's delicate manipulation of the equipment, my predictive powers were more or less foolproof, and soon I was winning so much that punters and waiters alike were drifting to my side. There is a finite period in which the management try to work out how you are doing it. After that, they simply declare you in breach of the laws of probability and politely ask you to leave. The bouncer looked at me with eyes like black snooker balls.

'University boy, aren't you? It's the way you talk. Yeah, maybe don't come round here with your smart tricks again. I know you boffins have systems . . .'

What did I care? I'd just won the term's rent, thrilling at the texture and smell of the new £20 notes in my pocket. It had been so easy, and where was the harm? Casinos sold hope to the vulnerable, didn't they? If I'd made the corporate machine cough up a windfall, then we were one cough closer to utopia. Someone had to rock the foundations of the gambling sector, and maybe that person was me, though I might have to put up with getting filthy rich in the process.

In a city as large as Birmingham, and especially one newly 'regenerated', there were plenty of opportunities for someone who could momentarily pinch the wings of the near future.

Not only were there casinos but also a wealth of betting shops that would take money right up to the wire, and even in-game for football matches. I hardly needed to skip back sixty seconds to tell them who would score next, and it gave me an excuse to watch a lot of sports.

These bookies were full of serious men, hunched in bomber jackets on high metal stools, grizzled from their standoffs with fate. After a few conversations, I learned the personal nature of their omens, the certainty that they would win today because they had not showered for a week, or they'd seen their nickname on the front page of the *Mirror*. To me, superstition has always seemed messy. Why substitute arbitrary rules for the laws of cause and effect? In these surroundings, I felt like the last champion of logic, the only one equipped to both expose and beat the universe at its game of chance. The men eyed me with suspicion, fearing I'd scupper their luck. Perhaps they were right, since I came away with hauls that kept me going well into second year, and there were still a few large casinos left untapped.

So now I was a rich student, the kind every non-student hated. In a lofty houseshare in Selly Oak, mine was the master bedroom, mine the cases of premium beer on top of the cupboards. I could have afforded to live alone, but who would want that? Being a student was a once-in-a-lifetime opportunity, and I had the luxury of never needing to choose between beans and beer.

I managed to buy a second-hand Audi TT from our football coach, just flashy enough to stand out in the sports centre car park, and developed a CD-buying habit that made my room resemble a record shop. When it was someone's birthday, I'd show up with a bottle or two of champagne, enjoying the reaction to my generosity. People wondered where I got the cash. 'Family,' I said. 'Rich family.' It was a classically boring response that invited no further enquiries, plus the thought of asking Nan for a handout from her pension was sheer comedy. For someone who'd grown up wearing second-hand shoes and eating yellow-stickered ready meals, a full wallet was new, exciting and very dangerous.

At parties, I was the one who had money for drugs, helping out a few friends and making new ones. Back at school, the world needed to be torn apart, but now it was my plaything. The beauty of being a short-term time traveller is that you can swallow a pill a hundred times, make the night last for ever. I'd fetch up at random houses, deep in the stench of some beer-soaked sofa, my tongue a similar texture and my cheeks chewed raw. If I'd undone a thousand things the night before, I wouldn't know. Amid the upward roar, the rush in my ears, it was impossible to tell which of my actions were real, and some of the memories left me shaking and shot through with adrenaline, hoping to God I'd wiped them out, or else forged them in a dream.

The trick was to ignore the lows. Why would you pay

attention to the shadows? It was all about getting to that bare, brilliant, eagle-polished peak, emerging from the flashing spotlights of a club, feet lifting from sticky floors, clothes splashed with vod-bull, bedazzled in the purest light. It was a rebirth into a world of pleasure, parent-free and purged of all darkness, in which I would sometimes believe I'd only dreamt the snake, that the ladder was a tree falling in the forest, and there was nothing I could have done to stop it.

In second year, I was guilty of being that languid, smiling bastard who sits around pointing out the vanities and hypocrisies of others, sometimes failing, through sheer lack of impetus, to undo a cruel jibe. It was not that I wanted to be offensive, just that words were smoke and I didn't understand why people paid them so much attention. If everything could be undone at the flick of a switch, so to speak, you lost interest in the short term. These minutes were just a sketchpad for messing about, or so I thought at the time. When I came to pay the price for this attitude, I'd berate myself for being so stupid, for not realising that the raw material of the long term is right here, right now.

Much to my surprise, I was discovering that there were others like me. After a rugby taster session one fine Monday, I found myself on an expensive bar crawl with a guy known only as 'Tomton' and some of the weirdest students I'd ever met. Their conversation ranged from mundane to insane, they flicked coins at bar staff and did coke on bathroom windowsills, and they chose which lectures to attend on the basis of entertainment value alone.

Immediately I was captivated, thinking I'd found a bunch of people who were on my wavelength, who did not fear making mistakes. Living off the fat of my reputation, I was welcomed into their gang and went on a bender that ended with me being kept in someone's room for about three days, not being allowed to go home. In the midst of the haze, questions had arisen: how did they dare to do all these things, to pop pills in front of bar staff, torment women and throw money like confetti? The answer was laughter, squeaky and burbling, like mice being emptied from a bucket, and always the same pleasing sentiment: 'What does it matter?'

Judging by the light, it must have been early evening when I awoke into a room full of smoke, my mouth tasting of grenadine and goose down. My fellow revellers were in various states of undress, playing cards on the bed and talking about hedgehogs, or maybe it was hedge funds.

'You, Arlo,' one of them snapped. 'What do your parentals do?'

I groaned at waking up to such a question, and smudged a hand across my face.

'My dad's an actor. My mum does nothing.'

They nodded with raised eyebrows at the actor bit, some unspoken protocol of discretion holding them back from asking questions about his fame. Tomton twisted his face into annoyance.

'See, I wish my mum would do nothing. She has these neuroticisms, like hiding the coffee grinder from the cleaner . . .' He carried on, his voice like a scratchy flute but I was zoning out. The weekdays lined up in my mind, and I realised how many classes I'd missed.

'Where are you going?'

It was so hard to get to my feet. 'Seminar,' I said. 'They can't cope without me.' Somehow, I broke through their almost viscous disgust and made it to the door. These student rooms were like mini-suites, the corridor thickly carpeted and the wall unscuffed. Now I was away from their little den I wondered what in God's name they were doing. Did they believe a degree was a souvenir scroll you purchased at the university gift shop? With every step, I slipped back into the shoes of a kid from south London, hating myself for pulling out the 'actor' card, shuddering at the way they'd talked about their mothers. They were fearless – it struck me at last – not because they secretly had powers matching my own, but as a result of having been fed and watered on money from an early age. There was nothing they or their families could ever do that would put them out on the street. They'd never tasted risk.

My knuckles, wound up as I was, somehow made contact with the glass of the fire alarm on the way out, and all I could hope was that their game hadn't left them completely naked. Being a rich student was all very well, but there was no way I was going down the same path as these guys, even though they'd probably end up running the country.

Arriving late, I earned a few caustic remarks from the Behavioural Studies tutor, but I have to admit my overriding feeling was pride at having made it to the seminar at all. While I hated Freud and sometimes Jung, and half the social sciences made no sense, the quiet voice at the back of my head had been making me get up for classes. If there was a deadline coming, I'd even been known to undo the double vodka I'd just necked at the bar, head back to my room and study.

That night, I went out to the lake, took off all my clothes and jumped in, just to see what it felt like, before sensing the dry fabric re-materialise around me. That was its purpose, wasn't it, this muscle in my brain? It was to give me an education over and above every other graduate of this university, a degree so rich and authentic that no scroll could contain it. I'd be the man who'd tried everything, in secret, and cared for nothing.

Twenty

This is the story of how the money tree met its end, sorrow-fully shedding its crisp green flowers and jingling fruit. Why couldn't I go on visiting casinos and betting shops instead of the bank? The answer came amid jazzy music, candy colours spelling out the word 'bingo' and a puff of hot air from the entrance heaters before the doorman stopped me. 'Wait there a moment, sir.' He ducked inside and then reappeared. 'You can go through to the bingo but we can't issue chips, just so you know.'

'I'm over eighteen,' I said, scrabbling in my back pocket for ID.

'It's not that, sir – you're on a list.'

'What list?'

'We reserve the right to refuse entry.'

'Why?'

'Your name is on a list.'

'You don't know my name.'

'Your picture too, sir.'

I took off my hat, a retro thing with a perky rim, cursing myself for not toning it down. No wonder they were recognising me.

'I haven't done anything wrong.'

'Not saying you have, sir, but you're on the list.'

We stared at each other. He had a cut on his upper lip, where a beauty mark might appear on a woman. It could have been gained in a fight, or simply from shaving.

'Are you saying I cheat?' I tried to keep the anger out of my voice.

'Not saying anything.'

He wasn't, but I was determined to make him. This was so unfair. It was only the third time I'd hit the place. They must keep an eye on the ebb and flow of fortune much more than people realise. Perhaps I had a bit of luck about me, but that wasn't against the rules, was it? I put this to him, but he was growing weary, wanting the conversation to be over. His hands burrowed into the pockets of his black Puffa jacket.

'Go be lucky someplace else.'

A good punch might have opened up his irritatingly closed face, but these bouncer types often had martial arts training and maybe he'd break my arm before I could blink. It would be undone, of course, but nobody wants to go through that, even for an instant.

The bus took ages to arrive, and I stayed on past the university and into town, where I buzzed around betting shops, seeking nectar. To my astonishment, the first one, which was part of a chain, told me they weren't accepting wagers on the athletics, the only option for a quick return. Did they have me on a list as well? When I reached the next bookies, an independent place full of Eastern Europeans, I pushed my betting float across the counter, reached into my back pocket and found my driver's licence gone. A panicked search came up with nothing. Had it fluttered onto the steps of the casino, several miles away, or did I only imagine putting it into my pocket? Sheepishly I scraped back my cash and went in a sullen mood to the nearest bar, an old man's pub that smelled of wet dog but where I could at least make twenty quid on a fruit machine, though its whooping, flashing cherries grated on my sanity.

It was not even chucking out time, but people swirled and stumbled and got in the way of traffic, girls with flawless legs and bare, chilly shoulders, tottering in heels, helping the one who had gone too far and was folding into a retch. I found a taxi rank and tucked cold fists into my armpits as I waited, standing apart from the only other person in line, a girl leaning on a bollard. Partygoers washed around us, tugging down the hems of skin-tight dresses, arguing about where to go. A group of them stepped on my toes, then had a full-frontal collision with a couple of guys, the banter escalating till I wanted to be airlifted from its midst. It was so monotonous and fake, so infused with desperation. At last they moved on, leaving the girl and me settling back into the road noise and fumes.

She was vulnerable, being on her own and ripe for taking home. Each time someone approached her, she would shake her head, making it look even more child-sized on its small, snappable neck. Though she was not really my type, I kept sneaking glances her way, just because she was so out of place, so sober-looking and alone. Eventually she unfolded her arms and, removing a polystyrene box from under her brown leather jacket, bit into a burger she'd obviously been saving for the ride. As she chewed, a guy in a baseball cap approached, twisting it round when he began to speak. Poor fella, I thought, wasting his time. She let him say his piece and then, in a lull between passing cars, my ears pricked up at her polite refusal, accompanied by a wry grin:

'So now I've wounded your ego,' she murmured, 'just imagine I've said something to bolster it, that you're a great guy or have an amazing smile or something – whatever gives you a high. Pick something, okay? You'll do it much better than me.'

It was so deadpan, her tone acknowledging it was a waste of breath, but she wanted to try it out loud anyway, to go off script and see if he could follow.

Sadly, he couldn't. A beat passed before he snatched the burger and threw it across the road. Shreds of lettuce were scattered by the wind, the smell of barbecue sauce dissipating. She looked sadly at the empty polystyrene, then stepped forward as a taxi pulled in, vanishing inside before I could think about the fact that we were probably both going towards the university. Not that someone like her would have wanted to share. Not with me, who had always been just another burger-throwing guy, though I'd probably reverse it just as quickly and let her eat.

My own ride turned up a second later, the cars coming in gluts, as they tend to, and I rattled around in the back. Things had gone badly today, but I felt better now, even a little pathetic for nearly having a meltdown. Perhaps something of the girl's calm acceptance had rubbed off on me.

By third year, even the wildest and most itinerant student has pondered what their next step will be. Much to my disappointment, the psychology classes had left me none the wiser with regard to my gift, and it was high time I made an effort to explore it myself, to categorise it as blessing or curse. Until now I'd spent my time dodging from one kind of denial to another: forgetting, pretending it would go away or that I'd grow out of it. Sometimes I even thought it was my imagination, that I was just a very indecisive person playing out each scenario inside my head, thinking it was real.

Since the world of betting had soured, my eyes were once

again on the prize. A lottery win would be simple and legal, with no petty cashiers or bouncers in the way. Beneath my other studies, I began covert research into the back and forth of my life. It took zero time. Housemates would pass me in the corridor, seeing me standing at the bottom of the stairs, never knowing I'd spent the last half an hour going up and then willing myself back down, going at a snail's pace – a snail would have been quicker – remembering the feel of the rail under my hand. The slowness was important, it added time, allowing me to undo three minutes rather than one. I thought it would be impossible to reach the top while still remembering what the bottom stair felt like, which exact areas of the ball of my foot had touched it, how I'd breathed. But memory can develop, and I kept at it, putting in an extra hour before football practice each week, training like a metaphysical version of Rocky.

Soon I could eat an entire breakfast and then go back to the moment it arrived steaming at my table. Imagine being able to eat as many breakfasts as you wanted, spending the equivalent of a whole day stuffing bacon and scrambled egg into your mouth. But there were no double portions; each time I was as famished as before, the previous satisfaction forgotten. Yet I liked the idea that if an experience was truly amazing it might be feasible to set up a little vortex in time, and live inside it for a while.

The big day was approaching. On the Friday I emptied out the sweets jar we had in our living room, full of condoms stolen from the health centre (big thick ones that robbed you of all sensation). I spread them on the table and began to build a drystone wall in slow motion, eking it out to forty-five minutes. Then I went to the health centre and stole another hundred. That gave me one and a half hours.

Saturday waned into a greasy twilight. My mate's house-share was right next to the newsagent, and I caused great hilarity by sitting in his living room building my condom wall over such a long period, forehead contorted with concentration, oblivious to every taunt. I was feeling each foil packet, absorbing the fruity fragrance. Red, green, blue; red, green, blue. The television was switched to the lottery draw as I instructed, my friend playing his part in my bizarre instructions. As soon as the numbers were announced, I memorised them, singing them back, confident they were burned into my brain. Then, with the biggest effort of my life, I held every sensation in my memory and undid the lot. An instant of disorientation found me at the table with the first condom grasped between finger and thumb, the wall unbuilt. It was before 7.30. I legged it to the newsagent, scattering forms as I snatched one, pen hovering.

Could I remember the numbers?

Not a damn digit. My mind was all graphite smudge. I filled out the ticket anyway, praying to my subconscious, and then it was back home for the agonising wait. Lottery ticket in hand, I was so expectant that the whole household crowded around to watch the draw. Balls were extracted from the tumbling drum with the usual fanfare, but not a single number matched. Even my nan's syndicate managed a tenner every fortnight or so.

No matter how many times I repeated this process, or how I tweaked it, time invariably fogged the winning line. It was like hearing someone rattle off a phone number and being expected to remember it at the end of the conversation, so much harder than recalling what else had been said. I could hold onto numbers if the backwards leap was only a minute or so, but any longer and they were spaghetti.

There followed a period in which I spent a lot of time sitting on the sofa trying to kill myself with alcohol. At least I'd proved I could go back all that way – wasn't that an achievement? Well no, it wasn't, because what was the point of an hour and a half?

Why bother with any time travel unless I could go back seven years? This was the needle that still jabbed me, broken off in my heart. If my abilities had been known back then, if I'd been less spoiled and careless, then maybe I could have blossomed a bit earlier, been a bit more Mozart-like about it. As soon as she started falling, I'd catch hold of a few seconds – so easy now – and be there gripping the ladder. I'd eat my Rolos and afterwards venture out and smash that slow-worm into a snake-shaped stain on the grass.

One evening my housemate Tim, who I was starting to

see as a rather pitifully nice guy, sat beside me and set up his erotic jigsaw puzzle on the coffee table. He claimed it was quicker than waiting for anything to download on our broadband, and I let him get on with it, pushing my cereal bowl under the sofa, only to see another one pop out.

'What's up with you?' he said, keeping his eyes on the pinkish puzzle pieces. It was Saturday night, and the house was just settling into the peacefulness that descends once the partygoers have departed.

'What are you thinking?' I asked dully.

'Right now? That I was dumb to start this conversation.'

An easy leap backwards and I gave him his thought.

'You're a clever guy, Arlo, that's your problem. You reckon you can read people's minds, and nobody thinks the same way you do.'

'Correct.'

'It's bull.'

I took a long suck on a bottle of Spitfire, my beer of choice, annoyed that I was running out and would have to face a trip to the Harborne off-licence that sold it before term ended.

'It's not bull, Tim. I can't share my innermost thoughts with anyone.'

'Yeah? Try me.'

'You first.'

'Innermost thoughts?' A challenge. As luck would have it, we were both drunk enough. After a ponderous pause,

Tim's voice quietened. 'Sometimes I think I've ruined myself,' he said. 'Like, I don't think I've got the tools to have a real relationship.'

A cough caught in my throat. This was way more personal than I'd expected, and coming completely out of the blue, but I could just about decipher what he meant. There was the instinct to mock, of course; a clockwork monkey already playing its cymbals in my head. I let it wind down before continuing.

'How do you mean? Too much shagging around?'

A nod. 'Some things about my "normal" aren't really normal for other people.' He sighed. 'Ironically, it's sending my libido the other way. I'm going to see the doctor about it, just in case there's a medical explanation that'll make me feel like less of a freak.'

He raised his eyebrows to indicate that it was my turn.

'Okay,' I said, 'For what it's worth . . . I could tell what you were thinking, just now, because I asked you and then reversed it. Shall I do it again?' I did it again and he frowned. 'It works with secrets too,' I said. My glance strayed to the television, which was back to the football, its jostling, bobble-hatted crowd hushing for a penalty.

'Haven't I just done a secret?'

'Yeah, but you're not convinced. Tell me . . . I don't know . . . where you had your first wank.'

'That's too long ago to remember.' He started hooking crockery out from under the sofa. 'There was this one occasion in the basement of a teacher's house . . . A bit vindictive really. I'm not proud.'

I looked at him, impressed. Then I skipped back to the penalty and told him all about his shameful activities. At once, I realised my mistake.

'How the fuck do you know that?' He was bolt upright, a spark of fear in his eyes, shaken by having something he considered a major secret thrown back at him so casually. The wickedness I'd admired only a second ago had backfired.

I sighed. Tim was my best friend at university, and some things are more important than others. With a certain sadness, I knocked it right back to his sex chat.

'So you're going to the doctor?' I took a draught of beer. 'Interesting.'

Twenty

At Christmas I learned that Erin was going blind. We sat on Nan's familiar thin-cushioned armchairs, the white plastic tree sparkling and glittering away. My sister took off her thick glasses and waved a hand in front of her eyes at arm's length, as though this demonstration might benefit the rest of us.

'It's degenerative,' she said. 'My eyes don't adjust in the dark any more, and I have to be three times closer to read anything.'

'Can't they give you something for it?' Nan said.

She shook her head. 'It's irreversible.'

My natural assumption, that it had resulted from over-swotting, was incorrect. Apparently it was more than just eyestrain, and the flashing lights and other symptoms had baffled doctors, until a specialist at the low vision clinic diagnosed a rare retinal dystrophy known as Visner's syndrome.

She cut a pitiful figure, wiping her lenses as though one less smear would make all the difference. Finishing university – which in her case meant a full-on doctorate – had not changed Erin, as it was changing me, but made her more like herself: even more moon-faced and cautious, uncommunicative except when she was painfully blunt. I could see from her black-rimmed glasses and dark, layered hair – my father's hair – that she had found some sort of style for herself, as we all do in our twenties, unconsciously choosing how we will dress for the rest of our lives.

'Can I try your beer?' she said, as I levered off the metal cap. It was my favourite brand, hunted and gathered at the supermarket by Nan. My eyebrows shot up.

'Are you sure?' I tipped a splash of it into the dregs of her water glass.

'I still had water in there.'

'That's good. It'll dilute it.'

Our current low level of squabbling was an achievement, though I still dipped my words in protective sarcasm. Any serious talk would still be dangerous. It was uncertain how much she remembered of the time I'd beat her almost senseless on the sterile floor tiles beneath Mum's hospital bed, and I was probably still hoping we'd go through life without ever having a real conversation about it.

* * *

Goalposts are slippery things. Over Christmas, quite by chance, I'd solved the financial crisis that had been getting me down. It was irksome not being able to remember lottery numbers, and I'd spent ages trying to work out why my memory was so bad after undoing. The brain has a lot of survival techniques, and perhaps it needed to erase stuff that had been undone to preserve the illusion of a cause-and-effect narrative, for the sake of my sanity. In any case, I'd found a new way of supplementing my student loan. Scratch cards, surprisingly, had their uses. Sure, you couldn't really ask the cashier for any card except the first one torn from the roll, but if there was no cash to be scratched you could undo the purchase. There were endless places to buy them and, after netting a few small wins, a haul of ten grand set me up nicely.

There was only one more term to go, and with exams just weeks away it was even harder to carve out time for what I really wanted to read: psychology journals featuring patients who could do something extraordinary. In the library I'd discovered this treasure trove, with examples of every imaginable brain. Finally my studies were yielding something interesting. There were individuals claiming telekinesis, foresight, time travel, mind reading or divine guidance, all categorised as delusional. Many of the cases were from decades ago, most of the subjects deceased. But how did the researchers know for sure that these people were lying? Could they prove that patient C. S. was not, in fact, Jesus? Even if there was no outward manifestation of unusual powers, within the person's individual reality it might still be true. With everyone wearing subjectivity specs, how could a clinical psychologist ever see the full picture?

I'd also given some thought to the blessing–curse spectrum. A Midas touch might initially sparkle, but sit it on the scales and they would soon tip towards misery. Mine was an additional bonus life skill that no one else had. It meant I could avoid mistakes, win people over, win money. Win. So why did it sometimes make me feel like a loser? As my chat with Tim had demonstrated, it was far from simple to communicate what I was going through. Even if I did make someone believe me – if I went on TV and did tricks until the audience were beaten into submission – I'd be ushered away from normality for good. A card-carrying freak.

It was the word Tim had used to describe himself, again and again, purely because he kept oscillating between intensive spells of one-night stands and periods of celibacy. To my surprise, his trip to the health centre had perked him up considerably. They'd given him a six-week course of counselling for his libido issues and, if not a whole new person, he was at least more optimistic. It would never have occurred to me that you could go to a medical professional, tell them you'd lost interest in sex, and they'd do anything but laugh their arse off.

If you could say that, you could say anything. Or so I hoped.

* * *

I put it off for months, booking the appointment amid a blur of post-exam drunkenness, certain it would be a complete waste of time. But what did I have to lose? My nervousness had grown considerably in the intervening twenty-four hours, but when I found myself in a warm consulting room I was reassured by the amiable appearance of Dr Mogg, whose stripy shirt was crying out for a bowtie. The large ceramic bowl of condoms beside his computer monitor announced that, dealing predominantly with students, he was thoroughly modern and unshockable.

'Mr Knott,' he said, 'what can I do for you?'

Think patient confidentiality, I told myself.

'It's a bit weird . . .'

'Good, I like weird. Makes a change from coughs and colds.'

'It might be called a mental thing.'

His eyebrows floated higher, grey cirrus clouds, but the smile remained. 'Go on.'

'I can do something . . . like drink a beer . . . and then my mind takes me back to before I've done it.'

It was late in the day, and he struggled to arrest the amusement spreading across his features.

'That sounds a lot like the phenomenon we know as memory, but do go on.'

I let my breath out slowly. On the grass bank outside the window, I saw two girls with crocheted hats and fingerless gloves pass by, smoking, and felt a tremendous desire for a deep drag, preferably on something a bit stronger than shop-bought fags.

'It's not in my mind,' I went on. 'I go back a few moments, sometimes more, in time and I can choose whether or not to do the same thing again.' Was I explaining it badly? He drew himself up to the computer and clicked the mouse, a screen of Yahoo results visible before it was closed.

'I see,' he said. 'And when does this occur?'

'Whenever I want.'

'Could you do it for me now?'

I went back to the W of 'whenever', and closed my mouth.

'And when does this occur?' he asked again, thinking I hadn't heard.

'Sorry, you just asked me to do a demo, so I went back a few seconds.'

He rubbed his chin, the sound of dry fingers against invisible stubble.

'I didn't notice.'

'Shall I do it again?'

'Yes.'

I went back to 'whenever'. The same thing happened, of course. By now I was no longer relaxed, and he was picking up on my tension. The convivial atmosphere had evaporated, and we were two people struggling to understand one another. He moved the bowl of condoms a fraction further from the blood pressure pump, and for an instant I thought he might be about to offer it to me, to make some crack about what I really wanted. In desperation I waited for more people to pass outside the window so I could go back and predict it. None came. The grass remained muddy and bare, the surgery quiet except for a distant whine, perhaps someone vacuuming. The walls were festooned with posters about STDs and meningitis, stubbornly refusing to peel away from their Blu-Tack. Nothing moved.

'So is it . . . a disease or something?' I asked lamely.

'Is what a disease?'

'This thing.'

'What thing?' He was leaning back, his answers pitched to meet mine, playing Snap.

'I've just shown you twice.'

'Well, I haven't seen anything, I'm afraid.'

'Look.' I gripped the edge of his desk, looking him in the eye. 'Tell me what you're thinking.'

'I beg your pardon?'

'Tell me what you're thinking, or tell me a secret, something only you would know.'

'I'm starting to think, Mr Knott, that you may be wasting my time.'

My fist made the condoms fly up like mortarboards at graduation.

'I'm not wasting your time.'

He sat up straight, eyes darting to the door. 'We have a zero tolerance policy on . . .'

I went back to pre-thump.

'I'm not wasting your time. Tell me what you're thinking.'

He reached to the desk and slid an A5 piece of card from a snug brown envelope, on which I could see my name.

'Psychology undergrad, yes? Is this part of an assignment. Because if so, I need to fill you in on the ethics of—'

'This isn't part of my degree.' I was furious at his unprofessionalism. 'I'm bringing you a problem. Why won't you take it seriously?'

'I take all medical complaints very seriously, but you haven't told me you are ill and you have described no symptoms. What exactly am I treating?'

'Tell me a secret and I'll show you.'

'I'm not here to tell you secrets . . . Honestly, if the student paper wants something, you can—'

I stood up, grabbed his monitor and hurled it towards the window, an upward thrust that, despite the trailing wire, put a spiderweb of cracks across the double glazing.

'. . . I'm not here to tell you secrets.' The window was intact again. I sat there calmly, realising I'd been completely mistaken in my first impression. This was a jaded, lazy medic, possibly with a few skeletons in his cupboard. It is a credit to my journey of self-development that I didn't storm out at this point.

'I know this sounds crazy or delusional,' I murmured, 'but if you could just humour me for thirty seconds, I'll be gone and you can shut up shop.'

'Take as long as you need.' I'd set a tone, and he had readjusted accordingly.

I scratched the back of my neck where my jacket label itched. 'Has there ever been a precedent for someone being able to do as I've just described, going back in time to before they acted?'

'No.'

'Is it possible?'

'You're talking about physics, not biology, so I wouldn't know.' A surprisingly open-minded response, considering what I'd heard from him so far. The distant vacuum hum came closer, creating an intimate feel to our conversation, as though we were the last people in the surgery.

'So if someone did have this weird condition, what would be your advice?'

'To consult a physicist.' He gave a short laugh. 'That's assuming there are no other symptoms to treat.'

'What about stress?'

He fell on the word hungrily. 'Stress I can do.' Back on solid ground, he proceeded to outline the usual options available to a student buckling under the pressure of exams, eyeing me in a way that said I'd described a common problem in some very strange terms. His facial hair moved as he spoke, thick hands slicing through the air to divide up the options, reminding me of the older medic who had spent so long trying to explain my mum's condition. As before, I was filtering out the sound of the doctor's voice, entering a sort of trance, and my stomach was becoming unsettled. I was anxious to leave.

By the time the printer was deafening us with its nasal racket, hawking up a prescription for diazepam that I would never use, he was almost jovial. 'You had me going,' he said, stuffing my notes back into their envelope. As I was leaving, he pointed to a poster on the door that featured the words 'Keep Calm and Carry On', not yet reproduced ad nauseam, and added: 'Found this in a bookshop the other day. Good sentiment, don't you think?'

Some years later, I read the story of that 1939 flyer and learned that its original two-and-a-half-million copies were never displayed. Dr Mogg's cheery, bright-red sign was meant only to be used in the event of total disaster: a German invasion or apocalyptic air-raid.

'Goodbye, Mr Knott,' said the doctor. 'Try not to worry.'

Try not to worry. His reassurance would mean nothing, even if my condition had been on his radar, on the first page of Yahoo results or treatable with antibiotics. The human body was a convergence of miracles gift-wrapped in skin, but he was blinkered to everything save his own tiny reper-toire of ailments. No wonder people got shut away in asylums.

It was clear by now that this wasn't my story, that going down the medical route would cross out my uniqueness and write the word 'freak' in its place. This visit to the doctor dispersed my last tattered hopes of finding other people who might share my condition, or an explanation of what it was.

There'd be no one to offer guidance or to help me work things out. Other people would pass me in the street and we would be walking on two different pavements, two different planes of existence. I was incomprehensible to medical science, which meant, rather worryingly, that I was potentially interesting to medical scientists.

As a psychology student you see so many slivers of brain. The brain of an epileptic, an insomniac, a pyromaniac, an amnesiac, someone with dementia, someone who'd killed fourteen people. I'd seen studies of patients who had Cotard's or 'walking corpse' syndrome, who believed they were dead and sometimes immortal, of prosopagnosiacs who saw apples and blank walls and hat stands instead of faces, studies of people who believed their wives or children had been replaced by imposters, people with multiple personalities or stroke victims who came out the other side speaking in a foreign accent. They all became slides for the microscope, eventually. Some were cited hundreds of times in journals, like the fascinating amnesia case of H. M., whose brain was carefully preserved and turned into a three-dimensional digital atlas. I may have aced half a dozen exams in experimental and clinical psychology, but the thought of any kind of career in this area was suddenly repulsive, as though one of those cases might rise from the journal pages, white and starchy as a clinic bed, and ask if I'd like to switch places.

Dr Mogg could keep calm and carry on if he liked, but I was damned if I was going to become patient A. K.

Twenty-one

Graduation day is another episode I'd prefer to forget. In many ways, it was the best day of my life, though for the woman I came to love, it was the worst. This jagged, broken bottle of a day started badly, with me going up to get my scroll amid palm-saving, obligatory applause. There were no parents clapping extra-hard in the crowd, and I'd never felt so invisible. Nan's voice had been sheepish as she'd explained on the phone that she finally had a date for her long-awaited hip operation, and could I guess when it was? Erin might have attended if I'd asked her, but I didn't, and as for Dad . . . A small part of me cast an eye over the crowds, almost fearing I'd see his inappropriately long coat, hair flopping over rimless glasses.

What do you do with yourself on graduation day once the compulsory throwing-mortarboards photo has been taken? I mingled in a sunlit plaza where people were chatting with their families, drinking Pimm's from a pop-up bar. Tim was nearby, utterly surrounded by his substantial kin, who were gangly and beaming and noticeably alike. A text beeped on my phone. I saw the name and could hardly believe it.

Since that awkward encounter at Nan's, when I was fifteen and he showed up at Christmas time, Dad had sent only two fairly meaningless texts. It was from the letters he'd exchanged with Erin that I learned it hadn't been all plain sailing back to stardom. He was still stuck doing adverts and – even better – the Vermont girl had dumped him. As I sought shade under one of the awnings, cupping the Nokia screen to try and make out the tiny black letters, I wondered if I'd misjudged him, since he'd at least taken the time to remember my graduation. The text read:

I thought you'd like to know I'm on the box tonight. Channel 5. *Dog Cops*. It's a lousy script but I'm not too dreadful. x x

Two kisses – what were they, fucking air kisses? It was some moments before I could free myself from a paralytic rage. There were a few people to elbow aside, but I grabbed Tim by the gown and whispered in his ear.

'Can you get away for a couple? I need a drink.'

He looked pained, but after a word to his sibling he lifted his robes and followed me away from the sickly strawberry odours and round to a union-run beer stand where I got us two pints straight away, and vodka chasers for good measure. We sat on a bench in the sun and I read him the text. My voice shook a little, until I took the shot. It was bad enough graduating when there was nobody watching who cared, but this was an unexpected punch to the gut. I cursed him, and hated Erin for giving him my number.

'I guess it's just what actors are like,' Tim said, sanguine as ever. I stared at his pale, almost translucent skin, already going pink in the sun. He'd got on the graduate scheme of a top law firm, shocked at his own success and hardly believing he was moving to London. I knew he'd be a brilliant lawyer, rational but human. He had a calling, while I still didn't know what I wanted to do except not be a psychologist. 'You didn't want him here anyway.'

I said nothing. Dad had sucked up so much glory from his stupid career. What was acting if not professional fakery? Lying wasn't difficult. On the occasions I'd seen him on stage during my childhood, it had always seemed as though he was playing a version of himself, much the same as when we were at home. He was cheating, and nobody but me could see it.

'I'm really going off actors,' I said, draining my pint, watching the last line of froth slide back down the glass.

'Celebrity is such a get-out-of-jail-free card,' Tim agreed. 'I had to work ten hours a day in the library for most of this year, but they hand out honorary degrees for free if you're famous.'

'They do what?'

'Did you sleep through the degree presentation? There were a couple during our ceremony; mostly scientists, to be fair, but at the 2 p.m. show I hear they're giving one to Stephen Fry.'

This made no sense. 'Why would they want to give him a degree?'

'I don't know, for fun? To get a free speaker?'

'But he's not an academic, he's an actor.'

Tim shrugged. 'They gave one to Simon Callow the year before last.' His eyes slipped back wistfully towards his family throng.

This whole day was bugging me, everything from the expensive hire of gown and mortarboard to the pomp and ceremony. Now, to top it all, they were trivialising our hard work by handing out degrees like supermarket coupons. Would I be watching Dad saunter up to the podium if he'd got his big film break? I could just envisage him saying a few smug words about his craft, his muse – and being honoured without having left so much as a fingerprint of sweat on any textbook.

I downed the vodka, and the pint, and went up to the bar again, as Tim was drinking too slowly. To my joy, they had

Spitfire in bottles. I picked up another shot at the same time. I wanted to feel the burn, the hurt in my mind transposed to my throat. To one side, a photo booth had been set up, where a photographer was taking pictures of guys and their girlfriends, groups of mates, parents with their fledglings in between. White umbrellas diffused the light over their faces, the snap of shutters stop-motioning people along the red carpet, because today they were famous, celebrated. They were celebrities.

'I've got to get back.' Tim was sheepish. 'They've come all the way from Hull. Will you be okay?'

'Me?' I clamped my lips round the neck of the bottle, drank and detached it with flute-like suction. 'Sure. I'll go see if I can get a glimpse of all these stars.' He must have noticed the bitterness in my tone, but the pull of duty was too strong.

'Okay, well don't explode with happiness or anything.'

I watched him leave, knowing that tomorrow I'd go back to appreciating him, but frowning with resentment because he was going off with his family while I had no one. Nobody to perform for, I told myself, so relax. Student days are over. Get smashed.

By the time I was halfway through my fifth Spitfire, big things mattered less, and small ones so much more. I took out my phone and re-read the text. It really was all about him, sitting in the windowless control-centre of his own ego. Putting yourself in front of a camera doesn't make you matter, I wanted to tell him. You see this piece of paper in my gown pocket? This is a fucking honours degree, three years in the making.

Without really noticing how the decision was made, I disentangled myself from the bench and began to march across campus, cutting corners over the grass, the beer sloshing in my half-empty bottle as though mirroring the toxic churn in my stomach. It was time to have a word with Stephen Fry. If Dad were here, he'd be heading to the 2 p.m. graduation ceremony rather than mine, far more interested in getting up close to his hero. Most of the grads were already in the great hall, but a few latecomers were frantically parking cars wherever they could and flying through the doors, parents puffing behind, coats clutched under sweating armpits.

A steward intercepted me before I could get up the steps. 'You can't come in with that.'

I looked at the bottle, tipped the last of its contents into my mouth and tossed it in a huge arc over my shoulder. I heard a clang, a screech, perhaps a braking car, and then the smash of it on the pavement. He started to ask for a ticket, but I shoved past him, grazed lightly by his lanyard. As I disappeared through the double doors, there was distant shouting, perhaps an altercation over the last parking spaces, but my eyes were locked onto the stage, and I was experiencing déjà vu from my own ceremony a couple of hours earlier. All those mortarboards held in laps, slicked-down hair, neat shoes.

A sudden hail of clapping accompanied the Vice Chancellor's

walk to the podium. It was all happening again. There would be some preamble, perhaps some poetry or music, then the degrees would be conferred. Someone touched my shoulder, startling me. The man had lanky brown hair and skinny corduroys under his gown, and I recognised my Behavioural Studies tutor from the year before last.

'You need to sit down.' He was looking around for a seat to push me into. Mr Pantoff was his name, rather unbelievably, a PhD student roped into teaching an easy course. During our seminars, he had been impressed with my contributions, and we had spoken as equals. But at that moment I was disgusted to realise he did not recognise me. He was being free with his steering, one hand on my shoulder and the other on the crook of my arm.

'Hey,' I said. 'Get off, Pantoff.'

People turned. That was my cue. With adrenaline geysering up through my body, I shoved him away and threw myself towards the stage, accelerated by every bemused look, a crimson sizzle on the edge of my vision.

'You don't know my name, do you? But you know Stephen fucking Fry,' my yell rang out. I'd stumbled up the steps, and the lights were in my eyes. Maybe someone was filming this, maybe he'd see me on the internet, or else I could text him. *I'm on the box tonight* . . . The Vice Chancellor was trying to contain me, raising his arms but not daring to intercept. Instead he turned to get help. Murmurs rippled through the audience as I kicked a pot plant from the stage out into the nothingness, smelling the soil as it exploded, and snapped. 'I'm Arlo Knott, and not only did I work for my degree, I'm also about a million times more talented than any of these dicking *dicks* they're about to wheel out.'

I clutched the chunky microphone, surprised at the thud which hit me – and everyone – in the ear. 'In case you don't know. I can make all of this disappear . . . but let's fuck that for a minute.' I wiped my prickling forehead and found my fingers dripping with sweat. The lights were absurdly hot. 'This is Arlo up here.' I hurled off my gown and hat. 'All of me.' I tore open my shirt. People were covering their eyes. 'There's more power in my cock than—' Two thickset security men tossed their earpieces aside and came running, their feet making a comic clatter across the stage. I was in my element, in a sort of dream. I watched as one slipped on my gown and was flung in a head-first dive towards the front rows, to the accompaniment of screams. The second guy wrestled me briefly to the ground but could barely keep me down. 'Where is he?' I yelled, not wanting it to be over just yet, not until I'd found the greasy actor and lamped him. 'Where's fucking Fry?' Already the Vice Chancellor was looming above me, a cartoon giant, reclaiming the lectern, cupping the microphone.

'I do apologise, ladies and gentlemen, for this unpleasant scene. Very unfortunate. But we must remember that mental health can be an issue for . . .'

The words fell on me like hot coals. I burned under them,

screaming. With a tremendous effort, I fought the bouncer and felt his elbow dig deep into my gut, and more men came running and it was time to go back, to go back, line them up . . . I pulled a thread, or so it seemed, to untie whatever slim bonds of time were holding my recent actions together. They came apart and suddenly I was back by the double doors, a few steps inside the hall, my heart starting to pound as a flashback of the reality I'd just undone barrelled through my brain. Pantoff was sidling up to me and I dodged, clutching my chest, slipping towards the rows of graduating students and easing myself into an empty seat.

The students I'd just squeezed past looked at me as I sweated and panted for no reason, probably interpreting it as a last-minute dash to avoid missing my own graduation ceremony. A girl smiled kindly as the Vice Chancellor's opening address was clapped.

'Don't worry, you haven't missed anything,' she whispered.

'What about Stephen Fry?'

'Sorry?'

'The honorary degrees.'

She hadn't bargained on a conversation, and covered her mouth to lisp a reply, as she passed me her programme. 'These guys?' A coral-painted fingernail stabbed at the list of honoraries, and for this ceremony it was someone called Siegel Fry, an award-winning linguist. I snapped it shut, earning the opposite of a smile now as the girl picked up on my contempt. I wanted to punch Tim. Typical Chinese whispers. Or maybe he read it wrong. I blew out a long sigh. No matter. I wasn't sorry. There was no harm done, and only a memory of the adrenaline. I'd already forgotten what it felt like to be busted silently in the gut by a man who really knew what he was doing. Much to the girl's annoyance, I stood up and started to edge out along the row, giving only token consideration to people's toes.

'We are very lucky to have the university's most promising violinist with us today,' continued the Vice Chancellor. 'Sabra Dil will be playing,' he checked his script, 'Bach's Partita no. 2, Chaconne. Sabra, we know you'll go on to great things.' I had reached the end of the row and saw a girl make her way onstage with a violin, the spotlight settling around her as she eased it under her chin. The scene was so tranquil I could hardly believe that moments ago I'd been up there with security guys encouraging me to taste the floorboards. She lifted her bow, and the phrase she played was not the harsh squeak I'd been accustomed to hearing when Erin practised violin after school but rather notes that ran into each other like water. Despite myself, I hesitated in the aisle. The light fell on her face, on the chestnut shine of the instrument, and I felt like something transformational might be about to happen. Another phrase lifted the pitch, and the heads of the audience, then abruptly she stopped. People waited. She took a few steps over to where the Vice Chancellor was seated and muttered something in his ear, one hand clasping her neck.

Perturbed, he rose and claimed the spotlight.

'Well, I'm sorry to say we will have to save that particular enjoyment for another time. Like a true professional, Sabra was hoping to soldier on regardless, however she has just informed me that only minutes ago she suffered whiplash from a minor car accident on arrival here.' He turned to the girl, who was already melting into the shadows, shoulders hunching up towards her neck, violin held awkwardly, off-balance in her hand, as though she'd picked it up and couldn't remember why. 'Ladies and gentlemen, Sabra Dil.'

There was scattered clapping, and you could hear, as always, the sentiment behind it – students applauding half-heartedly, resentful at offering this accolade in exchange for five bars of performance, parents supplementing out of sympathy. Then there was me, standing motionless by the doors, knowing I was to blame. That must have been the bump that sounded right after I'd hurled my bottle, not looking behind.

I closed my eyes and wondered if there was any way to undo such a complex period of time, some of which I'd already reversed. Trying nearly made me pass out, though that could also have been the effect of the booze. Damn European-strength Spitfire. My compulsion now was to find out whether the accident was definitely my fault.

Siegel Fry. Jesus.

Car parking had never been so haphazard. The wardens could have a field day ticketing these latecomers with their bumpers in bushes and wheels on pavements. A few dozen paces beyond the hall, it was easy to see where my bottle had landed – vehicles were still avoiding the patch of brown shards. Now I could place the metallic bump. The bottle must have bounced off someone's bonnet and then hit the tarmac, where it shattered. I followed the road to the overcrowded car park, puzzled at my dedication to this quest. Part of me was already heading back to the plaza and coaxing Tim into having another beer.

On one of the grass verges was a red Austin Metro – an old thing, very square, tilted at an alarming angle. The back bumper was crumpled, and the girl who'd been playing the violin was standing by the bonnet, staring at a crater in the metal. Her lips were pressed together around a tiny wrinkled roll-up, and she was desperately patting her jacket in search of a lighter. Feeling a bit of a fraud, I slipped one from my back pocket and stepped up.

'Cheers,' she said, holding the stub under my flame and sucking. She cupped her elbow and blew out an oblong cloud, eyes darting protectively to the instrument case at her feet.

'You all right?' I said.

'Yeah.' She shrugged. Near the windscreen wipers, I noticed she had placed a curved piece of glass she must have picked up from the road. The words 'a hoppy amber ale' were visible on its torn label. 'My own bloody fault for rushing. I thought this was a bird gone out of control when it hit me, but it was a bottle. Where did it come from, a plane?' She raised thick, dark eyebrows towards her fringe, which was dyed red and cut oddly halfway down her forehead. 'Anyway, slammed on the breaks, car behind comes straight into me. Hello, whiplash.' Her face bent into a lopsided grin before she removed the roll-up once more. 'Not great timing.'

I looked at her neck, pink from where she'd been rubbing it, and found myself rather impressed by her attitude. Many people I knew, including my sister, would have fled the hall crying.

'Are you going to get it checked?'

'Yeah. Got to do something about my car too.'

The violin case was a neat shape, perfectly fitted to the instrument. I imagined opening it and seeing the shiny curl of wood nestling inside. She caught me staring.

'I was meant to be playing.' A nod towards the great hall. 'Probably wouldn't have got me anywhere. These agents are next-level perfectionists; they'll write someone off for labouring a note.' Her head bobbed to indicate disdain, but it made her wince. 'So anyway . . . I need to go and sort out my neck. Probably by tipping something very strong down it. Thanks for the light, and for giving a shit.'

She hoisted the case, and tossed the fag away.

'Wait . . .'

Now I knew her. She was the girl from the taxi rank, minus the dark lipstick, someone who'd stuck in my mind for no particular reason. It felt wrong to be hearing her thank me when I'd been the cause of her injury. 'Would it cheer you up if I bought you a drink?'

She looked at me evenly. 'Are you seeing an opportunity to pick me up here?'

I held up my hands. 'Just trying to be nice.'

'Shame.' She gave a surprisingly wicked grin. 'Okay, let's do it.'

As she turned from her battered car and set off directly across the grass, I felt myself lurch after her, as though snagged in in a sudden magnetic field.

Part 5

ROLLING A SIX

Twenty-one

Whenever her instrument was in its case, Sabra Dil lived life as though it was a funfair: not too real and there for entertainment. Arriving in the nick of time was pretty good going for someone who was perpetually late. She normally got away with it – and would have again, if not for my bottle of Spitfire. Now she was dogged by injury when she should have been impressing agents and auditioning for orchestras. 'Think high-earning football player,' she said, trying to make me understand how hard it was to become a concert violinist. It required superior talent, an early start and a big break. Sabra's dream was to play the Musikverein in Vienna, whose acoustics she adored, but the odds of being noticed worsened the longer she was unable to practise. None of this stopped her laughing when we spoke about it though, as if though every rollercoaster got derailed once in a while.

I attempted to make up for my mistake, my unpardonable clumsiness, by accompanying her to the health centre and driving her E-reg Metro to the garage (where, unfortunately, it was written off). All this just made my halo shinier, and how could I bear to dismantle it when things were just getting started between us, when it mattered so much what she thought? There was something blissful about being here with her in this quiet restaurant, topping up her wine.

'What do you want,' she asked, 'the mini duck au Cognac or the vodka beetroot soup?'

I was too busy wrinkling my nose at the Pernod pâté to be able to decide. Although this booze-themed meal was her grateful thanks to a good Samaritan, she'd already made me admit that I liked her. Now all that mattered was sculpting the perfect evening.

'Pernod, the most disgusting drink ever invented,' I said. 'If you can't appreciate aniseed.'

Should I roll back? I decided not to – she was smiling, and it seemed to animate her when we disagreed. I'd had enough practice to know that too much skipping about during a date could make me seem sycophantic, or like an identical twin. Suppose my companion started lamenting U2's lack of output, I'd skip back a sentence and say: 'Yeah, and don't you think U2 have gone quiet?' *That's just what I was thinking when you said that.* 'We could be in *The Matrix* right now.' *Oh my God yes!* 'I really like cream horns.' *Shut up, cream horns are the best!*

A reliable gimmick which, tonight, I'd leave at home.

Instead I coaxed her, after the meal, into an impromptu cocktail-making class, which inevitably got us both hammered. Sabra leapt into the road whenever a taxi went by, almost throwing herself in the driver's path.

'Careful,' I said, possibly for the first time in my life. I was hyper-aware of her beautiful wire-sprung figure poised on the kerb, under the flickering street lamp, and the potency of my attraction made me wince. She was not even my type. There was a certain rural strength in her squarish fingers, not to mention the tree-root tendons standing out in her neck and wrists. She dressed in whatever she thought was fun to wear, and although tonight she was stylish, earlier in the week her waistcoat looked as though it has been snipped out of an old Turkish rug. In the evening, she wore dark russet lipstick to match her hair, and in the day no make-up at all.

A lesser man might have got lost in the twists of her conversation, her sharp wit turning to spear him at every corner, but I had the advantage of being able to double back, if it became necessary, and come across as more intelligent than I actually was.

'You never put a foot wrong,' she said.

I froze.

'What do you mean?'

She lined up her toes neatly on the kerb, gently humouring my caution, before her arm shot out again, yearning after some cab doing a hundred miles an hour. Her hand curled round to stroke my forearm so my hairs stood on end, a caress almost too intimate in this pocket of silence. Though we hadn't been hanging out for long, I'd accelerated our relationship by asking personal questions and then back-tracking before it started to feel like interrogation. By now I had a complete picture of her life up to the present, stretching all the way back to her parents meeting in Germany, her dad on his first summer away from Beirut. She'd been in this country since the start of primary school, though her passion for music had begun when she saw Vanya Milanova play Paganini in her mother's hometown. Sabra loved that I knew what she meant, first time round, when she described the pressure visited upon her by parents who had not achieved their own dreams, her mum having worked long hours on a hotel reception desk to pay violin tuition fees.

With her aversion to small talk, getting any trivia out of Sabra was difficult, and my spoils were only a passing interest in *Star Wars*, and a fondness for tinned mango – especially on a hangover. Instead of a diary she kept a small box in which she collected 'the flotsam and jetsam' of her life. She spoke two languages, plus a little Arabic, and had got herself a part-time job at the modern languages department of the university so she could learn Chinese for free alongside her music studies. She'd always assumed that playing concertos would take her all over the world, and liked the idea of being able to talk to everyone she met.

What captivated me was finding her so full of contrasts, so ready to be the soloist, the lone traveller, yet determined to connect. Like me, Sabra had grown up with at least one parent who saw her as larger than life, and she had been melded and shaped by that. We were both outsiders, outlandish even, never really planning for normality, and perhaps this quality was what made me notice her, even back when she was waiting for that taxi – a serene, isolated figure amid the Saturday night rabble.

Heat was building beneath the light touch of her fingers. Our cosmic resonance brought taxis flocking, and soon we were back at my house, where I could hardly manage to get the door open. It had been some time since I'd wanted anyone this much, and we threw ourselves into enthusiastic but slightly too-intoxicated sex. As with so many things, it was better the second time around, in the early hours of the morning, after she'd surprised me yet again by pulling a pixie-sized bag of white powder from her purse.

By the time we'd exhausted each other it was 7 a.m., and she had work at nine. I ran my hand over the length of her body, cupped her warm buttocks, the curve of her back perspiring under the thick duvet. It was hard to resist skipping back a few times to savour the sensation. Eventually I sighed.

'I guess I should let you go.'

'Well, don't put up too much of a fight,' she mocked.

Welcome to limbo. As fellow residents, we needed each other. Sabra had more going on than me, with her language school job, but the offers she'd expected to pour in had not materialised, and she felt as though she was drifting. It frustrated her, too, that only a few minutes of violin practice would leave her shot through with pain. Her gratefulness to me for being her distraction, a knight in shining armour, during this period was weighed down with so much irony that it sinks and falls through the bottom of the story. But how could I resist that hot-water joy bubbling up in her eyes, her laugh? Ancient emotions resurfaced, with the possibility that I could once again be someone's hero. The more effort I made, and the more she enjoyed herself, the further her dream, unbeknownst to us, corroded. The other irony, of course, was that university had left me stumbling around without a clue what I wanted to do, and if not for Sabra I would have spent that whole winter out in the cold.

She would never know, of course, that things were really backwards: I was the more vulnerable to limbo and she was my saviour. We'd been meeting as casually as possible for nearly three months, and one Saturday I took the train into the city centre to see her, even though it meant braving the Christmas market and – much worse – sharing her with a small child named Greta, whom she was babysitting.

The market was always packed, a squeeze to get through, and when I reached the central library I found myself in a nightmare wonderland of kids running everywhere among pop-up cardboard pirate ships, balloons, plastic hoopla and toy cars; some sort of children's activity day. It took me a while to locate Sabra, sitting in a fan of chairs around a man dressed as a clown. So many kids these days are scared of clowns, and this guy had really nailed the horror-film look, with red paint splashing blood-like from his eyes and the corners of his lips. I slipped into the seat Sabra had thoughtfully reserved and mustered a smile for the girl in plaits who sat mournfully beside her.

The sole benefit I took from the next half-hour was an intensified pleasure in stroking Sabra's hand, which I had to steal in order to keep my sanity. The clown was awful. He was a jack of all trades: juggling, blowing up bendy balloons, singing and even telling painfully predictable stories. His attempt at magic was to pick on someone in the audience, show them a balloon and say, 'Is this your favourite animal?' They would then yell 'No,' except in the case of one boy who said, 'Yay, snake!' He'd then twist the balloon squeakily into the usual stub-tailed Loch Ness monster, turn back and say, 'Ta da!' Astonishingly, this seemed to work about eighty per cent of the time. The little girl or boy would see a dog, a cat, a horse, an elephant or even, in one strange case, a whale. How did the man know their favourite animal? Magic. Either that or balloon animals all looked usefully similar.

'You, pigtails!' The plastic orange curls loomed closer. He was looking straight at Greta, who was frightened out of her skin. 'Favourite animal?' Painful squeaks sounded as he worked the balloon, talking to it all the while: 'I'll just do this, now twist that . . .' It was almost like a surgeon talking through a procedure with his patient. He held out some sort of creature with a spine and legs. 'Is this your favourite animal?' The girl whispered her answer to Sabra, who buckled with mirth before translating.

'Sorry, we were after an anemone.'

Amazingly the clown didn't laugh. Hesitation brought out the wrinkles beneath his eyes; a tired man in face paint.

'That's not an animal.' He snorted, and moved onto playing a tiny ukulele.

'Let's do a runner,' I said, glad of an excuse. We pulled Greta willingly from the seat and went out through the library, leaving the racket of tortured strings behind us. In the fresh air, I stretched. 'Well, that's forty minutes we'll never get back.'

Sabra didn't hear. She was crouched beside Greta, trying to use the girl's perfect plaits to brush tears from her cheeks. I heard a breathy voice say:

'It *is* an animal.'

In the distance there was the music-box momentum of the Christmas market's carousel and tempting mugs of hot, spicy wine. I squatted down too.

'Don't worry, Greta,' I said. 'He's a moron.' As the cold wind blew round us on the steps, something occurred to me. 'You want to see some real magic?' She was still crying, but her eyes flicked up to meet mine. Maybe she loved the idea of a magician and that was why she'd made Sabra sit through this whole disappointing performance. I could give her the hit she needed.

'I'll use magic,' I said, 'to tell you what you've got in your pockets.'

'Which pocket?'

I pointed to the left side of her blue coat, which bulged. 'That one.'

'Okay.'

Having darted my hand into the pocket, I skipped straight back.

'You've got a lovely pair of white, knitted mittens.'

She had to take them out to check. Now I had her attention. We did the same thing with her other pocket, then we guessed what colour coat the next man to come out of the library would be wearing, then what animal she was picturing (more anemones, as it turned out). She'd been cheered up in a few seconds, with zero effort, and I was rather enjoying her chubby smile.

Sabra's awe was palpable. She pushed herself up, took Greta's hand and led us off to get hot chocolate from the market, with a sneaky shot of rum in mine and hers.

'How did you do that?' she asked. Her eyes were green out here, hazel indoors. I liked her look of wonder, but knew I had to be careful.

'The gloves were hanging out,' I said. 'The 20p and the bird-warbler . . .' For the life of me I couldn't think of a logical explanation for this, or half the other stuff I'd predicted. Sabra was too smart to bullshit. I drained my mug and squinted at her, the slight down on her jawline catching the light. If I kissed her, she would taste of chocolate and rum, but it would not end this conversation. More than anything, I wanted to tell her all. But with other people that had always gone wrong. I stared at the empty cup and placed it on a barrel.

'You know some people have weird things, like . . . that friend of yours who named the metals in your ring just by touching it?' As I spoke, I was faltering, willing her to open her mind as wide as it would go. She fingered the ring on her thumb and nodded. 'Well I have a slight . . . sense of the near future. Sometimes. Just little things, like whether a light will go red . . .'

Fear rocketed through my system, my brain already trying to calculate if I could go back to before we'd left the library if needed. I was a man with cold hands, jiggling on my feet, stealing glances at her expression. Slowly, she placed her mug beside mine. Then she leaned closer, and from nowhere there came a sudden, rather violent kiss, her teeth biting at my lip. I staggered with pleasure and both mugs teetered.

'You saw that coming, right?' Up close, her smile was intoxicating.

'Ow.'

'I knew there was something weird about you.'

'Since when?'

'From the start.'

Greta was gravitating towards the *Schokokuss*, an array of chocolate domes, and before I could draw breath Sabra was in pursuit. Her outline, bobble hat and slim jacket, sank into my retinas. To be with this woman, I would pull out all the stops. Together, we would be unstoppable. The infinite sweetness of marshmallows in raspberry, Irish coffee, hazelnut, pear, mint choc-chip and vanilla closed in around me, and my whole past melted away.

Twenty-two

The limestone even smelled ancient, its chiselled graffiti illuminated by dusty Roman sunlight. I lifted the rope for Sabra. This sealed-off gallery had fine views of the arena and hypogeum below, and here, sure enough, were the metal rings to which the long banners were tied. I went along the line pulling the quick release of each highwayman's hitch, so they slithered down. No one seemed to notice.

'Arlo, don't,' she said.

'Relax, we won't get caught.'

Earlier we'd both agreed that the banners, with their pop-art gladiators and flashy superhero font, spoiled the otherwise spectacular arches. Heroes Unto Death was a tourist-milking exhibition that killed the Colosseum's ability to take you back in time. Since we were going off the beaten track, we might as well restore authenticity as we went, and, from Sabra's overdramatic tiptoeing and hiding, I could tell she was secretly pleased.

This was what it had come to. Full-fat risks, and no way to stop. She was still points ahead for this Rome trip in the first place, hiding the ticket in a prosciutto sandwich, even letting me start to bite. Apart from a smear of grease, the damn thing was fine. How do you beat a romantic gesture like that?

I'd tried my best since we got here. Little things like sampling all the flavours of gelato to find her the best one (pistachio), finding secret passageways and hidden bars. On the second night, we'd somehow found ourselves in the Trevi Fountain at four in the morning, its light trembling pink and green over our sweating bodies, the water deliciously cool. I was certain I'd have to undo it pretty quickly, that someone would yell at us, but miraculously no one came by and we splashed each other to kingdom come before trudging back to our hotel with soggy steps, leaving a trail of water down its tiled corridor.

Later, we'd lain under the sheets, gasping in the heat, playing Snap with all the little philosophies we had carried around since childhood. I tried not to meddle with our late-night conversations, even when I said the wrong thing or became confused and made her repeat herself. It was good to have them whole and perfectly formed, not honeycombed with things unsaid and evaded, that I might remember but she would not.

As we came out of the Colosseum, some burly Italians dressed as centurions converged around us, patting me on the back, complimenting Sabra, and saying 'How about a photo?' Before we could reply, they had our camera and we were squashed in between them. 'Now you give us five euros tip,' they said. I was sufficiently stunned to reach into my pocket, but then I saw from the corner of my eye that one of them was twisting Sabra away and forcing his lips quickly onto hers. A muffled squeal. They would take the money and be gone before we could do anything. In a wild rage, I flew across to the guy, aimed a useless jab at his chin and tried to knee him through the decorative metal pleats of his leather skirt. The others instantly had me by the arms and were starting to fold around me, angry faces and tanned flesh. Finally, I got my act together and took us back to the moment we emerged from the Colosseum archway into blinding sunlight. I seized Sabra's arm and steered her off to the left, where there was a gelato cart further along the piazza. 'Look, blood orange,' I said. 'That's unusual.'

The trip had coincided with an upturn in both our fortunes. Sabra had been offered a new and improved office job at the languages school, and she was once again shopping around for free courses. 'I'd like to learn Burmese,' she said, 'and visit before it gets touristy.' Although taking on more work than she could handle, she was also spending three or four nights a week at my new flat, so we saw plenty of each other. Mid-week was a time of sleepy bliss for me, while weekends were usually taken up by work. Some gigs were quite a drive away.

The easiest way to become a magician is with an agency. I'd planned it carefully, working on my particular bag of tricks. Early on, I decided my look would be smart and mysterious; a dark stranger rather than a goofy entertainer. I bought myself a neat-fitting suit of midnight blue, toyed with the idea of shades, and tied back my hair, which had grown quite long. Sabra thought the thin black scarf I draped around my shoulders was too much, enquiring sarcastically if I'd be performing at funerals.

My magic was of the mentalist variety, guessing people's thoughts and so on. I was not entirely without props. People liked to see some familiar tropes of magic, and props made it seem as though I was doing ten different things instead of the same trick over and over. *Pick a card, no don't show me. It's the three of hearts. Now pick a card, don't look, show everyone else, do you know what that card is? I do* . . . Amazing how much magic could work on this premise. I could also write down the name of an unknown audience member's son on a birthday card, or predict the contents of someone's bag. I'd tip it out, undo the process, and reel off a list of Cath Kidston purses, Revlon make-up, odd tissues and Lego bricks and sea shells, and sometimes a rape alarm. Once I'd perfected sleight of hand, I could get an additional laugh by slipping a furry thong inside the handbag as I squeezed it to my ear and mystically communed with it, shocking the owner when it was pulled out at the trick's denouement.

I'd point at a man in the audience and tell him he owned two cats named Asterix and Obelix, or suddenly know a child's guinea pig was the colour of a custard cream. I'd get people to throw dice in the air and already have written down a figure for what they would score. Or I would ask an audience member to sketch something, and, lo and behold, there would be a hazy copy already in my back pocket.

This kind of magic was a little sophisticated for kids, but I still got booked for parties, school events and the occasional bar mitzvah, so it was worthwhile adding items like a fake sawing-teddy-in-half kit to my act. There was a certain wild joy that flowed from a young audience, and I got used to smiling and bowing, reminding myself to notice the moment and drink it in, all this pleasure I was giving, reawakening wonder and broadening the boundaries of what people could believe. This was the nearest I'd come to having a mission.

It was satisfying to be using my particular strength to earn a living. Not a huge living, admittedly – there was still a little gambling on the side if I wanted to take Sabra somewhere fancy or to a country hotel for the weekend – but nevertheless it was a job, garnering respect. I could join the Magic Circle as an apprentice if I wanted, and already the agency was recommending me as the first choice for corporate entertainment, for any event that needed a little razzle-dazzle. I progressed from church halls to glitzy clubs, taking to the stage on cabaret evenings. There was no need to come up with a title for my act since, as Sabra enjoyed pointing out, I already had the name of a magician.

'The great Arlo,' she teased, dragging me down to bed by the ends of my black scarf. 'Oh, how I gasped.'

After a performance, there would always be someone coming up to ask how I did it, how I could possibly have known that he once plummeted from a balcony in Bournemouth, something he'd only just remembered himself and certainly had never mentioned to his wife. I would shrug and fall back gratefully on the magician's code, leaving him utterly perplexed. What other secrets could I see? The one or two audience members who always slipped out part-way through were probably fearful adulterers or criminals. I almost felt sorry for the man from Bournemouth, but this didn't stop me basking in the looks of wonder, hungering for more.

Sabra could see I was content in my job and was happy for me, enjoying her behind-the-scenes knowledge that being in harmony with the energies of the universe helped with my act – what harm could it do when I was bringing joy to children? We'd both come down a little, just a little, from the unruly start of our relationship – our battle with the fear of limbo – and had found ourselves on unexpected but sturdy new paths.

121

After working so long at the school of languages, Sabra was in two minds about a career in interpretation or a related field. Every day she took out her violin and practised for longer than I could believe, but the last few notes would sometimes be slow and melancholy, or she would just hold up the bow and stare at it. She'd lost her edge, and apparently it wasn't like a sports injury, where you could often work the muscles and get back up to speed. The intensive practice routine she put in place at Easter was more than she could handle: it resulted in a trapped nerve. 'How can I not be ready?' She was angry with the diagnosis, at being told to take it easy. 'It was almost a year ago, for God's sake!' In quieter moods she'd try to explain to me that there was damage below the surface, emotional breakages that were yet to heal, and she feared that, by the time they did, she'd have been forgotten by the musical establishment.

Sabra being Sabra, her spells of low spirits were rare, and when they did occur she would self-prescribe a massive injection of fun. The short term had always been cheap and disposable to me, but now I overtook her in wanting to hang onto it. I became the unlikely champion of seizing the moment. For the first time, all these throwaway minutes might be adding up to something, maybe even a future. I started to care what I did from second to second, to apply myself, and sometimes our relationship became almost frenzied with the effort we both put in, seeking ever more thoughtful, unexpected and romantic activities. She got double points, of course, because for me it was easy. I could take any number of risks. If I led Sabra beyond her comfort zone and she didn't like it, then it never happened.

Occasionally she'd coax me into showing off, loving it when I told her what birds would fly overhead or when her favourite advert was about to come on. No wonder she was so damn happy all the time, at least when the violin was in its bed. Here was a sensitive, attractive man who could not only keep pace with her lust for life but who was also improbably tuned into the universe. A man who washed up on a tide of altruism in her hour of need. Except that the more she let me save her, the more she would need saving.

Sabra once told me that a proportion of what you heard when listening to a violin – or any instrument – was just catgut scraping on wood, metal on fibre, rustles and rubbing. But when scientists recorded the music and extracted these elements to try and create 'pure' violin, it sounded unbearable, synthetic and wrong. The rough, raw materials were what rounded out the music, an idea that resonated with me. There was a great natural strength inside my girlfriend, a grain of visible goodness, but flaws that I adored. Her bad habits amused me, even the fact that she made me late for everything. No day went by without her surprising me in some little way, even if it was only a new, secret-passage way of seeing life. She came up with theories about the metre of people's beating hearts, the pulse synchronising among musicians. Sometimes she made remarks so rude I thought they'd melt a hole in the pavement, but she managed – amazingly – to charm not only Nan but Erin when she met them, though afterwards we acknowledged we'd both been on best behaviour. She knew my dad was an actor, of course. I introduced them one day when *Dog Cops* came on the telly. 'You see the guy sipping the port, levelling the gun? That's my dad. Dad, this is Sabra.' Bang.

I wished I'd been first to think of the trip to Rome, but this was her gesture and all I could do was out-romance her in little ways. So we ate the blood orange gelato and walked on until she found a Vespa with its key carelessly tucked under the seat cover and dared me to join her in taking it round the block. The panic that rose in my throat was nothing to do with this whirlwind ride, though I did have to cling on for dear life. It was our last night in Rome and she was still upstaging me at every turn. How little I knew about how relationships worked. That small, hollowed-out section of my heart told me that size mattered, that I needed to be larger than life if I was to keep someone like Sabra.

Returning the scooter, we passed a sumptuous building with a balloon arch over its entrance; it looked like the kind of place where we should be. Not a hotel, as I'd thought when I marched Sabra across the road, but even better: a brand-new casino. I told her to get ready to lose some serious money as I slipped the bouncer a couple of notes to get inside. In her elegant red tunic, Sabra was dressed perfectly, and with me in black we matched the roulette and card tables as though the place had been designed for us.

Entertainment was provided by a French barman doing the moving-three-cups trick, encouraging you to pick the right one and uncover a five-euro chip, while surprising people with unexpected items appearing magically in the two empty ones. When he reached us, I looked on with cynicism at the swirling pink tumblers, as he repeated, '*Cherchez, cherchez le prix.*' Letting the trick play out established that the bonus prizes, in this case mini macarons, were held in false bottoms and released with a squeeze. Takes one to know one.

Sabra was a little drunk and happened to pick the cup with the chip. 'Nice work,' I said, when she let out a cry of triumph, 'though you're pretty partial to macarons.' Impressed, the barman lifted the other two cups to show off the surprise sweets. He pinched an imaginary line between his spectacles and the opaque tumblers, and grinned at me. 'X-ray eyes, *non*?' he said, before directing an aside at Sabra: 'I hope you have the lead-lined underwear?'

At the card tables, with my hand guiding hers, Sabra won and won, and then really won. There seemed to be glitter in the air, or well-lit dust motes, or just my suspended exhaustion at having undone little pieces of time so frantically for the last couple of hours. But I was more than pleased with the result. The dazed look on her face, unaccustomed as she was to such raw, undiluted luck, was to die for. She touched her forehead, a little red from the sun, and started casting around vaguely in a way that meant she needed fresh air.

'Come on, that should keep us in magnums for a while.' I linked our elbows, and we headed to the foyer. 'And I'm not talking choc ices.'

Spotlights fell upon us as we passed mirrored walls, me glossy and well-muscled, Sabra elegant with her leather bag. My elation was such that I couldn't resist the handout provided so generously by the weather when we walked into the thick night. 'And now,' I said, turning her shoulders to face the river, 'lightning'. Down it came, the instant I'd seen it before reversing three paces, tearing the tinfoil sky and purpling the water. It was spectacular, but although Sabra's face registered a smile, her expression froze.

'What's up?' I said at once.

'I'm tired, shall we go to bed?'

Pure momentum made me reply in a suggestive tone, 'With pleasure.' But there was a disquieting silence for the rest of the walk. Something was up. One footstep followed thoughtfully after the next, and she didn't seem to see the Tiber, nor feel the first drops of rain.

Back at the hotel, I emerged from the bathroom to see her sitting cross-legged on the bed, watching puddle-sized drops dash themselves against the window. It was a pose for discussion, not sex, but I went over and began to massage her head and neck just in case.

'Arlo,' she murmured, 'there's something you're not telling me.'

My hands became self-conscious, trying to stay soft and give nothing away.

'It's not just the near future you see,' she went on. 'There's something more. Otherwise how could you know what was in those other cups? How much can you really see?'

The X-ray eyes joke had hit home. I sensed her curling up a little, protecting herself until she knew what she was dealing with. Mortified, I slid onto the bed and encircled her, kissing shoulders that still radiated the baked warmth of the Italian sun.

'Come on, darls,' I purred. 'You think I haven't seen that trick before?'

For a minute her head rested against my chest, but she wasn't satisfied. I'd gone too far and scared her, and now she was sullen, standing by her first question. I sighed.

'Look, Sabra, what do you want to know?'

'Whatever you want to tell me.' Her hair was filmy, so fine it fell away under my fingers, almost too delicate to exist. It smelled of Vespa fumes and orange sugar, or perhaps I'd lost track of reality; the prospect of telling her everything made me giddy, with equal measures of euphoria and fear. Mystery is sexy, and if I showed my hand then maybe I'd have nothing left.

I'd fantasised about introducing my secret slowly, building up her credulity brick by brick on the foundation stone of

127

what she already knew, testing her tolerance before I added something harder to believe. Was that why I'd been so frantic about making this the trip to end all trips? Naturally I wanted to reclaim my crown as king of carpe diem, but perhaps there was something more – the need to create a certain mood, as other men might try to engineer the perfect moment to propose.

'It's not smoke and mirrors.' Her hand lay in mine, palm upwards, my thumb exploring the calluses. 'It's completely real, just hard to believe. A bit like my sister's experiments in quantum physics.' Every sentence was more halting than the last. 'I just have an idea about the different ways things can go. Some things. Macarons, anyway.'

Just chew up this morsel, Sabra, and we can move on to the main course.

'So . . .' She raised an eyebrow.

'If you'd picked another cup, we'd have seen the macarons.'

'And that was enough for you to know they were there?' She turned back to the window. 'At least you didn't just say "I'm psychic".'

'If you don't—'

'Of course I believe you – I've seen it for myself. But how is it you have this power and you're not . . . I don't know . . . working for MI5?' She unhooked her bag from the bedpost and patted it, as though checking all the cash from our night of wins was still there. For a second I feared I'd set a dangerous precedent, but she tossed it carelessly to the chair. 'It's incredible, Arlo. My God, people talk about twenty-twenty vision, but yours is off the scale. You're so lucky, do you know that?'

Lucky, lucky, lucky. By then it had become something of a trigger word. In my mind it was caked with dirt, rhyming with mucky, yucky, sucky.

'You wouldn't say that if you knew.' My voice dropped to merge with the rumble of traffic. Inevitably it drew us closer, magnetised our limbs, so we spiralled round each other, cool skin against warm, watching the play of light on the ceiling. I hadn't intended to tell her the tale of the ladder, certainly not my part in it, yet here it all came, with me hardly aware I was speaking. For the first time, I drew no veil over my moment of stupidity. The story had been dammed up for so long that all I had to do was open wide and let it surge out. What amazed me was how different it felt, now that I was an adult, and how, for so many years, what I'd told people had been the official version, just one more ladder accident to add to the statistics, with no involvement from me, and absolutely no slow-worm.

When it was over, there was silence. The mattress bounced as she rose, and then I heard three words, spoken stiffly:

'Hindsight is shit.'

In an agony of confusion, I waited while she went to the bathroom, my tension not eased by the sounds of nose-blowing. Then she appeared in the doorway. For two awful minutes I'd wondered whether she might hate me, whether this conversation might have to be screwed up and tossed away, when I wanted so much for it to stick. It was a milestone, a change of direction. So imagine my joy to find her features softened, a wetness gleaming under her eyes. From an early age, Sabra had been taught to keep her emotions under more control than was really healthy, taking them off to a safe distance for disposal. My heart sparked into an inferno for this woman who'd just shed a tear for my childhood mistake.

She dipped back into the bathroom and emerged carrying two glasses of water. If I had a ring, I'd be fumbling for it in my shirt, sliding down onto one knee. For once, honesty had paid off, and now I hoped it would serve as armour for my final assault on her logic: the truth, the whole truth and nothing but the truth. She would know everything. No more disposable moments, no more conjuring up lightening from the sky. Not unless we were playing together, laughing at it. I could laugh now, but instead I drank the water, since my throat was dry and it was balmy and cool, a hesitation that turned out to be a terrible error.

'Imagine if we'd got together sooner, before graduation,' she mused. 'You could have stopped me getting into that car accident. Right now, you might be sat in Symphony Hall, listening to me smash the hell out of Bach.' Her lids half-closed, shoulders tensing as she mentally cradled her violin. 'Sometimes I look in the mirror and see the person I always expected to be, travelling the world and getting all my calories from alcohol, wooed by every philharmonic because of my quick . . . spiccato . . ' She petered out, an unnamed piece of music taking over.

My elation was struck a mortal blow. In this dark, over-heated room, sweat poured suddenly down my back. I was part of that sick little tableau from her past, tossing the bottle over my head, out of control and never knowing that all her chips were stacked on my instant of selfishness. She was too smart, too dangerously smart to be told the full story. Sooner or later, she'd piece it together, remember my beer-breath, my sheepish look, and start asking questions.

'Shall we party here?' she asked, brandishing a handful of miniatures from the fridge. The storm was still raging outside, and I may as well have been in its midst, drenched with loneliness. Maybe Sabra deserved better than someone who, despite having all the odds in his favour, kept messing up. Above the furious rain, I heard my dad's voice, ragged with giggles, telling my sister that I was unplanned. An accident waiting to happen.

Twenty-two

I waited at the school of languages reception, leaning against
the bookcases. Lingering in linguistics, wondering if the
word related to 'linguine'. As usual, my mind was straining
the world for anything I could use as a witticism in my act.
Most magicians have whole toolboxes of jokes, handy levers
that help their set run smoothly. But for me one-liners were
hard, and when I did start nattering away on stage, as I
shuffled cards, telling some story I believed was humorous,
a rustle in the audience told me to get to the point. Mostly
I relied on that old chestnut: ruthlessly sending up my
volunteer assistants, or an easy target in the crowd. 'So
you're American? Are you here on business or pleasure . . .
or just to learn the language?'

I looked up 'linguine' on my new phone and found the word meant 'little tongues'. The thought of steaming, swirling pasta made me hungry. Come on, Sabra. The delay was frustrating, or perhaps I was annoyed at myself for showing up early to meet someone who was always at least five minutes late. Distantly, I heard the slam of double doors, and then she appeared, coat still grasped in one hand, giving me the usual supernova smile that blasted away my gloom.

'Happy birthday,' I said.

'Get me the hell out of here.'

Now I was in good spirits again, enjoying her ignorance at what I had planned. She seemed a little twitchy as we walked out, fiddling with the zip on her coat, trying to apply lipstick as she walked and, most of all, not looking at me when she spoke. I knew her well enough to detect something negative, perhaps a bad day at the office, that she was suppressing, so I gave her a sudden, determined kiss on the temple without breaking pace and handed over a birthday card. She tore open the purple envelope.

'Nice.' An approving nod. It was a bear saying 'Many Happy Returns', to which I had added 'of the Jedi'. Doctored cards had been a running joke of ours ever since Sabra swore she'd seen one in a card shop that said 'Sorry You're Leaving Me', but the 'Me', on second glance, was just decorative curls. The idea of this card had us in stitches for the best part of a day, and we still couldn't bring it up without giggling.

133

Outside the language department, I steered her towards the car park, speeding up as my excitement grew.

'Where are we going?' she asked, looking around for my car.

'That's up to you.' The small parking area, reserved for staff, was almost empty except for one or two old bangers and a brand-new red Toyota Yaris. A rosette of white ribbon, the kind florists attach to bouquets (not knowing any better, this was where I'd obtained it) sat jauntily on the roof, just by the aerial. I saw her spot the decoration as we walked closer, yet it didn't sink in straight away. Then she slowed, stopped and staggered back a few steps, as though the car was a crouching beast, ready to spring with its tyre-rubber feet.

'No,' she said, her usual expression melting. 'No, Arlo, this is a joke.'

Her shock felt great. I was aware of a huge smile bursting out on my face.

'Don't you think the Audi has suffered enough?' I said this with sufficient levity that it didn't need undoing. Though she'd been on the insurance of my car for a year, I was always a little keyed up when she drove it, clenching my jaw whenever its perfect paintwork came within an inch of a car-park bollard, or if the alloy wheels grazed the kerb. Until now it had made sense, since we hardly ever used the car anyway, but now her mum's health was failing and I knew she would want to be driving to Kent much more often. That's what made it such a thoughtful, practical gift on my part.

'This is a ridiculous, impractical present.' She seemed almost angry, which amused me. I took her in my arms, her body well-padded by the quilted coat, her face red, breath smelling of cinnamon chewing gum. I tried to kiss her but she bobbed down, out of reach. 'Honestly.'

'Oh come on,' I said. 'You know I have money. Why do my presents have to be sensible?' I was rather taken aback at the strength of her reaction, and a little disappointed that it wasn't taking the form of ardent declarations of love.

Good of me, wasn't it, to expect worship and admiration when I'd been the one to write off her previous wheels? At no point did I remember the debt that was owed; instead I felt proud of the effort it had taken to forage in newsagents for scratch cards, of how I'd filled the vehicle with petrol and polished it furiously with Turtle Wax. Rarely had I spent big sums of money on anyone but myself. I wanted her to appreciate the car and relish being rescued from long train journeys and Sunday engineering works. 'If you don't like it, there's a nice deep lake just round the corner,' I said, handing over the keys.

After a few false starts – working out the car's high bite point – she got it out of the parking space and we went for a spin down Bristol Road. It did not take long for her to be seduced by the vehicle's light touch and horsepower.

'It's so responsive,' she exclaimed. 'My old Metro you had to wrestle.'

'Does it respond to your every touch?' I said, running a finger along the top of her thigh.

'Don't go distracting me.'

'Why, what would happen?'

This is how the banter began. It ended eight days later in the worst row of our relationship.

How does the saying go? The present is a gift. It was what I'd been trying to give Sabra, in as big and bold a way as possible. What harm could possibly come from living in the moment? With me around, there were no awkward or painful consequences, no regrets. We could dance to any tune and never pay the piper. It had taken me a week to get Sabra back into this way of thinking, and it involved physically preventing her, on two occasions, from returning the car to our nearest Toyota garage.

Now I was finally was back on form, and about to whisk us away on an exotic weekend break. Aberystwyth was a pleasant three-hour drive through the Elan Valley's steep slopes and silvery reservoirs. I told my girlfriend the roads were empty and that it was like being in a car advert. Predictably, Sabra had been confident handling the Yaris from the get-go, but since we were leaving so late I offered to drive.

'It'll be quicker, that's all,' I said, nudging her. She was having none of it and shoved me playfully away from the driver's side, into someone's Victoria creeper.

Once we were out of town, the countryside fell in around us, green and luxuriant. It was unseasonably warm, a lemony sunshine tempting me to open my window and sniff the tang of sheep. We saw them trotting along the edge of the road in ones and twos, dirty tails bouncing, before they scampered up the slopes with unexpected energy.

'The Devil's Bridge falls are almost en route,' I said, checking the road map. 'Maybe we could get there before they close?'

'Sounds great.' She put her foot down, much to my joy. Now the car was really being put through its paces, powering up hills and taking bends so fast I thought my body would meld to the inside of the passenger door.

'Easy,' I said.

'These are car-advert roads.'

We hummed round a corner and the V-shaped river valley opened below us, funnelling us deeper into its reedy, trickling lowlands. As we got to the bottom, we were going so fast that I had to close the window to hear what Sabra was saying, though she was yelling across the car. The belt cradled me as she took a right turn, following the road along the gulley. Two motorbikes were jutting out from a lay-by, and, instead of slowing, Sabra skimmed the ferns on the other side. She looked at me and laughed, but I'd stopped enjoying the ride by this point and was starting to feel the emptiness of my stomach. A cold sweat told me I wasn't in control and didn't like it.

Sabra's strong, deft fingers grabbed the gearstick, working between the two highest gears just enough to get us round corners. She was sitting well back in her seat, gunning the engine. There was a smudge of something at the edge of her lip, perhaps the bits of Kit Kat I'd been snapping off to feed her, logs tossed into a furnace. We climbed a little, past ruined cottages, hedges rising and falling alongside the road, then over the next ridge she picked up speed again. It was two-way, but basically a single-track road.

'Hey . . .'

She didn't hear me. An ice cream van was rounding the bend at the bottom, coming up towards us at a leisurely pace. I could see the driver notice our speed and open his mouth in alarm. Sabra slammed on the brakes. The seatbelt dug into my chest. By the time we reached the van, she had squealed to a stop, mounting a verge so we were at a tilt. I thought the ice cream guy would get out and give us a thrashing, but he just crawled past, grinding through the hedgerow, mouthing insults we couldn't hear and shooting us looks of the most potent disgust.

'Fuck,' was all I could say. I wiped the sweat from my hairline and shakily got out of the car, slamming the door. My heart was pounding so hard it hurt. 'That was too close.'

Sabra's mouth fell open. 'The roads are more or less empty, and we were trying to make the falls . . .' The Yaris seemed to exhale heat and the smell of oil, its bonnet almost sizzling. 'I'm a fast driver . . . but not a bad one.'

There was always truth in what she said. She was very fast, at all times, in everything, and I'd done nothing but encourage her to leap further and longer, landing somewhere beyond recklessness. Was that the root of my addiction to her? Was it Sabra I loved, or the way she was happy to toy with the world, as I did? All her strangeness over the past few days must have been weighing on my mind, because my brain was as overheated as the engine.

'We nearly hit an ice cream van.'

'Don't shout at me.' Her eyelids sunk to half-mast, shutting me out.

'I'm not shouting. I just want to know – what's with you?'

A coldness was entering her gaze.

'You're the magician. Why don't you read my mind?'

The wind tugged at my hair. In the distance I heard the tinkle of 'half a pound of tuppenny rice, half a pound of treacle'. It seemed to mock me, as did Sabra's defiant look. I turned and started up the steep gradient of the field, between the tussocks and sheep droppings, my trainers instantly drenched. All I wanted was to get away from the car, flop into the grass and look down on the road, seeing its twists and turns laid out ahead. It took me by surprise to hear the engine start.

The Yaris was pulling away, leaving me halfway up the side of the valley. Through my fury, I saw the danger. This time she was angry. This time she might be too fast . . .

The thought packed such an emotional punch that I found myself standing beside the car again, the hot bonnet under my palm, the idea of Sabra getting hurt obviously powerful enough to trigger an involuntary leap backwards. It made me stagger. Where was I? The taste of swearing was on my lips. Not quite far enough, I realised, to avoid my angry outburst and my stumble out of the car. The slam of its door still rang in my ears.

'You look like you're going to yell at me,' she said. By the skin of my teeth I managed a rather watery grin, relieved to win a smile in return instead of the look that had so terrified me, the narrowed-eyed expression that said I was dismissed and would never get access to her thoughts.

'Sorry,' I said, 'sorry, sorry, sorry.' I kissed the top of her head and folded back into the Yaris, urging her to carry on, for everything to be all right. We put on some music, which did not quite mask the tension. Despite everything, her mood seemed dulled, and my chatter elicited only token acknowledgements. It was so rare for Sabra to be troubled, as she obviously was, and I didn't know how to fix her.

We made it to the Devil's Bridge falls, down a hundred slippery steps, and she chose that moment, with our legs trembling and our faces flecked with spray from the cascade, to tell me she'd been offered a trainee interpreter's position at the European Commission – a career job – and was leaving for Brussels in the new year.

Twenty-two

The wind bit into Aberystwyth's ruined castle, and waves lashed its pebbles, turning them over and over, and sometimes blasting them with such force that walkers on the promenade covered their ears with gloved hands. It was a fitting backdrop, given that our every conversation was undercut by the cold, hard possibility of Sabra leaving the country.

On the last day the gales died down. At the crazy golf course, parents still stood over their children like penguins protecting chicks, but at least the balls were no longer being blown out to sea. Gulls coasted on thermals from bar and restaurant chimneys, and we walked along the length of the seafront and up the hill, so the town seemed to shrink below. Someone's bright orange hat came tumbling our way, and I fell behind to catch it, returning it to the woman who was giving chase and would otherwise have seen it go over the cliff. Since most of our breath was needed for the climb, Sabra had been fairly quiet, but as I returned the hat she took my arm.

'What were you thinking?'

'I know. That orange. Should have let it blow out to sea.'

We were back in step again. When we made it to the café at the top of the funicular, I sampled all of the cakes and, finding them lacking, brought two hot chocolates to our table along with two chocolate bars, since I'd heard you could bite the ends off a Wispa and use it like a straw. This proved to be a myth, but we had a lot of fun trying to make it happen. Sabra kissed a chocolate lipstick mark onto my cheek and, when she'd finished laughing, remarked:

'I hear the chocolate in Belgium is shit.'

'I've heard that too.'

'It's just . . .' She put on a glove, took it off again and seized my hand. Her fingertips were hardened with plucking and pressing, but always nimble. 'It's kind of a new and exciting opportunity. You know I've always wanted to live abroad. When I was young, I thought I'd be touring a lot, as musicians do . . . At least this job would involve some travel.'

I tried not to look too disdainful. From what she'd told me, it was a trainee role, not especially well-paid, and almost certainly office-based, transcribing boring conversations. 'I'd have to brush up on my Mandarin,' she added. 'It's almost as bad as playing the violin. If you stop for a week you forget four, five characters . . .'

Buying the car had given me such an aura of virtue; I really thought I'd progressed beyond self-interest, but I'm ashamed to say that integrity was still a speck on the horizon. 'What scares you most?' I asked, then skipped back and, nonchalantly stirring my drink with a stub of Wispa, parroted: 'Aren't you worried about being so far from your mum? And Brussels, don't some people say it's a bit sterile and bureaucratic?'

Deep in her eyes I saw the tiny craters made by having her worst fears catapulted back at her, the double impact of having them voiced by another.

'That's what I'm afraid of,' she said dully. 'And missing you, of course. Maybe I shouldn't go.'

A small, weak alarm bell told me I was being a dick, that I should stop and let things take their course. If this manipulation worked, it would only make me hate myself later on; but there was no time to think it through, and I was blinkered by a powerful fear of losing her, of having nothing left. Her hand was curled under mine, strong and warm and impossible to let go.

'It's not like life comes with only one opportunity,' I continued. 'It's a fruit tree, not a vegetable.' We smiled at each other, recalling an earlier conversation with an eccen-

143

tric local greengrocer. Life keeps giving, I wanted to tell her, and the best thing it's giving us right now is each other.

'Okay,' she said. 'Done. Sorted.'

We went down in the funicular, pressing ourselves against the front window and making screaming faces, a toddler looking at us in astonishment from its mother's arms. The trip, and our relationship, had been saved. Tension evaporated from my skin.

At Christmas she went back early to see her mum, who was still having a few health problems. For me, going back to Nan's was, much to my surprise, a pleasant prospect. They'd never seen me come through the door in such a jovial mood. Asda had been ransacked, and I brought in big carryalls of biscuits, cheese, wine and houseplants. Now that I had my own flat, and especially now that Sabra was about to move in permanently, the chains that had held me to Nan's house were well and truly broken. All the freedom in the world was mine, so coming back to the chaos of a steam-filled kitchen was novel rather than mundane.

Nan looked older, as she did every time I saw her, though she had long since run out of sandy hairs to turn grey. Her face was looser, her eyes more translucent and tired, but she also looked happier, having settled back into her third-age comings and goings, still appreciating our company at Christmas. We sat in the lounge and watched cheesy television, waiting for my sister to arrive, and I arranged my gifts under the everlasting white-tinsel tree. I tried to get the cat to sit on my lap.

Though it was hardly more than a kitten, this cat acted as if it had already lived eight of its nine lives and was now winding down. I watched it lap up its brown cereal and stagger, as though exhausted, to the lounge where a fluffy cushion was arranged a safe distance from the gas fire. It then fell into so satisfying a doze that its breathing could be heard above the television. For all I knew, this cat also had the power do to things repeatedly and, on seeing an empty bowl, would go back to when it was full and re-enact the eating experience twenty, forty times, before finally tiring of it and tottering off to rest. I looked at the sleeping curl of fur and considered that Smoky could be a hundred years old.

The strangest thing about my sister, when she emerged from the taxi, was that she seemed happy. Not a momentary, flickering, obligatory enthusiasm at seeing us, but real bedded-in joy. Her new job as a research associate in the physics department obviously suited her but it had never before made her glow. As she unloaded her shopping in the kitchen, I watched her like a hawk and chattered about all the things Sabra was probably doing right now.

'Will you shut up talking about your girlfriend?' Erin complained at last. 'You haven't even asked about mine.'

It was typical of my sister to reveal something so important in a throwaway line, a wry smile pasted over her feelings.

When Nan understood what was meant by this, she picked up the oven mitt and fanned herself with the burnt end.

'Well, I suppose it's the modern way,' she remarked, and my sister did not push her to say anything further. In any case, she seemed to forget the news quickly and was soon half-comatose in the armchair, relaxed by her second glass of sherry. Erin, as the only sober one, was left to finish the cooking, with me offering willing but rather tipsy assistance.

Before long we were seated at the table, and the delicious food seemed to send Nan back in time. She started reminiscing about collecting chestnuts with Mum, taking her to school. 'This bread sauce wouldn't have been to her taste,' she remarked at one point. 'Too many cloves. It's like perfume.' Hearing about Mum's good report cards and childhood scrapes suffused me with an odd emotion, sweet but somewhat overpowering. My room in this house still contained some of her things: a woollen hat I'd salvaged, some photos and coffee mugs, and the 'Top work!' and 'Star!' ink stamps she'd used for marking. I'd planned to take these items back to Birmingham, but perhaps it was better to keep them down here, leave plenty of room for Sabra's stuff.

'Your father hasn't been in touch?' Nan's voice filtered into my thoughts. 'You'd think he'd come over and visit us once in a while. Or you, anyway – I've no wish to see him.' Her tone brought a slight tension to the table, and I tried to sound casual as I addressed Erin:

'Is he still texting?'

She nodded. 'He says you never reply.' I always forgot her relationship with Dad was different, having had five more years of childhood with him. Even now she'd sometimes sound a little confused about how it all fell apart.

Later that day, when I was upstairs sorting through some of my junk, I came across a letter of his tucked into the pages of *Match of the Day* magazine. A crumpled sheet of paper with a hotel address at the top. Though I wanted to read it, the amount of beer I'd consumed made his handwriting squirm and, after several attempts, I gave up and thrust it angrily into my travel bag. For about a millisecond I wondered what Dad would make of Erin having a female partner, then I knew he would love it. Half his friends were gay, and no father liked the idea of a brawny lad climbing onto his little girl. I knew that Mum would have been fine with it too. Erin was lucky to have liberal-minded parents – or would have been if either was around. Instead, all she had was an immature little brother and an old woman asleep in front of *Die Hard*.

To me, this revelation about my sister, for all its shock value, made perfect sense. It bolted on naturally to her identity. As she boiled the kettle, inscrutable under her calm features but plum-cheeked and healthy, it occurred to me that we'd both come of age with a few secrets under our belts.

'So who is this girlfriend?' I asked.

'Just someone I work with.'

'Like a colleague?'

'Yes, like a colleague.'

'But not one?'

'Well, she's a PhD student.'

I could hardly contain myself. 'Dating a student?' My face exploded into a smirk.

'She's only a couple of years younger,' Erin said, turning to the kitchen windowsill where Nan had placed a row of apples to ripen. She picked one up and ran her fingers over its wrinkled skin before bringing it to her nose. I kept forgetting her eyesight was bad, that she was preparing herself for a world in which touch would take precedence. 'And she's brilliant. From Norway.' For some reason this gave me a vision of the two of them in their sensible glasses, leaning over microscopes, the student looking up admiringly at Erin. It struck me that my sister was, albeit in the cocoon of academia, a unique and fiercely intelligent person. I liked the idea that both of us were, in our different ways, high achievers, and attractive to other people as a result. Having got my imp under control, I gave her a verbal thumbs up.

'Well . . . Cool.'

In my mind's eye, the girlfriend juggled test tubes and conical flasks, and spoke in a sing-song accent. Less cartoonish were the images that entered my head when I relived Sabra's kiss goodbye, followed by a toast of festive schnapps. Despite myself, I started telling Erin how worried I'd been about the trainee interpreter job offer, how narrowly I'd avoided her being poached by Europe.

'So she's not going?' She bit the apple, so ripe it hardly crunched.

'No. In fact, she's moving in with me.' Since Sabra had already given up her houseshare, it was the perfect solution. It almost felt like fate bringing us together. She'd carry on with her university job for now, but I was already plotting some way of getting her back into music. 'Someone you work with . . . that's so convenient,' I mused, entertaining a brief fantasy of Sabra as a magician's assistant, wearing the hell out of a little sparkly dress. The prospect was delectable and, should I put it to her, guaranteed to provoke laughter. A shame she wouldn't see the appeal of being sawn in half.

'We're working on some really interesting projects,' Erin went on, starting to talk about electrons as I picked up the double-ended oven mitt and examined the patch that had been blackened against the grill. My sister was a career physicist now, desperate to make a name for herself. It was an aspiration I could understand, especially since I'd been enjoying a sizzling, out-of-nowhere reputation as a magician. But it had surprised me to find that what I valued more – what I really lived for – was time with Sabra, even if we did absolutely nothing and I was just Arlo, not the great illusionist, and not a word of hyperbole to my name.

I couldn't wait to feel her body press against mine, all the more pleasurable after a week apart. She would be waiting when I arrived back at the flat. Her plan was to drive up from Kent a day or two early with the rest of her stuff – she didn't have much – and I would walk through the door to be grabbed and rolled around under the kitchen table. She'd struggle with my belt and I'd make damp, evaporating handprints on the laminate, and afterwards, in our floor-level languor, we'd happen upon that half-bottle of cherry brandy that had rolled under the wooden bench the week before and been forgotten. I could already smell its sour-sweet vapour as I put my key in the lock, barely waiting for the crack to widen before I yelled:

'Anybody home?'

The heating was on, and I knew she was there because her car was outside, its shiny paintwork – had she washed it? – filling me with pride.

It was when I saw the piece of file paper on the kitchen table, weighed down with two sets of keys, that my heart stopped.

Dear Arlo,

I want to thank you for everything, and especially for being the one who picked me off the ground when we first met. I'll always be grateful.

I'm going to Brussels. I need to do what you would do and jump in with both feet, and I think it would be good for me to make a fresh start. It's nothing to do with you, only that being together makes me do things I regret. There's something wrong with me, and I don't know what it is, but it's been worrying me. I know it scared you when I nearly got us killed on the way to Aber, but by God it scared me too.

So, I'm sorry. I've never known anyone like you. I'm crying as I write this. I really think you are special, Arlo. Be happy.

Sabra

I held the paper in one hand, noting the scrunched edges, the blemish that could be a touch of salt water, her well-rounded secondary-school letters clustering in the centre of the page. A moment later I was at the window, scanning the pavement from end to end, searching for a figure with a suitcase heading for the trains, but there was nothing except that Yaris, two wheels on the kerb – a red devil mocking me. Why did I think it was a good idea? Sabra was never someone who valued flashy gifts. Too late I saw her thought process, the indignity of being bought a car because her promising musical career had morphed into a temping job and money was tight. Now she'd gone off to seize whatever career life could offer and had cast me aside to do it. I dashed round the flat, confirming that every scrap of her clothing was gone, along with her wire stand, shoulder rest and folders of sheet music. Even the wax-coated cheese she'd brought back from her trip to Germany had vanished from the fridge, though she'd left me the chilli wurst.

It was as though someone had slapped me in the face and

my ears were still ringing. Sitting at the table, I reached down, unblinking, and felt around for the bottle of brandy. I pulled out the cork and downed as much as I could in one long draught, hating its sickly sweetness, until it trickled like blood from the corners of my mouth. It belonged to Sabra and might contain some essence of her, something I could pour into my veins and thereby conjure her back. I thought about driving to the airport, trying to intercept her, though the idea of following the instructions laid out in romantic movies repulsed me. In any case, she could have gone yesterday or the day before, for all I knew. Her house key lay on the note beside the leather Toyota fob. She'd had plenty of time to pack up and leave in peace.

My stomach dallied with the idea of sending the liquid back up, but in the end I sat unmoving for half an hour and the alcohol played tricks with me instead. There was a card poking out of the bin, and suddenly I knew it would say 'Sorry I'm leaving you', butchered from the original 'Sorry you're leaving' well-wishing text. I flew across the linoleum and snatched it from the litter, certain this was what I'd see, but it was only a charity card with a fundraising message. Someone must have dumped it there.

I'd been dumped. 'Fuck,' I said aloud, remembering the conversations we'd had on this topic, Sabra telling me with a shrug that she'd always been the one to break off relationships. Being collateral damage in someone else's story was never my plan, and my charred ego smouldered with an almost physical pain. Sabra was disdainful of men she could predict; it was all those sleazy music teachers, offering to help with her fingerwork. Once she'd got the measure of someone, she lost interest. Could she have tired of me, even with all my secrets?

The letter refused to vanish from the table. Instead, its words huddled even closer and more claustrophobically together. It had never been so clear that Brussels was just a convenient and clear-cut exit route. What did she mean about doing things she regretted? I always fixed anything she regretted.

Didn't she love me?

She had never said she loved me because there was no need; I could see it when she took me warmly in her arms, when we were hurrying along and she'd look up admiringly. Reflected in her eyes, I was fit, smart, dark-eyed and devoted. Her words were mysterious. *The relationship makes me do things I regret.* Like what? She mentioned the driving, but that was nothing. Did she think I was angry about it? I'd already admitted to egging her on in the first place, and anyway there was no harm done. I was fairly sure I hadn't expressed any anger, only that short-lived fear, which was natural. She'd been scared too. Was she saying she had become too reckless? That hardly mattered as long as I was around. I remembered how she looked in the car: laughing, playing the radio at full volume, eating Kit Kats and taking corners as though they were just a suggestion. Did I teach her that?

I drained the bottle and smashed it across the floor, creating a hellish landscape of red drops and glass. The shards were so sparkly. I'd been an inspiration to Sabra. I'd inspired her all the way onto a plane and out of my life.

Twenty-two

I went to the airport twice in the next three days, whenever blind panic drove me there. The first time, I parked and then sat in the car for an hour, re-reading her letter. The second time, I was on my way to the budget airline desks when it occurred to me that I didn't have her address. Even if I made contact in Brussels, I wasn't sure I could handle the look on her face, the expression that would say *Arlo, I didn't think you'd be pathetic enough to follow me*, accompanied by mingled embarrassment and pity.

Was there nothing I could do? Occasionally I'd wake from a doze and my old mindset would hang around like morning mist, an aura of hopefulness. For years now, I'd had the power to see how things panned out and, if I didn't like it, go back and try again. It made no sense to be here in this desert of a January without a single option on the horizon. Just wait, I told myself: either she'll miss you and return, or you'll figure out what to do. Nevertheless, it was hard not to keep screening clips of our life together in my mental cinema, always ending with the kiss she'd given me when we'd parted for Christmas, the soft questing edges of her lips pulling at mine.

Aside from my mad dashes and beer runs, I became very stationary for the next few days, shuffling between bathroom and living room, ordering takeaways and letting them go cold, watching television until I lost the ability to distinguish between documentaries and dreams. The kitchen was difficult to use because it was still strewn with glass and sticky droplets. I'd been keeping the door closed to shut out the smell of cherry, which made me sick. Where did I keep the dustpan and brush? When the mess was finally wiped up, pathetically, with bits of kitchen roll, the nature of glass made itself known and put a big splinter in the pad of my thumb.

As I pulled it out, a vision appeared in my mind: Sabra's palm welling up rose-red, the blood flowing down her forearm and into the water, which was probably already stinging her with chlorine or whatever they put into these fountains.

It was summertime, and we'd been messing about by the Floozie in the Jacuzzi, as it was affectionately called, a statue with thick legs and arms that curled up rather than reclined in the Victoria Square cascades. On this beautiful heatwave day we were having some drinks and dipping our hands in the fountain to flick water at each other. When I tossed my empty pint glass end over end and caught it in the concave of my forearm, Sabra looked on with a competitive glint in her eye. She wanted to have a go, but was certain the glass would fall and smash.

'I believe in you,' I said, and undid her first two unsuccessful attempts, adding a lesson and a confidence boost before letting her perform a third time, in which the glass nestled on her light shirt, and her face was triumphant. I loved sharing her joy.

'How did you know I could do it?' she asked, and then nodded to herself as she answered the question internally. 'I forgot.' That mischievous expression appeared on her lips, the one that told me I was about to be tested. 'So tell me . . . what would happen if we got into this fountain to cool down a bit?'

We were perspiring in the heat, and it was a tempting prospect. I had us run through the motions, wading across to the statue . . . things happening, then I went back to beforehand.

'If we get into this pool with the floozie,' I said, 'a security guard from the council building will come over holding a sandwich and yell at us.'

'That's very specific,' she said delightedly. 'Okay, I'm going to try it.' Before I could stop her, she'd placed her pint on the wall, swung her bare legs over and launched into the pool.

'Sabra, no!' I'd forgotten to say we would also fall over in our haste and she'd cut her hand on some broken glass. But it was too late. Off she went, and I had to go in too, trying to stop her, my voice drowned out by the splashing. We made such a racket that people turned to look, and even though I'd dragged her to the side we got the security guard's attention anyway. 'What's the matter with you?' he began, but that sharp shout right by our ears, amid a hailstorm of tuna and breadcrumbs, startled Sabra so much she slipped. Her hand hit the bottom, and she stood up with dripping hair, unable to suppress a cry as the blood bubbled from her palm. I took a deep breath, calmed myself and took us all the way back to our fresh drinks.

'Cheers,' a clink and a blissful draught of lager.

The pint trick working for her. That's what she took away from that day, knowing nothing of the rest. I rewound the kitchen roll, to before the splinter went into my thumb, and retreated to the lounge, sinking onto a leather sofa that felt like cold skin. Here I was, in one piece, perfectly safe. I felt almost sick at how healthy and plump each of my hands appeared, my body a robust core of untested muscle. My thumb pad was covered in perfect, waterproof skin, unpunctured and turgid as the cushion. Once again, I'd saved myself without giving it a thought, and over the past year I'd generously extended this safety net to Sabra. My degree had included enough about behaviour reinforcement for me to understand how it happened, that every time Sabra had chosen the riskier route I'd validated her decision. There was no doubt her genetic makeup was two thirds daredevil, but perhaps I'd made it worse, made it even harder to keep a grip on reality. No wonder she was scared.

I read the letter again, read between the lines. *There's something wrong with me.* She'd let me influence her, and now she was terrified of herself. But it wasn't her fault. I sensed what she did not say, which was that she had been relying too much on my supposed foresight, assuming that if her actions could lead to any truly dire consequences I would warn her. Finally, I'd yanked myself out of my own thick skull and was seeing things through her eyes.

Despite all the crazy things we'd done together, no harm had come to us. No falls or smashes or broken bones – not even any minor inconveniences like being fined or losing valuables or even getting caught backstage at the Colosseum. We got away with everything, and she was losing the ability to sense danger. Perhaps she had started to look back on some of her actions with regret. We'd been quite wild at a time when she should really have been working towards whatever career was still an option, and this must have felt a little wrong. Sabra was the kind of person who would stuff these worries down the back of the sofa. She would ignore them and carry on. But then there had been the road to Aberystwyth.

I opened a bottle of wine – all I had left – and drank half

of it, spilling some on my Roma T-shirt. The bloody drive to Wales in my bloody sixty-eight-horsepower Yaris. Why was it so different from all the other near misses we'd lived through? Whenever we came close to disaster she would simply shoot me a glance, check the tiny yellow canary living in my dark pupil was still lazing back on its perch and know there was no cause for alarm. If I was cool, everything was cool. What was alarming was to see me drip sweat on the new upholstery and stagger, shaking, from the car. Escaping. I was *escaping* from her. That tamped-down fear of what she was becoming was out in the open, written all over my face. The safety net was in tatters, but she was trapped on the high wire with no way to get down.

The letter looped the loop gracefully as I let it fall from my fingers. With me by her side, Sabra could have done anything, but she left me for the same reason she should have stayed. I'd never let her know exactly what she was dealing with. She only had that one half-truth to go on – or was it a complete lie? I put my eye to the neck of the bottle and the liquid formed shadowy shapes, woodland creatures, a fawn-legs man raising his hand for half-truth, while another with a deer's head answered in favour of lies. If she'd known everything, she would have understood that we could take risks together but that her own actions couldn't be undone. All the uncertainty would be washed away. There was nothing wrong with her, and she wasn't turning into a monster; we were just special people.

How far had she strayed from the self she knew, and how

much had it frightened her? Even as I worked all of this out, I was berating myself for letting things reach a crisis point. The bottle of wine still had dust on its shoulder and a dark waterline within. Perhaps it would dissolve my brain with its acidity and these stinging thoughts would cease.

My fist made a crater in the leather sofa cushion. For someone who could grab onto bits of time and pull them back, being helpless in the face of someone else's decision was torture. Even if I could reverse the several days necessary to reach Sabra before Christmas – and that was far too many actions to remember – I still couldn't stop her leaving. Some deity was perfecting the concept of cruelty, handing me Sabra for a year and then snatching her away so I could feel the full whack of loneliness. There would be no going back, no scouring Brussels and working out the magic combination of words. There was no oxygen in the stale air of this flat; either that or I'd lost interest in breathing. Sure I was a screw-up, an arrogant, blundering fool, but did I deserve this? The stars must have found some toxic, quixotic alignment at my birth if this was to be my destiny, if everyone I loved was to slip through my fingers. The man who could make no mistakes.

Part 4

CHEAT AND MISS A TURN

Twenty-three

I read his letter in a hackney cab, keenly aware of the coincidence since I, too, was stuck in traffic.

Ritzy Cars Inc.,
2300 Venus Boulevard,
LA 400334

30 January 1995

Dear Arlo,

I thought I'd write you now while in the endless LA queues. This limousine has its own headed note paper! There is also champagne in a chiller but I'm trying to cut down. How are you, anyway? I hear you are now the proud owner of a Nintendo Game Boy – is that why you haven't been writing back?!

I'm still enjoying my role as the mastermind behind everything that goes awry in *Hillstation Nine Zero One*. Although I liked the other show, this one has writing that goes beyond the pale, and is much preferred by the critics. I know it's on a bit late in the UK but hope you've been taping it?

Playing the villain is such fun. Do you know why so many American baddies are English? The more I study other villains the more I've come to realise it's all down to classical story structure. If you boil down all plots, you find that they are always about the next generation desperately trying to break away from its parents to reproduce. Story of the human race . . . but, politically, also the story of the United States. That's why they love a baddie from the old country – it's the natural choice, and means they can play out endless fantasies of regaining their freedom.

Great news for me, and, thanks to *Hillstation*, there's been a very exciting nibble, my agent tells me, from the producers of a feature film that I think will be huge. But I'm not at liberty to say anything just yet. Fame is such a fickle thing – one moment you're up and they love you, the next you realise there's a big vending machine full of actors and you've been dropped and someone else pushed forward. Ah well . . . if I get the part then you'll be able to go around school boasting about me!

Anyway, Arlo, I'll come and see you at the end of
the summer if my schedule permits, but these directors
are such slave-drivers.

Yours etc.,

Dad

He never got to play that ultimate villain, although he did
get the part. For some reason, perhaps because of all the
pressure and expectation, his drinking escalated when
shooting began. There may have been drugs too; Erin didn't
say. He failed to turn up on set or learn lines, and he was
dropped in the same capricious way he'd envisioned, almost
in jest, half a year earlier.

This letter was the last that I received before Mum's death.
My intention had been to read it once more and then dispose
of it in a dustbin. Instead, I found myself folding the notepaper
neatly and slipping it back into my bag. These days, I was
sailing unexpectedly close to my dad's old haunted waters: fame
and fortune. With luck I would never be famous in the sense
of being exposed to the public. I preferred to remain inscrutable,
and was happiest with reviews that described me as mystical,
marvellous, mind-blowing and, most of all, a mystery.

As I got out, telling the driver to charge it to the agency
tab, I caught a glimpse of dark, dyed hair, a sharp suit and
sunglasses – the lip service I was paying to the idea of being
a magician. For some reason the agency had just rebranded
me as 'ArlO' with a capital 'O'.

'They love you,' said the director, shaking a copy of some trade magazine. He was a large man with a red, streaky face, despised by most of the staff because of the way he ran his other going concern, a lap-dancing club near Covent Garden. He wanted me to do television, telling me there was money in it and after a few appearances I would almost certainly get my own show. But I wasn't interested. A studio audience was half-asleep compared to its theatre equivalent. There would be so many breaks and retakes, and the last thing I wanted was to end up on some similar trajectory to Dad. There would be that inevitable phone call, brimming with glee, in which he would tell me he'd seen me on the telly, chip off the old block, and so on.

In the theatre it was close-up danger right in their faces. I could smell their fear, their aftershave and lip-balm, and my ears would ring for hours with high-pitched whoops and applause. Tonight was my biggest venue yet, and it would be packed. There would be a tiger in a cage (I was amazed they could get a tiger, but apparently it was okay if she was already in the business), who could exit either left or right, once the trick began. In one Perspex box was a bell, in the other there was me. I'd reel off some dubious stats about tigers being able to smell fresh blood for ten miles, always choosing live prey, but my animal mind-meld would keep me safe.

With this tiger trick, the latest in my repertoire and by far the flashiest, the cat had to push through a near-invisible Perspex flap to go either way, and the one on my side triggered a beep. Most of the time I detected the motion and undid even before the beeper began. My box was full of repellent scents, while the other was doused with meat juices. Normally the tiger went straight for the latter, snapping up the tiny hidden cube of steak tacked to the bell. If she went for me, I skipped back and changed position, pumping the cans of perfume in my pockets.

It was the element of risk that got the audience going, and this worked even better when I reset the whole thing and asked for a volunteer. Who the hell would put their hand up for that? Why do people trust magicians? Newsflash: we are ordinary people desperately hoping our tricks are good enough, plastering over the cracks with arrogance. Anyway, the volunteer was much easier. I could see what was going on and reverse things before any mauling took place.

I was one of the agency's biggest acts now, pulling in good money, in demand by the rich and famous. It seemed appropriate for my magician's backstory for me to be a loner, not someone who went home every evening to a girlfriend cooking chicken wings. I gave nothing away. Only if the applause was too rapturous, or if someone threw a rose on the stage, would my gratitude get the better of me, in which case I'd reward the audience with a smile.

For a while I'd seen no reason to leave Birmingham. It was only when I walked through Canon Hill Park and went for a coffee at the MAC without Sabra beside me that everything started to feel weird. Going to the supermarket, I found her 'trolley pound' in its little woven purse still in my coat pocket. I turned up late for things and was surprised when people thought I should have been on time.

One of these tardy occasions was a meeting in which my agency promised me stardom and serious money if I went on the London circuit, so I gave notice on the flat and closed the door – not without some relief – on the cherry-brandy smell that no amount of bleach was able to purge from the floor tiles.

I rented a beautiful apartment in Bloomsbury, earning its deposit from a single show at a Chinese New Year banquet in Mayfair. London fawned over me. Hardly a week went by without some celebrity or friend of the agency sending a car to bring me to a Michelin-starred restaurant, or through the pulsing Soho night to the private rooms of a club where champagne flowed over ice waterfalls. I would turn heads in my suit, still wearing shades because I was a magician and could look as weird as I liked, and the most stunning women – the most dewy-eyed, moist-lipped, worked-on Barbie-girls imaginable – would reach for me as I passed, their breath scented with honey and mint cocktails, sliding cool, thin arms around my shirt collar and begging me to come away and do some coke. I felt I could push them over like dominoes; they would topple so obligingly.

It was a relief.

A relief to be ArlO and not myself for a while, to let people's love and admiration rain against my titanium shell and listen quietly to its patter. People assumed 'Arlo' wasn't my real name, that I was a Gary or a Dave behind the scenes, though my olive skin and the near-black dye in my oil-slicked hair would keep them guessing at my nationality.

At the end of a gig, I longed to take off my sunglasses and admit to being a little kid from the wrong side of the river, just having fun with them, or even to ask what they really thought was happening. Wasn't it obvious that I was a freak and needed help? Perhaps on one occasion I did yell this out, or something like it, at the close of the act, but I undid it straight away, not liking to see the adoration fade from their faces, and with a sense that my career might depend on no one knowing the truth.

So the money rolled in, and it'd been some time since I'd bothered to buy a scratch card. You never knew when these gambling authorities would cotton on to a repeat winner, so it was probably just as well. Money was plentiful enough to allow for careless behaviour. I didn't chase up the deposit refund on my Birmingham flat, and Sabra's Yaris was still on the pavement where she'd left it. Occasionally I drifted into a reverie, imagining she would come back one day and nostalgically walk past the flat where she could have been happy, only to see the Yaris rusting away, orange clashing with red, and feel the waste of it.

Living in London also put me back in contact with Tim, who was holding down his lawyering job with difficulty. I was only now appreciating how absurdly nice he was, even in the face of personal misfortune. Since leaving university he'd been dumped by no fewer than three women, all of whom were 'the one', seen his dad develop cancer and his sister slip towards alcoholism, all in the gaps between twenty-hour days in the office. It was not unusual for him to come home, have a shower and return to work, unable to squeeze sleep into his schedule. Slate-grey half-moons had developed under his eyes, and his hair had begun to recede. Still, he laughed and bought endless lagers and enthused about my far-more-exciting lifestyle.

'I never could see you doing nine to five.'

'Yeah,' I said, 'but do you think it's illegal, with the tiger?'

'Probably. I could find out for you.'

I was grateful to have him back, one of the few people I could converse with as Arlo and not ArlO. That big expectant O. The big nothing. It was hard to be enigmatic all the time, and sometimes I feared becoming ArlO on the inside as well, strangely joyless among the spring bulbs, taking no pleasure in the parakeets in St James's Park. I'd walk past crowds at crossings, tourists deciding which way to go, living their closed little lives, never seeing the complex branching options that lay open to them at every turn. You went right, but what if you'd gone left? You ran across the road, but what if you'd waited? Sometimes I gave people incorrect directions just to nudge them from their set paths. I was a magician all right, twenty-four hours a day.

* * *

Sheila, the co-founder of the agency, was a woman with blue hair who'd been a clown herself before 'retiring from the field'. She was accompanying me to that night's gig but was currently being delayed by the director, who had chosen that moment to list all his issues with how she ran the business.

As I was checking the time, wondering whether to interrupt, the director stalked out of the office, spotted me and declaimed:

'Arlo will back me up on this, won't you?'

'On what?'

Sheila cut in: 'Throwing money at a problem doesn't always make it vanish.'

'Sure it does.'

We all knew that was how things worked at his strip club. It was cold, hard cash that had kept the recent attacks out of the papers. His phone started ringing and the director put it to his ear, while I noted Sheila's weary expression and tried to motion that we should get out of there while we could. But it turned out to be a good thing we stayed. After overhearing about a minute of the phone chat I decided to reverse back to the conversation, backing him up with gusto.

'Oh yeah, money and magic are the same thing,' I agreed, knowing he was about to take a call from a reporter who'd been undercover at his club for the last six weeks, that the blood was about to drain from his face. I leaned in and plucked the carnation from his breast pocket. 'But only if you have this lucky flower. Whoops!' I tossed it out of the window and he laughed, and the phone started to ring.

Out on the pavement, as we climbed into the taxi, it was Sheila's turn to laugh, though afterwards she fixed me with a no-shit glower and warned: 'Stay out of my head, Mr O.'

I smiled disarmingly. 'Scared of a few tricks?'

The gig had an odd sort of atmosphere, a cabaret venue hosting a corporate awards ceremony. I was the main entertainment and had been given a very nice dressing room. We'd ditched the tiger, since the wildlife charity the firm supported might disapprove, and instead I'd polished up my psychological tricks, ensuring all the senior staff were pointed out.

The lights came up – blindingly, as usual – and I was struck by the odour of heated dust, the endless glasses of wine stretching as far as the eye could see. A tiny piece of glitter had found its way to my cheek, and the mic was attached to my lapel. I launched into some card tricks, quickly involving the audience. It was like close-up magic but open to the whole room – my speciality. I got three of them on stage and we did various mind games, earning me half-laughing, half-angry shouts when I reeled off details about a guy's children and pets that I'd ostensibly obtained from listening to his wallet.

For the paint-off, I got the CEO drawing, so I could go back and create identical versions of his sketches. The hall was all expectant faces, waiting, watching me – my heart sank – as if I was a man-shaped television and they were wishing they could change the channel. I'd never noticed this before. From her position by the fire exit, Sheila was frowning, perhaps noticing my smile falter, my slight reticence to begin the next trick. She could tell something was wrong.

In the interval, it was a relief to be off the hot stage. My shirt picked up a smudge from the lighting rig, as though even the equipment had to wear powder. The MC was bigging me up in readiness for the second act, reminding the audience of my greatest triumphs. The applause may as well have been directed out of the window. I'd surprised them and they couldn't understand how I'd done it, that was all. No one really believed I could read minds. Most had probably left their insecurities hanging out at some point and seen them yanked; they knew people had tells. They could clap till their hands bled but what they'd take home was the belief that, underneath it all, I must be a cheat. Otherwise reality would not be reality.

A roar of laughter assaulted my ears: the MC making a dirty joke. It was brash yapping that continued for far too long, little screams spiralling above it. I wasn't sure I could bear to step back on stage. There were no exits on this side, only scenery boards printed with a silvery forest, leaning against the wall. I wished myself into the picture, up among the fresh hills and the bliss of silence.

The expectant gaze of the crowd restored me a little. Even if this was my last show, I wouldn't leave without my hit of rapturous applause. From the nearest table, I extracted a man whose face had been turned towards a pretty woman and asked, in cultivated, hypnotic tones, what he was thinking.

'Oh . . . just that I need another glass of white and our table only has red.' He was fidgety, tucking fingers into his tight trouser pockets then removing them self-consciously. He licked his lips, casting longing glances back to his table. I skipped back and launched into 'I will read your mind', pulling out imaginary tickertape from his ear: 'That momentary thought . . .' Never failed. They were always astonished to hear their interior monologue on another's lips, struck dumb by their own tone and vocabulary. I reeled off his line about the red and white wine. He squinted in the lights, shifted to one side, putting on a thoughtful expression. That was when I realised I'd caught myself a slippery bugger.

'Actually no, that's not it.' He shrugged, smiled, threw a look at the table once more and this time I saw where it landed – straight down the cleavage of that attractive woman, far too young for him. She was so new to the company that she hadn't dared to dress in anything other than her workwear, her A-line skirt and pinstriped blouse. I realised that he'd made up the thing about the wine because he was really thinking something quite obscene, something he'd not be sharing with colleagues.

'You weedy tosser,' I said, then undid it. But I left him standing. I could have undone the whole trick and picked someone else, but I didn't. Maybe I wanted to see how a mistake would pan out. I shrugged in supplication, admitting my wrongness, and let the bastard go. From this point onwards, everything became washed-out, only the thinnest sketch in my memory. There was the finale of the show, a prearranged crowd-pleaser where I would hurl a bucket of company-branded bouncy balls into the audience and correctly predict how many people would catch one. Then the MC reclaimed the microphone for the raffle.

It would have been a good idea to leave right then. As it was, I had to see the pretty girl, the source of Sleazy Man's sordid thoughts, win a car. And not just any car: a Toyota Yaris. What kind of company gives away a brand-new Yaris? Fine, I thought, congratulations, salesgirl of the year. Have it. These people looked right through me; I was done trying to broaden their horizons.

'They loved you,' said Sheila with a worried grimace. There was scattered clapping as we made our way out. Then a reedy, sneering voice reached my ears:

'Can't win 'em all, eh, son?' The guy I'd had on stage intercepted us at the exit, his breath full of cigarette. An unbearable smirk of self-satisfaction twisted his lips.

'Excuse me,' I murmured to Sheila. As my fist gushed into his stomach, so hard and unexpected it must have reached his spine, I said: 'You know why I can afford this mistake? Because I'm not cheating. I never cheat. And Arlo is my real name.'

I let him slump to the floor and enjoyed one last groan

before I took it back to his heckle, gave him a pleasant wave, and held the door open for Sheila.

'Chin up, sweetheart,' she said. 'You can bounce back. People bounce back from anything.'

She was right, of course. But there was something missing. Adoration was what I'd wanted – surely it's all anyone wants – but somehow this infinite supply was failing to hit the spot. 'They loved you' was all anyone ever said, but whom did they love? In my mind, when the great ArlO exited the building, there was always a small boy left on stage, scrabbling among the rose petals.

Twenty-three

Eleven days had passed since that gig, and I'd been roped into doing two more, not wanting to drop Sheila in it when the agency was in such chaos. The rest of the time I hid behind my flimsy curtains, beer in hand, leaving London to go about its business in the heatwave.

A top hat squatted on the television set, and by the radiator there was a case full of cards and other puny tricks, handkerchiefs and a toy rabbit. There was even, to my disgust, a black-and-white wand on the floor, pointing the way to the toilet. A suit dangled from the door, night-coloured with a mussel-shell sheen, just back from dry cleaning. It was my shiny exterior, hiding the fact that underneath I was soft and pathetic and still hurting like

179

crazy. I went to the washing machine for my shirts, turning the drum to get the last one out, wishing I could catch hold of the seasons and spin them backwards, summer over winter over summer, to where Sabra and I would be melding together under a fleece blanket on the sofa.

Now you see it, now you don't. How could I have thought being a magician was a good idea? I picked up the hat with incredulity, bending its felt rim, plucking at the lining. I turned to the mirror, rammed it on my head, then batted it off. My hair was loose, shoulder-length and a mucky colour, the black dye due for a touch-up. I hated trickery, yet I'd surrounded myself with illusions. Magician was the worst possible career I could have chosen; excelling at it meant being an even bigger fraud. I felt like an illusion myself, hardly real, floating desolately back to the couch and staring at my hands. Such white fingertips. All this power and I'd never used it for anything but parlour tricks. The sofa smelled of crumbs and copper coins, and brought me crashing back to the house of my childhood in Herne Hill: cupboards along the walls, flies circling in the kitchen, Rolos perched temptingly on the top of the freezer. Every detail was pin-sharp and three-dimensional. Would it be so hard? All this magic had made me practise almost daily and, while my body was not as fit as it had been, my mind was surely at its most muscular.

At the windows, the useless curtains wafted, filling their bellies with draught and then expelling it. 'Polonius!' my dad would cry, whenever we hid behind the long drapes in our house. The pain around my eyes was the tension of pure misery. So alone here in this flat, no one in the world to care about me. How eagerly my mum would have listened, nodding as I described the audiences and the prefabricated, archetypal magician they saw on stage. She would fold me into that soft crook of her shoulders, whose concave perfectly fitted my head, and all would be well.

I could do this.

It was happening quickly, but maybe that was the best way. The room was already teetering, even before I'd closed my eyes. The regret – oh, there was no shortage – like an iron cable dragging me back, yoking me always to that split-second when I let go of the ladder. There was no kidding myself that it was an accident: I needed to feel it keenly, to plunge into my own culpability and let it burn. All the events of the last few days lined up, and I tried to see beyond them to the years, searching for beacons I could skip between, to be a fire-signal sent through time. A mouth full of carpet told me I'd hit the floor, and the violent shudders made me knock into something, perhaps the coffee table, half-braining myself, and then I was no longer there but clicking back, faster than I'd thought possible, and all sensation vanished, and I reached, my mind reached so hard it frayed . . .

And pitched up, blind and blinking, with some hard surface below me. It was concrete, wasn't it? The light was warm on my face; it could be sunlight, but it was so hard to see, the turquoise blending with pink orbs as my eyes fluttered, desperate to open. A choking surge of hope filled my lungs, a gurgle that felt so strongly like it was from my young throat that I reached up to touch my face, to feel for a pre-stubble chin. No sensation. Who was I? The brilliance did not dim, and now there was a whispering, like wind through the Victoria plum. My lips chewed together, trying to find sound, trying to call to her.

'Arlo?' Someone was repeating my name; a quiet, musical voice, but full of fear. I'd got part-way to my feet, but now lost my balance again. There were shapes: other, less distinct people. My hands slammed against rough boards, and there was a huge space yawning and echoing out ahead. Someone I knew was effervescing from a fakery of light. Even before I saw her blue hair, I was shaking my head. 'No.'

'What's wrong, sweetheart?' she said gently.

My body curled up, arms wrapping skull.

'Do you need an ambulance?'

I need her to be here. Not dead. Not gone.

Sweat mustered in the crooks of my knees and beneath my palms. There was that make-up smell, along with hints of booze and even the slight musk of tiger that sometimes clung to my props. I recognised the MC and realised I was back at that godawful corporate gala nearly a fortnight ago. Seeing my head lift, Sheila crouched by my side.

'Are you okay to go on with the show?'

Mid-act I must have gone from owning the stage to crumpling into a ball. Worse, I saw that one of the shadowy figures was the arrogant guy in the ill-fitting suit, the one who'd kept his lecherous thoughts to himself. Had he just humiliated me? I possessed neither the energy nor the inclination to punch him a second time. Instead I gathered myself up, very slowly, the world still spinning, staggered drunkenly into the audience and smashed down the bar of the fire door.

It wasn't front-page material, but the next day I got a small headline towards the back of the *Times* and something in the *Metro*: 'Magician crashes out of show.' It needn't have been the end of my career. In fact, my bosses at the agency were almost frantic in their pleas for me to face the music and laugh it off, ready to risk me on the stage rather than cancel paid-for gigs. But I was a ruin. Reliving a week I'd already lived made me feel insubstantial, haunted by a ghost who had been sitting over there – not here – during that football match, who had been in the stairwell when the neighbour dropped his freezer, and helped out, rather than being in the kitchen making toast, hearing only a thump and an echoing 'Motherfucker!'

I had clinical déjà vu, but there was also something hard and painful behind it. Though Mum was gone, there had always been a seed of hope, cultivated alongside my gift. But giving it my best shot had spun the clock a mere eleven days backward, not to mention landing me head first in the middle of a deeply unpleasant experience. All that effort had resulted only in a tremendous, aneurysm-like pressure in my head as I pushed beyond my limits, and a sense of utter disorientation.

There really was no going back.

In many a legend, the hero loses his way, distracted by beautiful maidens, made soporific in a fragrant bower, or becalmed in a dead ocean, its mists full of spirits, forgetting his quest. Having neglected to eat for a day or two, I felt myself drifting, my fingers and limbs mere wrinkles in the bedsheet. Nothing was real, and I assumed the figure standing at the end of my bed was some manifestation from a dream, until I recognised the smell of Lynx.

'Take what you want and get out,' I said pleasantly.

The figure came closer.

'It's me, you moron.'

I still didn't recognise him. Tim, the perpetually clean-shaven, had at least a week of stubble and appeared half-starved. He was wearing a yellow sports shirt, too small for him, that looked like it had been found in a dustbin.

'What the hell happened to you?' Before he could reply, I added, 'And how did you get in?'

'A lady let me in the front, and your door was just hanging open.'

'Oh.'

I pulled the covers down and groped for a glass of water while Tim began his story, hesitant and stuttering. He'd made a bad call on an important case, a terrible call, and it had cost him his probation. If he had told me the next day, or even the same week, I might have been able to help, but now it was too late. As he rubbed his chin, seeming puzzled by the unfamiliar texture, I saw that, like me, he'd somehow ended up back at square one. No wonder he'd let himself go.

'Why didn't you tell me this earlier?'

He raised an eyebrow.

'What difference would it have made?'

Under normal circumstances I might have been the one to pick him up, dust him off and hurl him back onto some sort of positive trajectory, but I was weak from lack of food, and my sleep was unwholesome and patchy, like something worm-eaten. So instead I let myself succumb, nodding as Tim proposed a return to Birmingham, with free accommodation in a house his brother was converting to flats. We were both broke, and if I was going to spend my life in a tent-fort of bedsheets there was no need to pay an extortionate rent for the privilege of doing it in Bloomsbury.

'Back to Brum,' said Tim, holding up a flattened, corner-shop bottle of vodka, and somehow I found the energy to raise my glass and sup the last trickle of dust-mote soup.

It took me some time to rouse myself to the move. The landlord, rather pissed off with me, was pacified by the gift of my entire magical apparatus for his children, and Tim took my other few boxes in a packed-out van. I set off to Euston station through a warm, moisture-filled twilight. Russell Square was choked with vehicles, its grand buildings looming overhead. With every step, my pace became slower. A gaggle of children were lining up in twos, waiting to cross into the park. Amid the forest of pedestrian crossings, street-lamps and traffic lights, everyone was being directed one way or another, except for me. A strange sluggishness was stealing over my limbs, as though I could just give up and come to a standstill. My story might have ended there if it were not for a sudden flurry of movement behind me, the sound of squeaky footsteps breaking into a run and a horri-fied, heartbreaking cry.

I started to turn, just in time to see a guy with a checked scarf tied halfway up his face speed past. He'd grabbed an elderly lady's handbag and was now zigzagging through stopped traffic. Meanwhile, the woman had belatedly over-balanced and was now sprawled on the kerb, her face contorted in anguish.

'My cards, my passport.' Through her gasp I could discern a German accent. She looked bewildered, as though she would never rise again. Almost without thinking, I reversed my last few steps to the second before I'd passed her, a still figure in a furry coat who was gazing up to admire the square, her pudgy leather handbag hung on a thick stalk over the crook of her arm. I had plenty of time to glance back and spot the thief trailing a few car lengths behind, dirty-looking fingers tugging his scarf as high as possible, skittish in his trainers as he waited for the stream of people to thin. He began to pick up his feet. There was a yelp as he pulled the handbag free. At the right moment, I crouched low and stuck a leg out as far as I could, a lunge that meant his ankles caught against my shin and he barrelled forward, falling heavily onto the pavement. The bag tumbled end over end, spewing boiled sweets and tissues. I left someone else to get it and sat on the thief, putting all my weight on his shoulder blades, though I was slight enough that he could still wriggle. I called to two other passers-by to hold down his kicking legs, and a third was already pulling out her mobile to call the police.

While I reclined, with some satisfaction, on my man-shaped throne, the diminutive German woman was blinking back tears, as if the mugging, had it gone ahead, might have pushed her over the edge. Whatever trials and tribulations her trip to London had held, her faith in humanity was now being renewed, and I was feeling dry, soft hands clasping my arm, trying to mould it into a sculpture that would best express her gratitude. 'What's your name?' she was asking, and I told her. She repeated it twice. 'Thank you, Arlo.'

Amid the crazy kaleidoscope of pulsing blue lights, red and white traffic, the static of police walkie-talkies, hooting cars and rattling pushchairs, I was suddenly real again, sandwiched between two warm German hands.

Bobbies soon appeared, radioing for a car, and everyone visibly relaxed as they took over with handcuffs. I answered a few questions, rather impressed by the young officer's confidence, his sturdy body armour and thick belt of equipment, from which he'd also conjured up a notepad. 'Good job,' he said, squeezing that last, icing-on-the-cake endorphin into my bloodstream.

The adventurer was out of his trance and had found the path at last.

Part 3

A GOOD PLAYER

Twenty-three

The busker played on the steps of a bridge, violin case open on the floor, a few silvers within. She was young, probably a student, but her bow flew through Paganini's final Caprice, and I was so moved by her absorption in its rhythm that I grasped whatever notes remained in my wallet and let them fall into her case. If she'd seen how much it was, she might have broken off, but instead her elbow jerked and twitched and she thanked me with a blink.

What was the significance of money in the face of music like that? A sadness began in my chest and trickled down to my fingertips. We'd held hands along this stretch, a dozen times, ducking our heads under the low bridge, having a beer

191

or a burger at whatever bar took our fancy. Every memory of Sabra tapped into the pleasure centres of my brain, somehow managing to bypass the rest of it, though I suspected it was bad for me to reminisce. Tim was still friends with her on Facebook, and I hated it when he told me snippets about her life, that she was on holiday someplace or at a festival. The version of her I carried around in my head was delicate, not to be tampered with. Plus, it would be all too easy to track her down through social media, board a train to Brussels and settle into my own version of *Groundhog Day*.

Canada geese roosted beside the canal, raising their beaks when I came too close. 'Listen to how they honk,' my mum would say. 'Can you hear the accent?' She was being silly, of course, but it helped me remember the species. I'd been starting to hear her voice again, odd sayings or snippets. Sometimes I saw a woman walking along with her sort of gait, or looked at my hands and perceived her knuckles, her nails. The tenth anniversary of her death had slid by, not long ago, eyeing me dangerously like an alligator in muddy water.

But after years of flailing around, I was finally on a path that led somewhere, and she would certainly have approved. There'd be no cheering crowds, but who needed them? I could still feel the German lady's chunky handbag, those grey eyes teary with gratitude, but now I was the police officer, calm in the midst of chaos, cuffing the panting suspect, hardly out of breath myself, while the woman clamped my arm. 'You were so quick,' she was saying. 'It's like you saw him coming.' I'd allow myself a smile in response before blending back into the crowd, a part of it, yet apart from it. Later there would be car chases and foiled heists. I'd turn in my badge for going rogue then have it handed back in triumph when my unconventional ways brought the crime rings crashing down. It was about time I had a crack at being one of the good guys. As Sabra had once said, why the hell wasn't I working for MI5?

Let no one doubt the dedication of the new police recruit who volunteers (and everyone volunteers) to test the effects of pepper spray. It took place at the training centre and was categorically the most painful experience of my life. After one squirt, this is what happens: your eyes screw themselves up, making you fall over because you can't see, and then you crawl around the parade ground on hands and knees, turning your face away from the winter sun because even its weak rays are enough to amplify the fire.

It was pure pain in liquid form. Once I realised it would be torture, I undid my choice to volunteer. But, damn it, I couldn't bring myself to be the only chicken. In any case, it was the biggest opportunity to bond with my fellow trainees. Trembling, I went out to the grounds once more, felt the spray and collapsed onto my knees with the rest of them. It took two days of eye-stinging showers for the pepper spray to finally work its way out of my tear ducts. If only Mum could have been there to see what I went through; the agony, although intense, was nothing to the distress of not being able to tell her about it. There was something of penance, wasn't there, in having taken the punishment even knowing how it would feel? My pain was soothed when I thought of it like going through a fiery but purifying hell – coming out stronger, cleansed of the past.

Mum would have also been impressed that I was turning up on time to classes and playing well with others. Sometimes I'd be in a room with fellow trainees, quietly learning every single letter of the law, and would have a flashback to the great ArlO in his midnight suit, hair slicked back, sneering at a tiger – a tiger! It was like remembering a dream. I'd still toss and turn at night, as though sweating under a spotlight, seeming to hear the hiss of champagne, the cheering crowds. Had I been slightly drunk the whole time? Skipping backwards was essential to pull off the act, and maybe it had interfered with my sense of reality.

Recently I'd begun to see my gift simply as a way to correct myself if I went awry, like having a keen sense of balance, a sort of human gyroscope. So often I'd be sitting in a classroom hearing about risk: mitigating risk, anticipating risk, taking risks. I snapped up every instance of the word. I was built for risk, and this job was a lollipop-land of hazards. Would there be drug dealers in the next alleyway? Firearms in the car? Trafficked girls in the attic? Which way would he run? The work was full of twists and turns, and there was no question that I'd exceed expectations, give a performance that would shake West Midlands Police to its foundations.

Despite the recruitment process and training going on for the best part of a year, my sister and Nan still seemed to have difficulty picturing me as an officer of the law. When I spoke to them on the phone, they'd mention it hesitantly, like a hobby that might be out of date. To be fair, the figure of authority I'd glimpse reflected in shopfronts or car windows would often startle me. Neon yellow and black weren't really my colours, though a significant number of women seemed to disagree, judging by the way they eyed up my handcuffs.

It unsettled me to be 'the man', even if I was just toeing the line for as long as it would take to become a maverick. During those early days I would sometimes, almost subconsciously, rebel against my uniform. It was so much more fun behaving badly in a helmet. Sometimes I'd high-five protesters at a march, when the sergeant wasn't looking. They loved that. A police officer's mask slipping, a hint that I was human. These were the doses of anarchy I needed to keep me sane, to prevent me from becoming institutionalised. In any case, my superiors had nothing to complain about. Most of the time I blew them away with my aptitude for the job, my ability to spot things that even the most seasoned officers missed. The tutor constable I'd been assigned was a sturdy, steady woman in her forties, with hair tightly bound in blue-black ridges and a face that was hard to read. Her name was Alberta, and I stuck to this because of the slight slump in her eyelids when the others called her Bert.

Neither of us were big talkers. The first time we went out in the car, we were purring quietly through the traffic when we passed a couple of job – our shorthand for any police colleagues – pulling over a silver Lexus. It must have been somewhere around Aston, on the dual carriageway. Barely two minutes had gone by since we'd waved to them, but now panicked cries were blasting out of the speaker: 'Officer down! Backup, backup . . .' Three guys had leapt from the car and started shooting, hitting one constable in the hip, his partner barely able to radio us as she tried to drag him out of the firing line. A routine check, and it had turned ugly. Meanwhile, we were stopped at a red light, and I was zoning out Alberta's instructions, gathering my senses, my hands taut on the steering wheel. When the lights are turning green, urging forward motion, it is strangely difficult to go back. Nevertheless, I managed to get us to the car park where I'd last seen Remy and Jo, the two officers involved in the shooting. I found my mouth full of squishy, sweet stuff, then discovered I was holding a banana. I swallowed quickly.

'Watch out if you see a silver Lexus. I heard reports of firearms.'

'Silver Lexus, right,' Remy said, slamming his door, obviously just humouring me.

Twenty minutes later, the call for backup came while they

were in pursuit and, though I wasn't there to see it, the car was pulled over with plenty of firearms officers in attendance. No injuries.

'What are you smiling at?' Alberta wanted to know. I just shrugged and continued to observe the buses and cars and bikes flying past, serene as a person watching a movie. When we returned to the station, I slapped Remy on the back. Without me, he would have been groaning in hospital, probably awaiting an operation. Instead he was peering with bemusement from under his thick eyebrows, asking if he could help me with anything.

Unsung is the worst kind of hero you can be, and it would take some getting used to.

Twenty-four

For all that it devastated me, there was one good thing to have come from my failed attempt to leap back to age thirteen, tumbling backwards a mere eleven days. Previously, time in which I'd undone things was too messy to unstitch again later, once I'd moved on from it. There had been that heckler at the magic show, that annoying, seedy guy, whom I'd punched and then un-punched. The incident, gone over twice, was slightly blurred in my mind, yet in that huge eleven-day leap I'd gone back to the minutes before it. Was this a first? It felt like a milestone, one that would give me even more flexibility to fix things as a police officer.

Of course, like everything, it came with a kick in the teeth. If I'd managed to build up this level of control earlier on – at graduation, for instance – Sabra would never have been left standing by her battered Austin Metro, holding her neck and picking up that shard of Spitfire. Forfeiting my chance to play the good Samaritan, I'd have taken us both back to the start of the ceremony, and she would have given the performance of her life.

That regret aside, I was pleased that my mental muscles were in good shape. It was just as well. One morning, I showed up at the police station only to be brought face to face with a huge fuck-up from the day before. The cry wrung from Alberta during the shift briefing expressed my own anguish. There he was, flashing up on screen, a sneer stamped permanently on his lips. He had a string of violent crimes to his name, including several counts of GBH and armed robbery. Gloucestershire Constabulary had been tracking him for a murder there was little doubt he'd committed, though the sergeant expressed doubt we'd ever find him. The overlapping of his incisors was distinctive, but it was the yellow hue of his eyes that got to me, that look that said, 'Don't bother existing'. That was pretty much what he muttered to me yesterday, in the sportswear shop in Northfield, when Alberta and I gave him a slap on the wrist for smoking.

My jaw tensed, and I began lining up the twenty-two hours that would take me back there – not a moment longer than needed, since I was already clocking up an alarming number of unpaid shifts. All at once, we were at the retail centre, me yanking open the door of the pharmacy for

Alberta, who'd needed to buy some antacids. Our man was pausing to look at some discount trainers just inside the sports store, smoke curling round his fingers. 'Stop clicking your cuffs,' said my colleague irritably, but I was wound up like a spring. Amazingly, and probably because he was not expecting it, I got him secured on the first attempt, twisted an arm behind his back and told him the charge was suspicion of murder, while Alberta looked at me like I'd lost it, taking several seconds to regain her senses and help me get him in the car.

You can guess the rest. In fact, when we got back the sergeant was in his office preparing the morning briefing and immediately recognised the suspect being led past the desks. He came out to watch as I charged him – me, the fresh-faced newbie, not yet au fait with the paperwork but handing over the most wanted criminal in the West Midlands. Only yesterday the sarge had yelled at me for not wearing my flat cap on vehicle patrol. Now I could enjoy the astonishment on his face. 'Wobbles aside,' he was murmuring, 'it's a damn good start; a bloody good collar.' This was more like it.

In my first two months, I didn't put a foot wrong, and I helped a significant number of colleagues avoid their own slip-ups. Sometimes it was like Remy and the shooting, and I had to fix things with a throwaway comment, or even an anonymous phone call, but I much preferred it when they knew who to thank. This job was replete with even richer seams of risk than I'd imagined, and this was just the beginning. I'd been resigned to feeling like a fish out of water for these obligatory two years of beat duty, but once I was a detective the big wins would be within my grasp. Every department in the country would hunger for me: the antidote to ambush, the scourge of surprise. I couldn't remember who'd said it, but hindsight was a wonderful thing.

Beat work was mostly just keeping order, issuing warnings. Sometimes opportunities to shine were thin on the ground. A fortnight went by with nothing but a few traffic issues, and left me climbing the walls, boredom beckoning me into bad behaviour. Then, as Alberta and I were walking past a queue of cars, sweating in the pollution haze, we heard a smash. A man was leaning into a car, having obliterated its side window with the butt of a machete.

'Satnav!' he screamed. 'Now!'

My colleague started running, but I was faster. The guy clocked us with wild eyes, dropped the knife and fled down the street, my boots thundering after him as Alberta yelled at pedestrians to stand clear. I skittered round a wheelie bin and turned on a hairpin bend to give chase down a one-way street, then another, then into a hotel supply passage humming with kitchen fans. The guy was so quick; when I turned the corner he was fleeing upwards onto scaffolding, trying to toss the ladder aside but unable to detach it. In seconds I was climbing, dimly aware of yells from below forbidding pursuit.

The scaffolding chimed strangely as I rattled my way

upwards, hardly noticing the vertiginous space opening up below, the blue debris tube snaking down to a skip. If anything went wrong, I'd just go back. The thought was held lightly in my mind, ready to deploy. Everything would be fine. My hands grasped cold metal tubing as I hauled myself up, instantly aware of the flex of the scaffolding, the gaps in between, and a whisper of traffic noise reaching me from an odd direction between buildings.

Far away, my name was being shouted with increasing anger; then there was the buzz of Alberta's radio and a clang as she jumped onto the ladder. It pleased me that she was calling for backup – not because I'd need help making the arrest, but so there would be a few more officers around to see it. I crept along the boards, taking care. More heckles from below. If only she could read my thoughts: shh, Alberta, I need to listen. Where had he gone? The windows were brand-new double glazing, still with their frill of plastic; it seemed unlikely he could have escaped into the building. The scaffolding rounded a corner and I was ready with my baton and spray, poised to slip back for a few seconds of thinking time as soon as I spotted him.

'Knott, get the fuck down!' Why was she so worked up? I was in no danger. Bless her, she didn't know—

It hit my skull. From the side, as though there was no flesh in between. A brick – somewhere in the impact was the petrified foam of masonry – but the sickening *clink* made it feel like iron. I keeled over towards the building, one arm slipping through a gap, splintering, grazing, aware of a shape slithering down a pole from the level above, but far more concerned about this new hemisphere of darkness, night falling rapidly over my brain.

Death was accompanied by the sound of two Canadian commentators making droll remarks about a women's curling match. I traced the sound to a square television, high up on a bracket, becoming aware of the old woman in the bed next door stabbing a remote control. Fearing I would retch, I held the sheet over my mouth and nose and breathed through its starchy filter. A teal twilight hung over the ward, and the sheet was not enough protection. I'd almost take a whiff of pepper spray if it would keep this hospital stench from my nostrils. What exactly had happened to me? My face felt strange, swollen in places, painful around my neck, but there was no reason not to . . . I tried sitting up and rediscovered agony: the instinctive feel of a broken rib. My grunt attracted a nurse's attention.

'Watch it,' he said in a New Zealand accent. 'Still some healing to go.' He turned to address someone across the ward. 'Back again? You're in luck: he's awake.'

I half-expected family, but it was Alberta, ambling between the beds. My head sank into its pillow-indent. A shame it wasn't the sergeant. My erstwhile tutor's praise was usually understated, and with bones this shaken I needed the top brass to form an orderly queue and shower me with commendations, cards and chocolate.

There was a scrape as she took the chair, and I let my lids drift open, squinting against the whites of the ward and the Winter Olympics, every inch the injured champion.

'Well hello,' she said, 'you fucking idiot.' Calmly spoken, the words packed a punch. Her gaze was a shrink-ray. 'What did you think all that training was, a suggestion?' She plucked several grapes from a bowl which probably belonged to the elderly lady in the next bed. 'And me? Am I just background static?'

So they didn't want me feeling proud of this episode. Maybe I'd set a bad example. Her words hung in the air as I closed my eyes and began to line up all my movements, ready to unlace them. There was the sitting up in pain, the tilt of my head towards the television, but what was before that? My head throbbed, the concussion like a stretch of dark water too treacherous to cross. I took a deep breath.

'We might have lost him—'

'We did lose him,' she exploded, 'while I was trying to stop you bleeding to death.' A rush of exasperated air threw her head backwards. 'Do you think I don't know my own patch? We could have contained him up there, taken him down safely in custody.'

There was something both risible and humiliating about being recumbent in bed, dressed in virtually nothing, while a superior officer sprayed me with bits of chewed grape.

'I get it,' I said hurriedly, steeling myself to add, 'A bad job, right? I'm sorry.'

'If you'd stopped to listen . . .' She petered out, and something in her face told me she was on my side but somewhat helpless. There would be repercussions to my actions, perhaps even the forfeiture of a promising career. I didn't know what to say, though I wished she would end this awful silence and go back to lambasting me.

On the tiny television, an advert came on for – of all things – *Dog Cops*. I'd never really noticed, because it was so silly, that the damn thing was a detective show. It sent a ripple of anxiety through my belly. All of a sudden I was back on the scaffold, feeling the force behind the brick, that very intimate *thunk* as it made contact with my skull. Blood would soon flow and only shock was keeping the pain at bay, and my solitary, bone-sharp thought was 'This is it'. There was that split-second between the hit . . . and the black-out. No time to process, just the certainty of death. No way back.

'Got the shivers?' I heard Alberta say. 'What's up?' All colour must have drained from my face. I shook it off and tried to focus on the practicalities.

'Shame,' I said dully. 'This job was perfect.'

The permanent wrinkle between her brows deepened, her face taking on that expression I found so hard to interpret, as though she was calculating the trajectories of things I couldn't see.

'Can I tell you a secret?'

I shrugged.

'I used to be like you.' The chair squealed as she crossed her legs. As usual, whenever someone professed to know me, I felt an itch.

'Well, I—'

'Batshit insane,' she continued, leaning across to dump the grape skeleton back into the bowl. 'Walking a knife-edge between promotion and getting fired, coming close to a sticky end now and then. But what did I care? I was the first person in my family to get a job like this. I had to fight my arse off to get it, and the whole point was to change the world.' Her hands fluttered up to hallow these last words before dropping to her lap. 'Then what? I'll tell you: I had my first kid. Emmy – did I tell you his name? Emile. So I get back to work a year later, and everything's changed. What happened to the woman who'd confront car-jackers at night and be the first to grab the ram for a dawn raid?' Her arms expanded in a shrug so dramatic I felt my own shoulder blades twitch.

'Gone,' she concluded. 'I try to drum her up when I need to do something risky, but she just won't come back. It pisses me off, to tell the truth.' Alberta looked longingly towards the fruit bowl, rubbing grape must between finger and thumb. 'So I'm not going to haul you over the coals for this, Arlo. In fact, I'll do what I can to make you sound less of a lunatic than you really are. Because we need people like you. This city needs a helping hand and a smack up the arse. So don't get yourself killed, don't ignore me when I tell you to stop, but don't, whatever you do, lose your fire.'

Only something like the remote control giving this speech through its triple-A battery teeth could have shocked me more. Hardly ten words passed my colleague's lips during a typical conversation, and now she'd spilled her guts and was rising to leave. In the tension round her jaw, the brisk tug to settle her belt, I saw the passion, tamped down and controlled, the deep devotion and still-strong belief that the world could be made a better place, so profoundly anchored that I felt a slight pull of envy. At the end of my bed she hesitated, not looking round, and added:

'You're exceptional, Arlo.'

It was perhaps the most high-carat praise of my whole career. A shiver went through me as I watched Alberta march down the ward, picking up speed as she neared the exit. The smell of grape juice lingered around my pillows.

I'd done a good job of convincing them I was invincible, and now I'd have to somehow hide the fact that I was terrified of everything. A born-again coward.

Twenty-five

If life's a bitch, what is death? As I drove up the M6, sweating at every lorry that came too close, I sensed it everywhere – in specks of rain on the windscreen, in distant horns, in the sag of my eyelids when the heater was turned up for Nan – and I jerked awake, gulping air, gripping the wheel. If I died, would I carry on dreaming that I was alive, while in reality ambulances screeched to a halt, sirens blared and people hauled my battered body from the car? When the music faltered, when a van switched lanes without indicating, was that the moment the crash had happened, and was I just carrying on in my mind while my body was on a drip somewhere, or dead and buried?

Although the skin above my ear was still puckered with

a blister blush, it would eventually look normal again. Inside, it was a different matter. I'd always wanted to be a man who laughed at death. Who was this person shrinking away from lorries and potholes, seeking the safest path, keeping out of the way? Bridges flew over my head and I felt their weight, the blocks of concrete that could fall. Even Nan had commented that the Audi could probably go faster than the steady 66 I'd been doing, hesitant as I was to pass heavy goods vehicles which might swerve in the breeze. If I felt the impact, or if it took some seconds to unfold, then I'd have time to go back a few breaths, but what if some truck-monster jackknifed across the road? What if something crashed down and knocked me out? One blow to the head would be enough. Take out the brain, and I would be no more. You'd think my early experience of death might have made me a bit more comfortable with it. But years of care-free living had made me view mortality, like consequences, as something for other people to worry about.

So I sat beside a septuagenarian who talked about nothing but the new life she would lead when she moved to her sheltered housing complex, and I heard nothing but death. She may have got over the winter flu, but what other illnesses might be waiting to take either of us down? Not all disease had a known cause. If it came on too slowly, too stealthily, I'd never be able to go back to when the mosquito bit me, or when I ate the contaminated salad. Cancer might be caught a little earlier, but it could not be prevented. Why had I not thought about this before? In a couple of weeks, I seemed to have aged fifty years.

The trick, then, was to avoid disease, and anything that could deliver a sudden impact. It was important to protect my head; if someone shot me in the body, it would be fine because my brain would still be functioning. I reached up and scratched angrily beneath my soft hair – growing back now in its natural curls – wondering if I should go around wearing a crash helmet.

The worst of it was that being a bobby had felt so right, and it had been going well. After all I'd been through, I didn't want to quit, but what would happen the next time we went on a drug bust or a vehicle pursuit? Somehow, I doubted they'd let me sit out the more dangerous activities, and Alberta was counting on her spunky young colleague to dive into the fray. Much to my annoyance, a part of me had signed up to her cause, wanting, for some reason, to make her proud. All this time, I'd been scared of nothing, unfazed by the hairiest of raids, the fastest car chase, but how did you deal with cowardice? My fears had grown without my knowledge, like cannabis in someone's attic.

A snore made me jump. There was something very bear-like about the way Nan slept, one hand curling under her chin, turned against the seat. We were driving up to the Lake District for a few nights since Erin had taken a cottage there for the summer break. It would be the first time either Nan or I had met her partner, the brilliant PhD student she'd told us about so shyly a couple of Christmases ago. My sister was pushing thirty, which in itself was hard to believe, and had visited so rarely that if you'd asked me what she watched on television, or had for breakfast, or whether she believed in an afterlife, I wouldn't have known.

Finally, the nightmare of the M6 was over. We purred along A and B roads, surrounded by the sharp but strangely intriguing odour of cow dung being splattered across the fields, puddles leaping from my alloy wheels and hens pecking for worms on front lawns. At length, we arrived in Kendal, pulling up at a squat, whitewashed cottage with a pudding-bowl cut of thatch.

Nan said she was stiff, but the journey had left me so shaky that I could hardly help her from the car. Then suddenly Erin was there, waving and even – to my astonishment – smiling. Behind her, another woman emerged: younger, thinner and brighter than my sister, with short brilliant-blonde hair, her wide hips out of proportion with her skinny upper body. She wore a PVC apron featuring a Swiss brand of white chocolate, and was a long way from the mole-like scientist I'd envisaged.

'Hello,' she said, coming forward enthusiastically. 'So good to meet you.' Her voice deepened every vowel, as though she had a tiny bassoon in her windpipe.

'Nina,' my sister introduced us hurriedly.

'Oh yes, you're Erin's friend,' said Nan, as though she'd forgotten anyone else would be present. I thought Nina might be about to say something like 'and so much more', but instead she just smiled. My sister was taciturn as usual, yet she picked up on my delicate state, perhaps from the hoarseness of my voice.

'Difficult journey?'

I shrugged. 'Bit of traffic.'

Soon I was relaxing on the deep window seat, coffee in hand, drawing strength from the thick, ancient walls. Every surface was strewn with papers and books on quantum physics. At peak chaos was the dining table: a mass of laptops and cables, Post-its strung along the edge like bunting. When we were taken up to our rooms, the blackened boards squeaked underfoot and there was a heavy coolness in the air, perhaps due to the thatched roof. The cottage was disability-adapted and even had a stair-lift.

'Considerate to pick a place with Nan in mind,' I murmured to Nina.

'Oh yes,' she replied with a faintly puzzled look.

That night I slept well, and the country sounds to which I awoke the following morning took me a million miles from thoughts of death. Sparrows dust-bathing in the lane were much more relaxing to watch than computer screens, and birdsong a welcome relief from sirens. So deep was the respect for slumber in this building that even flies waited patiently on the windowsills until it seemed appropriate to start buzzing, when someone went downstairs to put the kettle on.

'These surroundings are very sensory,' Nina was saying. 'You can walk around the lake and hear the ducks, smell the water.'

'Great views too,' I said.

She hesitated.

'Yes.'

We were at the breakfast table, and I paused with toast in hand, detecting that an atmosphere had been created, though I wasn't sure why. As Erin went to fetch the Marmite, I asked:

'So you're from Norway originally?'

'Yes, though I'm really enjoying the UK. It's a great place for Europeans, especially if you're doing our kind of research. A few more funding pots around, and I guess it's more of a meritocracy.'

My sister stuck her head round the doorframe and said with unexpected gusto: 'The sky's the limit for Nina.' I wondered if she'd ever looked quite this cheerful in our presence. As she handed over the brown jar, I saw the relationship streaming out like the tail of a comet. Erin was so dark and intense and Nina so luminous and energetic. Perhaps my sister hoped they would become one of the great scientific couples of the century, like Pierre and Marie Curie.

Nan had decided not to attempt a hike that day, so the rest of us laced up our boots and got ready to leave. Nina pulled on fingerless gloves and gave me a smile that, for one split-second, belonged to Sabra. Nip that in the bud,

I told myself. I knew it was nothing to do with how Nina looked or even that she had a couple of Germanic mannerisms, only that I was in the unfamiliar role of third wheel and feeling a little spaced out, still recovering psychologically from the massive head trauma. Despite this, I was glad to be with family, to be in a safe environment as I worked out what to do. Here, at least, was a situation I couldn't mess up.

The path was a waymarked gravel trail, skirting boulders and yellow gorse that smelled of coconut. Nina would sometimes take Erin's wrist to pull her up a slope, though my sister had two of those walking poles that old people use. She was a bit clumsy, but when I asked her about it she said she was fine and tapped her glasses with a fingernail. The wind toyed with us, escaping our breath at first and then ploughing straight into our lungs, until I felt like a kite, the pockets of my coat ballooning.

'This wind . . . I'd like to stand naked and let it wash over me.'

Erin kept climbing slowly as she muttered, 'Excuse my brother.'

'And look at the lake,' I enthused. 'Like mercury.'

No one backed me up on this, though Nina turned and smiled, her new hiking boots pressing neat marks into the grass-edge.

'So, will you be seeing your dad, now he's back?' she asked.

'He's what?'

'Back in the country.'

I couldn't have heard right. Erin half-turned, her face a mess of whipping hair.

'Didn't you get my email?'

I stared at my sister, completely thrown by this non-sequitur. 'No, I didn't.' The walk had been quite a cardio workout, but this tightness in my chest was unexpected.

'This isn't how I wanted to tell you.' She stopped by a large boulder and steadied herself, looking down like an Old Testament preacher. 'It's in Luton, the flat. He gets better care in the UK. There is no health insurance to speak of, if you're a jobbing actor.' I could feel my body stilling, trying to absorb the words. 'He's been diagnosed with early onset dementia,' she went on. 'Quite lucky to catch it in the first stages. The dopamine will slow things. Anyway, the address is in the email. I'll send it again.'

Several goldfinches passed over our heads, bouncing on invisible layers of air. What struck me was it had gone this far, the diagnosis and the move back, the flat in Luton, without me hearing a thing about it.

'I was in Birmingham, not on the moon,' I growled, then undid it as I saw her expression. 'Why there?'

'It was the nearest he could get to London.'

So this was what happened with family. You took your eye off the ball for a few months, and the world turned upside down. Dad, struck down with signs of Alzheimer's and suddenly back in the country. I tried to picture him living in a flat, fussily arranging his coffee cups and lining up his shoes. What would he do in Luton? Act in some tiny local theatre?

'Why didn't he text me?'

She shrugged, rustling in her teal Gore-Tex. 'I don't know. Ask him.' Her tone held a note of exasperation. 'Shall we go on?'

Now I knew Dad was so near, I could almost sense his weight on the map, hear the slapping of his slippers. My phone was warm in my pocket, expecting his texts. Surely he was too young to get dementia, wasn't he, early onset or otherwise? I delved deep for feelings of sadness but came up empty-handed.

The track climbed higher, levelling off as we approached the viewpoint. When the wind paused, you could discern the whine of holiday traffic. There was a thread of cars in the distance. A couple of kestrels drifted at about our level, searching for shrews. When we reached the 50p telescope, I sank onto a nearby bench, enjoying the herbal aroma of the weeds tangled round its legs. Nina did not let go of my sister's hand as they sat down.

'So Erry tells me you're in the police,' Nina said. There was something a bit odd in sitting so close together, three of us in a row. The two women shifted to leave a decent gap between Nina and me.

'Been out of action for a few weeks,' I said, wondering if

my sister had passed on news of the assault. 'But when I go back I can apply to be a specialist.'

'Like?'

'Like a detective, for starters.'

'And do you think you'll get it?'

I yawned. 'It's more or less in the bag.'

'That's wonderful.'

My sister didn't look quite so delighted.

'I thought you spent most of your time getting hammered with Tim,' she remarked. 'Are you sure that promotion is guaranteed?' Though we were all out of breath, there was a sort of restless huff behind the words, making me smile. Erin might have a relationship and a summer cottage, but I could still make her jealous.

Families trudged past us as we rested, and from the corner of my eye I saw my sister twist handfuls of hair into an elastic, losing several strands that blew over the precipice. With Nan getting older and now this news about Dad, perhaps I was wrong to let our relationship keep reverting to adolescence. I stood up and went to lean on the semicircle of railing that enclosed the viewpoint, sensing the two of them eventually move forward to join me.

'Great walk,' I said in my mildest tone. 'Top views.'

Equanimity should have been restored, so imagine my surprise to hear Erin utter a strangled gasp. Her hands flew up from the fence as though it was white-hot and she stumbled back towards the path. Nina managed to drag at her sleeve but was shaken off with a cry of, 'I know the way.'

Her retreating figure left me bewildered. 'What's the matter with her?' Here we were in beautiful surroundings, all together for once, and Erin was stubbornly refusing to let me get on her wavelength.

'The view,' Nina said, taking a pale blue tissue from her pocket and blowing her nose.

'But she's got her glasses; she said—'

'She's always fine, if you ask.' The tissue was tucked away briskly. 'But the glasses mean nothing. The view is gone.'

Twenty-five

The clacking of Erin's sticks faded. It all made sense now: the hand-holding, the wide, easy track, her gathering irritation. Her little brother had always been wrapped up in himself, and had missed another chance to show he'd changed.

'Why come here, if she can't see it?' Distant windows winked invitingly, fairy lights in the hills. There was little point in undoing my last remark, not when I'd been going on about the scenery all day.

'It's like I said.' Nina's voice was measured, pleasant. 'The lakes are very sensory, and nobody can take away the fresh air.' Her eyes went to the path Erin had taken. It was a straightforward route, but there were one or two steep stretches. I saw what she was thinking.

219

'Shall we go after her?' We started back along the track, but my sister must have been going at quite a pace and was already out of sight. Nina's breathing quickened as we hurried through a kissing gate, hearing it clang coldly behind us.

'So how bad is her sight?'

'It's being eaten away at the edges, and even her central vision is becoming just shapes, weak colours . . . There's an ophthalmologist at Leeds who helped us do some research. It's genetic, you know. Erry said your granddad on your dad's side was blind, but I suppose the condition was never diagnosed, until now. You're doing well to have escaped.'

The world around me came into sharper focus.

'Oh?'

'It's actually more likely to present in a male. But don't worry, you'd know by now.'

This information tipped the scales, making it seem even more reasonable for Erin to think me a jammy bastard. On top of my ability to change careers at whim and my seemingly endless supply of money, I'd also somehow cheated the family illness.

It was strange to hear an outsider telling me things about myself. For the first time, I realised how unsettling it must have been for some of my magic-show volunteers.

'So why don't I have this thing, if it's genetic?'

'Luck.' The word echoed across the hillside, robust and magical. 'Pure luck. One of your gametes – most likely the

220

sperm – would have had some tiny mutation that stopped the Visner's syndrome from being expressed.' We crossed a patch of boggy ground, our feet sinking softly with each step. 'Luck is a funny thing,' she mused. 'The universe seems to dole out more of it to some people than others. As a physicist, I like the idea that you could measure it, study and stream it. That's what your sister needs, a nice beam of luck directed at her research, preferably with a Nobel Prize at the end of it.'

The image put me in mind of a pot of gold at the end of a rainbow. We had reached a jutting granite ridge that overlooked the gentle undulation of the hill. Nina exclaimed and pointed ahead. 'Look, there she is, right down there. She'll be fine now.'

'You don't want to catch up?'

'She'll be better for a little cooling-off time.'

That sounded good to me. Later on, I could make amends. Nina and I continued downwards, catching whiffs of livestock, crossing meadows dotted with dandelions.

'Not sure I remember this bit of woodland,' she said, going back to the field boundary to check the signpost, which declared Kendal to be one mile away. 'I think we should have forked right.'

'Let's just try it – there's probably another way down.'

The pines seemed to hush up as we passed, the air tangy with their antiseptic odour. My head throbbed, just once. It was impossible to bring the attack to mind without my heart rate doubling, an involuntary reaction that was getting on my nerves.

'Interesting what you were saying about luck,' I mused. 'I'm not powerless against it, but sometimes . . . how do we deal with the fact that death could just hit us at any minute?'

She shrugged. 'Just forget about it, I suppose.'

We emerged into a clearing of rusty bracken, the light just catching a peaty cascade splashing down between pebbles. Fungi were stacked like orange plates on a rotting log. Delighted, Nina crouched down and cupped the trickle in her hands. Then, as though having properly sifted my words, added, 'How do you mean, you're not powerless against it?'

I sighed, already anticipating her response.

'I can take back my actions. Like throwing that rock and finding it back in my hand.'

Her forehead wrinkled.

'Could you show me?'

I actually got as far as lifting a stone.

'It wouldn't work. You'd just be back at this second and never know I'd thrown it.'

She stayed very still.

'Do it anyway?'

I hesitated. But the talk of death, the sense of a skeletal hand on my shoulder, had made me even more desperate for human connection. The hope of being understood was never quite extinguished.

I shrugged and hurled it, then came back to the shrug, the rock once again wet and gritty in my palm.

'See?'

She shifted to perch on the log, taking care not to disturb the mushrooms. Her tone was cautious, trying to sidestep offence.

'Have you thought . . . that it could be your imagination?'

'Of course.' I fought the frustration, a lethargy coming over me as I realised this conversation would need to be undone. 'Okay, let's do tried and tested. Tell me something about yourself that I don't know.'

I got it out of her and went back to just before her mouth opened. 'Great,' I said, 'you just told me your child-hood cat once got into a beer lorry and was taken all the way to Sweden.'

Her lips remained parted. That moment I knew so well when the breath is being sucked in and the thought is just forming, neurons gathering momentum until enough of them fire in the same direction, conjuring up the words she was about to say. She couldn't quite believe it. For once, this was no magic trick. I was serious, sweating as I realised I wasn't going to back out. Maybe it didn't matter that much. Erin might break up with her within the year, or she might return to Norway. Then she'd be out of my life.

'Again?' We repeated the process, each time pulling up a secret even more dirtied by the depth of its concealment.

She slumped on the log, her wrist knocking off a piece of coral foam, though she never noticed.

'How are you doing that?' she asked at last. 'It's the most extraordinary thing I've ever seen, if it is what you say.'

This was uncharted territory.

'I just go back through the actions, undoing as many as I can remember.'

'Okay,' she said, 'let's say I buy into this. You go backwards in your own timeline, and the rest of the world knows nothing about it.' She scratched her neck, 'I mean . . . time is reasonably malleable, I guess. Someone who lives up a mountain will age more quickly than a person living by the Dead Sea. But I've never heard of a case like this.'

The word *case* put me on my guard.

'I'm not a novelty patient,' I said, the old fear coiling back to life. History was full of examples of sane but interesting people somehow finding themselves sectioned. I was poised on the edge of rolling the conversation back – when she said:

'Of course not – you're family.'

'Family?' Perhaps I looked as I felt, like a little boy.

'Of course.'

'You're pretty much the first person to believe me.' My voice was unsteady, and I kept my face turned away in case it was reddening. We began to walk slowly and thoughtfully onwards, needles crunching under our feet.

'It's a lot to get my head around,' she admitted, 'but in my line of work there are quite a few impossible things to believe before breakfast. I'm used to putting cynicism aside – for a little while, at least.' Her tone became lower. 'How long has this been going on?'

'Since I was a teenager.' I tugged at my scarf, hot around the neck all of a sudden.

'Interesting,' she said. 'You know, genetic stuff doesn't always manifest from birth. Take Huntington's, for instance. It only tends to kick in at reproductive age.'

Amid the haze of pine-sap, the intimacy of the woods, I realised that, over the course of this conversation, she'd more or less given me the diagnosis I'd been seeking for over a decade. Perhaps it was the lightness, the certainty in her voice, but to be told I was just coded that way sounded so obvious, so clear all of a sudden. The trees fell away and a marvellous vista spread out before us, the lake a concentration of light. I stopped blinking and let my eyes sting a little with the brilliance.

Everything was different, and I was giddy with it. Did she truly believe me? What I detected was temporary – rather than wholesale – acceptance, a willingness to run with it and suspend judgement. This was still enough to make my heart shudder with excitement.

'You don't know what it's like,' I managed, finding words at last, 'feeling you're a freak for so long.'

Her head tilted from side to side, weighing this up. 'I've had my moments.' A smile came to her lips. 'But that's the great thing about being with your sister, someone I can trust, who always lets me be myself. Why haven't you told her about all this?'

The path narrowed to a furrow, forcing us into single file.

'In all honesty, we're not that close.'

There was always the age gap, even more than gender. Throughout my childhood, Erin had been more of an occasional, slightly reluctant parent than a sister. Sometimes I'd wandered in while she was doing homework, or reading the *Children's Britannica*, and seen her start, as though she'd forgotten my existence. Perhaps she had been happier when it was just the three of them, herself as the sturdy third bar in an equilateral triangle.

'She'd be very interested,' said Nina.

'I'll think about it.'

She shrugged. 'Okay. You should have control of your own medical records. But if you were amenable, I'd love us to try one or two things in a controlled environment.'

'What are you hoping to prove?' A cure was unlikely. The thought arrived like an unusual scent on the breeze: Would I want a cure? For the first time I considered how much this uniqueness had been built into my identity, whether removing it would feel like cutting away a pound of flesh. Who would I be without the power to sidestep mistakes? It was hard to imagine blindly bushwhacking my way through life, tumbling into the same ditches as everyone else.

'It's an amazing gift,' Nina said, as though reading my mind.

'I mean, look at that caterpillar you've just stepped on . . .'

'Oh. Damn.'

'There's a universe where you step round and it's not smooshed, right?'

I went back and un-smooshed it, then told her what had just happened. She chuckled to herself.

'Schrödinger's caterpillar. Dead in one reality, alive in the other. In experiments, we can get things to be in two states at once – we can prove that an electron was in two places at the same time – but it never works with big stuff, nothing bigger than about sixty atoms. And look at you, effortlessly doing it with a caterpillar, a trillion trillion atoms. You've no idea how exciting that is.'

It was pleasing to watch the caterpillar undulate across the path, its body fat and unharmed. 'There it goes.'

'That's the reality you've chosen,' Nina said, 'but somewhere else a bird is pecking at a tasty green snack.'

I frowned. If that were true, then all the actions I'd wiped out would be stacked up like so many DVDs in the attic, a bunch of horror films full of punishment, injury and humiliation.

'You're in the police, right?' she added, shifting to the muddier side of the track. 'Imagine terrorists in a big building. They could use any of the exits to make their getaway, but then you come along, and they see you staking the place out. Suddenly their plans change, simply because they know you're watching. It's like that with quantum stuff – nothing is fixed until you try to observe it.'

'What exactly is quantum stuff?' It sounded like a rare substance, propping up one leg of the periodic table.

'Everything in the universe,' she said, adding: 'Einstein didn't like it either. Hated the uncertainty, the idea of God playing dice.'

Smart guy – I had to agree with him on that. Despite my ability to win at games of chance, the idea of a haphazard, accident-fuelled universe unsettled me.

We walked over matted twigs, crackling and fragrant, and Nina looked at me quizzically, as though several questions were forming and dissolving, all boiling down to one simple enquiry.

'What is it you want, Arlo?'

Surely everyone wanted the same thing: to understand their role in life. If mine was about winning, then why did I keep being sent back to square one? The reply that came to my lips took me by surprise.

'I'd like to be the person my mum always saw when she looked at me.'

Her voice softened. 'So why can't you?'

Hesitantly, I told her about the assault on the scaffolding and how, ever since, I'd felt like a hermit crab newly emerged and soft-shelled, unprepared for my own vulnerability. The worst of it was that this job had given me a new purpose, made me feel like I was going somewhere. It would be a shame to throw that away.

'You have a much better arsenal against death than the

average guy,' Nina remarked as we went through the last gate, back to the road.

'But it's not just that . . .' Ever since being in hospital, I'd felt as though death was present where it had not been before, as though I was being tailed. Even the evening shadow creeping across the hill made me faintly anxious.

'If you're worried, the best thing to do is investigate, shed some light on it.'

I knew she was about to suggest handing myself over for testing. 'Don't get any ideas,' I warned. 'I'm not a lab rat.'

She laughed. 'And I'm not a mad scientist, I promise. Don't you feel a bit isolated keeping this to yourself? If it was me, I'd want answers.' The cottage was ahead, its thatch thick enough to nurture any amount of wildlife. We stepped over the tiny stream that marked the road's gutter, and she put a hand on my arm. 'So, what do you say?'

Intelligence burned in her eyes. She was right, of course. I'd felt extremely lonely and had lived for too long with only questions. Nina had won me over with surprising speed; I trusted her. And besides, what choice did I have?

'I'm in,' I said, 'but leave the anal probe at home.'

'Deal.'

We went inside and found Nan and Erin chatting in a steamed-up kitchen. Nina went over and squeezed her girlfriend's hand, and it was so obvious now that my sister needed to feel her way around the room, hands loose as brushes, just to get a sense of things. Her head was tilted to the window at all times, drawn to the light, as she listened to Nan talk about how teabags could be saved up and fermented into wine. This was my family, a selection box of oddballs.

At first it had felt good to agree to Nina's proposal; a new chapter that would lead to a greater understanding and some sense of progress. But, as the day darkened and the thick cottage walls felt colder around the window seat, I became just a little uneasy. It was pure instinct, nothing much to go on, but something told me that exposing myself to the piercing gaze of physics was a bad idea, that it could shed light on all kinds of things that were best left in gloom.

In short, I feared it would open some whole new can of worms. Or *wyrms*, as my little figurine of Saint George would say. Nan had interrupted my thoughts by dragging out one of the board games that were stacked innocuously on a sideboard. She rattled the box and suggested we set it up on the table.

'No,' my sister and I replied in unison. We were old enough now to explain how our patience with board games had been ground to dust by our father's excessive playing. Nina helped me tidy up the pile, which had clattered onto the floor. I couldn't help deriving some pleasure from the secret look she shot me when Erin added, 'And anyway, Arlo always wins.'

Twenty-five

The drive only made it worse. By the time we'd pulled into the university car park, I was determined not to let anyone shut me in a room, to keep Nina in sight at all times. There would be no passing me on to other scientists in white coats, no group consultations. Laboratories had too often featured as the sets of my childhood nightmares; one whiff of surgical alcohol and I'd expect to feel rough straps tighten around my wrists and ankles, preparing to struggle and squirm as the experiments began.

For now, however, we were hanging out at Erin's desk, festooned with fat cacti and cat mugs, eating her chocolate digestives. I rocked back in her swivel chair, a pretty nice one, and thought how weird it was to be here, in her workplace, while she was staying on at the cottage a day longer with Nan.

'This desk is filthy.'

Nina laughed. 'Your sister usually works from home.'

As we talked, I was given to understand that, while the academics might conceptualise the experiments, it was the PhDs who got down and dirty in the engineering workshops. Nina was the one who fine-tuned their quantum experiments, who might spend days arranging equipment and soldering components together, only for them to crack when cooled to the right temperature. 'Which drives you barmy,' she'd remarked.

The time came for me to follow her into a 'controlled environment' – basically an empty room. I wanted her to stay with me, but she said her presence might skew the results.

'I'll be just outside, recording the infrared. You'll be able to see me through the glass.' Her tones were reassuring, but on exiting she turned to find me at her heels like a clingy puppy. 'Come on, Arlo,' she begged.

'Can't do it. Anything could happen.'

'Nothing will happen. Look,' she opened and closed the door, showing it didn't even have a lock, 'you've faced much worse than this.'

I was being a baby, and with that thought came new resolve. In the empty, clinical little room, my breathing shallow, I walked a few steps and took myself back to standing, again and again. Nina came in with a blindfold, a thermometer, even a Geiger counter, and made me undo speaking, inhaling, interacting with a rat and meditating, the latter of which I'd never tried before. Later, she made me remove a packet of fish fingers from the canteen's walk-in freezer, telling me she may as well see whether the chill made a difference. 'Are you kidding?' I asked, but she was deadly serious and came in with me to allay my fears. Her zest for the testing was infectious, and by now I was at ease, so much that I even let her colleague do a CT scan. Nina wanted to collect my DNA with a cheek swab, but the line had to be drawn somewhere.

'It's okay,' she said, 'there's already far more than I can analyse right now.' We were walking to the staff car park, which was almost deserted at this hour.

'What do you expect to find?'

She rubbed her eyes. 'There's a lot of noise. I guess I'll be looking for any kind of pattern in the data we've recorded, a sign of something out of the ordinary.'

I unlocked the car. Any order she could find in the randomness of my life would be welcome, but I was hoping for more of a detailed diagnosis, and said as much.

'Look, this isn't medicine, it's physics.' She smiled. 'Strange, unexplainable effects are our bread and butter. The phenomenon comes first, and then in the next decade someone comes along and solves the mystery. Take the Higgs Boson – we didn't know if it would even exist, yet we spent nearly five billion dollars to set up the experiment.'

'Did it exist?'

'Absolutely.'

This delivered a miniscule shot of comfort.

'Fine. I'd rather be a physics problem than a medical one. It's not like I'm sick.' I hesitated. 'What about my sister? Would she be interested?'

'Oh, you'll be fighting her off with a stick, honestly. Can I tell her now?' She draped herself over my open car door, still bright with anticipation despite our day of graft.

'Once I've put a hundred miles between us, you can tell her what you want.'

She kept waving even when I was halfway down the road. Those few hours in the lab seemed to have lasted for days, and I was wiped out, too tired to start thinking about whether it had been a good idea. What did Nina hope to discover? She'd just tested whatever she could think of, constantly apologising for such crude and ad hoc experiments. I feared they could still turn out to be a waste of time.

On my way down the motorway, my foot lifted from the accelerator for a split-second before I sped on past the junction that would have taken me towards Luton. There was way too much going on in my head without letting Dad get in there as well.

My embarrassing insensitivity to Erin's impending blindness kept coming back to bite me. Over the last year or so, I'd been all about helping people, yet I hadn't done much for my family. Following the trip up north, I felt a great compulsion to make it up to them, right away.

It meant dabbling in scratch cards for the first time in years, hoping no eyebrows would be raised by my name reappearing on the winners list. With hindsight, some of the gifts I bought might not have quite hit the mark. Nan wouldn't be able to fit many boxes into her yellow Corvette Coupe when she came to move to her sheltered flat, but at least she would arrive in style (and that cream Mini could finally be put out to pasture). For my sister and Nina, there were tickets for a spring river cruise down the Danube, which would surely be at least as sensory as the lakes by the cottage. The paper they were working on would be published by then, so they might appreciate a holiday. I hesitated to put my name on the accompanying gift card since there was still this thing between Erin and me about not trying too hard, but in the end I thought, 'What the hell', and went ahead. She would probably think I'd lost my mind. It was rather extravagant, but I had a lot of making up to do. Plus, I owed her for putting me in touch with Nina.

For all that being a part of experiments freaked me out, I felt strangely uplifted on returning from Leeds. Not only was my ability out there in the real world – categorically not a figment of my imagination – but there was someone on my team, working on it. I only hoped she would work fast and come up with some answers, as well as, more importantly, some solution to make me feel less of a scaredy-cat. How could I make a difference to people's lives if I couldn't put my own in danger? The old Arlo, the one who would plunge into lakes, jump on a Vespa or scramble up scaffolding, was gone. Once death is on your radar it never goes out of sight.

I was walking along a canal beside ruined factories, too restless to stay indoors, as these thoughts came. Though hours had passed since I'd called in sick, it wouldn't do to be spotted by colleagues. A dangerous raid had been lined up for this morning and, panicking, I'd reversed my decision to go to work and instead feigned dizziness from a healing ear infection. It was getting more difficult to avoid the risky parts of my job.

A buddleia iced my sleeve with fondant-white flowers as I pushed it aside. The further I walked, the more derelict the scenery, even though I was getting close to the city centre. Whenever the sun emerged, the canal water released mysterious bubbles. I passed a burnt-out warehouse resembling a dragon's cave, blackened on the inside, with cracks showing the red innards of bricks that had hibernated in grime for decades. Should I just write off policing as too dangerous and find something else to do? The thought of starting again was depressing.

Without thinking, I emerged from the scrubland around the old Curzon Street station onto a busy road. Ahead were sand-coloured tower blocks filled with shiny offices. I heard a shout.

'Arlo!'

I'd walked too far. What atrocious luck to be spotted by a couple of job, who were now crossing the road towards me: Remy and a trainee I'd not properly met. But maybe it didn't matter. A glance at my watch told me the shift would have ended by now, so it was just about reasonable to be out. My mood was so despondent I could hardly be bothered to mentally retrace my way back into the buddleias.

'You off today?' my colleague yelled above the traffic.

'I was on early.'

'Us too. We were just getting a coffee.' He motioned to a café, a chain where cops drank for free. 'Care to come with?'

I shrugged and joined them for a few minutes of leaning against the bar that ran along the front window, supping an espresso and making mundane conversation.

Then Remy stopped mid-joke. He was staring at something up in the sky. His jaw went slack as he tried to focus. Bemused, we followed his pointing finger across the road towards the shopping area, just in time to see a woman let go of the decorative stonework on the outside of an office block and give her body to the air, one shoulder turning gracefully as she fell, red skirt tangling round her legs, visible for only a moment before she vanished. Then we heard a delayed chorus of distant screams. The new recruit was clutching his head.

'Oh God,' he breathed. 'Oh no.'

It was so familiar now, the stilling of my beating heart,

the un-beating, sending blood backwards in my veins, several circuits of my body, several breaths and steps, till I was looking down at a galaxy of chewing gum on the first stretch of pavement beyond the scrub, vaguely aware that Remy was about to come into view and call out to me.

Where had it been? I craned my neck and identified the office block, already picking up my feet, scanning its higher reaches. The architect had added neoclassical finishing touches: a few flattened pillars and plaster garlands. A red whorl of fabric fluttered somewhere above, and I knew she was already out there.

Inside the foyer, I managed to drift straight past the security guards and into the lift on a tide of business people returning from lunch. Without my uniform, all I could do was try to muster up the same self-assurance I'd normally have in body armour. By the time the lift had disgorged everyone else and arrived at the highest floor – pure guesswork that she was here – I'd almost imploded with impatience. No one else was going this high, and I emerged on a corridor of closed doors. Server room, B store, C store. Silence. But at the far end my pulse raced to see the fire door ajar.

Beyond was a corridor of casement windows. The building had obviously been remodelled internally, its high ceilings plasterboarded off and the views enjoyed only by piles of IT equipment. Beside the third window along was a pair of red high-heeled shoes, placed together neatly against the wall. My chest tightened. Was I too late? When

I leaned out, I saw her skirt fluttering against the grooves of a pillar, a pigeon nest by her toe. She had edged a little way along the broad sill, as though easing herself away from safety and into the bleak idea of taking her own life.

'Stop,' I yelled. She took one look and fell forward. The horror of seeing it at close quarters is hard to describe. A piece of me seemed to break off and fall with her, a sensation hard to place but visceral and terrifying. I turned away and quickly went back to the shoes appearing in my vision, my hands flat on the chiselled windowsill as I leaned out.

'Hi,' I said, so softly she didn't hear. 'Hi,' again. Her head turned. I saw her eyes. Big, wet eyes in a face so pale it looked numb. Red lipstick and dark hair. It was like Snow White committing suicide. A sense of weirdness gusted around with the choppy winds. She said nothing. I waved timidly and smiled. 'Are you all right?'

Her head swung back to the sky, eyelids fluttering with emotion.

'Of course I'm not all right.' Her voice was gravelly.

I felt the great gap in my experience. What did you say to people who were in this condition?

'It can't be that bad, can it?'

She jumped.

Fuck. I reversed.

Again, my soft 'Hi'. I think it helped to let her senses cotton on to the presence of another person slowly. 'Sorry,' I found myself saying.

That look, same as before, the hesitation that told me she was weighing up whether to bother replying.

'What are you sorry for?'

I shrugged. 'For not being able to stop you jumping.'

Her skirt whipped at the pillar then sank back to her calves. I noticed she was wearing tights, seams awkwardly twisted across her toes, a couple of snags where the masonry must have torn them, already becoming ladders. All of a sudden I was desperate to get her to safety, maddened that I couldn't make it happen just by wanting it. I had to save her; there was no way I could leave this building until I did, no matter how sickening it was to feel that drop in my stomach. My innards were churning like never before.

'It's too late for reverse psychology,' she said.

'How about normal psychology?' I was floundering, trying to cover up my nervousness. 'What will it take?'

'Don't bother.' This was how people sounded when they were beyond speaking, almost a drunken slur.

'Why are you doing it?'

Another long pause. A shiver. Her feet must have been cold on the stone. 'It doesn't get any better.'

'What doesn't?'

'It doesn't change.'

Without quite comprehending, I said: 'And you're fed up with that?'

'You can't understand.'

240

'Well, maybe if you told me.' There was a chastening note in my voice; I heard her hear it.

'I appreciate what you're trying to do, but it's better this way.'

Almost reluctantly, she turned into the air, shoulder first, curling into the nothing, until she picked up speed and the skirt closed like a flower round her legs. I turned away.

Shoes. Window.

I only meant to go back as far as our dialogue, but it was hard to be precise. Now I had to go through it all again, my voice growing ever softer. This time she said something about the darkness, and I was the one to say it didn't seem to get any better. After this, she was silent for a while, and I felt I'd got it right.

'Everyone has bad times,' I said, something stirring inside me, 'but don't you think it's possible to come out the other side?'

'I'm not built for it.' There was conviction in her voice.

Some emotion, dammed up efficiently in a backwater of my soul, now burst its banks.

'God, I know how that feels.' I passed a hand over my forehead, resting my eyes in the warmth of my palm. 'Other people tick along happily, and you wonder how they manage it.' Don't do it, Snow White, I wanted to scream. Every amp of my brainpower was focused on trying to tap into hers. But nothing happened. She stood gazing out past the end of the city centre, into the industrial no man's land beyond.

Birmingham had yet to reclaim certain ruins from its past, and Curzon Street station rose up in the middle of our view, an incongruous temple-like building that no wrecking ball dared touch. Two men were bolting up the street towards us, and I realised they were my colleagues. They'd spotted the potential suicide, and this chat had bought them some time. They'd clear pedestrians from the area below and come bounding out of the lift in a matter of minutes. I had to work fast.

A million options opened up, and I tried them one after the next, begging her to come inside, telling her she was beautiful, to think of her family. Each time, the woman jumped. In a moment of frustration I told her to stop being selfish, and almost before I'd finished speaking she folded into the wind. The thump as she hit the pavement seemed to break every bone in my body.

I was back watching the toy policemen run, heroes heading for the damsel in distress. What the hell could I do? My body felt strangely raw and tender, and I'd been with Snow White for so long now that I could see an inch inside her mind.

'What's your name?' I asked.

The road below was filling up, people massing on either side. Soon it would be too late.

'Anne-Marie.' Her voice was remote, the name already having floated into the void, too small to see. I brought it back.

'Anne-Marie.' I was as helpless as she. All I had was this

name. We'd already come through the darkness conversation. I took her sense of isolation and imbibed it, got outside of it, like a pill I could swallow to become – just for an instant – enough like this woman to save her.

'Why should you carry on, when it will always be the same?' Some other force was playing me like an instrument. 'But do you know the one certain thing in this uncertain universe?' She was listening intently, despite herself. Her feet shuffled, one toe covering another. The ping of the lift in the distance. 'Change. You can trust me on this. I'm an expert.'

'So?'

'So even if you can't see any light, it will come back, because the darkness will always pass. Isn't it worth it, hanging on a little while longer, just to see that happen?'

Were tears good or bad? I couldn't tell.

'But how do you know?' she cried desperately. 'And this is so much easier.'

'This isn't easy.' My knuckles were white on the sill, voices drifting from the corridor. 'Taking two steps over here and getting a massive hug. That's easy.'

I waited.

'Please,' I said.

They were very near, easing the fire door open, spotting me. I waved them back wildly. Two legs in tan tights came into view, then she was clinging to the casement with hands that trembled, easing herself into a sitting position facing inwards. Her face powder was a shade too pale and had a delicate, floral fragrance. The brilliance illuminating my soul must have communicated itself to her in some way. I gave the promised hug, surprised at her slight shoulders, discovering the rippled texture of the skirt that had tumbled into oblivion so many times.

'Anne-Marie.'

She was whole again, really here and not down there. With extreme caution, my colleagues filtered in behind me, but I didn't let her go. Her hands were icy cold, and she muttered in my ear, 'This was a mistake.'

Twenty-five

Police protocol was to call an ambulance, but Anne-Marie begged us not to make a fuss, so instead we sat her down with a cup of tea in a room just behind reception. The walls were decorated with framed Cadbury's wrappers and sepia photos of the Bournville factory, and three glass jars of sugar cubes clustered beside the kettle. Once she was being looked after by office workers, I was able to step outside – into the corridor, anyway – and take a breath that made my lungs creak.

This was another level. It made catching murderers or stopping Remy getting injured seem all in a day's work. Today I'd cheated the reaper, saving a member of the public in what was probably a matter of minutes, and all without the slightest risk to myself. My colleagues had promised to buy me a pint later on, and it was clear from their fervent handshakes that, to any outsider, the whole episode had been a triumph, a huge win. No wonder it felt amazing. Perhaps suicides, or any other species of barricade, could be my forte. With a little training, I could save a life every day, easy as rescuing a fly from my coffee. My heart beat madly as I realised the police force would never give up an asset so valuable: someone who, while a bit reticent to run in front of bullets, could juggle the risks of others without ever dropping the ball.

Eventually Anne-Marie's husband arrived, a rather short, bald guy who had a soft voice and a calm, attentive look. He wasn't as surprised as I'd expected – perhaps there had been signs of her impending desperation – but he was all kindness and gentle humour, and I felt fairly confident leaving her with him.

'Come by the station and let me know how you are,' I insisted, wanting to leave before everyone's teary eyes got to me. I didn't know which dwarf Snow White had chosen, but in case he was the jealous type I held back from giving her another hug.

'I'll remember what you said,' she murmured, her voice now so much fuller than it had been on the ledge. There was still something broken in it, but a tentative hopefulness lingered beneath the Brummie accent.

'Stay safe.' I gave her a wink and slipped away, back to the bustling reception. I felt a touch on my arm.

'Excuse me.' It was the older of the two office workers, grey hair streaking back from her temples into a wiry bun. She wore a shirt with ruffles making a V down the front, and smiled through violet lipstick. 'Did you say your name was Arlo?'

I nodded.

'I thought I recognised you, though I couldn't work it out till I heard your name. Do you remember me? It's Ilsa.'

She had a very natural and honest-sounding voice, faintly familiar. An image came to mind of Mum at a coffee shop meeting a friend, me on my Game Boy and impatient to leave. Ilsa was older now, but she still had a look of energy about her. There were various unfilled piercings in her ears and part of a bird-heavy tattoo peeping from her sleeve. I got the impression she was still the no-shit activist my mum had known, modified only superficially for life in an office. We'd last met at the funeral.

'Hi,' I said warmly. 'Sorry . . . it's been a long time. You work here?'

'Third floor. I'm managing the volunteering programme now.' Her eyes glittered. 'It's so good to see you. I still think about your mum; she was such a legend. Do you remember that school fair she pulled off?'

Caught napping, my memory sprang into action and

summoned up the smell of icing and heaped teabags, butterfly buns and cornflake cakes on a stall alongside games that involved throwing hoopla rings or fishing plastic ducks from a paddling pool.

'That was all in aid of . . .?'

'Our Safe Soil Campaign. You bet it was.'

I'd never known a great deal about Mum's adopted charity, though I was aware she'd been much admired by staff for her tireless fundraising. It was easy to picture my mum being shaken by the idea of people losing limbs to landmines, devoting herself to making sure children could play safely in the jungle.

'Hell,' Ilsa continued, 'she was signed up to volunteer right back in the eighties, when it was still a new and risky business. She would have gone too, if it wasn't for the small matter of a baby boy.' Her smile was light, and she was obviously just joking, but I found myself slightly affronted. It was all I could do to keep my face in neutral. 'She'd be proud of you, saving lives.' Ilsa patted my arm. 'Anyway, keep in touch.' A business card appeared from her shirt pocket, printed in the same violet as her lipstick, and she waved me off.

Strange to meet someone who had known Mum in her before-me life. It was good to be reminded of how well regarded she'd always been, yet I didn't like hearing that there were other plans lined up when she became pregnant. Erin's words, so meaningless in childhood, now came back with adult vigour. An accident. Did that mean I was also an inter-ruption? I brushed the thought away.

Out on the pavement, the patch between the industrial bins and the kerb held demons for me and I gave it a wide berth, not liking to think of the blood that had exploded upon it again and again. The things I'd said to coax Anne-Marie inside were clear in my mind, but the attempts I'd undone were already fading. It might be a good idea to take notes, next time, so I knew what to avoid, but perhaps the knowledge would linger somewhere anyway, the same way a shout can echo undeciphered in your ear.

I crossed the road and slipped through the fencing into the scrubland. People walked their dogs here, around the forgotten station that was the oldest terminus in the world. As I ambled over concrete, crushing fragrant weeds with my boots, I was taken back to Mum's picnics, when we carried sweaty cheese sandwiches through the fields and she would show us how to open the heart-shaped pods of a shepherd's purse, or pull up a strand of grass and bite the mysterious nectar of its last millimetre.

We didn't have much money, especially when Dad was off on tour, and nature was our main entertainment provider, along with Mum herself. She told made-up stories inspired by childhood days in Whitby. A magic gravestone would send you back a thousand years, or a fish and chip shop was run by modern-day Vikings. They were choose-your-own-adventure stories where we could decide on the next move – and face the consequences. Erin didn't mind me being cast as the hero in these tales, but she did complain that they were never written down. It didn't seem to matter at the time. What was it Mum said? Something about enjoying the story as though it were a butterfly landing on your hand, no need to pickle it. The echo pinged back and forth in time, Mum intoning something like that and not really expecting us to listen, and me standing in a wasteland, hunting around for scraps of memory that had become so precious.

I refilled my lungs with a breeze full of traffic dust and thistledown. Already it seemed like hours since Remy had seen that hibiscus skirt flutter to earth. At least I'd stopped that from happening. The little bald husband would be rejoicing because of me, and Snow White would go on to find more colour in life. I hoped that, for a while at least, the tale would not be forgotten.

'There he is.' I hardly recognised them in plain clothes, but Remy, Alberta and two others were standing by the Gas Street sign, putting their mobiles away. They were beaming at me, here to celebrate, and I was touched. Lights twinkled from the pubs and restaurants on the other side of the canal. Thirty years ago, you'd only come down here to dump a body, but these days the water was the backdrop to a classy evening out.

Two pints in, I could hardly believe that only hours ago

I'd been on the brink of quitting. The superintendent had been told everything and, instead of being suspicious about my ear infection as I'd initially feared, he was preparing to heap me with commendations. Just a few more weeks on the beat and I could apply to be a detective, though my real specialism would be other people's risk.

'A detective?' said Alberta in disgust. 'You want to be one of those lazy snack-addicts who fuck off at 4 p.m. every day?'

This sounded even better. I answered in the affirmative.

Many joyful beers later, a slight figure in a white shirt passed by the window, and I recognised Tim, tentatively peering through the glass. I waved to him, glad he'd got my text. In typical fashion, he eased himself inside and over to the bar, careful not to let in a draught, but from his watery smile I could see something was up.

'What?' I said, sidling up to him.

'Nothing.' He tried to brighten. 'Sounds like you did good things today.'

'But what's up?'

'It doesn't matter. This is your party, isn't it?'

'Yeah, but I can't relax if . . . What have you just ordered?' His drinking-to-oblivion beverage of choice was a Negroni, and seconds later the tumbler arrived with its low-slung orange slice and bitter aroma. 'I knew it.'

He sipped the cocktail.

'I just thought, this time . . .'

Obviously his latest squeeze hadn't lasted beyond the usual

six-week expiration date. I ordered a Belgian beer and, glancing back to check the others were still happy, perched on a bar stool to try and fix Tim before I introduced him.

'Just remember there's no such thing as "the one", will you?' His breath was heavy with alcohol, and he must have had a few before coming out since he was drunk enough to reply:

'Not that you've ever been hung up on one person.'

I took it on the chin. 'I'm over her.'

The fridges behind the bar were well stocked with ales and, lurking on the bottom row, I caught sight of a distinctive red font and the word *Spitfire*. I felt a great longing to rejoin the party.

'Just as well,' he muttered. 'It's been wedding photos all day on Facebook.'

'What wedding photos?'

Bloody Facebook again, everyone addicted to its world of instant reversibility. Un-friend, un-follow, unlike. Tim's foot slipped and he repositioned it on the rung of the bar stool, gazing at me unsteadily.

'Did you know it was today?'

'What? What was today?'

As it hit me, I felt that slow turn of the atmosphere, from upbeat buzz to oppressive clamour. This was a bar for people who wanted to fake a good time. Through his orange fog, Tim seemed to gather, at last, that this was news to me. Except it wasn't possible. There was no way Sabra could be getting married. A bridal gown would be deflected by her body, would spin away into fractals. The whole thing was laughable, yet Tim's face remained grim.

'I was sure you knew,' he said. 'I mean, it's been on—'

'I'm not on Facebook.' He should know this.

'But I really thought . . . Why did I think that?'

My fist puckered, pulled back, then dropped. As if I'd punch a face that was stamped all over with awareness of the pain he was causing me. Yet to even contemplate Sabra as someone's wife . . . What kind of messed-up universe could make that happen?

Tim was saying, 'Are you all right, mate?'

I saved someone's life today.

'You don't look so good.'

I wasn't going to hang around and let the universe bring me down.

'Arl?'

It was noise rather than people I pushed aside as I made it to the door and ran out onto the street. But it tricked me: the stillness gathering not a ripple, not the smallest reminder that the gleaming black road was made of water. One life was not enough. 'You want more?' was the thought that came to me as I sank. 'You want everything I have to give?'

You can have it.

253

Twenty-six

If you spend enough time away, home becomes the foreign country. I couldn't get over the damp-flannel air, the toilets that you'd sit – rather than squat – on, the availability of paper and soap and drinkable tap water. The names of bus companies were familiar but strange on the way back from Heathrow, and seagulls looked greyer than I remembered.

When I heard about Sabra's wedding, I'd finally got a grip on how to do good in the world. With her lost, it was the only thing I felt like doing – as intensely and furiously as I could. My time in Colombia with the Safe Soil Campaign amounted to just under three months, plus a few days in Lima on the way back. It was as much sabbatical as I could beg, having just had my appointment as police constable confirmed, and they only let me have it because I'd made myself indispensable. Saving lives was the grade-A high I was looking for, and there was no greater risk to life than a field of landmines.

Of course, had I known where this hunger would lead I'd have torn up the plane tickets and locked myself away somewhere with a stiff drink.

When I rang Ilsa, not long after the Snow White incident, she seemed surprised to hear from me but was quickly thrilled at the prospect of a volunteer with my skills, especially the risk management stuff. The robust training of a copper was a solid foundation for team leadership, and the workshops and meetings came thick and fast. I'd hardly been aware of a landmine problem in Colombia, but it seemed they were killing or injuring hundreds of people every year. Whenever I read another case study, another farmer's anguished tale of working mined land and risking death with every seed, the emotion that welled up did not seem to belong to me but to Mum. I pictured her going through this training herself, and my determination to push ahead with this challenge, no matter how heartbreaking, grew with every briefing.

How the hell do you clear landmines? It turned out not to be my responsibility. The NGOs on the ground had a policy of training up locals to do the demining, since it was a useful skill to keep within the community. International volunteers were used for administration, detection and a certain amount of public relations back home. I pushed hard to be on detection duty, fascinated by the maps they laid out of grid squares, keen to start ticking them off, though everyone kept telling me detection was the slow part. In Cambodia, you could find two hundred mines in a square kilometre, but here it was far more ad hoc – there might be three or four. What's more, they were nasty bastards: TNT in glass or plastic bottles, and so little metal content that we couldn't always find them with a detector. So, with plenty of supervision, we would be digging trenches six inches deep, one square metre at a time. It would be a labour of patience, if not love. Working around the day's heat, each of us would cover about eight square metres a day.

Camping in the tropics was new to me, and sweating out half my bodyweight while being eaten by mosquitoes drove me to distraction. The tents were basic and the meals mainly rice and beans. Goats found their way to us from nearby smallholdings; if they didn't eat any bit of food you hadn't locked away then the ants would, and out here they were big biting things that took some effort to crush.

In the evenings, there were shared cooking duties, camp-fires and organised fun. Either I'd lost my ability to play well with others, or I wasn't in the mood. My brash, funny and obnoxious side resurfaced unexpectedly, made worse by the fact that three out of five members of my team got a kick out of me winding up the leaders. These rough-looking local bosses waited like hungry dogs for me to make a mistake, but of course it never happened. My team were ahead in every task, yet the seniors continued to regard me with suspicion. There was absolutely no room for error in this work. The inexperienced had lost limbs – even lives – blithely walking through an area they'd staked out as safe, only to find a mine shifted by a tree root, or in a dip, or beneath a bush.

Our grid squares looked like a lot of ground until you realised the whole operation was a pinprick in a vast territory of potentially mined areas. The pace was getting to me, and I could feel the frustration rubbing off onto other members of my team. Mines were blowing the limbs off hundreds of agricultural workers, women, kids . . . They should have been cleared by now. Nevertheless, we went on with our methodical work for a solid ten weeks, following instructions to the letter, crawling our way across the map, feeding bugs with our blood and forgetting that any carbohydrates besides rice existed in the world.

One evening, I got into the good books of a couple of local taxi drivers. It was easy to barter a few mind-reading tricks for a smoke, and I spent the whole night taking in some very strong, raw tobacco that I suspected was cut with something else. Dawn was just shy of breaking when I returned to the tent and looked at my fresh-faced gang of three girls and two guys. I'd never felt more like an old man. If I totted up all this extra time, what would my age be? At least thirty, I reckoned, maybe older. Sometimes I

tried to see myself through their eyes, with the multicoloured blanket I'd bought in Bogota draped around my
shoulders, hair creeping over my ears, looking tired most
of the time, skipping meals but always chewing on coca
leaves; brutally honest and funny and weary. They could
like or dislike me as they pleased, but they knew I was
never wrong. Somehow I intuited that Dan grew up the
youngest of a horde of brothers, Trudy had scuba diving
nightmares, Milenco was embarrassed about having no
sense of direction, Haji loved all things NASA and
Evangeline was raised on an apple farm in Terra Haute,
Indiana. Pre-saying their lines, especially when it was
something personal, was a sure-fire route to instant trust.
Instant. It sounded like a packet of powder, like the coffee
and creamer they had here.

The map was spread out on the rattan table. Each section
of the local area was divided up, with my marks showing
which belonged to our group. Over the other side of the rise,
a strip of land ran between the rocky base of the hill and
the road, terrain marked as scrub rather than jungle. My
heart was vibrating, and I wasn't sure if it was the tobacco
or what I was about to do. The jeep powered up, too loudly,
and I bumped along as the sun rose. This was our last day,
and time to brush aside the rules.

I was back just in time to see my team breakfasting, and
told them to get a move on, said I'd been up for hours. They
chattered sleepily as we walked to the jeep. Trudy, the

smartest girl and on track for a first in biochemistry, was gently ribbing the youngest, Evangeline, an American with Cheddar-blonde hair. A passionate belief in the good they were doing clung to all five of them like dew.

We drove to the coordinates and, throughout my explanation, no one asked to see the map for themselves nor questioned why our task should change slightly on the last day. We'd be working on pre-cleared areas, I told them, but doing a very worthwhile job. The village wanted to graze the land, but the team that did the demining, some time ago, had left the sticks marked with red paint in place. This made it look as though there were still mines around, so no one would come near. Our role was simply to walk the plot and remove them and – hey presto – a good mile free and clear.

It was not long before Trudy stumbled across the first of the javelins I'd thrown into the long grass from the road. She pounced on the metre-long stick and held it aloft. 'Hey, got one!' she cried in her bouncy Canadian lilt. As it was a year since the alleged demining, I was making them cut the grass with shears and stamp it down as we went, underlining the need for close attention with the second marker they found, which was in splinters. No one noticed the machete marks.

I promise I was quick, so quick to reverse it when someone got hit. The first was Evangeline, the explosion sending up such a geyser of soil and smoke that I could hardly see her, only the sense of a leg separated from a body. Before it landed, I was back several steps. 'Hang on,' I called, halting their walk so I could dart forward and drive in a marker just short of the mine. 'Bit of glass here, must have exploded. I'll go over these later in case there are TNT traces. Give it a wide berth.'

'Such a worrier!' the American ribbed me, as she skirted the mine. She was injured, perhaps killed, twice more before we reached the end of the plot. It had been mapped as a highly perilous zone, and no one managed the whole distance without a scratch, though I reversed everything, even the cut Dan received from a sharp palm-leaf. The sticks I'd thrown into the scrub made it seem like a clear-cut job, and we kept going along an unthinkable length of road, detecting and marking almost two dozen explosive devices using my new turbo-charged method of trial and error.

As I wiped the sweat from my brow, I heard a ringing and stuck a panicked finger into my ear, fearing the explosions and screams were making me deaf. But it was just the heat. All these sounds were already becoming muffled, disintegrating.

We swept the ground twice more, back the other way and up again. The whole thing had taken us just beyond lunch, and we'd marked up an area that would normally have claimed weeks. At the end of it, I stood listening to the whine of some insect from the palms and the distant bark of a dog. I thought I could smell gunpowder, or the iron of the soil, but when I sniffed there was nothing but pollen and the leaves beginning to be heated by the sun. My team were jubilant – a rewarding little job nailed, the afternoon free to drink Club Colombia beer and celebrate the end of the placement. I felt their strong arms hook round my shoulder, their bubbling laughter restoring me. They were full of life, good as new.

Once I'd pacified the project leaders with some whoppers about secret evening shifts and extra graft in the heat because my gang were so damn dedicated, the awards came thick and fast, and the guys deserved them all. They were presented with everything from Coolest Cooks to Awesomest Attitude and were seen off, alongside other international volunteers, with festivity and laughter, while I read the fond keep-in-touch messages they'd written in my journal.

For me, the reward was the end of that placement. Though full of congratulations, I could tell the people in charge were glad I was leaving. In any case, I didn't want to hang around any longer, not when I kept seeing Evangeline's smooth leg coming out of her stained white shorts. The vision wouldn't fade because I kept picturing it, making up the details even as they receded. Sometimes I would think about their sunglasses left lying around the tent, and how one pair had fallen broken at my feet as its owner was thrown upward amid smashed thorns. I kept reminding myself of the hugs they had given me at the end, so warm and full of sun cream and DEET, telling myself it was fine, it was worth it.

* * *

I got back to the flat to find Tim had moved some girl in on an optimistically permanent basis, and there was a clothes horse of washing steaming up my room.

'Sorry, I meant to take that out,' Tim said. He stared at me. 'Did they feed you in Colombia?' I fingered the fabric of my travelling shirt, worn thin from use. Perhaps I'd lost a little weight.

'How did it go?'

He'd been apologetic about not being able to pick me up from the airport, having already expended most of his annual leave on minibreaks with various women.

'It was mad.'

The attic didn't feel the same. It smelled of onions and some sort of incense, and there were patches of mould all along the window seals that I'd never noticed before. I was suddenly uncertain I could even spend the night there. It was someone else's place now. Exhaustion wanted me, but I made it outside and into my Audi, damp and cold itself, before drifting off.

Amid the dregs of darkness I woke with dreams of Sabra still flavouring my thoughts, like a sweet just disintegrated. My body was stiff in the driver's seat and I turned on my phone, hoping one ghostly light could displace another. I looked up stats on landmine deaths and injuries, but avoided the pictures. Could I give myself a score for these three months of graft? If so, where would the next points be coming from?

As the morning brightened, I thought about calling the police station to say I was available, jet lag-permitting. There might be bad things happening that could be prevented. I checked my messages and found an email from Nina asking about my trip, inviting me to give her a bell on my return. I checked the time. Nearly 8.30. Was that too early?

'Hi, Nina.'

'Is that Arlo?' She sounded like she'd been awake for hours. 'How was Colombia?'

'I did what I could to make it less deadly.'

'Nice work.' I heard the clink of ceramics, and water starting to gush.

'Did you publish that paper?'

A hesitation, or was she just finding the washing-up liquid?

'It was published. I've got some good news for you.'

'Yeah?'

'That wavelength analysis . . . the infrared put me onto something.'

I could hardly believe what I was hearing.

'You've found out how it happens?' This was what I'd quietly been hoping for: the discovery of a simple equation, something that would pin it down.

She laughed. 'Not quite – it's way too complex and needs a lot more work. But I was very excited by what showed up. It's hard to explain . . . There were little variations, like heat signatures, in the places you'd been before you undid your movement. So when you walked to the window and undid, there was the tiniest disturbance in the light, and the same when you walked to the table.' She paused for breath. 'Tell me, have you noticed any effect on the world around you when it happens?'

'The world around me? Like what?'

'I don't know. Anything.'

My car rocked slightly as a lorry sped past.

'Is that all you've found out?'

'Don't be downcast, Arlo. It's nothing short of miraculous. At the very least, you have evidence of your ability being visible to others. You could get a lot of scientific attention, if you wanted to, by exploring this further or making it public.'

Horror seized me.

'But we're not doing that.'

'Of course not.' The easy, light tone I'd come to trust in the lakes was still there. 'It's your body, Arlo. Your choice.'

Once again, she'd reminded me why I respected her so much, why she was the only one who would ever be allowed to wield scientific instruments in my direction.

'Well, just keep it under your hat, will you?'

'Nobody knows outside of me and your sister.'

'And what does she say about all this?' I'd been slightly surprised not to have been, as Nina put it, fighting my sister off with a stick. There was something a little petulant in the way I wanted her attention, even though I might have said no to more experiments. When the phone didn't ring off the hook I assumed she was being churlish, determined to forgo the scientific discovery of the century rather than ask favours of her little brother. But it turned out to be nothing to do with me: apparently her paper had made quite a splash within the physics community and she'd been in constant demand at conferences and symposia ever since.

A slurp, then a bang as the mug came down too quickly. 'Your sister? You'll have to ask her yourself. I haven't seen her in a few weeks.'

'You haven't . . .'

'We separated.'

This was dismaying. I'd liked Nina, but Erin seemed crazy about her. I couldn't believe it had all gone wrong.

'Oh shit. What happened? No, it's none of my business . . .'

I could sense her rising, pacing, fuelled by some well-controlled pain. She might be looking out through the metal-rimmed windows of the lab kitchen, across a concrete campus.

'That's life,' she said, not offering any explanation. 'Just to warn you, though, she'll be zoning in on this once all the current publicity has died down. Be prepared to be kidnapped.'

Despite myself I laughed. 'Seems unlikely.'

'Tell me more about the landmines. You must be feeling pretty chuffed.'

My fingers curled over the leather of the steering wheel.

It was still early enough for kids to be going to school; they came walking along the road and enveloped my car, one boy glancing in nervously. Multicoloured backpacks over navy blue jumpers.

'Yeah, it was pretty good,' I said. 'Marked up quite a few mines.'

'Did you find yourself . . . going back, at all?'

Skinny legs sprouting from shiny black school shoes. Kids fanning out across every inch of the pavement. An old lady coming the opposite way had to turn sideways to get through.

'Arlo?'

It might just have been the oddness of sitting in a car with people passing me instead of me passing them, or what Nina had just said about little scratches of light after I reversed something, but a sudden queasiness came over me at what I'd done in that last day of the placement. My team were fine and would never know that they'd been blown up repeatedly, but in a way it had still happened, because it happened to me.

'Hello?'

It had been a bad idea to hand myself over to science. Nina had said herself that there was too much noise to get any meaningful results. What she'd observed could have been something else, perhaps even a trail of body heat. The gift was mine, it was in my genes, and its effects stayed within the confines of my own skin.

'No,' I said, my voice rebounding off the car windows. 'No, I didn't.'

We exchanged some final remarks and promised we'd stay in touch, though I think she could tell I was in a hurry to put down the phone. The next line of schoolchildren was about to sweep past, one of them kicking a stone, the others taking turns at trying on a pair of red sunglasses that were huge and garish. Had they found them abandoned on a bench or something? I turned on the ignition and roared away in the opposite direction as fast as a cold engine could go.

Twenty-six

Of course you'd want to save as many lives as possible. Anyone who went all the way to Colombia and saw the chance to clear a full mile of land would take it. But perhaps my approach was rather bloody-minded. Loneliness had been swilling round my system, since hearing about Sabra, and had sent me on a rampage of destructive altruism. While my team had emerged unscathed, I was starting to recognise that I'd taken a bit of a mental beating, and perhaps the accomplishment was also undermined by having been a little too easy. Mum had always despised those who cut corners, people who slap-dashed their way through life. Mine was a win made of shortcuts, like superman flying to the final square of the board game.

Gravel crunched as I passed gnarled orchard trees aromatic with apples, lost in thoughts of my track record at work, my effortless brilliance. Since becoming a full constable I'd made so many seat-of-the-trousers arrests, perfect predictions and last-second saves that a quiet day gave me withdrawal symptoms. Hence it pained me to be here, at a tranquil Georgian mansion, snagging my sleeve on climbing roses as we investigated a petty theft of lead from the roof.

While Alberta talked it over with the management, I walked round the building trying to ascertain the most likely spot for the thieves' ladders. With hopeful eyes, I scoured tarnished drainpipes and acres of flashing, imagining terror-stricken faces looking down, caught in the act, metal sheets slithering as they fought to get away. But the criminals were long gone, and swallows darted around the vanilla walls.

My boots were drenched as I slid down a bank and onto the main lawn, the scent of wet grass irritatingly wholesome. Whenever I turned to the house, curtains twitched, revealing grey-haired folk with puzzled faces, not used to seeing police officers wandering the grounds, and perhaps forgetting their green island was surrounded by a chaotic metropolis.

There was something here, mown into the lawn. From a distance it was a ripple-like pattern, complex as a brain, like a crop circle with interlocking, concentric rings. The shorn path was a couple of feet wide, and I found myself drawn to it, compelled to take that first step, like Dorothy on the yellow brick road. A clanking sound distracted me, and I turned to see a long-haired gardener with a wheelbarrow of clippings.

'Expect you're here about the roof,' he said, as though I was a tradesman. He noticed where I was standing. 'Go on, give it a go.' Most people direct their remarks to the uniform, so his chummy smile was refreshing.

'Is it a maze?'

'A lawn labyrinth,' he said. 'A maze has lots of ways to reach the centre, a labyrinth only one.'

He lifted the handles of his wheelbarrow and trundled off, giving me a nod. There were people behind the closed windows now seeing a police officer nonchalantly follow a pattern mown into the grass, but I didn't care what they thought. The wind sank, and it was like spiralling into another dimension, the garden left behind. I became aware of the hot fluids pumping through my system, my expanding lungs pressing against the body armour. I was conscious of every cell, every molecule buzzing, waiting for me to summon a modicum of regret – except it was now something more functional and coarser than regret – and go back. With one sidestep, it would be possible to cross to an outer ring of this labyrinth and find myself further from the centre.

Be careful where you step. The mantra of the landmine detection crew, of anyone living in fear that the earth beneath their feet could attack. Be careful, Snow White. The ledge is shallow, not made for feet in frayed tights. Though the circling could be blamed, this wasn't the first time I'd felt dizzy recalling everything that had passed. What was undone was gone for ever, but I was in the habit of sketching it in my mind, as you might mentally note what you dreamt about.

Memories would sometimes catch me unawares, and I'd realise certain things really did happen, but only to me. I'd once had to see Alberta pulled from a car wreck, the paramedic kneeling over her and slicing her armpits to relieve some of the internal bleeding pressure. It was a scene that had completely vanished until one night when, boiling the kettle, I instead saw the steam rising from her blood and remembered the smell of it, like the early stages of cooking a very fresh steak. As far as my department was aware, this had never taken place, along with all the other non-happenings that probably made those two years the most successful and uneventful on record. Yet Alberta's pain was inside me somewhere, along with all the bursts of soil, the yells and the sounds of snapping sunglasses.

My bravery was no longer about risking my life; it was about witnessing terrible things to ascertain how they had come to pass. The realisation had the smack of a wave, making me teeter between steps yet filling me with a strange relief. This was the exact opposite of a shortcut. It meant doing things when no one was watching, patiently absorbing each wrong turn, each dead end, without anyone ever knowing what it had taken to get there. Flying to the end of the board game wasn't cheating, not when it came at a cost.

* * *

'Retrocausality is being redefined, thanks to Dr Erin Knott of Leeds University . . .' Only now was I reading about the famous paper, perusing a crumpled copy of *New Scientist* that had been passed round all of Nan's friends. From what I could gather, it was some sort of theoretical breakthrough, though I felt the 'many worlds' stuff should have been left in science fiction where it belonged. Funny to see my sister quoted like this, to hear her 'public' voice, if only on the page. I didn't see Nina mentioned anywhere, but perhaps she hadn't been around for the interview. Erin herself had been in Switzerland for most of the year.

It still saddened me to think that Nina was gone for good. There was that tiny part of her that had reminded me, faintly, of Sabra. Not just her in her quirks, but in the way she ploughed cheerfully onwards without ever considering the possibility that she wasn't totally cool in every way. Nina had all the personality traits my sister lacked, not to mention the much-needed lighter view of life.

Even taking into account that I'd called when she had the flu, my first chat with Erin had gone phenomenally badly. Without thinking it through, I'd asked about the river cruise, and failed to keep the disappointment out of my voice on learning that she never went. Instead of pointing out the difficulties of travelling alone when you are visually impaired, she just said in acid tones: 'I can't imagine how you got the money.'

The remark hit home. She'd obviously given it some

thought and was starting to work out the sort of things I could do. Would she mention it to colleagues, or leave Nina's research lying around? My trip to Leeds had sown a small seed of fear that someone might expose me, intentionally or not, and throw a spanner into my currently well-oiled, high-velocity career. I put the phone down thinking things had been better when my ability was a secret.

Now, though, after a night shift that had left me deeply unsettled, I needed to talk to someone. It was paperwork that had kept me at my desk just late enough for Remy to swing by and tell me the last thing I wanted to hear. That girl I'd talked down – Anne-Marie, aka Snow White – had been in a vehicle collision on the Aston Expressway, the only one in the car to have died. By now I'd attended countless crashes and it was all part and parcel; you couldn't get too upset or you'd stop functioning. But because she had been my first real damsel in distress, the first person I'd saved, however long ago, this piece of news stayed in my head and bugged me all the way home.

Erin wasn't my ideal choice for a friendly ear, but she was pretty much the only option if I wanted to chat to someone who knew about my skills; and she would want to talk about them too, of that I was sure. Only when the phone was ringing did I realise my capital error the last time around: not bothering to butter her up. The science magazine was still splayed open on the breakfast bar.

'Dr Knott? Is this *the* Dr Erin Knott?'

'Yes?'

'Congratulations! Only a year late, I know, but Nan's been hogging the article about you. She's to blame completely.'

'Is that Arlo?'

'None other.'

'I was just thinking I should call you.'

'Well, I got there first.' Competitive habits die hard. My stomach rumbled and I reached towards the bread bin. 'Nan told me you were famous. Are you pleased?'

'It went down well.'

'Offers rolling in?'

'A professorship. Mainly because of the publicity . . . People never noticed my past papers before.' She spoke as though someone might be about to punch her in the gut.

My toast was charring nicely. I transferred the phone to my other ear. 'So, that's good, isn't it?' There was a slight rustle on the line, but no reply forthcoming. Maybe she was overwhelmed by it all. Erin was unused to getting a lot of attention. I remembered the weirdness of being in demand back in my magician days. 'Oh well,' I soothed. 'Enjoy it while you can.'

'What do you mean?' Oddly, her usual combative tone had been replaced by something that sounded almost fearful. 'It's all right for you . . .' she continued, making me think we were finally getting onto what I wanted to talk about, but then she lapsed into silence.

'Seriously, Erin, what is wrong?' She was annoying me

now. I plucked a grape from the fruit basket the next-door neighbour had left me. Fortunately, I'd been around the other night when her collie had an altercation with a car – now merely a near-miss.

'Nothing,' she insisted. I pictured her curled up on an Ikea chair, surrounded by cat mugs with murky peppermint rings. Was she too shy, all of a sudden, to interrogate me? Maybe she had decided that, despite the evidence, I was making it up. Or perhaps there was no evidence, if Nina hadn't shown her the results before they parted ways. I was just about to voice some of this when she burst out: 'I've been to see Dad.'

That knocked me out of my trance. 'Oh . . . and?'

'A few times. He's getting—'

'Worse?'

'I don't know . . . insular and a bit obsessive. He doesn't go out any more. The warden was asking if we wanted to get him a few more private support hours.'

'And what did you say?'

That old frustration broke through her voice.

'Nothing, Arlo. I said nothing. I can't make all the decisions.'

There was a slight echo on the line, as though every word had a shadow. It was so easy to slip back into my passive little-brother role. Things should be different now.

'I guess I should get my shit together and go visit him?'

'That would be good.'

275

My problems would have to wait. The toast and Marmite was cold between my fingers. I used to loathe this tar-like spread, but had slowly allowed it into my diet as a source of B vitamins. Maybe these days I did have some sanity to spare – enough to seek out, for the first time in my life, the man I least wanted to see.

Twenty-six

The lift ejected me into a corridor of natural wood doors, each with a chrome knocker and spyhole. He would doubt-less still lean towards that white, show-home perfection he'd always tried to carve out in the midst of family mess. His kitchen in particular would glisten, all surfaces clear except for something very useless, like a jar or two of decorative beans. The windows would be nondescript with teak blinds, the dining table topped with some interesting mini-sculpture, and there would be an Italian coffee grinder, ensuring each cup took a respectably long time to make.

I was unprepared for the sight that greeted me, even after I'd got over the shock of seeing my father grinning in the doorway. There was a softness to his attire: the collar of a polo shirt protruding from a huge cream jumper, and jersey trousers with a drawstring waist. His hair was longer and lankier, though still not fully grey, and his face was almost feverish with delight. The dimples under his eyes suggested patchy sleep. I'd forgotten he was supposed to be ill but now found myself searching for the signs. He'd always had a certain air of distraction.

'Oh hello,' he said. 'I'm so glad you're here.'

'Good to see you too,' I said cautiously, as he dragged me into the flat. It was the smell I noticed first, a sugary, milky scent I couldn't quite place until I saw the three bowls of cereal on the breakfast bar, guarded by monolithic boxes of chocolate curls, Frosted Shreddies, Cheerios and Corn Flakes (with the cockerel crossed out, for some reason). Back when I ate cereal before school, he'd enjoyed the odd bowl, but I was fairly sure that in the intervening years he'd been a strictly coffee-and-toast person. Plus, it was about four in the afternoon.

This kitchen array was nothing, however, to the strange world I entered as we progressed to the living room. What was I looking at? Instead of the clean surfaces of my mind's eye, everything was cluttered, though there was a certain precision to the arrangement. A chair was pulled up to the fold-out table where he seemed to have begun playing – and making – the board game. A large piece of ply had been decorated with a curving ladder of squares in orange and green. One counter, a lion, still languished here, three paces in. Pots of model paints stood empty by the rust-red lava of a volcano, made from an upended plastic funnel with the tip sawn off. It made me think of the photos that rotated so long ago on Mum's screensaver, of volcanoes in Indonesia she'd circumnavigated. The board game climbed up and across this obstacle and beneath a copse of model trees before escaping the extended flaps of the table onto another board propped up with an empty poster tube and a long box still containing its extra-wide turkey foil. Everything was taped and nailed together, and when the game ran out of board there was an actual helter-skelter that brought it to the ground, made from a traffic cone with a long slice of card spiralling around it. Fascinated, I took a marble from a neat stack and rolled it down.

'Did you make all this?' I was almost expecting him to say he'd befriended some lonely child with a lot of paints and glue. But he just nodded and looked proud of himself. 'How come?' I asked.

He shrugged and picked up a counter on the far side of the room, twirling it in his fingers. 'So it can be played, naturally.'

I looked over at the next bit, towards the window. Sections of a Monopoly board had been cut and laid end to end so they were linear. The man I'd known would never have done something so sacrilegious.

'How long have you been at this?' I said.

'Oh, I don't know. It's just something to do in between

filming.' Dad flustered about, bustling me up the length of the game till he found the dice, uttering a cry of happiness at rolling a six. He moved the lion half a dozen spaces, muttering, 'Courage, my boy.' The game did a U-turn at the wall and headed back up a ramp, then over several chairs. 'Sorry, have I been going on?' He looked at me with faint confusion, as though trying to calculate how long we'd been talking. What little I knew of dementia came to mind; the sudden slipperiness of the short term.

'Filming? You've got a new part?'

'Oh, have I got a part,' he beamed, floating across to a section of game that went straight up the wall and unsticking a little iron figurine with an air of triumph. 'Magnets,' he chuckled, carefully replacing it on the square. I had to admit the construction was ingenious. He hovered over the game with arms slightly raised, poised to dabble. Beneath the table there was a preponderance of cereal packets and washing-up bottles – construction materials for future sections. *Blue Peter* was back in business. I crouched down and prodded a pewter dog, only to hear my dad's sharp voice:

'Don't mess with the board.'

I shot him a placating smile and turned back to the table, fascinated to see a tiny cardboard cut-out of Lawrence Olivier, black-and-white and carrying a colour Helena Bonham-Carter across a river, the game following on plasticine stepping stones. A willow tree made from a sprig of real willow was taped to a pencil to dangle languidly over the water. Then there were rolling hills, a battlefield, long-bows, labels and annotations here and there. A cauldron blocked the path, and a slip of paper inside told the player to roll a six if they wanted to outsmart the weird sisters. I knew without asking that the red-brown markings that followed were drops of blood, partially absorbed into the cardboard as the plasma diffused.

'What's this about, Dad?' There was an involuntary wobble in my voice.

'Arlo?' It was as though I'd just appeared. 'Look at you! You're ancient.'

He hadn't lost his knack for annoying me.

'What does it mean?' I persisted. 'The game.'

'What's the point of any game? You play it.'

'How do you win?'

He gave me a sly look, indulging his competitive son. 'It's not quite finished.' He went over to a section on the far wall, where the pathway of the game became squares dangling from the ceiling. Several ladders grew up to them, sometimes forking, and there were stars, too. The black reverses told me he'd cut these out of the same magnetic sheet as the other vertical elements. Attached to one of them, and dangling upside down, I spotted a tiny knight, not unlike the one I'd played with as a child.

'Over here.' His voice was soft. 'It will end over here somewhere, when I finish it, but I'm not sure . . . Not sure if I'll go back. I mean, it's long days, the filming. They want you there at 6.30 a.m. Sometimes I can't face it, I don't know why . . .' A hand passed over his face and he looked up as though it was a cloud, casting a shadow.

'So you might quit?' My face remained neutral, but I was barely holding it together. All the father-son angst I thought we'd grapple with had been eclipsed by this new, precarious reality, measured in little squares. Was this the only way he felt he could move forward now? He took a long-nosed watering can and topped up a pool that players could cross on two wind-up boats as long as they threw a five. After this point, the board became erratic, the next places marked by beer mats, jar lids and cut-out faces from magazines.

'Who are the other players?' I asked. But he'd become intent upon winding up the steamships until they croaked in protest. When he let them go, they chugged across to the edge of the upside-down bin lid then began to chase each other in circles.

'As I said,' he continued, 'I don't have much time. My agent's got me the most amazing role and I need to prepare. You've probably heard I play the villain?'

'Yup.'

'So I need to understand everything that's going on. What's the word for it?' Concentration fudged up his brow. I wished I could help him. 'Mash . . . Machinations.'

'Machinations?'

'You might not know quite what I mean, but it's something I've been looking into.'

He'd taken over the entire apartment with this crazy board game, yet the place retained a sense of emptiness. How could a person become so lost, so quickly? Only two, or maybe three, years had passed since he'd abandoned the tradition of sending me a text on my birthday. I sought my mildest voice.

'Hey . . . you're retired now.' I looked around for a place to sit, but there seemed to be nowhere. 'Maybe you could get out a bit more?'

He looked up sharply, his mouth becoming very small. 'Get out more? Do you want me to get papped? They lie in wait, you know. That's why a certain actress shows up in the same New York sweater day after day – the vultures hate getting duplicates.'

His finger and thumb framed some starlet in the camera lens, and suddenly I could see him on set, tossing his jacket over a director's chair, tanned skin lustrous under the hot lights, laughing delightedly with fellow actors between takes, in the haze of all his dreams coming true.

A crunch alerted me to him taking a quick bite of cereal. 'Can I offer you anything?'

I shook my head. Evidently he was eating well enough.

'I've got to get going.' I lifted my coat, but he flew round the breakfast bar, hurriedly wiping his mouth.

'No, you don't. I'll get the dice. Come play with me a while.'

I took in the endless game writhing across the floor.

'Dad—'

'It does take a while,' he admitted, 'but play anyway. We used to enjoy our board games.'

This was him reaching out a finger and prodding the bit of my heart that still had feeling for him. I'd begun to assume he didn't really know who I was, or not for the best part of the conversation. My hands smoothed the air. 'Let's just take a break from all this. Go out and get a beer. What do you say?'

The quizzical expression was hard to read, but he didn't say no. I put on my jacket and handed him a surprisingly grubby trench coat hanging by the door. He put his arms in, shrugging it uncertainly over his shoulders. I went out to press the lift button, then looked back and saw he wasn't coming. The doorway was an invisible forcefield. He was almost flattened against it, head pulled in and feet together.

'I just need to finish . . .' he murmured, a little sheepishly. 'I'll come next time, is that okay?'

'It's fine, Dad.' I treated him to half a smile, the best I could muster, then let the lift take me back down to earth.

A day later Erin emailed and I rang her back.

'What do you mean, he won't close the door? Can't the warden just close it for him?'

'He waits by it,' she continued. 'Apparently one of the players – or counters, I forget which – went through and will be coming back the same way.'

'Are you sure this is dementia, Erin? He's very delusional.'

A silence. The line up to Leeds always seemed to have some strange scratchings and fidgetings on it, starlings twanging the wires.

'Maybe you caught him on a bad day.' She was hesitant. 'Sometimes he's very lucid.'

'But the game . . .'

'I've seen the game. It's good for him to have hobbies.'

'There was something not right about it, about him . . .'

'Your visit has made him much worse, Arlo. It's my fault for egging you on.' She sighed. 'It would have been better if you'd never gone. He didn't go to bed last night, the warden said. Just sat in a chair by the doorway. I'm worried about his nutrition too . . . once people get weaker—'

'Okay, okay.' Perhaps her mind wasn't going in the same direction, but to me it was obvious. 'I'll just not go, all right?'

A long pause.

'Two days?'

'Easy.'

How unknowable I must be, and how strange that she had asked me nothing, even though I'd long since overtaken her as the more freakish sibling. Congenital blindness was nothing compared to this.

'All right,' she said.

The next time we spoke was more than fifty hours earlier, Monday where it had been Wednesday. I felt a little light-headed, as though I hadn't eaten for a while. Erin had called just before I'd had lunch. Toast, Marmite, fruit – each mouthful un-eaten back to hunger. I let her get to our father in the conversation before taking a deep breath and interrupting.

'Sorry . . . but we've done all this. I went to see him, all the way down to Luton. It was a bad time. I made him worse and you asked me to unwind the whole thing.'

She was rightly suspicious, but once I'd recounted details of the board game and bowls of cereal, speaking faster as they retreated into the haze, there was no doubt in her mind. 'Wow,' she said finally, that long overdue reaction. 'That is simply amazing. Two days. More, even, if you rang me at around 3 p.m. on Wednesday. How do you keep all those actions in your head?'

A rush of excitement as I realised I was finally getting to talk about it. My quest had been completed: a visit to Dad in his tower, with all the accompanying anguish. Now I was through to Erin, reaping my reward.

'It's not easy. The trick is to be very still and quiet.'

'Like meditation?'

'I don't know about that. Like the moment before going to sleep, when you're calm enough to reflect on stuff that has happened during the day.'

There was silence for a moment, the echo of a distant truck. She must have been sitting by an open window.

'Well, Nina was right about you, like everything else.' A sigh escaped her. 'But it's quite remarkable. You are something special, Arlo, but I guess you've always known that.'

A hundred miles apart, and it was the closest I'd ever felt to Erin. I almost wished I could see her, and wondered if she'd still be able to see me. My tone had a rasp of affection as I mumbled, 'Runs in the family.'

She absorbed both the compliment and – I realised – the irony.

'There's some bad stuff that runs in our family too, but I take your point.' The phone line crackled, and I clamped the mobile tighter to my ear. 'Have you . . .' She hesitated. 'Arlo, have you ever . . . unwound something that happened to me?'

'Like what?' The leather sofa squeaked as I rose, nerves coming to life.

'Well, I wouldn't know, would I?'

She could have no inkling of those fractured minutes in the surgical-smelling room, where every ounce of my thirteen-year-old bulk battered her away from Mum's bedside. I clenched and unclenched my hand, the skin stretching over the white nubs of my front two knuckles, toughened by the threadbare punchbag in our gym. The Arlo who would win gold for confession was there, on a pedestal just out of reach.

'No,' I said. 'Not that I can remember.'

A shrug was in her voice. 'I just wondered.' We went on to talk about the tests Nina had done and how there were still files on her computer that my sister was too shy to request, though she was working on it.

I hung up with the certainty that Erin had found the

subject of her next paper. What she'd done was very clever, and it took me two more rounds of toast and Marmite to see it. Was Dad really worse after my visit, or was that just part of her plan? Either way, she couldn't pull the wool over my eyes. I knew when I'd been the subject of an experiment, however subtle.

Twenty-nine

I first met Detective Superintendent Steven Green, the man who'd give me my big break and then horrify me, and whom I'd ultimately betray, in the briefing room the evening before Operation Changeling. He'd come up from London specially, but his train was late, so when he entered the room he'd already begun speaking, as if we were the ones lagging behind.

His voice had a tremendous thrust and an impressive range. It wheedled and curved around objections, then flung you against the wall until you could do nothing but nod mutely and agree. For me, it was fascination at first sight. About eighty per cent of the time, he was the most focused person alive, eating up backstory and setting out action plans for every eventuality. Otherwise he was vaguely absent, so if you spoke to him a beat would pass before he showed signs of hearing. He wore these blue-green Nike trainers, half-concealed under the trousers of a grey suit, and brimmed with the most puerile and filthy jokes I'd heard for some time, all gritted with a deep Hackney growl.

'What's the matter, fella, lost the plot? You wait till it hits the fan. What? What's brown and sticky? Don't look at me like that. A stick, that's what. Now get me a dead-animal sandwich from that shithole you call a canteen.'

Since becoming a detective, I'd stepped it up a notch, and people had started to see me as a sort of unofficial risk specialist. Being right, time after time, got you noticed. The trick was to adopt an open, artless stance and speak in a way that inspired complete confidence, with a drop in tone and sentences folded under at the ends like well-made beds. While a cocky schoolboy would be dismissed out of hand, someone who'd done risk management training – who'd done landmine clearance, for God's sake – would always be believed. Every superintendent knew my name, and there were even a few emails of congratulation when I gained my promotion to detective sergeant.

This operation was pretty much the biggest one I'd seen so far, involving a lot of officers. By the skin of my teeth, I'd managed to make a case for being on hand, both to collect evidence for the investigation that would ensue, and because my expertise might be useful in such a volatile situation. It was only when we were briefed about the cordons and the full kit we'd be wearing that I realised it would also be important to keep out of harm's way, though conflict was unlikely.

The two gangs had been padding out our incident logs for some time, especially now they were at each other's throats. One was more established and therefore furious at these newbies, the Marlow Road boys, homing in on their rackets and territory. There had been regular scuffles over the last six months, plus a nasty stabbing that closed a pub for a fortnight and probably left it bankrupt.

The guy who had taken the kid hostage was around forty, bald with a tattoo of dark roses on his scalp. He could apparently sweet-talk officers fairly well, all while hiding a backlog of evil deeds that were straight out of a horror film. If his demands weren't met, an individual named Ivy, the sister of a Roader, would die, and we didn't like to think about how.

All this was supposed to have happened under our radar. From their point of view, the police becoming involved was a huge spanner in the works. Our super was in command of the operation, and Green had been drafted in at short notice because of his expertise with gangs. It was a delicate situation, especially since the hostage was being held at a residential address – in leafy Moseley, no less.

The grubby, floral curtains were closed, and I wondered if our intel could be trusted, whether there really were only three people inside. While my gut tightened, Steve Green was sticking on a nicotine patch, whistling quietly and polishing his sunglasses as though he was about to go on holiday. Finally, someone leaned out of the window; not Rose-head but an older guy.

'Go home, will ya?' he yelled. The Brummie accent came as a surprise for some reason. It had a sort of in-built indignation, as though we were the ones being unreasonable, lining up a potential bloodbath.

'None of the Roaders are coming,' boomed the negotiator. 'You're stuck with us, I'm afraid, so relax and bring out the girl.'

'There's no girl.'

I was locked onto Green, studying his moves. He'd bumped the driver's side front wheel up onto the kerb so his vehicle was diagonal and he could lean more casually on the open door. He looked more vulnerable this way, closer to the house, but that window was bulletproof. It would take him but a moment to duck, or even to get in the car and reverse. His notepad was open on the dashboard, and I could see his trademark mind map, a pathway to the best-case scenario underlined in red.

'We got a message.' His hand traced an imaginary missive. 'Girl's missing and we know you want Max to back off. But not today, bud. Let her walk.'

A pause. Then the guy I knew from the mugshots came to the window. He had a slightly more nasal voice than his companion, and big, clean teeth that added precision to his words.

'You got the wrong intel, officers. We don't have no girl here.' A slight hesitation. 'Come in and look if you want.'

The negotiator checked his notepad, more a twitch than anything else. Even I could tell this wasn't going as expected. I was hoping we could go inside, then we'd find out a bit more and I could skip back if necessary, but he said:

'You know that's not going to happen. We'd settle for you coming out, though, so why not play ball?'

'Ditto, cap'n.' The face vanished in a flash of floral tattoo.

Green swore quietly. He strolled over to where the other superintendents were hovering and they began to reassess the situation.

'Ivy is there,' I heard him say. 'I believe she's there. But they won't come out, and we haven't a clue what's inside.'

'You're thinking firearms?'

He shrugged, peeling the back from a second patch and rolling up his shirtsleeve to add it. 'They've been caught by surprise, I'd say, trying to move her quietly. This residential address was dark till now, right?'

My hands had felt their way around a car bonnet, inching me closer to catch every word, and now I realised they were staring at me.

'Can we help you, Detective Sergeant Knott?' The super leaned more heavily than he needed to on my rank and, slightly embarrassed, I skipped back a few steps.

But nothing much came from their meeting. We returned to the barricade and I began to battle the gnaw of an empty stomach. My eyes strayed to the police tape strung across the end of the street, dreaming of burger vans. Telephone calls had warned the neighbours to evacuate before we moved in, but two kids stood watching by the barrier, their skateboards propped against their legs. Good luck seeing any action, I thought.

Minutes later, I was roused from my stupor by a one-sided shouting match.

'We don't fucking have her. We don't have anybody,' Rosehead was yelling, while Green, an emotional intelligence wizard, kept his voice low and steady.

'Okay, I hear you. But look at it from our point of view – why'd we get the message?'

'That's your problem, cap'n.'

'So come out and have a chat with me. What's the issue?'

'You're the fucking issue. Get away from my house.'

'I don't want to be—' Gunfire cut him off. It was wildly, unexpectedly everywhere, the brick wall exploding in terracotta shards, dimpling his face with blood. Officers took cover, then they shot out the windows, hurled canisters of tear gas, stormed the door and kicked it down. I was frozen behind the car, counting breaths – a habit I'd gotten into – but I couldn't remember what I was supposed to do. The scene unfolded like a dream: men coming out of windows with guns, police swarming, shooting, cracking mortar from Victorian brickwork. I saw black fingers scrape weeds from a crevice. *Officer down.* Up, around and behind. Green

294

shouted commands that sounded like the names of children's games. Someone tapped me on the shoulder, but otherwise they let me be. Then two men were marched out of the front door. Then another. Then a woman, though it was not the girl. A third and fourth man followed, struggling in cuffs. They kept coming. It was the whole bloody gang, sweaty and angry and demanding lawyers.

No girl. I couldn't believe it. Somehow I was up and running through the doorway, wanting to see if they'd pulled up the carpets, knocked on every wall. It was a lofty place, bay windows but no storage, attic already converted, no room for a body between the skins of brick. I came out with a sense that something had gone horribly wrong. Rose-head had been right; it was a set-up. If we'd known there were so many of them, clearly at a gathering of some sort, we'd never have kicked the hornets' nest.

Before the quandary could take hold, before it could muddy my thoughts, I lifted the plastic barrier and walked calmly past the two teenagers, who were now holding their skateboards up like shields, and found a front wall I could perch on. An unseen pigeon cooed a couple of bars of the *Star Wars* theme, a strange phenomenon I hoped never to hear again.

Back, rocking dizzily, sensing the grit of the road, over actions no more substantial than spikes in cortisol. Then I was standing with one hand on a car, noticing my breathing. Still normal. Nothing had happened yet. Green pursed his lips in frustration and consulted quietly with the senior officers. I shuffled closer.

'Ivy is there, I believe,' he was saying. Then they became aware of me staring.

'They don't have the girl.' My voice sounded robotic.

'Who's this joker?' Green looked me up and down.

'Knott, sir.'

'See you, Knott.' He turned his back.

'There are nine men and one woman,' I said. 'No kidnap, no hostage, no grounds for arrest. We should get out of here.' Desperation slurred my speech. He was almost laughing, about to flick me out of his way, and then it would all happen again. It did.

This time I got to the same point and said, 'New intel, sir. Those kids saw the girl moved out, saw a bunch of people arrive too. It's rammed in there, and they're armed.' My nonchalance was honed to such perfection that I nearly added, 'Take it or leave it.'

They looked at each other, then turned towards the teenagers, who, rather prematurely, ran away. I'd warned them in confidential tones that they were in big trouble for an unspecified reason, and if any police started coming their way, they'd do well to scarper. Luckily, I was ready to stake my reputation on their veracity, exhorting every undercurrent of the universe to make the people in charge believe me, thinking longingly of when I'd be promoted high enough to avoid their tiresome doubts. Finally, the super stepped in.

'I know what you're thinking,' he said, 'but Arlo's one of our best. He's a trained risk analyst.'

Nice lie, boss, I thought. Green looked at me, measuring the gulf in rank against this high praise. The conflict in his eyes resolved into a nod.

'Fine,' he sighed. 'My assessment is that we can't risk action based on this intel, not without more firearms support. See what you can muster.'

Orders were relayed, some of us were sent away, and I could hardly keep the smile off my face. As we drove, I kept staring at my new CID colleague's hand on the steering wheel, fingers that had earlier been smeared with blood. He could have thanked me, but instead he said, 'Something fascinating about my driving?' and stayed grumpy till we got back. I'd acted strangely, seeming to turn tail like a scared rabbit, then marching up to the chiefs to boldly state my opinion. No wonder my colleague was rattled; he didn't know what to make of me.

A day later, the girl was found hidden elsewhere, and the snout who'd given us the Moseley address was exposed as having links to the rival gang. It could have been a costly blunder, and the debriefing took place amid an atmosphere of edgy relief. Green barked my name as I was leaving the room, and I hung back, feeling like one of those students called out by a teacher because they've been either intelligent or disruptive.

'How did you think to speak to those kid gawkers?'

I shrugged. 'Instinct.'

'Instinct's *my* thing. Get your own.' His frown reversed. 'Really we should all be giving you the bumps.'

'I'd settle for a pint, sir.'

He laughed, pulling out a chair for me. 'Call me Steve. No really, just do it. I'll level with you, Knott, my wife's sick and at some point in the not too distant future I'm going to need to take a sabbatical. We don't normally train anyone below inspector level, but I reckon I could swing the overtime if you'd be interested?'

'Are you offering to mentor me?'

'No, no!' He looked disgusted and drummed his fingers on the table. 'Well, yes. Frankly, someone like you should be in the Met.'

Turquoise trainers with grubby white laces dangled before me, one on the floor and one airborne, as he perched askew on the table. If I followed in his footsteps, where would they lead? He was a master of risk, an expert in matters of life and death. Importantly, the life and death of other people. My face betrayed my enthusiasm.

'It's settled.' His gruffness was back. 'Be at Scotland Yard, next Tuesday, not earlier than 10 a.m.'

We left it at that, and I soon discovered he was a man who didn't bother about little details like there being no desk for me, or that I might need to find a hotel at very short notice when he kept me in the capital for three days at a stretch, out drinking into the small hours. Luckily, I could mine the betting shops now and then to finance these sojourns, and Tim later called in a favour from his mum so I could stay in her apartment when she was out of town.

I think my old housemate missed me, having once again broken up with a girlfriend. He'd coaxed me onto Facebook, where photos showed him with a glacial expression I'd never seen before – and not just because he was clutching skis in Austria, determinedly riding out the holiday he'd planned with her on his own. Tim had let his stubble grow into something long enough to catch the snowflakes, his cheeks almost blue and his eyes unsmiling. Sometimes he'd call, but always when I was on an errand for my mentor or tied up with other people. As time went on, I moved back to the capital, so I hardly saw him.

Shadowing Green took me to interesting places. Instinct, which he'd rightly bragged of, told him I had huge potential, and his way of bulldozing opposition meant I got to make decisions way above my rank. It may not have been hard work, compared to the beat, but it was long hours. When Green wasn't in the office, he was drinking or eating out at expensive seafood restaurants. His favourite dish was octopus, 'The most intelligent of the cephalopods.' As he savoured each purplish, lemon-marinated mouthful, he envisaged its intelligence passing to him, restoring his mental powers.

He was a Londoner at heart, and deeply knowledgeable about gang culture, including Scotland Yard's blind spots, and the drug trade routes that shifted almost hourly. He'd say yes to any summons, with the exception of work for the Foreign Office.

'I bloody hate flying,' he said. 'They claim you won't need to, but then suddenly the meeting is in Frankfurt or Brussels or somewhere. Overseas work can be a lot more dicey, and crotch-deep in politics.' He stuffed a tentacle puckered with suckers into his mouth at this point and, as an accompaniment to the word 'crotch', it made me feel a little nauseous.

'And what's the secret?' I asked once we'd moved on to a ratty old bar near Blackfriars and were blowing sepia foam off a couple of stouts. 'You said there are three types we deal with: terrorists, professional criminals and the depressed . . .'

'Mad, bad and sad.'

'Right. So how do you predict someone so unpredictable?'

Green took a peanut and absentmindedly began to plot a map in the air. 'It's a combination of targeting the outcome you want – those hard lines I keep going on about – and empathy. Underrated, is empathy. Do you have it?'

'Isn't it the same as sympathy?'

'Empathy is better in our line of work. Just feel them, let them know it and work from their point of view.'

Whatever I was drinking, it was strong stuff, and this was my fifth pint of it. Though he was probably at his most insightful, my brain was struggling with anything complex. I took my own pinch of peanuts and lined them up on the table.

'What say . . . what say you could, just theoretically, have someone on hand who could try out every option and then just cancel it if it didn't work?'

'I've no idea what you're talking about.'

'Trial and error. You refuse a demand, and the guy blows a fuse. That's where the magic colleague comes in, undoing the mistake so you can try again.' The consonants were like an assault course and I'd stumbled over a few of them. Green was staring at me, a certain malevolence always at the back of his eyes. Then he roared with laughter.

'You're as much a fantasist as the next one. I'll tell you what I'd do with this talented fellow, this magician who'd make my job a piece of cake: I'd milk him for every drop, then I'd hand him over to the security services so they could lock him up for use as an alarm bell.'

He shook the foam-ringed glass and made a *tingalingaling* sound before his gaze settled back into his own personal middle distance. The ache in my jaw turned out to be my lips biting together. He'd just raised a mental image I'd thought had been long since laid to rest. The freak locked up in a cage, only this time with security services rather than psychologists outside the door. As I swirled the last of my black, bitter liquid, watching my mentor stride towards the bar and slam down a fist to get attention, I recognised a passion inside him that was not so different to my own. He was the first person I'd known who was properly larger than life, as I wanted to be, but sometimes kindred spirits are those you end up despising the most.

There was no real need to worry about Green boxing me up because, although we had similarities, he was inferior to me. All he had at his disposal was a rickety apparatus of guesswork, albeit one well tested over the years. Since we'd been working together for such a long period, it came as a shock when I told him I'd got a better offer and was switching departments. The people who mattered had already begun to send me emails behind his back, finding it refreshing to receive advice without a side order of mockery, even insult. He'd made himself so big, bold and brash that no one wanted to deal with him, not when they could have a crisp-shirted, bright young thing who always made the right call. The nicest of them was a lady from the Foreign Office, who was currently putting together a team for a delicate little job: an eighty-foot yacht in the hands of pirates, just off the coast of Somalia. All in strictest confidence, since the skipper was a close schoolfriend of the prime minister's. It was a dicey situation, but could I help?

Of course I could. 'Dicey' was my middle name.

Part 2

LANDING ON A SNAKE

Thirty-four

The journey from Bangkok airport left me wilting and moist under my clothes, and I was glad to escape into the air-conditioned hotel lobby. Lotus flowers floated in low pools beneath fragrant frangipani. The five stars of this Thai palace glittered in its spotlit marble, its silk cushions comforting my flight-weary bones. These days, there was no gambling required to cover my hotel bills. If a foreign government was paying, I flew first class and was allotted a driver on arrival.

Not fancying Khao San Road and its pushy invitations to ping pong shows, I decided to spend the evening at the hotel's sublime cocktail bar. In the morning, I'd be driving out to the tourist town where the barricade was in progress.

There was a stalemate involving a local businessman with several rackets to his name, mainly prostitution, who'd escaped from the police station and was now holed up at his brother's guest house. According to the accounts of staff members – two maids and a chef, who had fled when the hotel was seized – there were three rooms occupied by tourists at the time. They thought the guests were English, as that was the language they spoke, but couldn't be sure. Either way, it was enough to warrant an offer of assistance from the British government, who would provide long-distance support as well as sending me and a secondary negotiator.

Had it been high season, with the hotel fully booked, it would have been unviable to take hostages. Even keeping a handful of tourists was a messy, stressful tactic, and I hoped the fugitive would be keen to negotiate a way out. My part in the operation was to take the commander role, of strategy and decision-making, while the primary negotiator would be provided by the Thai government.

It was the kind of assignment that suited me perfectly, working with people who knew me only by reputation. That's Knott, they'd say as I entered the boardroom, carrying my trademark chai latte with an island of demerara sugar still sinking through the foam, my cuffs un-linked and ready to roll, tie loosened further with every hour of talks. The trick was to be aloof and inscrutable, a person whose thinking transcended their own. That way, I could behave as I liked and they would still follow my commands. All the standoffs, barricades, kidnaps and impossible situations I'd been through had strengthened my instinct for people, for the way these scenarios would go. It was hard to hide my joy at being handed this high profile Thai job, ripe for media attention. My prediction that it would be the final feather in my cap would turn out to be spot on, though not in the way I'd anticipated.

Showered and changed, I made my way sleepily to the bar, yawning despite having slept on the plane. 'I'll have the fish,' I'd told the flight attendant, and, unlike everyone else when they unwrapped the fetid, slime-surrounded fillet, I was able to go back and change my mind.

I eased myself onto a tall chrome stool.

'Would you like to try our cocktail of the day?' asked a perky bartender, who looked about fifteen.

'No thanks, just the local beer.'

It was good to sip something ice-cold and a little too fizzy, watching the girl thread wine glasses onto an overhead rack. Bottles of many-coloured liquids twinkled on mirrored shelves. I was just sliding out my travel journal, hunting for a pen, when I heard two women speaking English behind me, dragging heavy wooden chairs from beneath a table. Almost before they had seated themselves, the bartender was there, plugging her Monday cocktail, which they both ordered with enthusiasm.

Beyond stealing that first glance, I stayed facing the bar,

amused that I could hear their conversation so clearly. The pan-pipe mood music barely reached this side of the foyer, and the marble surfaces amplified every sound.

'Shame I'm only here one night . . . there's a nice wee pool in the basement.'

'Where is it you're off to in the morning?'

'Oh, some tourist place. Leaving at the crack of dawn.'

Odd that the woman couldn't name her own holiday destination. Their cocktails arrived amid appreciative murmurs. They said their room numbers to the bartender, and I wondered how they knew each other. One American and one Glaswegian, by the sound of it.

'If you're only here tonight, are you sure you don't want to go out and see the city?'

'God no, I'm knackered. I'll join you for dinner though, if the offer still stands? It'll be good to eat real food after that rancid . . . I can't even describe it.'

'Don't.' A laugh, accompanied by the tinkle of ice in glasses. I began to suspect they had met on the plane; perhaps two women on their own, one more of a frequent business traveller than the other. I hoped they'd get drunk quickly and come up with something to entertain me, ideally of a sexual nature. At present their talk was turning to the person-alities of their kids – or nephews, in the case of the Scottish woman – making me zone out and begin to flick through my journal. Just at that moment, I heard the Scot say, 'No, I tell a lie, I do know one of them. At least, I met him once, when he was a keynote speaker at the Arbitrators Association dinner, though I'm sure he won't remember me.'

My spine pinged me upright an inch or two, so suddenly that the businessman beside me glanced across before returning to his typing. The woman continued:

'He was coming from London, so he'll probably have got a direct flight.'

'So he's a hostage negotiator?'

My head turned just enough to scan the Scottish woman's face, and it seemed marginally familiar, perhaps someone I'd seen at a conference.

'They say he's a bit of a mind reader . . .'

'Aren't you worried about working with him, then?'

'I'm excited about working with him. I'll just have to watch what I think!'

I was no stranger to admiration, but to be doused with it so unexpectedly, so delightfully, ignited me with glee. I felt like sending a few more cocktails to their table, spinning round and embracing this woman – who was clearly the secondary negotiator I'd been assigned – and skipping back if she thought it inappropriate.

'Some people shit on him quite hard,' she continued, shedding a few brownie points. 'But he's the same person who got twenty-three people safely out of a hijacked jet in Tunis last year, who extracted five children from the attic of their bonkers father without him having to be shot . . . Criminologists have written whole papers on this guy, trying to come up with a theory for his technique. I'd be surprised if the FBI haven't tried to poach him.'

There were a few little beeps, and a glance told me the other woman was typing something on her phone. 'So much more interesting than selling insurance,' she mumbled in token response.

'I'm hoping I can learn something.'

'What did you say was happening? A kidnap?'

'It's a crime in action,' she said. 'I can't say more.'

Attagirl, I thought. Sticking to protocol. Over the next half-hour, she said a few more things, more than her companion wanted to hear. If only she could have known how much pleasure it was giving me. I hardly dared to gulp my beer, lest it block my ears and make me miss some important detail.

'Do you want another drink?' the negotiator asked her friend.

'I'd better go answer a few emails, Melinda. But I'll see you in the restaurant?'

When I greeted Melinda the next morning, as though for the first time, I couldn't keep the smile from my face. As usual, I had the advantage, and could meet her nervous chatter with quiet charm. Don't get me wrong, she was not my type romantically, though I got the impression she would have liked to be. She was quite tall, with a ponytail and angular glasses that had something of my sister about them.

We had a beautiful drive down to Tamrieng, passing through palm plantations and dodging skinny chickens as we cut through villages. I tried to work out where I'd seen her before. At the arbitrators event, certainly, but perhaps earlier in my career as well.

We took the minimum amount of time to settle into our simple but pleasant hotel before heading over to meet the team. The crime was taking place at a guesthouse called Hotel Oasis, and the local police had set up a cordon around it, requisitioning an annex of the restaurant opposite to use as their base of operations. I was surprised to learn that they had already been in situ for three days. Clearly this was a slow-burn sort of case.

Everyone greeted me with much deference and even jittery excitement. I'd worked with one or two local police chiefs before, and had tended to find them humourless and even brutal, but Lamon was a surprisingly charming man. I'd later learn there were other sides to him, but for now I accepted the cigar he forced into my hand and we exchanged some ice-breaking comments about English football teams.

He took me to the annex, which smelled of charred grease, and showed me mugshots of Somsith, the main perpetrator, and the two other men they believed to be inside. There were files for each of the seven tourists suspected to be trapped in the hotel, though one was a child so hers contained only a single sheet of paper.

'Brits?' I said.

'Could be.' They could just as easily be Australians, in this part of the world, or any other English-speaking nationality, not that it mattered much to me. The photocopies taken of their passports were, of course, still inside the hotel.

I was introduced to the primary negotiator: a grey-haired Thai named Boon-Nam who spoke perfect English, having lived in Sydney. He filled me in on the dialogue to date as we went to take a closer look at the perimeter. The limp vegetation was still in the midday haze, and guys with machine guns loitered subtly at each corner.

I heard birds and frogs in the undergrowth as we looked around. The hotel was set back from the road, surrounded by a simple garden and with a bamboo fence at the back to keep the forest at bay. It was towards the edge of town, the tarmac crisscrossed with mud where farm tracks led off on either side. The building had seen better days, perhaps during the sixties or seventies, when it must have been thrown up to meet the growing tourist tide. Now it was one of the shabbier options for accommodation, the ponds flanking the doorway choked with fallen leaves, the two dragons overhead weeping flakes of pink paint. Not much of an oasis.

I handed back the binoculars.

'Fifteen rooms, you say?'

'That's right.'

'And not many options.' I was referring to the shutters. Barricaded windows made it much harder to throw in gas canisters, if the need arose.

'Plus, he's very whimsical,' Boon-Nam replied. 'He only answers you at certain times of day.'

The negotiator walked around with a megaphone constantly bouncing against his thigh, attached to his belt with a carabiner, as though I might ask him to open a dialogue there and then. It would take a lot more groundwork before we were at that stage.

'Are you okay?' I asked, as he bent forward. I thought he might have dropped something.

'Yes, just a cramp.'

He showed me his teeth, which looked as though they were made of solidified cooking fat, and wiped the sweat from his brow. He was wearing a sports jacket despite the heat, though perhaps to him the temperature was just mild.

Later on, I took a call from London and went over the details. A staff member from the restaurant brought us coconut curries and baked fish wrapped in banana leaves, washed down with chilled lime juice. We ate them perched on windowsills and tables, seeking the faintest breeze.

By the time an evening balm was settling, I'd finished speaking to everyone and was ready to brief Boon-Nam on our opening tactics, but he was nowhere to be found. I realised he hadn't been with us at lunch either. It rubbed me up the wrong way to have a primary negotiator skipping out at such a crucial stage. Eventually one of the officers stuck his head through the window and told us Boon-Nam had been puking among the trees, that he'd been bitten by something while he was doing it, and that he had now been rushed to the clinic with a combination of gastroenteritis and a rapidly swelling lower leg.

This left me at a complete loss. There was no way I could help him, lacking knowledge of what he'd done to get ill in the first place.

'What's the plan?' Lamon muttered. 'Get someone else? That could take a lot of time.'

He was right. We sat around in the hut, drowning in paper and our own sweat, the officers not even bothering to go outside when they smoked. Melinda coughed, fanned her face and addressed me.

'I mean, they wouldn't bring in a negotiator with as much experience as you anyway, would they?'

I could see what she was getting at. It would go against the normal way of things for the commander to do the negotiating himself. But she would be there as a second, and it wasn't as if I could mess it up.

'Just one problem,' Lamon added. 'Somsith, he has very bad English.'

'Can we get an interpreter?' Melinda said.

'Don't know. Ask London?'

We asked London, and Lamon asked his regional commissioner. Neither could do anything quickly. Then Melinda made some calls and came up with a friend working another translation job in Bangkok, who could get here tomorrow.

We spent the rest of the twilight hours planning our tactics.

I would negotiate, with Melinda acting as my second, keeping me on track. If things went in an unexpected direction, we'd halt and adjust the strategy. It wasn't perfect, and the Foreign Office was less than pleased, but I knew it wouldn't fail. In fact, I liked the idea of gaining credit as both commander and negotiator. When you're at the top of your game, the only thing you can do is break new ground. This was turning out even better than I'd expected.

The interpreter arrived promptly at midday, just as my Casio watch flickered to twelve. The car door opened. I didn't see her at first. Then I saw a woman with flicky ear-length hair, sunburned shoulders and russet lips, with a polka-dot rucksack slung over her shoulder. Just a stranger who had, for some reason, paralysed me in a strange outer-second of time. I still wasn't ready to breathe, but my body obligingly stepped forward and held out a hand.

'Hello, Arlo,' said Sabra.

Thirty-four

I had no reaction. When something truly mind-blowing happens, all you can do is nothing. But the moment I gripped her hand, surprisingly cool and dry given she'd just completed a journey in a stifling taxi, something made me drop it and twist away. I let out a breathy cry that dragged at the very base of my lungs. 'What the hell' – I was talking to the universe – 'are you playing at?' It's blurry, but I still remember my trunk buckling, that tangled-tree sensation, every muscle curling round itself till my skin was taut enough to split, to crack like bark. Of course, I undid it back to the handshake and motioned her politely towards headquarters.

As she passed through the doorway, removing her light cardigan, the scent floating from her body nearly did for me. Once so familiar. Physiology was taking over, pure chemistry flooding my veins with excitement, overriding my brain, but I was determined not to let her see. I masked my joy with a tone of professional courtesy.

'Good of you to come. I understand this is a little outside your usual remit?' All Melinda had told me was that her friend was working for a lawyer attached to the European Court of Justice. I didn't even ask the interpreter's name.

Sabra put her bag on the floor and leaned back in the chair to look up at me. 'It's great,' she said. 'I couldn't believe it when Mel texted. I never get to do anything exciting.' The weighting of her make-up had changed, favouring eyeliner over lipstick. Though her face looked older, the sharpness suited her, and a healthy brown tan dotted with freckles made her look wonderfully earthy and real. Her hair was still red, though a touch lighter than I remembered. Overall, the vampy paleness she'd sported at university was gone, and she looked considerably different to the woman who'd lived inside my head all these years.

I poured her a glass from the jug of hibiscus iced tea, which she took with grateful eyes.

'Are you hungry?'

'I can eat later.' As she drank, I noticed the silver bands encircling her ring finger, one with a tiny diamond.

At that moment, Lamon bustled in and began pumping her hand, talking in Thai and introducing her to an endless succession of officers, screaming at them to get inside and say their names. I suspected he was testing her prowess with the language, but she answered swiftly enough and he was soon content. Of course she would be an expert; Sabra didn't do things by halves.

Not understanding the conversation, I took the opportunity to slip out and fetch some snacks from the restaurant. Moon Bay Diner must have seen its out-of-season profits quadruple since the barricade began. As I waited for the cook to prepare our noodles, I stared at the curls and flourishes of the Thai menu. It was hard to believe I'd seen the wedding ring with my own eyes. That curl of silver, or perhaps white gold, its off-centre jewel with a genuine sort of glitter. My heart felt a pinch. Sabra was a married woman and had shown up when I least needed distraction. She would rub her happy relationship in my face and make me miserable.

How difficult would it be to go back? I thought of the hours of discussion I'd have to bring to mind and reverse, then there was the long journey by car and plane, all the way back to that first phone call I'd taken in London. Several days.

The elderly woman making lunch had a milky eye and looked like she could see things which were not of this world. I half-expected her to weigh in on my internal argument, but instead she just turned back to the wok. I inhaled the spicy vapours, suddenly aware that I wouldn't try to get out of this situation by rewinding the clock. For one thing, my body forbade it. Every cell reached out to Sabra, buzzing with a thrill hard to suppress. She had come out of her way, and could easily have refused the job – there must be a reason she agreed. Instead of handing me a chance meeting, fate had brought her deliberately onto my turf, to see me in my element, working magic and saving lives.

The old woman clucked her teeth to get my attention. Warm boxes were put in my hands.

'Bring back?' she said.

I nodded.

The food was moist with nut oil and smelled very tempting. When I got to the hut, Sabra's eyes sought mine and I could see she was hungrier than she'd let on. As I watched her roll up some chicken in a flatbread, I was pleased to note her fingers hadn't changed. Still the same square nails, a little dirty from travel. All the imprints they'd left on my flesh resurfaced and began to glow. I cleared my throat and picked up where the chief had left off.

'We hope he's smart enough not to harm the hostages. Somsith is an educated man, to some extent, a business owner in this town, and he knows any violence would be unwise.'

'What business?' she asked.

'Brothels,' said Lamon, not without a hint of glee. I wondered how many backhanders they'd had from this guy over the years. Sabra began to flick through her briefing papers.

I stepped outside, letting her read, and the chief joined

me, taking two cigarettes from the packet in my shirt. He'd become pretty familiar in a short space of time. A quiet minute passed with birds singing tentatively overhead, until a shout came from one of the perimeter guards. We ran over and saw him point eagerly to a ground-floor window. The shutters were open, and a man was keeping his head carefully in the shadows, cupping a hand over his mouth.

'What's he saying?' I was impatient.

'They want food,' said Lamon. 'It's Somsith talking. He . . . he wants to speak to the man in charge.'

I told the guard to go and fetch Sabra. She'd be a little green, but I only needed her to translate. Lamon barked something that made the officer pick up his heels.

It was unsurprising they needed supplies – the hotel's stores must be running low by now and the scent of curry drifted continuously across the street. Somsith carried on shouting, his voice occasionally breaking at the end of a sentence, making me wonder whether he was nervous or even a bit manic.

'Guns,' said Lamon. 'He confirms they have much firepower. He . . . he's on a rant about how the police used to be okay with him, that we used to . . . never matter. He asks . . . why everything has changed.' The police chief was giving me his edited version, leaving a few choice bits out. Another reason we needed an independent interpreter.

'What does he want?' Sabra came up behind me. I saw someone had handed her Boon-Nam's megaphone. She was perfectly calm and ready to begin.

'Tell him I'm here to help,' I instructed her. 'He knows I'm nothing to do with the local police. How can we help him?'

There was a pause as Somsith digested the addition of a woman's voice and took his time staring at Sabra. The light caught his nose, forehead and cheek, giving them an almost greenish tinge. Soon he started up again.

'Rice, eggs, soup, bread, roast chicken, milk, beer, bottles of water.' She matched his speed. 'Unless you want the hostages to starve.'

'What else?' I said.

The replies flew back, drowning out the birdsong. 'That you get out of here. What is your business? I've done nothing wrong.'

I hesitated, then told her to translate my response: 'That was how I understood it to be. Give us the innocent people and you can go free.'

A contemptuous laugh and the window slammed shut. Much as I'd expected, but it was worth a go. I went back to before he'd shut us out, and asked, 'Then what can we do to bring this to an end?'

Sabra's voice bending around the Thai vowels was something I could listen to all day. When he replied, she screwed up her face trying to understand. I put out a hand to stop her creeping forward. His words spurted out and then became rasps of air, sentences with their insides scooped out. With a look of impatience, he ducked back inside. Sabra was translating what she could.

'I want you to clear out. Leave a car. No, to guarantee you'll let me go back to my humble . . . I'm not sure.'

'It's okay.' I patted her arm.

When he reappeared, his voice was still a wheezy hiss. 'Food from restaurant. Leave on back doorstep.'

As we drew away, the window having been firmly slammed, Sabra said:

'Does he have asthma, perhaps, or laryngitis?'

I turned to Lamon, who shrugged.

'It's not in the file.'

'Keep a close watch and call me if he appears again.'

Nothing was heard from the hotel for the rest of the afternoon. Its curtains were closed, its frontage like a sleeping face. Even the food they'd requested sat on the doorstep until steam stopped issuing from the bags, until well after twilight, when an officer finally reported it had been drawn inside. Somsith was going to be a tricky customer, but not – I hoped – a dangerous one. Since he'd not tended to communicate during the hours of darkness, I left the chief playing dice with Melinda and went back to the hotel.

Some part of me knew she'd be there, waiting in the little bar that doubled up as reception, just a counter with a fridge of beers behind it. She looked over without surprise. What must she have seen when she stepped out of the taxi? A man slightly more solid than before – I hoped she could tell it was muscle rather than chub under my shirt – my face unshaven but fashionably so, my shirt rather more sweaty than was attractive, hair plentiful but shorter, with no sign of the silly black dye and ponytail I'd sported as a magician. Would she notice the dark drag of time beneath my eyes? Would she see how much I'd changed on the inside?

'Two beers.' I held up fingers to the receptionist, then sat down. 'Of all the hostage situations in all the world, you had to walk into mine.' It was about the worst line that had ever fallen from my lips and I chewed it back immediately. Unfortunately, this left me with nothing else to say.

'So, is this good or bad for you?' She grabbed the beer and wiped off its condensation. Sabra's aversion to small talk was intact.

My vague instinct to obscure my feelings lasted only a moment. 'What can I say? Disastrous.' Her face softened at my grin. She brought the bottle to her parched lips, and I added: 'Have you known Mel long?'

'Ages.'

I nodded. 'There was something familiar—'

'But you wouldn't have met her. She never came to Brum.'

So much for that theory. The beer was cold, its foaming bubbles eclipsing any flavour, yet it was quenching a world of thirst. My plastic chair squeaked as I leaned forward, noting the crook of her tanned elbow, the touch of moisture on her forehead.

'Anyway . . .' I continued. 'You're married?'

She nodded.

'Happily?'

'Yes.'

It was refreshing to have a conversation like this without needing to undo every other question. How easily we slipped back into habits of old, half-reading each other's minds, daring the other to take offence.

'You?' she asked.

'Yes.'

'Oh?'

'To my career.' That sounded naff, but I left it. I wanted to know what she thought of me now that I was an international risk specialist, not to mention the youngest DCI in the Met.

'I can see that.'

'What does your husband do?' I fished.

'He's a journal editor.' She gave me a warning look. 'A Clark Kent type.'

What the hell did that mean? My look of disdain made her laugh. 'He just looks a bit like Christopher Reeve, that's all. I've got it into my head now . . .'

Whatever she was saying, it wasn't a cry for rescue. Later, I'd use a few wiles to discover he was German, perhaps almost on a par with me in terms of looks – she had photos on her phone – though rather bland in the face. His main strength seemed to be devotion, and he'd apparently been trying to get Sabra to step away from interpretation work, which had brought her close to burnout on occasion, and focus on her music, even if it didn't pay. He sounded too nice by far.

'Are you allowed to drink on duty?' There was something sly in her tone. The idea of me being in the police clearly tickled her.

'Special dispensation,' I said. 'From myself.'

There it was, the old unprofessional me, coming out of its cave. I'd played by the rules – more or less – for so long I'd forgotten what it felt like. With a thrill, I pictured seizing her petal-smooth hand and pulling her into the jungle with me, where we'd go swimming under the waterfall that featured on the tourist leaflets. The torrent would massage our aching shoulders, and as night fell we'd peel off the little we were wearing to let it dry, or not, in the humming heat, our aquamarine ballet watched only by a small stray dog, who would later run off with my boxers.

'You've become quieter in your old age.' She delivered the equivalent of a verbal slap.

'Old age? I don't believe I'm the most vintage wine at this table.'

'That's why I can get away with it.'

We talked about Brussels, about her job and what she'd been doing. It sounded like she had managed to seek out and befriend all five of the interesting people who lived there, and, though she'd given up on Chinese, she'd done a postgrad diploma and was now a freelance Thai interpreter, working mostly with the EU. The woman she was assisting at present was very important, but also apparently 'a great laugh', and kind enough to put up with someone else for a few days while Sabra did this favour for the UK government.

'So once we're done here . . .' I prompted hesitantly.

'I'll be drowning in conference prep.'

My beer had grown tepid, as I nodded and took a last sip.

The next day, Somsith hailed us at about 10 a.m. We'd hardly been talking for more than fifteen minutes before his voice began to give out, but he seemed determined to hammer out terms. No one in that hotel could be getting much sleep, and the signs of strain were there in his gulping breaths, in the way he rubbed his forehead.

'Say that again,' I requested, as Sabra signalled difficulty understanding.

'We leave in car. Then you can come in and get the tourists.'

Two paces from my elbow, Melinda stood hugging her clipboard. The nature of conversation meant that tangents were inevitable, and it was important to stick to our agenda. Her ears would have pricked up at the car suggestion, since our top priority was always the safety of the hostages, followed by our own staff. She pulled her hair over her shoulder and I noticed it was tied with one of those fluffy bands popular with schoolgirls. An overpowering temptation squirmed in my soul, standing here amid people who looked up to me, who waited on my word of command. Somsith, in his window, looked sickly, hardly much of a threat. Melinda caught my eye and gave me a shy smile. It would not be hard to convince her that there was no single way to handle a barricade, no benchmark for how long it should reasonably continue. Everyone trusted me to the hilt. I looked at Sabra, perfectly turned out in a yellow, thigh-length tunic dotted with tiny bicycles, and came to a decision.

'How do I know you have hostages to bargain with?' I said.

Melinda's head swivelled round in surprise, but Sabra had already translated.

'You don't get to ask the questions,' snapped Somsith. I took a deep breath, letting the sensations of what I was doing imprint clearly in my mind.

'If you want something from me, I need to see a hostage.'

'Commander . . .' began my secondary. This was not in the list of tactics we'd discussed, but that didn't matter. Sabra was like my echo.

'Bring one to the door,' I said.

'No.'

'Bring one, or you have nothing to bargain with. I have it on good authority that all the tourists were outside the hotel when you arrived.'

A silence. His face remained in the window, waxy and malevolent.

'A lie.'

'Prove it.'

Melinda was actually tugging my arm, going white. We were there to dampen emotions not fan their flames. 'I'm just trying something,' I muttered, shaking her off.

'Do it,' I called again, 'or I go home and you take your chance with the army.'

The face vanished. We were so incongruous in this place. Night rain still seeped from the porous wooden boards above the entrance, gathering on the left-hand dragon's tail and dripping onto the tiled portico. A gecko crept along the edge of the rock where my foot rested.

Then a noise made us snap to attention. Contrary to all logic, one of the hotel's double doors was opening. A leg emerged, very pale and hairy, then part of a vibrant pink shirt. Finally, we saw a man in his early twenties, perhaps younger, held by the neck, his chest thrust awkwardly forward, indicating that Somsmith's gun was digging into his spine.

As soon as he saw us his eyes widened.

'Help me.' He was British. Welsh, if I wasn't deceived. His captor gave him a jab, then started to haul him back. Before the door could close, however, the young man turned sideways, wrenched away and ran at full pelt towards us, his knees lifting awkwardly, almost comically, to keep his balance with hands tied. There was a moment of horror while we all, Somsith included, watched to see what would happen. Then his gun jutted out into the air, firing a couple of angry shots – not too well-aimed – in the boy's wake. I thought the kid would reach us, but at the last instant I saw he'd been hit. The blood was a horrible clash: red all over his fuchsia shirt. We stood paralysed, ears ringing. His groan was the catalyst I needed to gather my wits and close my eyes.

'How do we know you have hostages?' I was saying, with Melinda looking up at me. This time I drew his antagonism just enough to flatten the negotiation into a stalemate. He didn't really know what he wanted yet anyway, and his communication was getting worse. I was okay with him being a little confused, uncertain what to request in order to secure the best deal for himself with the least likelihood of getting shot.

The Oasis Hotel floated cerise and serene in the heat, and Sabra lowered the megaphone. She hooked a strand of hair from across her face and raised her eyebrows, awaiting orders.

'I can't believe he keeps retreating,' Melinda exploded. 'This is going to drag on for ever.'

My voice was soothing. 'These things can take a little time.' I motioned them both away to headquarters, where the chief was brewing coffee. He made it with condensed milk, much to the silent disgust of the other officers, but Sabra and I each took a cup and smiled at the hit of outrageous sweetness.

These things could certainly take time, though I was a fool to think we had it.

Thirty-four

Imagine my chief super at Scotland Yard getting this report: *Having taken on the additional role of lead negotiator, DCI Knott was off-site for the best part of two hours, swimming in a waterfall with his interpreter.*

Luckily, he would never hear such scurrilous rumours because the only one who would tell them, even if she found out, was Melinda, and I'd already won her over heart and soul with my usual instant-connection formula. The moon rose above the canopy as Sabra and I emerged from the water, and we shook our garments vigorously since it was too dark to see any ants. Perhaps it was foolhardy to be in the jungle at night, even on a concrete trail, but when else would we get the chance?

'Arlo,' Sabra said, pulling on her plimsolls.

'What is it?'

'You're making me remember things.'

'Such as?'

She teetered on one foot and I steadied her, the smell of the waterfall still in her hair. She brushed a bug from her thigh.

'The person I used to be. When I was young.'

'We're both still young.'

'I've been feeling very old.'

I wiped droplets from her forehead with my thumb. Whenever anyone said that, it made me indignant, as did complaints about overtime. But I liked hearing her say it, imagining she knew what I'd suffered and we were somehow in harmony. We exchanged a monochrome smile and walked on, our shoes making lonesome taps on the concrete. The air was thick as soup.

'I haven't done anything like this in forever,' she went on. 'I've stopped doing it.' She grabbed my arm, her fingers tense. 'Here you are, a bloody hostage negotiator, living on the edge, and what have I ever done?'

'You got married.' This might have worked as a compliment, but right now I saw it was salt in the wound and took it back.

'I've forgotten how to live in the present,' she said. 'Like jumping into the waterfall, just because it's there, even if I'm more mosquito bite than woman.'

The edge of the jungle was near. Ahead was the road and

331

the lights of a garage. I ran my hands along her arms, finding I could create goosebumps. She batted me away and scratched both elbows furiously.

'They're hungry for you tonight,' I said.

Unable to resist any longer, my fingers slid under her damp hair, onto her scalp, and before I could say anything else she had reached up her lips to mine.

In the morning I was afraid I'd find her gloom-eyed and troubled, but she looked up brightly and waved a chopstick.

'Some sort of rice for breakfast.'

She snipped a formation of egg yolk in half and put one rubbery piece in her mouth. I was content not to talk about it if she didn't want to, but it meant the conversation happened inside my head: *What of your husband – aren't you happy? You sounded happy.* Then her response: *It's not that. The two things aren't mutually exclusive.* The conclusion of the made-up debate was that she loved her husband but missed the person she'd used to be. *The trouble is, Arlo*, said her imaginary voice, *I never stopped loving you.*

As I sat down, swirling my medicinal-smelling fruit juice, she seemed to nestle into my presence. I was everything I'd been before, only grown up at last, doing the things she'd had in mind when she asked why I wasn't working for MI5. Under my steady gaze, she pushed the plate away, took a sip of coffee and licked her lips. Damn, she was irresistible. I wanted to take her straight back to my room.

Readying myself for a reversal, I said, 'No guilt at all, then?'

Her spine straightened. 'You worry about yours, I'll worry about mine.' It was delivered with a watertight smile, but I could see she took it as a dig. There was no point trying to make her reveal her feelings; interrogation didn't work with Sabra and, in any case, we were having a nice breakfast. I went back to the medicinal fruit juice, pushing it aside and offering to get her another coffee.

Minutes later we were walking to the annex for another day of strategy and slow progress. The town was sleepy that morning, the road so quiet we could hear the sizzle of cicadas in the surrounding forest.

'So what's the plan, boss?'

I loved this so much. It was like being in some fabulous movie with an exotic setting, in which the bad guy and myself would dance the dance, outmanoeuvre each other, with Sabra in a supporting role, quietly astonished at my every prediction coming true. Did she still believe I could see the future, or had the miracle faded with time? I wanted her to see that there were no tricks here, that she could trust me completely.

Now that the negotiation had been strung out for a few days, deliveries of food to the hotel had taken on an almost domestic feel. We started getting empties and rubbish left out for us to take away. I no longer noticed the heavy humidity, the orioles ringing out at dawn.

My technique was to progress talks up to the point at which a decision could be made, then reverse at the last second, swapping my last remark for something that would puzzle him slightly or make him storm off. I saw it as a pattern in my mind, or a game: helping Somsith climb towards resolution, with a few unexpected leaps of progress, my team's anticipation growing, and then the magic words that would make him slither back down. His voice was often too rasping for us to hear, but when we offered him an inhaler he swore at us so ferociously we took cover in case it was followed by gunfire.

'So erratic, his behaviour,' Melinda sighed. She never questioned my decisions, but sometimes Lamon looked at me as if to ask whose reputation I'd pilfered.

Was the constant manipulation having an effect on our quarry? As a cornered criminal, his mental state was already under pressure, and if I'd stopped to think about it, if I'd delved, for even a moment, into everything a psychology degree had taught me, then the insanity of what I was doing might have hit home. All the signs were there. He was becoming impatient with us, quick to anger, his abuse sometimes so extreme and colloquial that Sabra could translate it only into question marks. He'd accuse us of laying traps, of trying to wear him down. Once he threw the boxes of rice out of the window, saying the food smelled of poison. Why would we send in poison when there were hostages? Amid bamboo wallpaper and uncleaned bathrooms, the tourists must have been in quite a state by now. At night, our generator gave the perimeter a stark, unnatural brilliance, but the windows betrayed an inner glow, an alive-light of people deep within. The thought of these hostages, the child especially, plucked at my conscience.

Finally, and perhaps fortuitously, the day came when I ran out of middle ground. Somsith's potential for dancing around the issues had been exhausted. With every demand I queried, he proposed to shoot a hostage.

'Come back!'

His head vanished for a terrifying instant. He brought the same young man to the window, still in the pink shirt, and bent him over the sill, a gun at his temple, and it was all I could do to soothe the brothel-owner enough to continue our conversation. Clearly Somsith was too exhausted to go on. He needed to bring this to a close, which meant I was out of time.

Unfortunately, his ragged mental state made him ask for things I could not give – ridiculous things, like having Lamon flogged in the hotel garden. After an hour or so of insults and threats, when I tried to keep everyone calm, a new plan was born. While we had him tired and talking here at the front, officers would attempt a stealthy entry round the back. Since we'd not tried anything like this to date, he'd not be expecting it. We would use his stress against him, coming in with several officers all at once, overwhelming him with a firm hand.

The group split in two, some men quietly climbing a tree that grew towards a first-floor window, while others waited to storm the back door. Because they were out of sight, the first I knew of the operation's commencement was a series of gun reports. These were followed by thuds as the officers' bodies fell limply to the ground, one man tumbling into view as he crushed a border of canna lilies. These were men who looked barely out of adolescence, yet who all had families; men who, the evening before, had made up an impromptu game throwing beer bottle-caps into a hat. A little shaken, I undid the assault, and when I said goodbye to the officers later that day, I shook their hands with a fervour that amused them. It was inconvenient, but bloodshed upset me more and more as I got older.

When Somsith had shot the fleeing hostage, he hadn't really been aiming. He'd fired primarily out of panic. Now they'd gunned down our men, shooting to kill. Up until this point, I'd felt I could handle the situation, but this was a new level of volatility. The time for stalling was over. Sabra was sticking to me like a limpet and it was time to pull out my A-game and end this.

As if that was all it would take.

The reality of the situation was coming slowly and dreadfully into focus. I'd been coasting along on my own arrogance, thinking we had all the time in the world to gather information, when in truth I'd gone past the point of no return and dragged everyone else along with me. Still, we hunkered down and put our heads together – Melinda, Sabra and me – with one goal. There were no more evening walks in the jungle. We were up late plotting scenarios, getting Lamon to call up anyone who might have information, some leverage or a piece of the perpetrator's history. Also inside the hotel was his brother, the only one with no prior criminal record, and the unseen bodyguard. But few local people were willing to talk. Somsith had fingers in many pies, including a human trafficking route that went all the way to Europe, and even to Britain. Extra kudos, should we manage to capture and interrogate him.

It was Melinda who found a beer girl in a local bar who'd once worked in his brothel. She would speak to no one else, and made my secondary come to an outside table and promise to ask loudly for tourist tips if the bar's owner came near. I'd never realised that these beer girls were employed – with the complicity of a large European brewery – to sell beer with a side order of sex. I'd begun to see the town as a sort of paradise, all flowers and rainforest, but now the paint was peeling. The Oasis Hotel got into my dreams more often than not, smug and ugly and impenetrable, its dragons razzing us. I yearned to crack it open and smash every pink fragment.

Melinda and I agreed our hard lines, our final tactics and timings. I hailed Somsith and he came to the window. I'd become so used to seeing his head in the darkness, cheeks that bunched and chewed over his words and spat; hardly a man so much as a creature in his lair.

'I'm bored of you, Englishman.'

It was a bad beginning. Whenever his voice gave out and we asked him to repeat something, he'd change it slightly, which would begin a whole new round of debate. I lost my patience several times, and then it took longer as I went backwards. The whole thing seemed to be going backwards.

'It's about goodwill,' Melinda kept prompting me. 'We're building trust.' No wonder she was trying to keep me on track – I was dying for a quick win. But he was tiring too.

'We don't want to be here for ever, even if you do.' His last words drifted into breath, into pain. Sabra was struggling. He was maddening himself with his own inability to negotiate. I wondered why he didn't feed instructions to his brother to do the shouting. Perhaps he didn't trust anyone else.

Finally, he slammed half of the window closed, making us jump, then directed his words inside the house. I became aware of a change taking place, something subtle in his tone. It did not occur to me that he was about to find the gap in my armour, that my confidence handling other people's risk – almost a motto by now – was about to disintegrate. Out of nowhere, a child of about ten appeared at the window. She was a girl with short dreadlocks, or perhaps just very matted hair.

'We give you this kid and you give us interpreter.'

'What?'

'Easier if we tell her demands. No shouting.'

Fury made me grab the megaphone.

338

'No deal,' I said. 'Why don't you write them down?'

Sabra took it back and translated.

'We discuss.'

'We're discussing right now.'

'No.' He said other words that were lost inside the room. For the first time, another man appeared – the bodyguard. He was at the door, opening it and shoving the girl out.

'Here, goodwill. When the lady interpreter comes, we'll do the list.'

His barked words were coolly converted into English. The door closed, and the girl teetered, looking at her feet. As one, we beckoned to her, and eventually she started moving, rubbernecking over her shoulder the whole time.

'It's fine,' Sabra comforted the girl, and damned if she didn't try to set off right then towards the house. I caught her arm so roughly she winced.

'Are you insane?'

'I'll be okay.'

I dragged her back as far as the road, leaving Melinda and the police to see to the kid.

'Sabra, he's an unknown quantity.' The very idea of her coming face to face with this lunatic made my voice crack.

'You said yourself, we need this to end. How mad will they be if I don't go in?'

I turned away, lifted my face to the white linen sky and asked why this was happening. It was my doing: I'd steamed away Sabra's hard-won professional coating to leave someone blithely trusting, happy to leap into the jaws of death. We were speeding towards the ice cream van all over again.

'I can't protect you.'

'You don't need to.'

There is no reason to recount the days and weeks that followed, all lived in that one tiny slot of time, my undoing back through the conversation, through our nights of frolicking. No matter what I did, Somsith always ran out of breath and wanted his own interpreter, and I would watch Sabra shrug off my entreaties and walk with determination through the hotel gates.

The instant itself seemed calcified in time, a hard nodule that I could not circumvent. People came and asked why I was white as bone and shivering beneath my sweat. Yes, I was ill, sick at the very thought of seeing blood spread through that pale-yellow top, drowning the bicycles. Or worse. The beer girl had showed Melinda the puckered stepping stones that traversed her belly: cigarette burns when Somsith thought he'd been double-crossed. Sabra was fiery enough for anything; she would always fight back, she would take every opportunity to escape. The situation was brimming with danger, yet she was annoyingly fearless. This was her chance to make up for all those years of office work, her personal claim to bravery. I'd been doing it for a decade and now it was her turn, now that she felt, much to my distress, safe in my hands again.

I begged Sabra not to go, I told her my life was on the line, that I loved her. My arms spread wide and prevented her from going, causing scenes that made police officers run in to intervene, that made Lamon punch me in the face and hogtie me on the ground. I went back to the night before, kidnapped her, put a bag over her head, drove her to Bangkok and left her in a café. She came back and things played out the same way, only with a day's delay. I changed tactics, I told him to shoot everyone. Nothing worked.

I tried being mean to her, hoping she'd quit or at least be unwilling to give her all. It was going fairly well, until she looked at me with such sadness that my heart broke. Even a flicker of affection was enough to set things on their usual course. Damn it, I was out of practice being a bastard. An easier prospect was to make her ill. Sickness had done for Boon-Nam, after all, and Melinda got slightly ill after every curry. It would be a plausible thing to happen in rural Thailand. But all those years of beetroot soup and offal had given Sabra an iron constitution. She could smell a rotten egg a mile off, and I couldn't find anything non-dangerous to put in her food that she wouldn't detect.

Though I was loathe to give up these golden days we'd had together, I lay on my bed and prepared to go back to the beginning, though a week would leave me disorientated and useless as a commander. My eyes closed and the actions swam in my head. They were viscose, melting together, the exhaustion making them interweave and pile up and merge and refuse to get into a line. Her arrival, the moment she stepped from the car, was so powerful it seemed to have petrified, and all I could feel was my twisted-tree shape as I turned away in shock. My eyes opened and filled with tears.

How strange it must have been for her to glance back, as she walked towards the dragons, and see me folding to the floor, broken by a thousand attempts to stop her. All I could picture was blood through fabric, blood through bicycles. Whatever I said to make him kill her, even if it was unsaid, would stay with me, along with the knowledge that a knife had penetrated her flesh. I had a voodoo doll for a heart, and it was Sabra.

'Stop,' I said weakly. The same meaningless words over and over. 'Don't do this.'

She turned, slowly, and retraced her steps. I rose up to meet her, my whole body shaking, imploding with hope, and she gave me a brief, fierce kiss on the lips.

'I'll keep the room service to a minimum, okay?'

That was it. What a time to wind me up, even as she hurried towards her doom. They must have been watching. The door opened as if by magic, and then she was gone.

Thirty-four

One of the first incidents I attended, soon after taking over DCI Green's patch in London, involved a man who had climbed up to the mezzanine of a book store and was threatening to immolate himself. Some clumsy officer dropped a fire extinguisher in the stairwell, and it made such a racket he thought we were storming the place. He tipped the petrol can over his head, and before we could get to him he'd coaxed a flame from his lighter and gone up like a torch.

Of course, with my involvement he was saved, as were many others: people who had been stabbed or hit by trains, or who'd jumped into the Thames; individuals caught up in rare situations involving terrorists and all-too-common cases of domestic violence. Each time, I would keep going back until we got it right, dreaming and re-dreaming the nightmare until seeing a skull flatten or a knife going into flesh meant nothing to me. I might have done the whole eighteen-hour standoff several times already, colleagues never knowing. But I was damned if I'd let a man send himself up in flames or turn his family into pools of type-O blood. Not when I was in charge. Other people's risk – that was my business.

Melinda had told Sabra all of these tales, had conveyed to her the depth and breadth of my reputation, still with tiny stars in her eyes. No one died on my watch – or, at least, no one stayed dead. Little wonder Sabra trusted me so implicitly. Now that anarchy was in charge, the idea that she might be suffering stopped my heart with a cold finger. I was balled up so tightly I could hardly drag myself over to the hotel walls to investigate the crash we heard as something was hurled from a window.

'It's a vase,' said Melinda, turning over a concave piece of ceramic with her toe.

A little design of flowers showed she was right. I looked up at the shutters, which had been closed again. My secondary had already extracted the sheet of paper inside the vase, and when I recognised the handwriting I snatched it from her. The script was so recognisable, so familiar, though her scrawl had become smaller and more confident since university days. The hostage takers' demands had been listed and were, for the first time, reasonably clear, though completely in the realms of make-believe. They had presumably put the paper in a vase so they could throw it a distance, rather than having the list flutter down awkwardly below the window. I would not have been surprised to learn that it was Sabra's idea. The last thing written was that they would keep the interpreter until the requirements were fulfilled.

Lamon exhaled disdainfully. 'That's enough,' he said, waving their ludicrous requests in my face. 'We go in tonight, round the back first, then storm the front.'

Terror seized me. 'We'll assess the situation properly before doing anything rash.'

'You've been assessing it for a week. What progress have you made?' His features clouded over, eyelids coming down as he mentally took himself off my team. I later found he'd complained to his superiors about my failings, requesting authority to take command.

This, and other things, came to light when London called, furious at the delay, fearful of being embarrassed in an international setting. Didn't I know the Australian government were clamouring for news of the situation? Why hadn't I been able to ascertain what other nationals were involved? Why hadn't I immediately requested another negotiator? Where were my reports, and why the hell had I let a civilian interpreter affiliated with the European Court of Justice enter an armed barricade?

The treacherous nature of the situation cut no ice with them, nor did our suspicions of mental instability. I'd lost control and, worst of all, had nothing up my sleeve. The only way I could stop Lamon, who now flicked ash my way more often than he spoke to me, was to come up with my own cast-iron tactic to end the standoff.

When I outlined my proposal to the police chief, he looked incredulous.

'Give them everything they want? That's your plan?'

I bristled.

'Our priorities are the safety of the hostages and ourselves.'

'Have you read this?' He waved the now-crumpled and nicotine-stained slip of hotel writing paper in my face. 'An armoured vehicle, a million baht to be handed in for counting, no police, no chasing, and even then we must believe they will leave the one hostage they take with them at a roadside garage. Let me tell you, that will not be on this side of the border, and what if he changes his mind again?'

'This is what we're doing. It better meets our priorities.'

'It better meets *your* priorities,' he snapped. 'But I've got no confidence in you. Some of the things you've said to this guy. Couple of times he's been ready to strike a deal, and you let it fall through your fingers. You think I don't see it, but I do. Pay is good, yes? Or maybe you don't like your wife. I don't care. All I know is, you wasted my time, and my men's time. You were meant to be such a big-shot nego-tiator, they told us it would be worth it, even though we'd have to translate, but we should have handled this ourselves.'

There it was, the disintegration of my pedestal. I stole a

glance at Melinda to see if she felt the same way and was horrified to detect, beneath her supportive grimace, a hint of doubt.

My jab caught him on the chin, eliciting only a grunt, but at least it knocked that self-satisfied, predatory expression off his face.

Then we were back at my explanation of the plan.

'Both governments have agreed.' My hand flew up to silence his interjection. 'This is an order, not a discussion. I'm still the commander here.'

I knew London would back the plan, and I got them to email me a written confirmation to forestall the imminent mutiny. Lamon wanted blood, but objectively my proposal was the safest course of action. Better to covertly pursue a vehicle and have only one hostage left to extract.

Besides, the pink, dripping frontage of the hotel with its stinking ponds was starting to make all of us a little sick. I stood looking at the dragons for a long time before hailing those inside. Seeing Sabra's face at the window, where we'd been so accustomed to Somsith appearing, packed a punch that made me dizzy.

'Are you ok?' I said. There was a racket behind her.

'Will you meet our demands?' Her expression was neutral, her delivery wooden, though in a voice as strong and clear as ever.

'Sabra, are you ok?'

A tremor crossed her expression. In between translating

the phrases that were being hurled at her from behind, she managed a nod.

They were impatient, Somsith soon appearing beside her to make sure there was no gesturing or funny business that he couldn't see.

'All the demands?' he double-checked.

'We can't get the armoured car until 1900 hours tomorrow.'

'The money before.'

'Affirmative.'

'The police gone.'

'Yes.'

'How do we know they'll be gone?'

'They'll send you postcards from Hawaii.'

Fucking moron. I hated how close he was to Sabra. If I didn't think he'd shoot me in the face I'd walk straight up to the window and lamp him. Back I went.

'They'll be gone.'

Somsith's attempts at cunning would be his downfall. He was terrible at this. It was a testament to his loosening grip on reality that he thought the gang had the smallest hope of getting away, even under cover of darkness, in an armoured vehicle. Particularly in view of the trafficking connection, governments would collaborate to ensure their security services never stopped hunting him.

'Do you swear?'

'As a representative of the Metropolitan Police Service, I swear. We want the hostages safe. That's all that matters.'

I held my breath, fearing Sabra would relay a dull 'I don't believe you.' He was slippery enough for anything. Instead there was a long pause. The jungle insects whined as though being twisted. Then Sabra said:

'The money must be here no later than 1700 hours. Any tricks, and they will be executed.' Somsith, on her left, prodded her, and she added, 'I will be executed.'

I put down the megaphone, afraid Melinda would see my arm shaking, and we retreated, keeping a close watch.

As evening fell, officers reported sounds coming from the hotel, on one occasion a frightened squeal. Obviously, things were being shifted around, a few defences shored up in case of last-minute treachery or escape attempts. We had a day to wait. I lived with one foot inside the grisly funhouse I imagined to be Somsith's mind, willing him to keep a clear head, worrying that the passage of time might make some new idea occur to him. Perhaps he'd want a helicopter, or to inflict retribution on the police, or some other wild request that his temporary position of power might make him think plausible.

I walked up and down the road, occasionally getting in the way of someone's farm truck, staring at tarmac discoloured by oil leaks or roadkill, puckered as tree roots burrowed underneath. I'd become so used to winning every game of dice, always knowing what everyone's next step would be. Here I was powerless, a figure who could do nothing but put one foot in front of the other, on a road that smelled of sour milk and curry and rotting leaves, everything made fetid by the slow fermentation of time. I'd sleepwalked into this nightmare, and now there was no way out.

Sabra appeared at the window once. Just the curve of her cheek, ashen as soap. If there was so much as a fingernail-scratch on that face I would cut them in two.

'The armoured car is here,' Lamon said, beckoning. 'They've had the money already. I'm happy to say that if it's not recovered I won't be held responsible.' He smiled thinly.

Although the police would be gone, as agreed, there would be a small number of specialist army personnel concealed at strategic points. There would also be a security detail along the probable escape route, poised to follow the car undetected. I was not happy with this adjunct to the plan, but I couldn't do much to stop it.

The armoured vehicle was a jeep with a reinforced body and no window that wasn't bulletproof. It could have been booby-trapped, but they knew we wouldn't dare. I'd made Melinda go back to the hotel, but had insisted on being present myself, furnished with a handgun from the army supply truck. It felt heavy in my hand, an omen of what was to come. Earlier we'd packed up the perimeter lights, the best way to make a show of leaving; now the Oasis was as sleepy as any other hotel out of season, lit only by its own yellowy garden and porch lights, just above the dragons, who looked longingly towards the clouds of circling flies.

Where I was concealed, the wall been damaged and

re-patched, but not to its original height. The palms were completely in darkness and scratched my face as I climbed down into the hotel garden. Now I was a watcher unseen, and thoughts came unbidden to my mind: a flashback to Nina and her quantum behaviours, atoms like terrorists in a house, with the viewer influencing how they act. I hunkered down even lower, wanting to be certain no beam of torchlight could pick out my head. The drive was just yards away, and at 1900 exactly an officer reversed the vehicle towards the hotel entrance – Somsith had been very specific – leaving the key in the ignition before hurrying off.

The hotel door opened.

The person who appeared was Sabra, staring into the dewy light. My heart thundered joyously. The deal was that they'd leave the hostages in the house and we'd release them afterwards, but Sabra's work was done so she was free to go. Perhaps she'd even charmed them enough to be seen as an ally. Her slim legs navigated the doorstep, one arm held behind. Then a chill struck me.

Her wrist was gripped by a man too stocky to be Somsith. It was the bodyguard. He marched her forward to the jeep and opened the door. The cogs of my mind were so gunked up with fear that it had taken me all this time to realise Sabra was the hostage going with them. The injustice of it, when she'd helped so willingly. A tremendous anger boiled up inside me. They were monsters, snakes swallowing people and sucking out the money, gobbling up hostages, trafficked women, beer girls and my beloved Sabra. With superhuman effort, I stilled myself, knowing her life now depended on the getaway going like clockwork.

Once the bodyguard had motioned her into the back seat and closed the door, he went round to the driver's side. The hotel was now disgorging the other two men. Every instinct told me to do something, anything, to stop this happening, but she was already in the jeep. It would be no good returning to the minute before, because she'd still be in close proximity to the bodyguard's gun. The one thing I knew, above all else, is that I was not capable of seeing Sabra shot. So there was no choice except to bite down on my agony and let her be driven away; the start of a whole new ordeal for both of us.

Then the gap. The dangerous gap. Sabra saw it. That span of seconds between the bodyguard getting into the vehicle and the other two not yet having reached it. Her eyes went to the door handle, her body shifting to get a grip. I heard the click, the slight scrape as it opened. They heard too. She was out and dashing towards the road, and they were lunging forward into a firing stance, huge weapons drawn, both brothers together, and her feet slapped the concrete, and before I heard the shots I sucked back the last ten breaths I'd taken – sucked them fit to choke – and rewound to that first palm leaf I'd held back from my face.

The memory trace sent my heart into overdrive, giving me a strange ache in my lungs and the sense of having hyperventilated. It had never affected me this badly before. From between the trees to either side, and along the top of the wall, I sensed the invisible sightlines of guns, men camouflaged as I was, all working to a plan and bound by orders. Now Sabra was out of the hotel, there was only one safe place for her to be. The course of action I was about to take was not heroic. Our protocols, not to mention years of training, clearly outlined the dangers of going rogue in the middle of an operation. That was how people died. It was how you skipped disciplinary proceedings and went straight to dismissal. But I was going to do it all the same.

Once again, the bodyguard was closing the jeep door behind her – that sight of her knees tucking in, so childlike, dragged at my heart. I took three steps forward, aimed and shot him in the chest.

Sabra's shriek was dulled by the thick glass of the vehicle. She started to rattle the door, but I dashed over and stood against it, ducking to be less of an obvious target for Somsith and his brother, who had run out but were now confusedly trying to retreat.

Shouts came from the perimeter like the first rumbles of a thunderstorm. The brother had got back inside and was shooting through a window. Somsith was still out front, fixated on the bulky crocodile-shape of his dead bodyguard. He raised his gun. I shot and missed. I needed cover but couldn't risk Sabra opening the door. Men in dappled combat gear appeared, guns blazing all around. I remember the little dots of light they made, flashing against the ponds, reflecting up the walls, like noisy fireflies. When he fired again, I felt the punch of bullets – no pain, just something like the finger of big Glen, the bully at school, jabbing into a bit of soft skin between my arm and chest. Again and again and again, between my ribs, though what I noticed was my arm smacking into the concrete, the close-up of the jeep wheels and the creature sheltering beneath. It slithered away, quickly as a thought, into the long grass.

Thirty-four

In heaven, they wake you with music. That's the strangest thing. They rouse your senses one at a time, so you hear the flutes, the plucking of a mandolin, then finally a breeze full of nectar drifts through the French window, and your eyes open.

Beyond my room was a courtyard garden. Four trees stuck out leafy tongues to catch snowflake flowers. The people outside wore in white, emerging through their own individual patio doors. One patient who passed by looked familiar; I swear he had the face of the bodyguard, but he turned away and I couldn't be sure.

My room consisted of a bed, two generous armchairs and an en-suite bathroom. On a sideboard were vases, a marble

Buddha and a bowl filled with plastic fruit. The military hospital where I'd been before seemed like an uncomfortable, sweaty dream in comparison. Melinda had visited me there, on her way back through Bangkok, but I was in a stupor and nothing she said made any sense. I got the impression I was in big trouble, but that was it, and this information just got in the way of what I really wanted to know.

Now, for my sins, I was recuperating in a place that seemed to be part hotel, part nursing home. There was a fountain in the courtyard, splishing merrily, and someone was cupping the water – I heard the trickle as it was released, flicked from fingertips. The woman was wearing a loose tunic top, cream with a motif of two coral-bright birds, and skinny jeans beneath. I sat up. The sun appeared to ignite her hair as she came towards me and stepped through the open door.

'This is much nicer. No soldiers staring.'

Sabra perched on my bed, tucking one leg beneath her. I noticed bare ankles – my hands longing to touch the jut of bone.

'You came to the army hospital?'

'Once, but you were out of it.'

I closed my eyes, sifting the images of Sabra's face for one that was not from a dream. There had been so many dreams, nightmares too, where the car exploded, or she got out and was shot. Sometimes I was killed and drifted above the scene like a ghost that could haunt only that one moment, eternally rueing my mistake.

'What is this place?'

'Suan Som,' she said. 'It means "the Orange Grove".'

'Ah.' I glanced at the bowl on the sideboard. 'That explains the imitation oranges.'

A smile. 'These are real.' She handed me a waxy sphere. 'Go on.'

With strange reluctance, I dug a thumbnail into the fruit and it opened perfectly; a fat clementine, flowering into segments.

Outside, someone chuckled, a ripple of sound that merged perfectly with the falling water. Perhaps the trees blossomed all year round, the air always sweet. Though my body still ached with every breath, I felt at peace.

'You nearly got yourself totalled,' she added. 'Melinda told me your supervisors are pissed.'

I shrugged.

'I know I am,' she continued.

'You're pissed?'

'Livid. I even got you this card.' She handed me an envelope from which I extracted a greetings card, rather battered, probably bought from one of those convenience stores that sold English newspapers. The front bulged with a grey teddy bear in a car. 'Well done,' it said. The words 'for passing your driving test' were crossed out, replaced with 'for not dying stupidly'.

A grin spread involuntarily across my face.

'You nearly didn't get this card,' she said.

'Well, I appreciate it.'

There was a pause as she crumpled up the envelope and pitched it neatly into the waste paper bin. A cyclone of memories swirled in the back of my head. I sat a little straighter and asked her to fill in the blanks, to tell me how the barricade had ended.

'What do you know already?' she said.

'No hostages killed. That's the main thing.'

She nodded. 'Just that one hippy guy hurt when he tried to climb out of the window.'

'The bodyguard?'

'Dead.'

She spoke matter-of-factly, but for me the words fell like blows. I had killed a man. Not injured . . . killed. It felt so obvious at the time, so necessary to put him out of action, almost as though we were playing a game and it was my next move. I could have maimed him, but instead I'd gone straight for the heart.

'Arlo?' Sabra must have seen the blood drain from my face. Her hand covered mine, so warm and good that I could focus on the feel of it and nothing else. 'The brother was shot by the army, and Somsith—'

'He was shot?'

'Yes, but he survived. He must be out of hospital now, but I expect they've put him somewhere very secure.'

Hearing he was still alive unnerved me almost as much as knowing the other two were dead.

'I never thought I'd kill anyone.' My lips squashed and slurred the words. 'I mean, there might have been some sort of shoot-out later—'

'You stopped me being trapped with them on some godawful joyride.' She moved closer, lowering her voice. 'Arlo, there's a good chance you saved my life. You do know that, right?'

Every time she said my name, the dozen years we'd been apart flickered like a faulty lightbulb. We were exactly the same as we'd always been.

'How long are you staying?' I said.

'As long as you need.'

'What if that's for ever?'

She just smiled. I tried to hide my disappointment.

'So I'm definitely in the shit at work, then?'

'Sorry.'

'Not your fault.' Before this began, the thought of falling from grace would have terrified me. My self-respect was built entirely on an untarnished reputation, but how little it seemed to matter now. I'd throw away a thousand admiring handshakes in exchange for one squeeze from Sabra's strong string-hardened fingers. It was almost a shame my chief super wasn't flying to Bangkok to give me a damn good bollocking, right here in the recovery centre, so she could watch. Endangering the operation, the hostages, myself, not to mention shooting one of the suspects stone-dead . . . He'd demote me on the spot, and Sabra could witness the fireworks of a glittering career going up in smoke.

'You should rest,' she said, registering the twitch as my eyes yearned for sleep. I floated upward an inch as she rose from the bed.

'Don't go.'

She waved away my pathetic entreaty and went through the other door, vanishing into a corridor. Once my imagination had walked her back to some local guesthouse, I tried to formulate a plan, think about tactics . . . but drowsiness was overpowering me, suffusing every cell in my body. Or was it that voice again, the one that always reverberated somewhere just below the level of hearing? Rest now – it seemed to say – rest and recover.

I woke sporadically throughout the day and during the night, but lacked the strength to stay conscious for long. Nurses drifted in and out, pristine in their starched uniforms. I dreamt of treacherous landscapes, seething with sounds and tastes and colours, and then snapped into a lucid state, my brain firing on all cylinders even while it acknowledged being asleep.

One scene was another hospital room, the chamber Mum had lain in, I think, or one very similar. A figure was in the bed, under the sheets, and that doctor with grey hair was explaining to me in low, careful tones about blood flow, tears in arteries and how long she had left. It wasn't like before, when it had all gone over my head. This time I heard and understood, believed him when he said she would not recover, choked in anguish when he told me to say goodbye. When I awoke, I must have been yelling. A nurse ran in – how things recur – and was yanking open a drawer full of syringes when I managed to convince her, uncertain she could understand my breathless English, that I didn't need sedating.

Perhaps it was just a dose of that old hospital fear returning, too many long-forgotten associations, but because my mind was too muddled to patch together the right images, the person lying in the bed had been Sabra, red hair limp across her forehead. Little wonder, since she'd been on my mind constantly, and hers was the face I longed to see; but the dream had been particularly unpleasant and, once the hospital's morning pan-pipes were fluting delicately into my room, I forced myself to stand, walk around a little and generally reassure myself that I was in the land of the living. They brought me orange juice and a breakfast of lava-hot curry and rice with a fried egg on the side. I was just savouring the smell, wondering if I was ready to eat, when she appeared at the door.

'What's up?' The shoulder bag slid from her arm.

'Nothing. Now.'

We took a moment to smile nonchalantly at each other, almost shy. Then all the questions I'd been too self-absorbed to ask yesterday bubbled up, and Sabra told me how she'd been looked after following the traumatic incident, given the once-over by a female military doctor, allowed sick leave by her employer and generally handled with care. During her time as a hostage, she'd been subjected to nothing more offensive than sly questions designed to make her reveal our weaknesses, and it had not been difficult to plead ignorance as a lowly interpreter. Too valuable for them to harm, she'd been kept with whichever of the three was on watch at the window, fed with rice and water and put to bed on an armchair infused with cigarette smoke.

My admiration for her resilience was renewed. Her husband had offered to fly over and accompany her back to Brussels, and she had turned him down. Even as Sabra described the phone call in her most casual voice, I was reading what my dad would call 'the subtext', trying to detect any mixed feelings, until she changed the subject abruptly.

'What about your nan? Your sister?'

I came out of my trance and took a sip of juice. 'Next of kin do get told about these things. I'm sure the flowers are in the post.'

The world and everyone in it seemed a long way away, and far less interesting than the person in front of me, chewing her cinnamon gum.

In fact, I received a call from Nan later that day. It had taken her until now to track down the right hospital, and she was touchingly concerned, almost tearful, though I think it was partly joy at having finally got me on the phone. Erin would have called too, apparently, but she was busy moving house for a year-long sabbatical in Cumbria.

It was easier to talk about Erin than describe what I'd just gone through. I wasn't ready and, in any case, Nan seemed too emotional to handle a blow-by-blow account. Instead I played it down, assured her I was recovering and would soon be on a plane home. The cold, clear air of the English countryside was a pleasant prospect in the midst of this unremitting heat. I'd drink ale in a pub with picnic benches and eat a steak with thick-cut chips. Perhaps I'd visit Erin in the lakes, though the thought made me remember, with shame, how I'd unwittingly rubbed the stunning views in my sister's face.

'I don't think she should go,' I told Nan. 'Not on her own.' What if she had a fall? There would be no Nina to keep an eye on her. Nan assured me her granddaughter was confident, and, while her new course of drugs could not cure the partial blindness, it was at least slowing the progression. I pictured my sister feeling her way around a living room, making a mental note of every jutting corner, every bookcase and sideboard, every light switch and socket. It must be a terrible thing to lose your sight. Why had it not struck me before? Perhaps in my weakened condition I could feel it more keenly, the helplessness of it, the dependence on others. No wonder she was so grumpy. When I got back, things would be different between Erin and me. There would be a proper family bond, and no more one-upmanship. It was nothing short of a vow, made here in the Orange Grove. I didn't have the least suspicion it would lead to anything bad.

When I put the phone down, I realised that Dad had been absent from our topics of conversation, and I'd forgotten to ask about him. The duck-down pillows rumpled under my shoulders. If Erin told him I'd been shot, would he even remember who I was? He'd be gluing a path of squares to a checkerboard, wiping the stickiness from his thumb, searching his memory for a son. Even then, it would be a boy he found, fifteen at the oldest. What did he suppose had happened to me? His mind was a backwater of time in which his children enjoyed an eternal youth; Erin had told me as much. Even if I travelled to Luton to see him every day, on leaving his flat I would vanish, like a thought. He had too strong a need for his board game, and on some level it made sense: what charms did reality have compared to a game you could win?

As I improved over the next few days, my routine was built around Sabra – waiting for her in the courtyard each morning, while it was still cool. The fragrance of the citrus trees was like a beautiful remnant of the night's dreams. We earned a stern look from the head nurse for splashing each other with the fountain, making other residents crane their necks to see what all the giggling was about. The staff were ready for me to leave before I was. As the day approached, I found myself hardly able to eat or sleep.

When Sabra showed up, my suitcase was still not packed and I was shivering in bed.

'I think I've caught a chill.'

'Here?' That amused her. 'Come on, Arlo, think of that steak waiting for you at home.'

'And what's waiting for you?'

She was silent. It had become too serious for banter. I'd seen her come in with red eyes, refusing to talk lightly about her husband any longer. She'd already given me an inkling of her feelings since we'd been together in Tamrieng, even before everything went crazy. Life is short and bumpy – the gun whispered as much when it was held to her head. She was no longer certain about returning to another existence.

I got down on one knee, resisting her attempts to drag me up again. 'Sabra Dil, will you eat steak with me?'

'Oh, fuck off,' she said. But it was our last day together and I needed an answer. My gaze was unblinking until she added, 'I can't just up and move.'

'You've done it before.'

'It's different when you're young.'

'Sabra.' I stroked her arm gently. 'There's nothing you can't do. Every path is open to you.' My tone hinted of secrets, of the special knowledge I'd claimed to possess about the future. There were three cups and she should trust me to know what sweet things lay beneath. All the lessons of the past fled my memory, everything that trickery had cost. The texture of her skin absorbed me completely, so it never occurred that I might be repeating the same mistakes, turning the ignition on that same cycle of trust, recklessness, fear. 'Come on,' I said. 'How often does someone invite you to eat steak?'

And how often does someone save your life?

'It's rare,' she admitted, then allowed herself a smile at the pun. 'But I can't.'

As she shook her head, a desperate longing came over me. This couldn't be all it meant, to have emerged on the other side of death like this, with Sabra in tow. Surely she wouldn't just vanish again? Her hand was restless and boiling hot. In times past, I would concentrate my whole being into tracing its maze, the cul-de-sacs, knuckle-twists and alleyways of her fingers. There was nothing I wouldn't give to keep hold of it.

'There's just one thing I don't understand,' she added. 'You always had that slight ability to foresee outcomes, didn't you?' Her choice of language was more formal than it used to be, affected by a few years in diplomatic circles.

'So?'

'So . . . didn't you know you'd be hit?'

A scattering of petals drifted through the French windows, settling peacefully on the carpet. Without knowing it, I'd been chasing this moment for a long time, unaware what it would take to get here, or how it would feel. There was nothing more I needed to say. Asking the question was enough to make her guess the answer, to understand that saving her was only half the story, because even if I'd known what would happen, I'd have done it anyway.

I'd have given my life.

Part 1

THE LOST PIECE

Thirty-six

It had been slow around the edge of Birmingham, often stationary. We were behind the van of a tour company with a print of Iceland across its back window. Being somewhat exhausted, I kept reading the 'Diverse' in *Diverse Landscapes* as 'Divorce', picturing a tundra of cracking earth, tufts of grass splitting, its inhabitants uncertain where to step. The longer we were in traffic, the wilder my daydream became – perhaps there were a few too many exhaust fumes seeping through the air ducts.

Sabra rested her head on my shoulder while she fiddled with the stereo, seeking the most static-free version of Radio 6 music. Above the lines of traffic, the sky was dominated by a fortress-like cloud that trailed off into a line, as though letting down a drawbridge.

'How about a bouncy castle for the kids?' I asked. She shot me a look of fond derision.

'There will already be a trampoline, a soft play area and my cousin's Xbox.'

'Well, let's get a bouncy castle too.'

Sabra had to keep reminding me it was not a wedding, that we didn't need to go overboard. But I was taking delight in organising everything I could think of. The first words she said to me, once her marriage had been officially terminated, were: 'Don't even think of proposing.' Once had been enough. Instead we'd hold a summer solstice party, inviting all our friends and family, who would hopefully grasp the importance of this euphemistic occasion from my gilt-edged, hand-printed invitations. Sabra had a soft spot for things that were a bit new-age, for Celtic jewellery and stone circles, so our party would have a broad theme of 'ancient times'.

We'd been looking for a place to erect a marquee, and, much to my delight, a family friend was willing to offer his field, in a prime location near Glastonbury Tor. Luckily, the eponymous festival was having a fallow year, so we wouldn't have to compete. People could stay in town, and the more intrepid attendees could camp between the cowpats. I'd narrowly failed to persuade Sabra to have a local druid perform a handfasting ceremony, and I kept leaving his business card around the flat in case she changed her mind, even though there was now only a week to go. Religion was immaterial; it was tying the knot that mattered.

What a year it had been. When people told me how fortunate I was, it took me a minute to realise they meant surviving three bullets rather than having Sabra back in my life. It was hard to describe the pleasure of seeing her put her violin to sleep each night in its case. Her strong fingers would run along the length of the bow, always fearing to lose a few hairs, as even a dust-pinch change in weight would make a difference. Our flat had views of Brockwell Park, and I'd never thought it possible to derive so much happiness from the simple task of boiling two eggs on a Saturday morning, waiting with childlike anticipation for Sabra to return from her run.

She was subsisting on translation work while she investigated orchestras and chamber groups, being quite choosy and often finding fault with their standards. Where there were opportunities to get her feet under the table, I came along, clinking glasses of wine in echoey concert halls, helping her backtrack if any part of the schmoozing didn't go to plan. I made sure she was offered auditions, and if they were a waste of time I went back far enough to strike them from the diary. It was all about cushioning her from disheartening experiences, though I must have overdone the fairy godmothering because somehow she detected it. 'I've had plenty of time to make peace with the idea of not being the world's greatest violinist,' she insisted, giving me a talking-to after a particularly brutal audition. 'Quit trying to help.'

But it was difficult to sit by and do nothing, especially when she put herself through periods of practice so intense they made her forget everything, even meals. She would go over a single note again and again to get it right. Sometimes, as I climbed the stairs to our top-floor flat, hearing the piece pick up speed until the bow was almost squeaking, I felt an anxiety in the sound, as though she'd staked everything on perfecting the tricky final phrase of this concerto. Once she'd decided to leave her husband, no word of regret passed her lips, but she'd been settled in Brussels and enjoying her job. We both felt the need to validate her decision.

After a few disciplinary meetings, I was back to regular CID work, escaping worse punishment purely because the hostages happened to have survived. My penance was some hard graft on volume crime, and while they would still ask me to help with call-outs involving barricades, I'd more often be given the role of secondary negotiator. They wanted me to be in no doubt of the price of my arrogance. But being downgraded had its advantages. Fewer terrorist situations or standoffs between gangs meant I was safer and Sabra less worried. These days, the urge to use my special skills had dwindled. All those years of undoing had worn me down, made me thin. I still got a kick out of saving the disturbed, the troubled and victimised, but trial and error was no longer my go-to approach. I preferred to proceed with caution, living for the evenings and weekends, when I could relate my stories to Sabra over a cup of chai tea.

Like a soft red carpet, the June days were lengthening, drawing us closer to the party. It was time to make good on my promise and fetch Erin from her cottage, since it was now unviable for her to manage country bus routes and read train departure boards. As I'd decided in Thailand, things would be different between us. I wouldn't let her slide into darkness alone.

When we finally got onto the M6, dreading the congestion, it was almost deserted. 'This is uncanny,' Sabra remarked. We purred along in our new Volvo, overtaking a row of army trucks and a horse box, and then for a while we had three lanes to ourselves. From nowhere, Erin's 'many worlds' theory came into my head. When the wind buffeted the car, I imagined it was the traffic of all the other dimensions, bumping against ours. She would probably tell me that was plausible, on an atomic level. It made me put my foot down.

We arrived at her cottage just before seven, earlier than predicted. The address said Windermere, but the nearest town was Bowness. It was a white house with inverted-V shapes over the dormer windows and grey slate on the roof, sitting on a little rise above the lake. On the phone, Erin had said it belonged to the head of department, who'd allowed her to keep renting it beyond the term of her sabbatical. She was finding Leeds too stressful, and preferred to stay away unless she had teaching commitments. As Nina had wryly told me, the technicians did all the work, while the academics conceptualised.

When I slammed the car door, struck by the sudden quiet, I saw that the house was in a bad state. Not derelict exactly, but as though it had been left for a year or two with no maintenance. A sprawl of weeds and knee-high grass hid most of the front garden, the casement windows looked greenish and grubby and the overgrown hedge had made the path to the front door almost impassable.

'I hope she has a strimmer,' I muttered to Sabra, lifting the heavy brass knocker. The sound seemed to bounce across the lake, and birds chittered as we waited. My sister was clearly in need of help, and before we could sit down and have all the amiable, adult conversations I was anticipating, I'd need to sort out a few things around the house.

What I noticed when Erin appeared was how sad she looked, a habitual droop that lifted when she smiled. Her eyes were unfocused, obviously just able to make out our shapes against the light. She'd cut her hair shorter than I'd ever seen it, and wore a dark-green knitted vest on top of a white shirt, together with a denim skirt. It reminded me of the sort of thing Nina had worn when we spent that week together so long ago, and I wondered if her style had rubbed off on my sister.

'Nice place you've got here,' I said, shouldering our bags. The interior was in a worse state then the garden, fluff massing under every radiator. The kitchen and bathroom were not too bad, but black mould nestled in the grout between tiles, in shady corners. All the lighting seemed to be clustered around her workstation in one half of the living room, which she'd set up by the largest window. A big computer screen was equipped with magnifiers that slid over it, like an optician's testing lenses, plus speakers and headphones. Our bedroom was airy and pleasant, a converted attic room at the top of the house, though it looked as though it had last been decorated in the forties.

The next morning, we found a hedge trimmer in the shed, encased in cobwebs, and Sabra insisted on attacking the greenery while I donned Marigolds and tipped bleach into a bucket. I unwound the extension cord for her into the kitchen, through the window, and soon an ear-splitting buzz rattled through the house, doubling in volume when she forced the trimmer to sever an especially thick branch.

At length, I peeled off my sticky gloves, perspiring under my clothes, and carried my bucket of dank water out to the front, where my girlfriend was still tirelessly working. She'd beaten the hedge back to splintery gnarls all the way along and had nearly reached the front gate. When she saw me, she gave a thumbs up but didn't stop; I knew she'd want to get the job done in one go, no matter how exhausting it was. The vibrations were making her readjust her grip, and I went over, determined to make her rest. That was when disaster began to unfold. She was making the power tool chew through a looped branch, nearly wrist-thick, when it glanced off to one side. Sabra overcorrected and brought it up towards her shoulder, where the blades caught in strands of escaping hair. The rest was tugged from its clip and the tangle worsened. She let out a gasp, trying to hold the trimmer back from her head. 'Turn it off,' she was yelling. I spun round.

'Shut it off!' I bawled to Erin, who was in the kitchen. It was plugged in right in front of her. 'Erin, turn the trimmer off now!' My voice was thunderous. She just stood there, a cardboard cut-out. With crazed steps, I ran towards the window, thrust it wide, reached inside – scraping a long graze up my arm – and yanked the plug out of its socket. The noise stopped. I dashed back to Sabra who, as the clippers slowed, had managed to detach them from her hair, leaving plenty in the blades.

'Ow.' Her breath was ragged as she clutched the left side of her scalp. I tried to hold her and help massage it, smelling conditioner and fresh hedge sap. Shredded leaves were caught in her matted locks. We stood there for a few minutes until she recovered, letting out a sigh. 'So much for the style I was planning.'

My heart was still beating rapidly as I walked her back inside and went to put the kettle on. Erin had collapsed onto one of the stools by her fold-out table.

'Jesus, Erin.' My hackles were up.

'I'm sorry.'

'Couldn't you see it?' The sockets were equipped with red

lights, and she'd already demonstrated that she knew every inch of her kitchen. 'All you had to do was flick a switch.'

'I know.' Her stricken face took the edge off my rage. Tears marbled her eyes and she wiped away fingerfuls of moisture. 'I just couldn't. I don't know why.'

I stood there, conflicted, but couldn't bring myself to comfort her, not when Sabra had been screaming and my sister standing here, doing nothing. The most I could manage was to pour a second cup of tea and place it silently in front of her, while I took the other mug into the living room. My girlfriend was squinting at herself in the bleary antique mirror, continuing to massage her head.

'What a moron,' she said. 'Are there any scissors in the kitchen?'

'Were you attached to that hair?'

She took the tea. 'Aren't you the comedian?'

'It's a serious question.'

In the end, I didn't reverse what had happened, not only because I was out of the habit with Sabra unless it was absolutely necessary, but also because Erin's reaction had troubled me and I didn't want it the memory of it to degrade until I'd given it some thought.

It was a sign of how much the incident had upset me that at midnight I still wasn't asleep, despite my exhaustion. Erin had gone to bed early, subdued and silent.

'There's something wrong,' Sabra whispered.

'She needs a cleaner, that's all.'

'It's more than that.' Her voice was feathery. 'She's lonely, and then some.'

Sabra rolled closer, so she lay in the crook of my arm. I tried to tell her that my sister had been self-sufficient almost from birth – it was her thing.

'We both know you're right quite often,' she murmured, dozing off, 'but trust me on this.'

The cottage was cold underfoot as I went downstairs, pulling a coat over my dressing gown and slipping into Sabra's pumps. Her feet were almost as big as my own. The night air was fresh and the lane took me downhill, all paths seeming to lead to the lake.

Oil-black waters sloshed against the gritty beach. I thought of my sister standing by the socket, staring at the red light that showed it was turned on. I was pretty sure she approved of Sabra, and she'd apologised shakily all afternoon, so it seemed unlikely any harm was meant. A psychologist would look for some internal source for Erin's sudden paralysis, and the one that came to mind had awful implications.

Wet pebbles slithered beneath my shoes, and I kicked a rock into the shallows. What I was contemplating, out there in my dressing gown, was that something in Erin's past had rewired her to avoid flicking a switch under pressure, especially when someone was in pain. What other episode could have instilled this except the day when, heart breaking and mind in chaos, she felt she had no choice but to turn off our mother's life support? I picked up another stone, pockmarked but smoothed by millennia. Erin was not supposed to have felt the beatings I gave her on the way to turning off that ventilator. Every one of them was undone – subconsciously of course, since I had no idea what I was doing. But how many times had her lip been split? How bruised would her skin have become if all my punches had been allowed to ripen? Much as I wanted to deny that any traces remained, I feared what I'd seen in Erin's frightened eyes.

If there was any truth in this, it meant that going back and forth across a moment really did spin out a cat's cradle of time, threads that jostled together, even influenced each other. My fingers itched around the rock and I wished it was a cigarette, though Sabra and I had given up months ago without a single relapse. It was easy to follow my will-o'-the-wisp imagination into treacherous thinking. Things that were undone were wiped from existence – I felt it in my bones – the memories evaporating quickly and naturally. I weighed the stone in my hand, thinking of Erin's pale face, her figure frozen in the window. My guilty conscience had been taking me for a ride, making me forget that turning off our mother's life support was a traumatic enough experience on its own. Not to mention that, for a visually impaired person, hearing someone yelling from the garden in distress would create tremendous confusion. Anyone would panic in those circumstances.

The stone made a satisfying plop in the lake, and I wiped my hand. Then I went back inside, being careful not to wake Sabra, and took my travel journal from the deep pocket of my coat, settling down to write a few words about Windermere. The light from the Tiffany lamp fell upon the pages, rippled where they had become damp and dried out. There were countless work trips, dating all the way back to my first entry, the volunteering in Colombia. So long ago. The notebook fell open at a tally of the number of mines we'd marked, a picket fence that, on the last day, crossed the entire page in triumph. It had seemed like such a win, but now all I saw was my blinkered progression towards a goal, falling back on my gift again and again, when there could have been far more creative ways to handle things. There was a photo of my team slotted between the pages, and I was surprised to discover everyone's email addresses on the back. So that's where it had got to. I thought of pretty Evangeline, setting the world to rights in her naïve drawl, and stocky Dan with his attempts to impress me. On a whim, I slid out my phone and sent a group email to the whole team. Years had passed, but I was curious to know what they were doing. I hoped they'd all be saving the world, as intended, and that I could claim some small credit for inspiring them.

It was not until late the next morning, waking in the armchair, that I looked blearily at my phone. Tea was brewing, and I was desperate to get a cup, but four emails had appeared – a pleasing and speedy response – and needed to be read.

The contents shook me so much that I immediately broke several police guidelines to obtain a phone number.

'Is this Mrs O'Hare?'

'Yes.'

'Evangeline's mother?'

'Yes.'

'Could I speak to her please? It's Arlo, an old friend.'

A long pause. I gripped the phone with both hands, my shoulders fused with tension.

'I'm sorry,' she said at last. 'Evangeline passed away three years ago.'

I forced myself to wring a couple more answers out of the anguished parent, just enough to confirm that, like the rest of my team, Evangeline had taken her own life.

Thirty-six

This was the first moment I'd had to myself since we arrived in Glastonbury, and I wasn't enjoying it. In this noisy café, there seemed to be no logic to how people loitered, staring at the list of drinks on the chalkboard, randomly stepping forward to order. In the chrome-patterned tabletop, my face was a flat disc, nose protruding. Factor in your own arrogance, I told myself. It might seem like a juggernaut of a coincidence for five people to have taken their own lives, but consider the bigger picture. At Bogota airport, everyone was fine, radiating youthful vitality as I shook their hands. But say they stayed in touch after the trip – not unlikely – and went down some dark path together, to drugs or a cult; or if they picked up on each other's suicidal thoughts. All five were in the business of humanitarian aid or international development, in close proximity to natural disasters, war, poverty, displacement and bereavement. These factors had to be taken into account.

My decaf flat white arrived, overfull, and I managed to spill it. What was I supposed to do anyway? Other people's lives were out of my control. There was no option except to get over it, chalk it up to experience. This was not the time to be thinking about these things, not when I had a huge party to organise. In truth, the more I dreamt about Dan and Evangeline, Trudy and Milenco, and quiet little Haji, the less real they became. They were like fairies, sprung from my imagination, as though I'd been the one to draw up the landmine clearance plans and had fantasised that they were helping me.

Doubtless these thoughts represented a whole new level of delusion but any hard facts would have to wait for me back in London. I was in Glastonbury now, and the summer solstice was approaching. As the sign above the cake stand proclaimed, this town believed in fairies.

At sunrise we went to the Tor, Sabra and I, and though we were not yet wearing our medieval garb, it felt like a ritual. As we climbed the steep, grassy bank, we met others coming down, people in robes with flower garlands in their hair who'd been saluting the rising sun. Every tree cast a mile-long shadow, the grass luminous with dew, and the roofless

385

church whispered in the voices of all those who had stood there over the centuries. Our ancestors, our previous incarnations. Her small shoulder nestled beneath my arm, and I leaned to kiss the top of her hair, close-cropped again, as it had been when we first met. In times past, we might have felt the urge to do something wild, even make love, but now it was crazy enough to be here, on a site that claimed to be the ancient Isle of Avalon, at the apex of the year.

Everyone's wedding must pass like a sort of dream, timeless until that midnight chime turns it into a pumpkin. Our non-wedding was no different. There is a particular euphoria that comes with mixing groups of friends and family, and I felt almost lightheaded as we greeted everyone at the marquee, pointing out the bouncy castle, the kegs of ale and the buffet food they could take outside to eat on the hay bales. It was delicately warm, and everyone was in high spirits, happily comparing their home-made costumes. Sabra had gone for a simple white smock gathered in at the waist with a plaited garter, a ring of saffron rosebuds in her hair. My outfit was the classiest knight costume the internet could provide, complete with chain mail and all the trimmings. As the day went on, I'd shed bits and pieces, so kids would be seen sporting my huge helmet, wielding my wooden sword or my red-cross shield. Nan had made her own wimple out of a floral tea towel and part of a flan dish, and others had gone for full reenactment gear, gowns, religious robes or variations on the muddy-peasant look.

When I issued Dad his invitation, it didn't occur to me that he would show up, yet he came along with a young Polish guy, introduced only as 'Jan'. It transpired that Jan worked at the supported housing complex and had been very impressed with Dad after watching a box set of *Dog Cops*. My father seemed to enjoy pottering around as long as this fan stuck by him. They picked at the buffet and talked to Nan, holding conversations in which Dad came across as merely a little dreamy and absentminded. The only time he struggled was when the gypsy ska band started up (we hadn't let our theme restrict the music too much), and he caught my hand and asked to be moved as far away as possible.

I never thought I'd be escorting my dad to a comfortable hay bale on a warm June day, much less that I'd feel good doing it. As he settled down, and we waited for Jan to catch up with the drinks, I looked at the comb tucked into his top pocket and the lines on his dry face, eyebrows raised expectantly. He seemed at home in the world again, though who knew which world it was. I too had wrestled fame and fortune, and survived, so I took a beer and clinked it against his, and Santa and Satan, like Erin's matter and antimatter, cancelled each other out.

Because Sabra knew so many musical types, band after band took to the stage. There were silly games like ringtoss and apple-bobbing outside, and a hog roast at supper time. Alberta had come down from Birmingham with her little son and looked stunning in a vermillion dress. A shame Tim hadn't been able to make it, the only blip in our otherwise perfect plans. He'd come back from chasing his dreams, volunteering on a Caribbean island, a stone lower in weight and with a bug that had kept him in bed for the best part of a fortnight. We'd had an odd conversation on the phone, in which he told me I was a bad influence, that for me every wild idea seemed to work out, whereas he always got stung. It was so unlike him to be bitter, and when he began to rant vaguely about blue and red rain, Coventry and kings, it became clear he was still feverish. I told him to rest, and began to reassure him that everything was fine, but he hung up midway through.

I missed my old housemate now, amid all the fun. There had been plenty of ale-quaffing and clashing of pewter tankards. As we jousted with breadsticks, the children drove me backwards until I tripped on someone's robe, finding myself sweaty and panting on the grass.

A little way off, Sabra was sitting cross-legged on a hay bale with Erin, deep in conversation. That morning, when my sister emerged from her guesthouse bedroom, we'd shared a moment of shock at what she'd found to wear. The flaring green velvet sleeves overflowed her arms and the skirt was full enough to hide a sheep. Right now it was bunched up on the hay, pooling around her knees. She had been quite chipper earlier on, but had slowed down as evening fell.

Sabra was gesticulating wildly, clutching her neck; she undid her woven belt and offered it to Erin, perhaps to tie up that green dress, which must have been a couple of sizes too large. I'd always said my girlfriend would give away the clothes on her back if anyone asked, and now she seemed to be doing just that. My trajectory curved to take me in their direction. Not a mean bone in her body, Sabra, though her sense of humour was downright evil. It might be time that I stole her away from Erin for a dance.

But I was too slow. A gaggle of old schoolmates converged around the bale and dragged Sabra off towards the tent, where the tempo of the music was climbing. I was about to follow when I noticed Erin escaping from the throng; she was not the dancing type. Her brow creased, trying to recognise me, until I called out a greeting.

'What were you talking about?' I asked. Bats flitted above us, catching mosquitoes.

'How you met.'

'At graduation?' I raised an eyebrow, wondering how much Sabra had said. My tunic had to be hoisted right up before I could climb onto the bale. The straw had the texture of dusty butter.

'You helped with her car.'

'When you see a damsel in distress . . .' My grin was wasted on her. One of my soft leather boots, which looked authentic but were now very damp, slid from my foot. I laughed. Here I was, done up like Saint George and not feeling remotely out of place. Maybe the alcohol was to blame, but nothing felt more natural than to be celebrating, now that we'd been through the hell of Hotel Oasis, followed by the purgatory of divorce proceedings, and come out the other side. Why would I question Sabra's decision, or our joyous new life together? It was the reward for conquering my terrible, disproportionate fear of death, putting her life before mine. 'You heard what happened in Thailand, right?'

She did not look over; presumably eye contact meant nothing to her now.

'Your big moment.'

'I did get shot.' Shifting position, my sword struck something that produced a ringing sound, and I reached down, thrilled to find a half-bottle of prosecco against the hay. 'Though I was more worried about Sabra.'

'Didn't you get her into it?'

I choked mid-quaff.

'No,' I said, coughing out the fizz that had gone down the wrong way. 'She went into the hotel herself.' Of course, it might not have come to that, nor degenerated into a bloodbath, if I hadn't spent several days wearing Somsith down and rattling his cage. I tried to make out my sister's expression.

'Walking away with the glory,' she said, reaching for the bottle. 'You can get a taste for it.' In the tent, the drums stopped and the fiddles raced each other. Erin felt her way across to my shoulder, plucked at the chain mail, and she sighed. 'How much do you enjoy being . . . this? Do you think it's all over and done now, the dragon slain?'

I laughed. 'It's only a costume.'

Her hand fanned out, framing a concept in the air, and I waited for words to follow, but the breath she'd taken went unused. A guitar solo from the tent lowered the volume enough for us to hear calves lowing in the nearby barn.

'Dad's enjoying himself, isn't he?' I remarked.

'A shame Mum isn't here.'

The stalks were hot and prickly under my fingers. I'd lifted the bottle to my lips, but now my heart was racing.

'Look, Erin, I need to tell you something.'

She turned her head, but her eyes reflected only the pale lilac clouds of twilight, as though she was already peering into my soul, into my past, and knew it all already. I was still the little boy who'd done something terrible and never owned up.

'It's about Mum.'

Telling her the story of the ladder, of my stupidity, was like coughing up bees, every word stinging. My vow that we would be closer was being fulfilled, and even as I struggled through the confession a small trickle of peace ran into my heart. I kept checking her face for tears. But this was Erin, and true to form, her expression did not flicker. When I was finished, she nodded, and we sat listening to the distant drums, the babble of voices. Her serenity was such that I started to suspect some prior knowledge – just a hunch, perhaps. The way I'd behaved over the years, whenever the accident was mentioned, must have given something away.

'Why did you wait until now to tell me?'

The midges rose and circled round us, invisible to her.

'Why do you think?' I said, trying to keep a lid on the emotion. 'Maybe I didn't feel so great about it.'

The pain in my words didn't affect her measured tones. 'A single moment . . . with such awful consequences.' Was she being cruel, or just reaching for the irony? 'You can fix your mistakes,' she went on, 'but not this one. That must be hard.'

'It is.' My whisper was from the distant past, when I was four or five and Erin seemed like a grown-up.

She folded velvet round her hands. 'Even if they seem like accidents, these things come from somewhere,' she said. 'From something inside you.' The sleeve slithered back down onto the bale. I shifted an inch away, realising there was something else on her mind, something that made my confession small beer in comparison.

'What's bothering you, Erin?'

Her head rotated slowly in the direction of the music and the marquee, where Sabra was just emerging and peering across to the field, searching for me.

'There'd be no way you could go back and change it?'

For a second I thought I'd misheard. My mouth hung open before I managed to slur out a reply. 'You're not talking about . . . are you? It happened more than twenty years ago.'

'Is that too long?'

'Yes, it's too long,' I snapped. The very idea was insane,

so why was there a defensive undertone to my voice? I sensed her detect it. 'In any case, it would be before I had this ability. That's an unknown variable, as you might say.'

It would be utterly perilous, the most likely outcome being to fetch up at some random point along my timeline, wherever my memory faltered, and then I'd be stuck, having to slog through the years all over again. I closed my eyes, overcome with weariness, then started seeing, as I'd trained myself to do, the past like a long path, all its rises and falls and detours. I jerked awake quickly, fearing that I'd feel that tug and start reaching for it. Across the field, Sabra wandered a few steps out of the marquee, saw me with Erin and saluted before disappearing once more. It firmed my resolution.

'I'm not going backwards any more, even day-to-day. I've spent enough time airbrushing out mistakes.'

Beneath all the whirlwind celebrations, that news about my landmine team was still sinking in. Almost certainly I was reading too much into it – there were far stranger coincidences in the world – but I knew that when back in London I'd want to probe a little further and approach it with a detective's mindset, the one I used to investigate unexplained deaths.

A breeze rippled the sleeves of Erin's dress, releasing more of its musty-wardrobe odour. She might be a bit odd, but here beside me was someone who had rocked the foundations of quantum physics, a woman I should feel proud to have as my sister. For some time, I'd suspected that fame and fortune had left her feeling short-changed. It puzzled me, and I wanted her, just for once, to stop being so hard on herself.

'Let me run some tests,' she said, surprising me with another curveball – she had an infinite supply. 'That data you gave Nina is about the only interesting thing I've got to work on.'

For the last few years, I'd been willing, even keen, but Erin's paper had created so much fame, so much follow-up, that her brother, a miracle of science, had been put on the back-burner . . . until now. Her timing was terrible.

'Sorry,' I said. 'There'd be nothing to test.'

'Oh please, are you really going cold turkey?'

'Absolutely.'

'Not even a few tweaks, today, to make things go better?'

There had been speeches over lunch, informal and jokey, referencing the fact that this was absolutely not, in any way, a wedding. The food had been good, the bands well-timed. Erin could be forgiven for thinking that I'd nipped back over any hiccups.

I shook my head. 'Surprising, isn't it?'

She was in darkness now, the colour gone from her dress. Why hadn't we thought of outdoor lighting? Even the longest day had to end eventually. People would find their way back to tents or guesthouses by the glow of mobile phones. 'You know I was demoted after Thailand?' I slid down from the bale. 'But I'm happier now than I've ever been.'

'Lucky you.'

It was not sharp, only sad. The gloom was drawing me involuntarily into my sister's universe, into a lonely mono-chrome landscape. More than anything, I wanted her to realise that she was brilliant, to celebrate her success, as I was celebrating mine.

'For the love of God, Erin, give yourself a break. We're going nowhere until you admit you're a great physicist and your paper was gold.' With some distress, I saw her lurch to one side at these words, as though avoiding a bat. 'Retro . . . something or other . . . is being redefined,' I quoted. 'You'll go down in history.' My arm shot out, but it was too late to prevent her from losing her balance and toppling into the meadow. I leapt up, but she'd scrambled to gather her skirts and was striding off in the opposite direction to the marquee, the source of light. 'It's the other way, Erin,' I called, wondering if she was confused, but she kept going, stumbling over the tussocks, and I gave chase, my increasingly plaintive cries ringing across the hill. The only brightness was from pinprick stars, and the field was grey, otherworldly and completely empty. A chill gripped me, slowing my footsteps; the wet, lumpy weeds made it too similar to that mile of scrubland that fragile young legs had tentatively trodden, not expecting the earth to explode. My socks were soaking, and I began to shiver uncontrollably. My sister had vanished.

Thirty-six

It happened while Sabra and I were dozing under a tree, later that summer. A memory returned without warning. At first it was the sensation of parched earth and grass tickling my arms, just the same as this, but in a huge park in Coventry. There was a hiss and a smell of lager as Tim cracked open his next can, just me and him, taking a breather even though the main act was on the stage. Go West were hoping people would remember their glory days, still the kings of wishful thinking. How could I have forgotten all this? On the phone, during the solstice, I'd assured Tim that neither of us had ever been to Coventry, and he'd said, 'Yes, yes, I know that.' Yet now the war memorial was swimming into view, along with a stage, food stalls and bunting. Images that felt invented, or from a film, solidified into memories. The Godiva festival was obviously an episode I'd unstitched, though I couldn't think why.

Trying not to disturb Sabra, I rose and got into the position I'd begun to associate with meditation. I calmed my mind, trying not to be impatient, and at length it began to come back, fuzzed with decade-old dust. As usual, everything was Tim's fault. He'd let slip that, on Facebook, Sabra had mentioned she was attending this festival – she must have been in England visiting friends – and, now that the seed was sown, I couldn't resist. Coventry was minutes away by train. As the memories drifted back, so did the emotions. Even the weather couldn't settle that day, alternating between dense sunshine and sudden downpours.

And did we see her? Of course we did. I was like a bloodhound. There was one of those awkward bumping-into-your-ex moments – for her, in any case, since I'd orchestrated it carefully ever since spotting her. She looked different, a little plumper, sort of dishevelled as though she'd been couch-surfing, which she probably had. Her friend was called Mel – Melinda! There was my secondary negotiator, younger and lacking glasses, but with the same brassy Glaswegian laugh. It felt slightly wrong to hang out together, but we were all drinking, so this was easy to ignore. Unfortunately, Tim had a bit too much and got himself lost, until we found him, after darkness had fallen, in a ring of paramedics. The ambulance's two-tone lights flashed like a sinister disco in time to the music.

A bunch of posters had made the rain-drenched path even more slippery, and Tim's foot must have flown out in front, his spine hitting the concrete. He couldn't feel his legs. I remember Sabra crouching down as we spoke to him, blackcurrant cider on her breath. My mind was chaotic with noise and booze, with my own unpleasant memories of being concussed by a brick and rushed to hospital only weeks before, and most of all with Sabra, who knew I'd have to go with the paramedics and was trying to say goodbye. It was sweet. Why would I have erased all this?

'So . . . good to see you,' she said, as they loaded Tim up.

'I don't want to go,' I muttered, still trying to muster an hour, or even less, to go back and get us out of this. 'I want to marry you and have your babies.' It didn't matter what I said, only that I lined up the footsteps, the food I'd eaten . . . Meanwhile, Sabra was examining her left hand.

'Did you notice this?' The ring had a very small diamond at its centre. I was normally so observant – had it been invisible until now? 'I kept waiting for you to call me on it, but you never did.'

Her face was illuminated blue and red, so she didn't look quite human. The paramedics were hassling me to get into the vehicle, a latex-gloved hand pumping the door handle impatiently.

'Married?' I said.

'Engaged.'

'Is it serious?'

As I was bundled into the back of the ambulance, she mouthed 'goodbye', then the doors slammed and we were bouncing away over the field, Tim recumbent in front of me, the disinfectant pungent enough to kill even the worst bacteria, and perhaps humans too. Dying was just what I felt like doing, after being reminded how happy it made me to be in Sabra's company, how my memories of it were shadows in comparison, only to have this . . . this closing door.

I didn't go back an hour. I wanted this whole episode gone, this feeling out of my system, a surgical wipe across the brain. I went back a full three days, to that Wednesday night on the sofa, Tim on his laptop, about to tell me there was a free festival in Coventry and Sabra had marked herself as 'going'.

'For the love of God,' I said to him. 'You haven't seen her in years. Un-friend her.'

Without regard for my health, I then set about getting us both drunk as skunks. That was all I remembered, a little mire-pit of memory with alcohol melting off the edges. But it worried me to have erased this so cleanly until now. Were there other scenes so painful that my brain had intervened and, as a defence mechanism, blocked them out entirely?

The grass was a sun-baked stubble with hints of cigarette – one or two butts lay among the roots of the tree – and Sabra stirred, moving her head so she could use my belly as a pillow. Her left hand encountered a leaf skeleton and she twirled it.

'Daytime dreams are the weirdest,' she murmured.

'You're telling me.'

'I kept nearly falling, like you do in dreams, but into an orchestra that was a bear pit full of animals, the holes in the cellos and violas like mouths with splintery teeth, catgut hair and metal horns, and there were still bits of humans clinging to them, trying to play them . . .'

I smiled. We'd both been overdoing it. No wonder we'd passed out on the grass. I ached to tell her what I'd remembered, but to explain my gift now would feel like confessing an affair of the past. Sabra might feel cheated if I admitted all the mistakes I'd undone in our relationship. She might look back on our best moments and wonder if they were the product of trial and error.

'Oops,' she said, noticing a touch of lipstick left on my T-shirt.

I just smiled. Right now, I was down with 'oops', rediscovering the joy of getting things wrong, of mistakes small or large, foolish, deliberate, unconscionable or accidental. I was fine with slips of the tongue, unwitting insults, getting people's names confused or boarding the wrong train. Every hit was a badge of honour, every embarrassment toughening me up for the next. Like someone who'd spent their whole life numb, I wanted to sample all the different knocks and scrapes and feel their distinctive tingle, burn or sting. I was awake to the possibilities of blagging and shrugging and apologising with aplomb. The novelty of error would doubtless be temporary, a honeymoon period, but something told me I needed it to last as long as possible.

As I played with her hair – she was stubbornly growing it again – I thought about the other reason I didn't want to jeopardise things. All around were the sounds of children shrieking, pushchairs rattling on pavements. As if running straight out of my thoughts, a toddler with blonde curly hair stumbled past us, nearly tripping over Sabra's outstretched feet. She retracted them, losing a flip-flop, and scratched a mosquito bite on her neck. Her eyes squinted up at me against the dappled light.

'I felt it again just then,' she said.

'What?' I sat up in fear. It would be typical of Sabra to be tardy in mentioning something so important. Surely she couldn't be pregnant? I'd taken every precaution.

'Everything went black, and my head spun, like I was about to pass out.'

We definitely needed to see a doctor about these dizzy spells, yet my overwhelming sensation was relief, and I wanted to laugh at myself for the wild, surreal thought that Sabra might feel the kick of a baby in that too-flat stomach. Although in general I was no longer using my ability, there would be one exception: I needed to know that, in the event of a risky childbirth, it would be possible to go back nine months. Sabra meant more to me than any child, and conception would have to wait until my head was clear enough, until I had a sense that whole months were within my reach. Some time ago, Erin had introduced me, via email, to meditation as a way to manage stress, but I'd also found it made my mind as still and sharp as a mirror.

Sap was falling from the tree in a light rain, spattering the lenses of my shades, so I proposed a walk, though it was getting fairly hot. Sabra brought along the leaf skeleton to add to her box of keepsakes.

'A perfect day,' she declared. 'In everything but sweatiness.'

The moisture was running down my back too. When we reached a bridge, I looked down into the tempting teal waters and stopped, a flicker of old wickedness kindling.

'Come on then,' I said, easing off her sunglasses and tucking them behind a stone. 'Let's jump.'

'In there? It's not safe.'

'Sure it is – I promise I'll save you if it's not.'

'Yeah, yeah,' she said, stealing back her shades. 'Any excuse to save me.' Her flip-flops slapped their way over the rest of the bridge, where she made a beeline for a small ice cream cart under a willow. It took me a minute to crank into action, a whiff of the Serpentine reaching me from below. I'd been laughing, but it hit me that she was right: my heels were twitching, my system already flooded with pleasure at the thought of diving in and rescuing her.

What the hell was wrong with me?

Thirty-seven

I missed the thank you cards. Mistakes had lost their sparkle and I was hungry to do big things again, but there was no going back. The irony was of anvil proportions. I'd never regain my infallibility as a hostage negotiator because to skip back over time was now too much of a risk. Or, at least, I feared that it might put others at risk. On my return to work after Glastonbury, one of the admin managers had kindly taken the time to look up some of my old cases, to contact people whom I'd saved from various grisly fates and check on them. It was rather unorthodox, but the punters didn't know that. She made a few phone calls, and I waited anxiously, my desk spread with burglaries, gobbledegook reports and a copy of Strindberg's

Ghost Sonata that Dad had given me as a non-wedding present.

Finally, the results came back, and they were ambiguous enough to be worrying. It was unremarkable that individuals who'd been – or nearly been – in traumatic situations found life a little rocky following the event. Some of the ex-victims were fine, but others had got into trouble, and one particularly disturbing case involved a young man who had been wrongly tasered by a colleague. This teen had been tricky to save, since the tasering just seemed to keep happening at different points of the chase. A very sad story, the admin manager had told me. He got electrocuted while doing some work in his girlfriend's house. She saw it happen.

This was one of a few calamities that looked like accidents. But if Sabra had cut herself with the hedge trimmer it would have been written off as misfortune, and I'd seen for myself that there was more to it. The mixed bag of evidence still weighed too heavily for me to risk saving lives, not when I had no idea what it was doing to people. My true enemy was uncertainty. If only I could be sure there were no ill-effects, it could be business as usual. But I'd been in such a blissful stupor with Sabra that it had taken me until now to remember what a brave man was supposed to do when chased: turn and face it. The time had come to place myself in the probing, surgical hands of science, and this time I'd let them shake out all my secrets.

What no one understood was that I didn't just appreciate

the thank you cards; I thirsted for them. If my future wasn't one of great deeds, then it was nothing. Even my past seemed in jeopardy, if all the good I'd done could just crumble away. As I flicked through the *Ghost Sonata*, my imagination put me on an island, like the one at the end of the play. If there was nothing ahead of me, and nothing behind, then I was stranded. The idea filled me with an icy dread, yet I'd find myself on that island sooner than I thought.

We drove up to the lakes in early August, under brilliant blue skies. 'Do what you will with me,' was what I'd said to Erin in an email that she must have been delighted to receive. I wanted all the answers physics could give, and was willing to face what I knew would be a cold and clinical interrogation to get them. By now, it was clear that no amount of effort could crack open Erin's hard shell and reveal an affectionate sister inside. There was a bitterness that had grown within her, ingrained itself in her very fabric.

Hence my jolt of disbelief when she came hurrying out, greeting us as though nothing had ever given her such joy.

'Come in, come in,' she almost sang. 'You have the top room again. I hope that's acceptable? It's been redecorated.'

On the table were six bottles of wine alongside a bowl overflowing with fruit, and the whole place was transformed. A woman from the village now came twice a week for cleaning and laundry, we were told. The guestroom had become crisp and white, smelling of potpourri, and struck me as oddly matrimonial. Its vast iron bedstead was draped with lace covers, a dressing screen in one corner and a vase of dried flowers on the windowsill. I put our suitcases on the dresser and bent to peer through the glazing, dazzled by the view of the lake. We would see it when we woke up, quietly reflecting the sky.

As Sabra and I settled in, we noticed that more adaptive technologies had sprung up around the house, with textured strips announcing the end of stair rails, a clock speaking the time in the kitchen and a big microphone attached to the computer. I sat in my sister's swivel chair and spun. 'Do we have to start right away?'

Erin felt around on the table, locating a corkscrew. 'Of course not. You need to relax first. This is Windermere in August – think of it as a delayed honeymoon.'

Sabra laughed and put up her hand. 'Not married.'

Nevertheless, we took a day or two to enjoy the area, greatly amused by my sister turning tour guide, bouncing her roller-ball cane along lakeside trails, explaining the raised platforms where charcoal-burning had decimated the forest – until the romantics replanted it. Commentaries from tourist boats drifted distinctly across the water, and streams trickled down the hillsides, branching and re-forming until they reached the lake.

'So, you've had a chance to explore,' I said, pleased at this new relaxed version of my sister. 'Has the work eased up a bit?'

'Are you still doing quantum mechanics?' Sabra cut in. 'I don't even understand what that means. Someone told me it was about cats being dead and alive at the same time, but that didn't help.' She laughed at herself, plucking a floret of cow parsley.

I knew Erin well enough to sense an internal eye-roll, but she replied, 'That particular illustration is about several realities existing at once. In one, the cat is dead. In another, it's alive. Maybe in another it's sick. They're all as real as each other, but once you look at the cat a single reality is chosen, and the others collapse.'

'Is that true?'

'It's been proven on an atomic scale, but not with cats – quantum states are very fragile, and all the heat and outside influences mean you can't observe them in anything big.' Like a weathervane, her head tilted towards me at this point, sending a flush to my cheeks.

'And it's hard to observe things anyway, isn't it?' I piped up, remembering Nina's descriptions of cracking solder and finely tuned equipment. 'One look, and all the options close up.' It put me in mind of a card trick, the deck fanned out and at your disposal, until you chose.

Erin's stick hovered ponderously, like a long white lollipop. 'Well, there's a thing called the quantum eraser, where you measure where everything is, then un-measure it – look away again, so to speak – and that seems to reset the uncertainty. The universe resumes its game of dice.'

408

Sabra had been concentrating and was now reaching up to massage the crick from her neck. She'd managed to injure herself again, trying to get under the skin of Bazzini's Dance of the Goblins. 'I'll do that,' I said, repositioning my arm, quantum physics forgotten.

A white cross further up the lake marked the spot where a couple of young men had capsized in the 1800s.

WATCH THEREFORE FOR YE KNOW NEITHER THE DAY NOR THE HOUR.

This was the inscription that greeted us as the rowing boat came near. For the last two days, the weather had been having tremendous mood swings, its horizontal sheets of rain keeping us indoors. Now the water was calm again, though it was the colour of shadow, a single swan dragging at its surface. Were there shipwrecks in its depths? I asked Erin, who continued to row and nodded not quite in the direction of the cross. 'At least one.'

Sabra was back at the cottage, having done her best to conceal how queasy she felt after my sister's attempt at a fish dinner the night before. I'd sat around reading all morning, and when Erin suggested going for a row in the neighbour's boat, I jumped at the chance to get some exercise. It was not quite as expected, since I was needed for my eyesight rather than my biceps. Erin rarely got the

409

chance to row. She grabbed the oars and seemed to take pleasure in the smooth push and pull, while I gave directions: 'A bit more to the right, more on the left,' lounging back like Louis XIV in his barge, trailing my fingertips in the water. The air was exactly at body temperature. We were slightly north of Bowness, a fair way from the tourist boats, and it was exceptionally quiet. Then, from nowhere, a violin sang out across the lake. Sabra must have roused herself and begun practising by the open window. Astonishing how the sound carried.

There is something a bit too intimate about a rowboat. Erin's sandalled feet were braced against the bow as she pulled, her breathing heavy. Twice I offered to take over and was rebuffed. As we circled back, she proposed landing on an island where there had once been an ancient chapel, a pretty place with a smaller holm nearby where the monks had kept chickens. Readily I agreed, keen to be out of the boat, and we manoeuvred with care around the warning buoys and rocks.

'I came here once with Nina, though you aren't supposed to land in a tourist rowboat,' she said as we slid up the gravelly beach, disturbing a couple of gulls and Canada geese. 'Before I met her, it never occurred to me that you could ignore the rules and still have a healthy moral compass.'

Though I was curious to know where this was going, the prolonged splashing of oars had made it imperative I find a bush as quickly as possible. My restless limbs also wanted to work off the weirdness of the journey, so I left Erin removing a picnic rug and food from the boat. The island had a craggy little topography of its own, and I picked my way between lattices of roots, silvery foliage and mossy rocks, while cormorants took flight.

When I made my leisurely way back to the beach, the sight that greeted me was so bewildering that I took the last few steps at a run.

'What the . . . Hey!'

Too late: she'd walked the boat out into the shallows and given it a mighty shove, the oars rocking inside. It slid away, helped by the wind. Old fury filled my veins. 'What the fuck? What the actual fuck, Erin?'

Our boat was drifting out into the vastness of the lake.

'Stop.' Her hand shot out. 'Don't go back. You won't have to.'

'I wasn't going to.'

She felt around, sat down and began to remove her wet sandals. It was a miracle she hadn't slipped on the lake's pebbly bed. My curiosity was piqued. Erin had never done anything like this. Caution was in her nature, and it had only become more prevalent as her sight waned. This recklessness was out of character.

'I thought we could talk about your abilities.' Her tone was eager. 'It's really the only thing I want to work on.'

Despite myself, I felt relief, pleasure even.

'You set our boat adrift for that?'

There was clearly something up her sleeve. She lined up her dripping sandals, running a hand lightly over their shape to check they were neat, making them look like two petted creatures.

'You've reached a sort of perfection with it, haven't you?'

'I wouldn't say perfection.' It was true that in former days I'd have to feel my way through the actions, whereas now they could be totted up with a certain deftness.

'Meditation gives you access to your subconscious,' she went on. 'You just need to be still enough to hold your mind like a book and turn to the right page.' There was something a little odd about her enthusiasm, her words a bit too studied. I began to detect an agenda.

'Are you looking to formulate some sort of hypothesis here?'

She shook her head. 'I'm suggesting that . . . you really could go back.'

Beneath thickening cloud, the air was growing strangely warm. Water scented with decay lapped at the beach. Now I got it – this was personal. I felt the lake turning inward to stare at us, the intruders on its navel. Perhaps confessing to Erin at the solstice hadn't been such a good idea.

'It's too long ago,' I said gently. We'd been over this.

'No—'

'It is, Erin.' My hand reached for her shoulder and I was

surprised at the tension. Was this her resting state? 'Do you think I haven't considered it a thousand times? It was my fault, after all. But going back to that ladder . . . it would be uncharted waters.'

Nothing moved, and then she dislodged my hand.

'You're on about Mum?' Her body swayed with incredulity. 'No, Arlo, I'm talking about something completely different.'

Thirty-seven

I blinked, and there before me was a woman in her forties. Of course she didn't mean Mum. Her face told me I'd been silly to think she was yearning for a parent at her age, even though it was something I had done for most of my life. What exactly was she asking then, and why did it require us to be marooned on an island? The wind offered up a snatch of tourist-boat audio, a whiff of smoke from someone's barbeque.

'I'm not asking you to go back that far. You only need to go back to when I published my paper. The previous week will do, or even the day before.'

'Your paper?' Now I was lost. It was her greatest moment, and all I could think was that she wanted to live it again, to squeeze out even more glory the second time around. 'Did you wear the wrong outfit or something?' My tone was cutting. 'Did someone not clap hard enough?'

'Don't mock.' She stepped back, tripped over a small pile of driftwood and fell onto the sand, clutching her foot. 'You don't know what I did that day. Normalisation is a terrible thing.' Her voice grew hoarse. 'It was so common, until recently, for academics to work with a PhD and ... I convinced myself it would be fine. Nina never cared about fame. She was the purest of academics, only interested in knowledge. People leave doctoral students off papers all the time. What would it matter if only my name appeared?' She buried her head in mottled, sandy hands, knuckles battered and grazed. They had been so white and tiny when I'd snatched them away from the machine by Mum's bedside.

'I was naïve.' Tears eased down her cheeks. 'Nina knew she was the driving intelligence behind our work; I could never match her brilliance. I just joined the dots, connecting up her flashes of inspiration. She was right to feel betrayed, but how I ... how I begged her not to go.' Her voice was flooded with emotion, leaving me completely out of my depth. If her crying wasn't so real – and she searched her pockets desperately for tissues – I'd have believed this beach was a stage and we were playing out some strange melodrama.

'Erin, come on,' I said. 'People forgive. If they didn't, I wouldn't be here today.'

'It was not as though we could forget about it,' my sister sobbed. 'Not when it was all over the internet, my name and her discoveries. She must have come to hate my name. I know I did.'

The name 'Dr Erin Knott' sprang into view, clothed in newsprint, kite-tailing from Google searches, sneaking into cross references. I remembered how I'd come to loathe seeing 'The Great ArlO' splashed over posters and event invitation, as though a piece of my identity had gone rogue.

'It was a long time ago,' I said gently. 'Why don't you get in touch? Maybe she'll say it's water under the bridge.'

Her fingers wormed into the soft grit. 'She's married.'

A sigh escaped me. I wondered whether there would be any harm in jumping back half an hour, just to get the boat, or if I should swim out to where it was rotating. In the distance, the dormer windows of Erin's house caught my eye. With super-sight I could peer all the way into that attic room and see Sabra's head on the pillow, probably grimacing as the trout roiled in her stomach. If only I was beside her.

'There's no going back,' I murmured. 'I'm sorry.'

She flinched. 'You don't understand.' Wiping her eyes left a trail of sand across her face. 'The visual world I can take or leave, but . . . she's the light I need.'

A cormorant skimmed over the water and alighted regally on a rock. I'd have been less surprised if it had opened its beak and started telling me it was a star-crossed lover. Erin had always been proudly independent, passionate only about her work.

'What else do I have?' she continued, her voice flat. 'If you knew what it was like to be hauled backwards into the cave . . . no more petals on flowers, no flowers in the grass, no grass in the fog.' Her arms spread wide, smudging out the scenery, and my heart buckled. It was clear that she saw turning back time as her only hope.

'Erin—'

'All you have to do is go back and tell me to include her name on the paper. If you demonstrate your ability at the same time, then I'll believe you and do what you say. I was having doubts in any case; deep down I knew it was wrong.' Her hands built a mound of pebbles as she outlined the plan. 'We'll publish on the post-selection, and then on your germline mutation too. We'll be famous together, Arlo.'

The water wrinkled as a breeze dragged it. Hadn't Erin learned anything? Here she was walking into the same old trap that had tempted me – and eaten Dad whole. Her cheeks were flushed, a small figure wrapped tightly in her own daydream.

'Did I tell you that, when I was at uni, I tried to win the lottery?' The feel of foil condom packets returned to my fingertips. 'Do you know why I never managed it?'

She shrugged.

'I could never remember the numbers.' There was a bottle of pop on the picnic rug, and I reached for it. My mouth was so dry. 'The memory fades too quickly. If I went back several years, I'd probably end up dazed, even concussed. I wouldn't remember anything about your paper. Do you see what I'm saying?'

A poor choice of words. To my dismay, I heard her whisper, 'You don't want to.'

'I've just explained—'

'You have to do this for me, Arlo. I know it'll work. You might not remember numbers, but anything emotional is much easier, like when you undid the visit to Dad.'

There it was. I knew she'd been testing me.

'Did I really make him worse?'

A certain discomfiture was apparent in her hesitation.

'No,' she said. 'He loved seeing you, and I hated having to take it away from him.'

The cormorant spread its wings and soared off, while I just stared at my sister, hardly believing what I was hearing. She really had pulled out all the stops in her desperation to fix this, her own big, broken-bottle mistake. For a moment, I entertained the possibility of going back several years. It wasn't so much about losing the time or the promotions at work; what mattered was that crucial period in Thailand. If not for the Hotel Oasis, Sabra would still be married and I'd be alone. Who knew how things might play out the second time around? She might be borne away in the 4x4 and later caught in crossfire. A sudden image of her gravestone chilled me as though I was touching it.

'You can't ask me to gamble my future for the slim chance of sorting out your past.'

If I awoke some years ago, disorientated, I'd get over my headache and carry on as before. We'd reach this point again, and she'd make me go back. The thought made me crumple with weariness. That circle of hell already haunted my dreams, an eternity of getting everything I ever wanted, only to throw it away again, to be tested repeatedly by some devil who didn't really believe I could risk my life for Sabra and had to keep rewinding.

'Jesus, Erin, we could have gone through this whole thing ten times already. That would make me about eighty-eight years old, and right now I feel it.'

How long do slow-worms live? I had a fleeting image of it growing, ageing over many lifetimes, becoming scalier, wings unfolding, uglier and more monstrous with every year, and better at hiding. I tugged at the neckline of my T-shirt, stuffy despite the breeze, and scanned the lake for the boat. The idea of stripping to my pants and plunging into the water, cold though it would be, appealed greatly. My imagination, which Sabra had once described as 'gothically inclined' was even now painting this island in familiar colours, adding dark cypresses and conjuring up the unnerving idea that I'd been here before.

'Don't talk to me about feeling ancient, Arlo,' Erin snapped. 'You made me old before my time. Once you came along, and especially after Mum's death, I had to do everything.

They kept telling me I was mature for my age, but I didn't have a choice.' Halfway to taking off my shoes, I stood on one leg like a heron, taken aback. 'Do you have any idea how many times you've messed things up, for me and others?' she continued in harsh tones. 'You've caused untold harm in the world, letting people die repeatedly because you wanted to look like a hero.'

The words made my skin crawl, latching on like biting insects. People dying? I'd never even said it aloud. My body slumped to the picnic blanket so forcefully that a dry airing-cupboard smell was thumped out of it. Erin had been my hope, my one hope of clearing up this notion that I might be causing damage, and now to hear her condemn me so thoroughly, as though there wasn't any doubt . . . It left me reeling.

'I didn't . . .' Where had this voice come from? It was about five years old.

'Of course you did.'

'But if they died . . . it was all undone.'

How I regretted being so candid in the email I'd sent, telling her about the checks my admin manager had undertaken, about the landmine crew.

'I know.' Her mouth twisted. 'But how many times did they die? You picked the reality where a person zigzags through a field of explosives and lives, but you also created ten other versions where they die. Things resonate, Arlo. Worlds influence worlds.'

It was too much. This wasn't science. None of it was real. The island itself was otherworldly enough to spook me out, and I was suddenly desperate to escape. Some raw, unfiltered terror volcanoed up through my body, propelling me to my feet. Grasping the hem of my T-shirt, I tore it over my head.

'Don't get any ideas,' she said. 'I still need that favour.'

I tugged off my socks. A wild laugh, part-gurgle, escaped my throat. 'I fancy a swim.'

'You seem to think there's a choice.'

Erin was now standing with her toes planted in the sand, hands on hips, a thin, hard figure. Nothing she could say would stop me getting the boat and rowing to shore. She could stay here and stew for a while.

Her next words were spoken lightly: 'Sabra doesn't know, does she?'

The wind dropped, the canopy falling silent.

'Tell her if you want.' I was down to khaki shorts and heading for the lake. It wasn't ideal, but if Sabra had to know about my gift then I could handle it.

'For someone who can't make mistakes, you get a lot wrong,' she remarked, using that teacher-like voice I'd always found so irritating. My feet were like white fish in the shallows, but I didn't care that the water was freezing. The best thing was to take a run at it, and I was just about to do so when she added, 'Did you know she keeps a memory box of things – a sort of journal, only in objects, not words?

421

I didn't grace this with a reply.

'Of course you do,' she went on. 'But are you aware of what's inside?' Shivers migrated upward from my submerged legs. I was moored by my ears, straining to listen. 'A piece of brown glass labelled 'Spitfire' is one of the items. Remember Spitfire? All those photos of you drinking it at uni, Nan getting it in specially at Christmas? Funny how you went off it. People's tastes change, I suppose.'

I froze, my thighs two stakes driven into the lakebed. She raised her voice, gathering pace. 'Sabra says you approached her after the accident to help. It doesn't take a genius to work out that the person who threw the beer, especially that beer, was also the one who showed up afterwards to lend a hand. What was it, some other rampage you didn't quite manage to undo all the way?' Her eyes blinked, fixed on the sky, as though she could see my whole life sculpted in the clouds.

'That's not—'

'Does Sabra know it was you who made her mess up that crucial, most unforgiving moment of a musician's career – the start? Does she know it was you who stole her dream?'

Thirty-seven

Every splash of the oars was vicious. My bare upper half was rock-hard with cold, dotted with droplets, while rivulets ran from my hair. It had been an effort to heave myself into the boat, shivery from the swim. Leaving her yelling on the beach felt cowardly, but – damn her – she'd given me no choice. As my eyelids closed against the sun, I saw nothing but a red glow, but what did Erin see behind hers? Tunnels leading to every secret. Deep, distraction-free thinking must have been required to burrow around beneath the surface of my relationship and find this unexploded bomb. In the tranquil surroundings of the island – and in the shadow of this threat – she'd expected me to settle into a deep meditation. Next, we'd both find ourselves back wherever we'd been in the lead-up to Erin's publication date. As a quantum physicist, she had plenty of experience believing in the impossible.

Did she only befriend Sabra to sniff out some leverage for her plan? I could imagine her delight when she pieced together what had happened on graduation day. A few calculations and hey presto: beyond reasonable doubt, it was I who had robbed my girlfriend of the chance to fulfil her potential. Sabra's smile came to mind, a crinkle to her eyes like the sparks a child might draw around the sun. She would pardon my secrecy, my strangeness, my unnatural nature, but would she forgive the theft of her life's work? One brown curl of glass, propped on the bonnet of her car. It had such power. There were photos of me drinking Spitfire, plus I'd been there at the crime scene, approaching with sympathy. Even if there wasn't so much evidence, I'd be undone by the simple fact that, now I'd given my life for Sabra, there would be no denying her the truth if she asked for it.

I moored the boat to the slippery jetty and clambered out. In my mind, Erin was already buzzing to shore in a flagged-down speedboat, marching to the house. Sabra would say 'Hey . . .' in surprise, before being quickly transfixed by the story, warmed by the nostalgia of our first meeting, then chilled as the full picture was revealed. She really did feel the deepest bitterness for whoever had cost her that crucial performance. It would be absorbed, made a part of her, this long-held poison Erin had finally imparted.

I couldn't let that happen. The darker parts of me were already contemplating more desperate measures. If only Erin could just be left on the island and forgotten. Perhaps her phone would run out of battery. But, while it was a lot of lake to cross, a determined person could swim, or hail a tourist or a fisherman. My hours were numbered.

Though I had not cried, my face was puckered, screwed up painfully and denied the comfort of tears. When I stumbled through the door, Sabra looked at me in alarm.

'You're soaking wet.'

'I went for a swim.'

Amusement coloured her face. She went to put the kettle on, obviously feeling better. The kitchen was a mess of cooking utensils, a huge pot of Thai curry boiling on the stove.

'You cooked.'

'I slept all afternoon and now I'm full of beans, like this pot. Where's your sister?'

My eyes went instinctively to the blue-lit window. 'She's staying somewhere else tonight.'

Sabra spun round, wooden spoon in hand. 'My God, how did you engineer that?' She came in for a kiss, slipping her fingers up under my hair, pressing against my chest in a way I normally struggled to resist. 'I'd take advantage of you being half-naked, but this would boil over.' Her spoon dived back into the gingery magma that was bubbling away.

When I came down in a dry hoody, she was going over the difficult bits in Biber's Mystery Sonatas, so I took over at the hob, the steam warming my icy hands. I pretended to stir the rice and mess about with plates but kept stealing glances through the doorway at her arm dipping and weaving, the tiniest motion producing the sweetest arpeggio. Then a stop, a quick in-breath which I knew was her fighting the pain, a tendon twanging in her neck, before she'd adjust her fingers and try something more legato. Her eyes were closed and her head tilted, as though she was not playing but listening to something no one else could hear, compelling her elbow and wrist to move until they ached, fulfilling the music's whims. It was a relationship, I realised, of a kind that was beyond my comprehension.

Outside, the light was almost gone, yet the sky was pale enough for me to make out the silhouette of the island. Part of me was still there amid the damp, acid-green moss, under trees stripped to the bone by the caustic droppings of cormorants. As I watched, a cloud of these dark sentinels lifted from the highest boughs, then resettled, filling me with foreboding.

Was there a pinprick glow? Erin probably had her phone with her; she could easily call for help if she wanted, or perhaps she'd just bed down in the blanket and wait, biding her time, hoping I'd calm down and come to get her, or do what she wanted right here.

All that anger, kindled over a lifetime. I used to sneak into her bedroom as a child and jump on her Rainbow Brite duvet, surrounded by Impulse deodorants and dusty crystals from the museum gift shop. She had a framed picture of herself at a waterpark, both parents swaddling her with towels. I'd seen it at Nan's too, always perplexed as to why she would keep an image of my dad. Only now was I beginning to understand its significance, grainy and badly composed though it was. The fluffiness of the towels, the thrilling slides and her grin – so whimsical, goofy and childish – all the things she was once allowed to be.

A trill alerted me to Sabra, still playing for all she was worth, wringing out the notes, telling stories with her bow. It would be the hardest thing I'd ever done, but Erin had left me no choice. The sonata vibrated through my skin, and I let it continue, delaying the moment I'd wave and get her attention, in case this turned into our last evening together and I'd never get the pleasure of hearing her again.

Abruptly, she stopped and swayed like a tree cut at the base, one elbow starting to droop. I was there in an instant, just in time to catch her as she fell, collapsing into a twisted position beneath her on the rug. She opened her eyes, groaning as she regained consciousness.

'An actual faint?' She looked over to the instrument lying nearby, its bow fluffy with broken hair. 'Arlo,' she remonstrated, 'always save the fiddle, you know that.'

A growl escaped my throat. How could she expect me to let her soft body hit the floor? In my ignorance, I kept thinking this occasional dizziness was a sign of pregnancy, or fearing

427

it was early menopause, though the doctor had told her it was probably just low blood pressure. In every other way, she was fit as the proverbial. I held her close, smelling the salt of the kitchen, or perhaps sweat from her exertions, her warm-tea arm flowing past mine as she reached up to her neck. We were just starting to melt into one another when, from nowhere, an oppressive heat closed in, heavy with jungle sap and gun smoke. I felt my skin go clammy. Something was coming to me, a split-second vision, like a brick to the temple.

'What's wrong?' She pulled away.

Her beautiful neck, the first feature ever to catch my eye. All those twinges, the sudden cries of pain in the night as her head turned on the pillow. It was just another injury, the kind caused by something as insignificant as a draught and exacerbated by excessive practice, the sort of sprain every violinist got at some point in her career. But now she was blacking out, falling, and I was back beside the hotel driveway, hiding amid the border's hot mulch, watching her flight from the jeep, crushing sugary leaves beneath my boot as I plunged forward, catching her in my arms while she clamped a hand to her neck. The lurch backwards came straight from my gut, before I saw the blood, a frenzy of back and forth – blocked out, erased and vetoed in my memory until now – before I finally reversed the two minutes needed to bite down on my decision, ensuring that whatever happened I would make that dash across the open ground and stop her getting out of the vehicle.

Flawed heroism. Heroism that fucked up, that pondered things too long and then on second thought decided to spring into action. One bullet, again and again, and it was in her neck, damn it, the strong, flower-stem neck I loved so fiercely.

'What's wrong?' she asked again.

If I'd been one notch smarter and had anticipated her sprint up the driveway, so there had been no patter of her flip-flops on tarmac, no bullets needed to rouse me, then this would never have happened. With a will of their own, my hands checked over her shoulders, stroked her, my thumb detecting the dip in her collarbone, a light wax to the skin. So solid and sensory, not the smallest mark of a bullet. It was just a neck injury. But it had gone on for weeks, and now she was dizzy too. The gunshot was echoing, bouncing around in a dozen different realities, one for each of my heartbeats, and something bad was going to happen.

'You drama queen,' she said gently. 'I haven't eaten, that's all.'

It was true. I allowed myself one deep breath. That trip to the island, coupled with all Erin's strangeness, would have unnerved anyone. Set against the fear of a moment ago, all my secrets dwindled to meaningless whispers.

In the kitchen, the curry glooped and burbled and started to smell like it was burning around the edges, becoming a chewy honeycomb. It was Sabra's go-to meal, full of spices. When we sat down to eat, my eyes continued to rove over her neck, questioning every undulation and wrinkle, so I spooned far too much chicken onto the plates and sat staring at my mountain of food, my mouth dry. Sabra ate with relish, grunting appreciatively.

'So obvious why they eat this for breakfast, lunch and dinner in Thailand,' she said.

The odour was already taking me back to the Orange Grove, where I'd once stared at a meal like this one, steaming with flavour but failing to conjure up my appetite. Then, as now, my fork moved lightly over its surface, ploughing furrows in the sauce.

There had been that dream, one in a long line of nightmares set in a hospital room, where Mum had been replaced with Sabra. It happened when my brain was tangled, still in shock. The doctor's tone was the same as it had always been: purposefully low, measuring out the bad news dose by dose. A small tear in the lining of the vertebral arteries, clot formation, blood flow to the brain . . . This detail, where had it come from? With a numb, trickling sensation, it dawned on me that perhaps there had been no dream, that the vision was something else entirely.

Sabra paused mid-chew and looked over. This time there was no hiding it. My face was a landslide of terror.

'The two things, they're connected.'

'What two things?'

'You being . . .' I couldn't tell her she was shot. 'I'm afraid there's something wrong with you.'

'Arlo . . .' She went through the stage of almost laughing, wanting to joke, but was stalled by such authentic fear. 'Don't—'

'I thought it was a repeat – everything's a repeat – just another dream about Mum.' My chest was solid with tension, each breath shallower than the last. It was hitting me so hard, this hell-blast of specifics: medical words, bits of art on the ward walls, hospital parking charges, wills and testaments, things I knew and shouldn't know. 'But it was you there, and the doctor was telling me to say goodbye . . . to say . . .' My voice dried up.

Say goodbye, they would tell me, but I wouldn't do that. There was no way future me would have said his farewells. Instead he would gather his ragged thoughts and, in desperation, perform the miracle I'd just told Erin was impossible. Recklessly, I'd thrown myself backwards, reaching out for that scabby hotel with its pink dragons, hoping with razor-thin hope that I could somehow do my bravery right, or change the course of events. But instead I'd fallen short, just a little, into the sweet citrus hum of the Orange Grove, and that hospital room of the future had wound up its cold-metal smell and white walls into what seemed like a harmless nightmare.

The last two years were detaching, floating apart. Why shouldn't things feel familiar if you are going out with an old girlfriend? I'd thought nothing of it. But the déjà vu was real, because this was my second time around. It might be

431

in six months, or six years, but we would end up in that hospital room together. I knew because I'd already been there, and these neck pains were the first raindrops of an unstoppable storm.

Sabra's mouth was partly open, a smear of saffron at one corner, and she reached across and laid a hand – so cool – on my forehead. 'You're feverish,' she said. 'Maybe that swim wasn't such a good idea. Where's Erin?'

It was ludicrous, beautiful innocence, and made me feel like I was someone in a play who had broken character, telling her all the lines still to come. That pre-lived week, back when I was a magician, was nothing to this. With every movement of my body, every word, I was acting out something that had been done before.

'My sister's on an island,' I laughed. 'She can't get us now.' This was my part, at last, the madman. No reason not to play it well. It switched on a faint light of concern in Sabra's eyes, which she covered by hauling me viciously to my feet, prodding me towards the staircase.

'Go on, get some rest.'

A cloud would have offered more resistance. I drifted across to the stairs and took them like a sleepwalker. The flight up to the attic room grew narrow, almost to a funnel, all wattle and daub, and I didn't bother turning on the light. Only now did it occur to me that I'd just told her about her own death, and she'd done pretty well not to get freaked out. But what did it matter? This time was already cardboard, ready to be crumpled. Nothing was real except that hospital room in our future. What the hell could I do to prevent it? A great weariness was already coming over me, slowing my climb. There was nothing to do. Nothing except try again. Like never before, the bleakness hit me, the sheer tedium of being able to go back; one of those things in life that, because it can be done, must be.

The bed received me with its starchy sheets. Daunting, to burn through the events of not only months but years, even jet-fuelled with urgency. One desire reverberated through my being. *Save Sabra.* Save her life. Already I was feeling the pull of all the actions I could undo, queuing them up, until I could almost sense the rumble of a white taxi on a dirt road, the slam of the door and my love standing travel-worn before me. Was there the smallest chance of changing the course of events? Failure seemed guaranteed. And what if I fell short again . . . or overshot the mark? I feared being stranded somewhere along the way, no signposts to guide me.

Sitting in a meditative pose on the bed, among pillows scented with lavender, there was silence for what seemed like hours, then finally the strains of violin music – a softer piece, in case I was sleeping. We'd developed these habits. Something about the tune bypassed all reason, all reasoning. Then it halted mid-phrase. *Stop listening.* I told myself to concentrate, to think of palms and orioles and a snake beneath the jeep. Another burst of music, and it stopped again. I could hear her frustration, that abiding fear that her work was too full of faults, her ambition fragmented into fantasy.

Always save the fiddle. But I'd always saved her. If I went back and tried again to preserve her life, what sort of life would it be? The sonata restarted, sweetly gathering pace, and when it broke off there was something more than a silence: a chasm, as though she'd given her all. She was hurling this music out into the universe, waiting to see if such passion would elicit a faint echo of applause.

I pictured my dad's apartment: the board game coiling beyond the table, between the chairs, beneath the combi boiler. If I was that little Saint George figure winning its way through life, I was bending the game around me, warping it for everyone else, throwing their stories askew. 'Untold harm' was how Erin put it. But she'd also told me that the position of every atom in the universe – including flying bullets and bottles of Spitfire – is not fixed, not until it is observed, and if you take away the observation the possibilities fan out again. If there is no other way to beat the dragon, you simply remove the knight and fold away the board. Things would have been different for so many people, had I never played the game.

My hair still smelled of lake water. I let the silence settle over me, not fighting it, till my lungs were almost motionless; hardly a need for breath, for a pulse. From nowhere, a sense of what I'd done wrong last time came to mind. Too many moments, all those faint ones loitering in between, like counting stars. Stories stick in the mind for a reason, and it need not be anything epic, just the kind of tale Mum would tell, a choose-your-own-adventure that twists and turns, ducks and dives, labyrinthine before vanishing. If I fetched up by the ladder, this life might fizz up before my eyes just enough to make me turn away from the slow-worm, keep my grip firm until the danger was past, the Rolos consumed in triumph. All these years would have been one long battle with the same beast, leaving me ready only now to raise my sword, the winner about to be decided.

Choose this, and face its consequences. But the violin is advancing in trills, slides and grace notes, like children running, and Sabra is already playing at the Musikverein, incandescent as she reaches the finale, people closing their eyes, holding their breath, and I don't dare to stop, to listen, even to play out my battles. They begin, slowly at first, to sink into the earth, the matrimonial bed, the dark room and the cottage itself, deeper and deeper, beyond feeling, the percolation of memory. Hotel Oasis is keen to appear, with its stagnant pools, the fag ends roasting to nothing between my fingers, the tangy soil scattered unexpectedly, gunpowder greasy as stage make-up under the lights, where a pinch of orange tiger fur is snagged . . . But there must be no wild leaps; my pace must be measured if I am to make it all the way, even beyond my mother examining my eyes for dust. Rather than being two sunlit shapes in her pupils, I am being teased apart – or rather, my smallest coils of code were never entwined.

We will resonate for each other, as atoms do that were once together, even as the bowing moves from figure-of-eight to knots so fast and intricate that the arm blurs; Sabra herself is the instrument, creating sound that unlocks, that undoes people, until the audience is raw, unravelled and exposed. The applause doesn't stop.

Acknowledgements

With thanks to Matt Ashby for his police knowledge, to Dr Michael Brooks and Dr Mairead Butler for tips on quantum mechanics and physics, to Patricia Butler for violin expertise, Mandy Espey for medical matters, Helen Stafford for optical insights and also to Leoni Munslow and Chris Paines for details on all the firefighting Arlo did and subsequently undid and forgot (sorry about that!) As usual, my agent Julie Crisp went above and beyond, giving me great advice on this book all the way through, as did Jenni Hill, who helped make Arlo a better person. Thanks also to Joanna Kramer, Nazia Khatun and everyone else at Orbit. The enthusiasm and support I've received from my partner and family, as well as from some wonderful friends and colleagues, has been hugely appreciated.

Look out for

EVERY
THING
ABOUT
YOU

by

HEATHER CHILD

Think twice before you share your life online.

Freya has a new virtual assistant. It knows what she likes,
knows what she wants and knows whose voice she most
needs to hear: her missing sister's.

It adopts her sister's personality, recreating her through a
life lived online. But this virtual version of her sister
knows things it shouldn't be possible to know. It's almost
as if the missing girl is still out there somewhere, feeding
fresh updates into the cloud. But that's impossible. Isn't it?

www.orbitbooks.net

extras

orbit
www.orbitbooks.net

extras

about the author

Heather Child is based in Bristol, and previously lived in the Midlands after studying at the University of Warwick. Her debut novel, *Everything About You*, was published by Orbit in 2018. Alongside writing she has had an eclectic career in marketing and communications, working for various non-profit organisations. If she had Arlo's powers, she would reappear back in that charity shop and buy the deluxe pirate outfit for only twelve pounds.

Find out more about Heather Child and other Orbit authors by registering for the free monthly newsletter at www.orbitbooks.net.

if you enjoyed
THE UNDOING OF
ARLO KNOTT

look out for

THE GAMESHOUSE

by

Claire North

*Everyone has heard of the Gameshouse. But few
know all its secrets . . .*

*It is the place where fortunes can be made and lost though
chess, backgammon – every game under the sun.*

*But those whom fortune favours may be invited to compete
in the higher league . . . where the games played are of
politics and nations, of economics and kings. It is a contest
where* Capture the Castle *involves real castles and where hide
and seek takes place on the scale of a continent.*

*Among those worthy of competing in the higher league,
three unusually talented contestants play for the
highest stakes of all . . .*

Chapter 1

She is gone, she is gone. The coin turns, and she is gone.

Chapter 2

Come.

Let us watch together, you and I.

We pull back the mists.

We step onto the board, make our entrance with a flourish; we are here, we have arrived; let the musicians fall silent, let those who know turn their faces away at our approach. We are the umpires of this little event; we sit in judgement, outside the game but part of it still, trapped by the flow of the board, the snap of the card, the fall of the pieces. Did you think you were free of it? Do you think yourself something more in the eyes of the player? Do you fancy that it is not you who are moved, but is moving?

How naïve we have become.

Let's choose a place and call it Venice. Let us say it is 1610, six years since the Pope last declared this place heretic, barred from the blessings of his divine office. And what was this to the people of the city? Why, it was no more than what it was: a piece of paper stamped with wax. No Bishop of Rome could shake this sinking city. Instead the black rats will come, they will come with fleas and plague, and the city will rue its impiety then.

But we run ahead of ourselves. Time, to those of us who play in the Gameshouse, stretches like kneaded dough; fibres split and tear away but we persist, and the game goes on.

She will be called Thene.

She was born at the close of the sixteenth century to a cloth merchant who made a fortune buying from the Egyptians and selling to the Dutch, and her mother was a Jew who married for love, and her father fed her pork from infancy and made her swear never to reveal this terrible secret to the great men of the city.

– What will I be when I am old? she asked her father. – Can I be both my mother's daughter, and yours?

To which her father answered, – No, neither. I do not know who you will be, but you will be all yourself, and that will be enough.

Later, after her mother dies, her father remembers himself speaking these words and weeps. His brother, who never approved of the match and dislikes the child as a symbol of it, paces up and down, rasping:

– Stop crying! Be a man! I'm ashamed to look at you!

She, the child, eight years old, watches this exchange through the door and swears with her fists clenched and eyes hot that she will never be caught crying again.

And a few years later, Thene, dressed in blue and grey, a silver crucifix about her neck, leather gloves upon her hands, is informed that she shall be married.

Her father sits, silent and ashamed, while her uncle rattles off the details of the match.

Her dowry is greater than her name, and it has purchased Jacamo de Orcelo, of ancient title and new-found poverty.

– He is adequate, potentially a fine husband given your degree, her uncle explains. Thene keeps her fingers spread loose across her lap. The act of keeping them so, of preventing from them locking tight, requires a great deal of concentration, and at fifteen years old, Thene has not cried for seven years, and will not cry now.

– Is this your wish? she asks her father.

He turns his face away, and on the night before her wedding day she sits down with him before the fire, takes his hand in hers and says, – You do not need my forgiveness, for you have done nothing wrong. But as you want it, know that it is yours, and when I am gone I will only remember the best of you; only the very best.

For the first time since her mother died, he cries again, and she does not.

Jacamo de Orcelo was not a fine husband.

For the sake of Thene's dowry, this thirty-eight-year-old man of the city swore he would endure the snickering of his peers who laughed to see his fifteen-year-old bride, whispering that he had married the merchant's daughter, and murmuring that beneath her skirts there was only cloth and more cloth, no womanly parts at all for a man to grapple with.

The first night they were alone together, she held his hands, as she had seen her mother do when she was young, and stroked the hair back from behind his ear, but he said this was womanly rot and pushed her down.

His aged mother told her that he loved fresh shrimp cooked over a smoky flame, the spices just so, the sweetness just right, and she learned the secrets of this dish and presented him a platter for his supper, which he ate without thanks, not noticing the efforts she had gone to.

– Did you like the meal? she asked.

– I had better as a boy, he replied.

She sang when first she came to this house, but he said her voice gave him a headache. Then one night, when she was walking alone, she sang one of her mother's songs, and he came downstairs and hit her, screaming, – Jew! Jew! Whore and Jew! and she did not sing again.

Her wealth bought him some redemption from his debts, but money dwindles, and the laughter persisted. Was it this, we wonder, that made their marriage so cold? Or was it the fumbling of the old man in the sheets with his teenage bride, his love of wine, his affection for cards and, as she failed to produce an heir, his growing fondness for whores? Which piece of all of this, shall we say, was it that most defined their home?

We watch their house, proud and tall in the heart of San Polo, hear the servants whisper behind their hands, see the wife withdraw into her duties, witness the husband spend more on less, see the coffers empty, and as the years roll by and Jacamo grows ever more reckless in the destruction of himself, what do we see in her? Why, nothing at all, for it seems that against the buffets of fortune she is stone, her features carved into a mask of perfect white.

Thene, beautiful Thene, grown to a woman now, manages the accounts when her husband is gone, works with the servants and hides in the lining of her skirts those ducats that she can best secure before he finds them and spends them on whatever – or whoever – it is that today has best taken his fancy. And as he grows loud, so she grows quiet, until even the whispers against her character cease, for it seems to the gossipy wives of Venice that there is nothing there – no merchant's daughter or gambler's wife, no woman and no Jew, not even Thene herself – but only ice against which they can whisper, and who has any joy in scheming against winter herself?

All this might persist, but then this is Venice, beloved of plague, reviled by popes, the trading heart of Europe, and even here, all things must change.